CRIMEUCOPIA

Great Googly Moo!

A Murderous Ink Press Anthology

****

CRIMEUCOPIA
Great Googly Moo!

First published by Murderous Ink Press
Crowland
LINCOLNSHIRE
England

www.murderousinkpress.co.uk

Paperback Edition ISBN: 9781909498624
eBook Edition ISBN: 9781909498631

Acknowledgements

To those writers and artists who helped make this anthology what it is, I can only say a heartfelt Thank You!

To L. N. Hunter, for help with the grunt work of proofing

And to Den, as always.

Contents

James Fletcher
Illustrator
Open for commissions
from portraits to fully illustrated
comicbook pages
Contact:
flexographics2001@yahoo.co.uk

I Remember the Dame Well...

(An Editorial of Sorts)

...Mainly as she had a laugh that reminded me of two cheese graters energetically fornicating in an iron bathtub. I looked out the open window at the Johnson Memorial, standing resolute and upright in the persistent rain. The clock on it said it was 3:15 in the a.m. and I figured, what-the-Hell, it was time to review the 14 case files scattered across my desk.

Daryl Wood Gerber had labelled her report **In Dying Color**, and it concerned a PI who seemed to have a thing for DIY — and a problem her mother had, in regard to the dead man in the other room.

I put it to one side and picked up the next. **Don Magin** had turned up a shyster, who was a reluctant investigator in regard to **The Slivered Princess**. Talk about taking money from working gumshoes...

I took a long pull from the seemingly bottomless cup of cold black coffee, savoured the rush of caffeine, then pulled up a file marked **Man with a Limp**. A limp what? I read on... The report was from **James Donzella**, about a *Blackmoor Agency* operative, known as Dixon Webb — before I let **J. T. Seate**'s report ask that age old question, **What's in a Name**?

I turned to **S. B. Watson**, whose report was worrying — was someone really undercutting us? — as it talked about **The Five Cent Detective**. Jay-zus, I knew this business was often called 'nickel & dime' — but literally?

I looked out across the skyline and wondered: *Why is it* always *raining in Noir City?* I got up and moved over to the chess board. I hadn't seen the cat in several hours, so I rearranged the pieces a little in order to give myself a bit of an advantage...

Back at the file-scattered desktop, I picked up **Wil A. Emerson**'s folder. I didn't know what concerned me more — the file cover being marked up **Cracker Jacks and the Granny Cases**, or the fact her report was on *J and L Detective Agency* headed paper...

Below her folder was another simply marked **Twink**, and I recognised the penmanship of **Michael Bracken.** It wasn't long before I started to wonder if blonds really did have more fun, and whether at my age I could still pull off a shade usually referred to as *Honey*...

As I stacked it in the IN tray, I saw that it had been covering a thick airmail package from **Glenn Francis Faelnar**, and when I opened it, out fell a glossy 5-by-7 colour photo. On the back was written *Eddie's Girl* in black ink. At least he'd had the good grace not to include a photo of his landlord.

The tray was starting to overflow, so I pulled out the file from **Michael Thomét**. He has a long term thing about reporting back on Bear and Bird — this time the latest was marked ***Bear and Bird in the Snow***. If he kept on reporting then he would need a filing cabinet drawer all his own. I'd assigned **Jay Andrew Connor** his own drawer years ago. Still didn't stop the *Willerby Trenton Retirement Village for Discerning Seniors* from forwarding ***Memindip and the Persian Poet***. Why couldn't they just take him out the back? .22 revolver, spade and a bag of quicklime. A definite mercy. For all of us....

I looked down at the desktop, surprised I could actually see some of it now, and picked up something marked ***Barely is Good Enough***, with a *Post-It* note from **Martin Zeigler** saying there was no way he was genetically related to a guy called 'Cooper.'

Another long pull of cold black coffee made me smile. Down to the last three — one was from **Michael J. Ciaraldi**, who had sent in his initial report on one *Summer Cum Laude*, College Detective. On the top of the folder was written ***Film Blank***, so I wasn't hopeful of there being any photos of the chick.

Of the two remaining folders, one had a particular odour that reminded me of a polecat. I picked up one of the pencils from the shambles of my desk tidy, and with the rubber-tipped end I flicked it open. I was mistaken — it wasn't polecat, it was ***Ferret***, and I made a note to tell **Jeff Burt** that, like himself, I also take my Absurdism neat and straight up as well.

That just left the file with the curious claw marks gouged into the cover. It came from **L. N. Hunter**, and was marked: ***The Case of the Saintsville Cat*** — and I for one would never have called *Solomon Granger* 'pussy whipped'.

I put it on top of the IN pile in the hope that anyone reading this would find something they immediately liked, as well as detecting something that took them out of their reading comfort zone — and put them into a completely new one.

Because, in the spirit of the *Murderous Ink Detective Agency* motto:

> *You never know what you like until you investigate it.*

In Dying Color
Daryl Wood Gerber

I'd decided at three a.m. that I needed color on the walls. Not ecru or eggshell or whatever the heck they were calling cream nowadays. Fire engine red. I wondered if my neighbor, Declan Gannon, a handsome Irishman not much older than me, would approve. I spied him through the living room window, clipping the box hedges between our properties. With thick dark hair and eyes that twinkled with something bordering on sassy, I had to admit he made me swoon.

Focus, Hope. The walls. Back to the walls.

When my clients entered my house, I wanted them to feel *zoom*, not *gloom*. Most, when they rang the doorbell, would be in a deep funk. My aim was to perk them up, provide positive feedback, and hold their hands.

Note to self: fix doorbell.

I am thirty-one, single, and a private detective in Los Robles, California, a bedroom community located twenty miles north of the valley, aka San Fernando Valley, Los Angeles County. Most of my clients expect me to assure them that I, Hope McAn, can do the job. I tell them I sure *McAn*. In fact, I'm pretty good at what I do. I've tracked errant husbands, served papers, and even solved a few cold cases that the police threw my way. The agency has been open ten years and counting. Not bad.

Energy zinged through my body as I painted the wall in easy, even strokes. Smartly, I'd donned a baseball cap. Who needed red hair to become redder? Actually, I leaned more toward a natural reddish brown, if my hair dye color was telling the truth, which was why I wasn't averse to the color red—on me or around me. I looked good in it as well as other jewel tones, though no one would call me a gem. I was a girl-next-door-type: expressive green eyes, good bone structure, but Hollywood wouldn't be calling.

My cell phone rang. I scanned the readout but didn't recognize the number. "McAn Detective Agency. You bet I can. What's your problem?" I perched the paint brush on the edge of the can, but it flopped onto the Chinese cabinet beneath. I groped for the brush, but that sent the puzzle box holding my prized pair of silver earrings to the floor. I wasn't a jewelry person, but I treasured the ones my mother had given me on my sixteenth birthday. "That's where I left you," I muttered at the box. Ignoring the mess I'd made, I said into the phone, "Hello? Anyone there?"

"Help!" Barely a whisper.

"Mom? What's wrong?"

"Help!"

A year ago, my mother bought a house in Santa Monica and invited her older-by-ten-years sister to move in with her. Aunt Alicia protested saying she wasn't frail, but my mother insisted. Mom had been rejuvenated by the move. She told me Santa Monica was a *happening* town. I didn't counter by saying that was because newer residents were now dot.com kids one-third her age.

"Mom, are you choking? Isn't Auntie there?"

"He's...He's in the other room."

He wasn't the proper pronoun for my aunt. She identified as she/her. "He, who?"

Not my father. Of that I was certain. When I popped into my parents' lives, my mother named me Hope. Good thing I'd come out sort of cute, or my father might have named me Failure. As it was, he walked out the next day without a backward glance. Why my mother kept a picture of them on their wedding day on the wall in the living room was beyond me. It sure didn't go with the rest of the fine art she'd displayed. But she made me swear I'd never take it down. As a reminder, I supposed, of when things went wrong.

"The man," my mother replied in answer to my question.

"Which man?" I was terrible at playing guessing games. I liked cold, hard facts.

"I quit!" my British-born assistant announced as she stormed across the foyer and fled through the front door.

"What? No!" I shrieked. I couldn't let her go. Okay, she'd quit before and she'd always come back, but what if she quit for *real* this time? "Wait!" I was efficient, but I needed a full-time assistant. And a tarp for paint spills. *Note to self.*

"Hope," my mother hissed. "The man is dead."

My stomach plummeted. "What do you mean he's dead?"

"I think I killed him."

Chills swizzled down my spine. The house telephone rang. "Felix, get that!"

Felix Farnsworth, my hum-loving intern, snapped up the phone. "McAn Detective Agency. You bet we McAn." He was always upbeat, certain that we could solve any problem. I wished—prayed—I could be more upbeat like him, but life in general made me a little jaded.

"Robo-call." He hung up.

"Hope, darling." My mother was near tears.

"Dead man. The other room. Yes, Mom. I'm listening."

Felix raised an eyebrow. I waved him off.

"I thought he was the delivery guy. I'd ordered food from that little Chinese place. Your aunt didn't want Chinese, but I insisted." My mother loves Chinese food. I'm partial to good old American cuisine, particularly a rare hamburger. "I was sick and tired of pizza." My mother couldn't cook a lick. Her sister, either. It was Nana's fault. "I opened the door and he pushed his way in."

I gasped. "You didn't look through the peephole?" All my life, she'd drummed into me to be super cautious. Check and double check. Be safe.

"I thought he was the delivery guy," she repeated with exasperation.

"Where's Auntie?"

"On her way home."

"From where?"

"The salon. Why does that matter?"

"Let me ask the questions, Mother. He pushed his way in. Then what?"

"He aimed a gun at me."

My stomach tensed. "What kind of gun?"

"A big one."

Okay, she wasn't an expert. She owned a pink Sig Mosquito. *Pink.* To her, a Glock or Colt Lightweight Commander might look the same.

"What happened next?" I asked.

"He ordered me to give him all my jewelry."

When Dad left, Mom was gainfully employed as a high-powered lawyer who defended white collar criminals, so she didn't go looking for him. Over the course of her career she'd made beaucoup bucks and invested and, subsequently, retired extremely well off at the tender age of fifty-eight. My shrink often told to me that I became a detective because I wanted to pay society back for the sleazy clients my mother had gotten off.

"And did you give it to him, Mom?"

"Of course not. It's not here."

"Where is it?" I glanced around. My mother had gifted me the house, lock, stock, and barrel. I'd refi'd it to keep the business on track. I'd never seen any of her jewelry. Had she hidden it in a safe I didn't know about?

"It's at the bank. In a vault. I don't need it. It's not like I'm hobnobbing around Beverly Hills."

"You haven't been slumming it, either." I happened to know she and my aunt went to the theater once a week, and she went out to dinner with friends at least three nights a week. She always wore some piece of flashy jewelry.

"Alright, fine. Yes, it's here. Under my mattress. But I refused to give it to him, so he waggled his gun and told me to get it, or else."

"Or else what?"

"Or else he'd shoot me."

"What did you do then?" I mean, after all, he was dead in the other room. Or at least she thought he was dead.

"I grabbed the baseball bat I keep by the door and clobbered him with it."

"And he didn't shoot?"

"I think he was stunned that I would defy him." She sucked back a sob. "There's blood everywhere. Your aunt is going to be very upset."

I was pretty sure Aunt Alicia would be more upset if my mother was lying dead on the floor.

"Should I clean up?" she asked.

"No, Mom. Don't do anything. I mean, do something. Call nine-one-one."

"I can't."

"What do you mean you can't?" My voice rose to a near hysterical pitch.

"Because I have outstanding speeding tickets. They'll arrest me."

"Mom." A nervous chuckle burst from my lips. "They'll be too preoccupied with the body to even think about your speeding tickets."

"You're wrong there." She clucked her tongue. "Don't you remember that client I defended? The one who owned three Mercedes Benz dealerships."

I did. One night, he was pulled over for a busted taillight and, lo and behold, he'd racked up over thirty parking tickets. They were stuffed into his glove compartment. My mother tried to get him off with only a slap on the wrist as long as he paid the tickets and the fines that had accrued. But no-o-o. The cop that arrested the guy was a stickler and sent him to prison for a year.

"Mom. Hang tight. I'm on my way."

*****

A cool breeze caught me as I hurried across the lawn to where my Jeep stood in the driveway. I tried to walk-jog, but my bum knee—the result of a grand jeté as a preteen that went sideways—made it hard to kick myself into high gear. The scent of gardenias and jasmine wafted on the breeze. If only I had an hour to enjoy it.

"Morning, Hope." Gannon waved his hedge trimmers. His black T-shirt clung to his muscular body. Perspiration glistened on his tanned skin. "You look like you're in a hurry."

"My mother."

"Say no more. Stop by later if you're up for a beer." Gannon made his own craft beer. He was also a genius at the barbecue, he rebuilt most of his house by himself, and he listened to jazz, which was pumping out his outdoor speakers. He was a real renaissance guy, different from most of the cops I knew. For a nanosecond, I wondered if he'd moved into the neighboring house two years ago because my mother put him up to it to keep an eye on me.

A car door slammed behind me. I spun around. Not my wayward assistant returning to the fold. It was my cousin Blaze, my long, lost cousin—lost because she'd been in jail for the past five years for robbery. She was removing a backpack and duffel from the backseat of a Ford Escort. She handed the driver cash through the front window.

As he drove off, she yelled, "Cuz!" Blaze was a large woman, taller than me by a good six inches and meatier all over. She looked even taller in her three-inch-high, sexy-beyond-belief sandals. Her hair was white-blonde, streaked with blue. She could pull it off. I'd look ridiculous. She grabbed me in a bear hug and lifted me off the ground. "It's so good to see you. Have you lost weight?"

"Um, no."

"You're light as a feather."

"You've put on muscle."

"Time in the clink does that." She set me down and eyed the house and grounds. "Wow, looks good."

"Why are you here?"

"I was talking to Dad. He asked how you were."

Often when we were girls, her father, a gambler and a roustabout, would drop Blaze off, and she and I would play. My mother had felt empathy for Blaze. Not her father.

"And he thought it would be nice if you and I..." Blaze began to use her hands to paint a picture.

"Go inside." I pointed at my Craftsman. "Felix will take care of you. We'll catch up later." I shook the keys I was holding.

"Where are you going?"

Softly, so Gannon wouldn't hear, I clued her in about my mother's predicament.

"You're not going alone, honey girl." Blaze tossed her luggage in the backseat of the Jeep and climbed into the passenger seat.

"Honey girl?"

She waved her hand. "It's just something I've gotten used to saying."

"Yeah. No. Not to me."

As I sped down the 5, Blaze pelted me with questions about my mother's predicament, but I didn't have answers. When I merged onto the 405 Freeway, I grumbled. Los Angeles traffic had increased five-fold over the past ten years to a point where it was maddening. A snail could slither faster.

My mother touched base right after I'd crossed the 101 Freeway and was nearing the Getty Museum. I had yet to go inside the place. I should. I wasn't much of an art fan, but I knew the difference between a Picasso and a Monet, and I was quite partial to Degas because I'd often thought I would end up a ballerina...until the accident.

"Alicia just got home," my mother said. "She's hysterical. What do I do?"

"Sedate her."

"With what?"

"She likes gin. Give her a shot."

"Gin." My mother snorted. She was a wine snob.

"Do it."

"You know"—Blaze swiveled in her seat—"she's probably a nervous wreck." My cousin had the most beautiful eyes, naturally outlined and brilliant blue, and a little intimidating. I'd bet she could find work as a hypnotist if she wanted. "There's a dead guy—"

"On her floor. Got it. Why? Why is he there? Is he really a robber? How did he know she owned a lot of jewelry?"

"You said it yourself. She goes out. She flaunts her stuff. People like me..." She rolled her lip between her teeth. "Like I used to be, pay attention to stuff like that."

Way back when, even though I was younger than Blaze, I was protective of her. I realized early on that she was a petty thief. To keep her out of trouble, I returned things she stole, like CDs and hair ribbons and lipstick. When she graduated to larger items, specifically shoes, pretty ones—five-inch stilettos, sassy wedges, strappy sandals like the ones she was wearing, and yes, even high-end tennis shoes, the brighter the better—she got in trouble, and I couldn't save her. She went to jail for stealing a pair of Manolo Blahnicks.

"I can help today," Blaze offered. "I'll get the truth out of the guy."

"He's dead."

"In case he's not. I mean, c'mon, your mom is a pipsqueak, no bigger than you. Do you really think she killed him with one whack to the head? He's probably just out like a light."

Worry knotted in my stomach. I needed to get to my mother ASAP. If Blaze was right, if the man wasn't dead and he woke up.... If he hurt my mother.... If he hurt my aunt....

"Relax, Cuz."

"I'm relaxed."

"No, you're not. You're doing that curl thing with your hair, twisting it around your finger."

Long hair, short hair, I did do that curl thing when I was nervous. In truth, I was wondering about the guy. Why follow my mother? Had he been stalking her? Was he a former client with a grudge against her?

"Hey, after we wrap this up," Blaze went on, "I was thinking maybe you could put me to work. I'm great with files and getting things in order. I ran the library at the prison for the past year."

An ex-con working for a private detective? What were the ethical rules on that? I'd have to make a few calls to be sure.

"We'll see." I headed west on Wilshire Boulevard and veered right on San Vicente.

As I was passing the Cheesecake Factory, Blaze gestured to it. "I'm hungry."

"Can't stop."

"But their avocado spring rolls are your mom's favorite."

She wasn't wrong, but we couldn't spare a precious minute. I pressed redial on my steering wheel.

My mother answered. "Are you close?"

"About five minutes." Three, if I went over the speed limit. "Has he roused?"

"Roused? He's dead."

"And Auntie? How's she?"

"She's kicked back two jiggers of gin and is lying down in the living room with a cold compress."

A few minutes later, I arrived at my mother's house. It wasn't ostentatious. She hadn't wanted anything ritzy. Or anything gargantuan, either, like the Craftsman I lived in. She'd wanted a cute Mediterranean storybook home, something *charming,* within walking distance of boutiques and restaurants. Her silver Lexus was parked in the driveway. Aunt Alicia's more modest Toyota was parked beside it. There wasn't a Chinese food delivery vehicle in sight. Or any vehicle for that matter. Did the robber come on foot?

I parked on the street, jammed on the brake, and bolted from the car. Pain from my bum knee radiated up my thigh. I bit my teeth to fight the ache. That made me inhale hard. The scent of the ocean was strong. I rarely took the time to drive to the beach. When I did, it was to enjoy a long walk or to visit the Santa Monica Pier. Memories of my mother and me riding the Ferris wheel and playing carney games on the pier scudded through my mind. Those were the times I'd grill her about my father, how they'd met and why they'd broken up. *Because* was the extent of her answers, causing me no end of frustration.

"Hope!" Blaze yelled, yanking me back to the present. She pointed at the front door.

It was hanging open. I pressed it aside and stepped into the foyer. Blaze followed and closed and locked the door. The man—the presumably dead man—was lying prone on the patterned hardwood floor at the foot of the staircase, his head turned to one side. Blood the color of the walls—the same red color I was painting mine—pooled beneath his silver-black hair. He was wearing what looked like a retro Members Only black jacket. The big gun—a Beretta 92X if I wasn't mistaken—was lying about five feet from his left hand. A Dodger's souvenir baseball bat, covered with his blood, lay beyond that. My mother must have released it after she'd struck him.

"Mom?"

"In here." Her voice echoed because of the beamed and coffered ceilings.

I stepped into the sunken living room. Light was pouring through the stained glass windows. My mother was sitting on a royal blue Queen Anne chair, her golden hair hanging like a curtain around her petite face, her hands pressed between her knees. Her linen trousers were splattered with blood. Her linen blouse, too. In particular, the cuffs. Aunt Alicia was lying on the sofa, her hands holding a wet compress over her face. So much for the new hairdo. The moisture from the compress would ruin it. I wanted to pull down the skirt of her shirt-waist dress but thought it might embarrass her to know we could see all the way to her panties. Instead, I grabbed an aqua blue Pashmina throw from the back of the sofa and laid it across her lap. A delivery bag from Jin's Chinese Kitchen sat on the coffee table.

Mom lifted her gaze and saw me gawking at the bag. "I didn't answer the door. He left it on the porch. Alicia brought it in. Why is Blaze with you?"

"She just got out of jail."

"Congratulations."

"Mother!" I barked.

"What? I was afraid she'd be in there for ages. I should have helped more."

Yes, you should've. Water under the bridge.

"Did you go through the man's pockets?" I asked. "Did you find some ID?"

"No. I..." She shuddered.

I got the distinct feeling she was holding something back. "Hey, Auntie." I bent to touch her arm. "How are you doing?"

"I can't believe it," she muttered from beneath the compress. "I can't believe it. I just can't believe it."

Blaze rolled her eyes at me. "I guess she can't believe it."

I stood up and knuckled her arm.

"Why don't I dish this up?" Blaze grabbed the bag of Chinese food.

"I'm not hungry," I said.

"I am."

"Don't pinch a thing," I warned.

"Ouch! That hurt." Blaze cackled.

"Mom, is there anything else you need to tell me about what happened?"

"Why?" she asked, her voice girlish.

Oh, yeah, she was holding something back.

"Don't be evasive," Blaze yelled from the other room. "Hope hates evasive."

I did. Being direct was something my mother had instilled in me. Tell the truth, no matter what. Always.

"Why?" my mother repeated.

"What do you mean, why?" I snapped. "I have to figure out who this guy is. I want to get the story straight so when I call nine-one-one—"

"No!" Aunt Alicia cried, sitting up abruptly like a corpse come to life in a coffin. "No, don't."

"I have to."

"But..." She sputtered and looked at my mother and then back at me.

I stared at her. What was going on? What weren't they telling me? I glanced over my shoulder through the archway at the body. "Do you know him, Aunt Alicia?"

She lowered her chin.

"Mom?"

She kept mute.

"Oh, crap."

*****

Blaze yelled from the kitchen. "I found sweets, Hope. Want some? I know how much you love dessert."

Too much, I feared. Double-chocolate fudge cake came to mind. Or espresso chip ice cream. To die for. I choked back the last thought. How gauche to think in those terms when there was a body in the foyer.

The doorbell *rang*. I startled. My mother mewled.

Blaze yelled, "Want me to get that?"

My mother and I yelled, "No!"

I tiptoed to the window and peered toward the street. A car was parked behind mine. Not just any car. Gannon's muscle car. Holy heck. Why had he followed me? Did he have a nose for ex-cons? Would he think Blaze killed the man? Would he run her in? I needed to get rid of him, but how?

I returned to my mother and crouched down. I took her hands in mine. "Tell me who the man is."

Aunt Alicia moaned.

I shot a look in her direction. "You know him."

"So do you." She mewled.

I peeked into the foyer. Nope. Didn't know the guy. Never seen him before in my life. Though the shape of him looked vaguely familiar. Broad shoulders. Long legs. My father had a similar physique.

"No!" I gagged. "No, no, tell me no!"

My mother nodded.

"Dad? It's Dad?" I ran into the foyer. Knelt to inspect the battered face. His eyes were open. Light green. Like mine. The only thing I'd gotten from my father. The recessive gene. I returned to my mother and aunt.

Gannon pounded on the door. "Open up! Police!"

He didn't have jurisdiction here. I ignored him.

Blaze hurtled into the living room. "Did you call them?"

"No. They...*he* is not here for you. He's my neighbor. He followed me."

Why had he done so? I hadn't looked guilty of anything, had I? Had he sensed my mother killed someone? No, that was a stretch.

Gannon triggered the doorbell again.

Blaze's eyes widened. "I'm not going back to jail."

"No, you're not," I said. "You didn't do this." I turned to my mother. "After all this time, why did my father"—my *jerk* of a father—"come after you?"

"He wanted my jewelry."

"No, Mom. That's a lie." I folded my arms, waiting.

"He claimed if he'd stayed with me, he would have gotten half of everything I owned in a divorce. He wanted me to pay up."

"I'm not buying it."

Aunt Alicia whimpered.

I cut a look in her direction. "What do you know that you're not saying?"

My mother left her chair and sat beside my aunt. She took her sister's hand in hers and stroked it.

What secret were they holding onto? I cycled through the facts in my mind. My father came to the house. He brandished a gun at my mother—unless she planted it beside him, but I didn't see that as a possibility. He wielded the weapon and demanded her jewels. That much sounded like the truth. How did he find her? How did he target her? How did he know she owned expensive jewelry?

Sunlight prismed off the stained glass. The distraction made me turn. I took in the art on the walls. The petite ballerina statues my mother had collected. The ornate puzzle boxes that she'd brought back from her many trips to Asia, one of which was in my living room. None of the items were my aunt's. They all belonged to my mother. Throughout her life, my aunt hadn't been able to hold down a job. Mom had always lined her sister's pockets with cash.

I spotted a photograph of my mother and Alicia as girls and flashed on the framed wedding picture that hung on the wall of my house. In it, Alicia was standing beside my mother. Blaze's father, beside Dad. My mother looked radiant. My father trapped. And Alicia? She looked as dour as a spinster. If looks could kill.

"You loved my father," I said to my aunt. That explained why she'd been loath to live with my mother. "And you"—I stared daggers at Mom—"were pregnant with me when you got married."

I'd come into this world seven months after their wedding. My mother had tried to hide the information from me, but, as I stated previously, I love cold, hard facts. The timing of it was seared in my brain.

Right then, standing in my mother's living room, everything gelled. My father hadn't wanted to get married. Not to my mother. He'd been in love with Alicia, and she with him. Did my father run to her after he walked out? If so, how did they conceal their affair all these years? Today, did he come to the house to demand the jewelry from my mother so he could cash it in, thinking he and Alicia could live a life of luxury? Did Alicia, knowing what he was up to, go to the hair salon so she would have an alibi if things went sideways?

"The wedding photograph, Mom. Why did you make me promise to keep hanging it on the wall?"

After a long moment, she said, "Because it was my first picture of you."

Tears pressed at the corners of my eyes. "Aunt Alicia, this is your fault. You told my father about the jewelry. After he stole it and pawned it, you and he planned to run away. You wouldn't need to live off my mother's dole any longer. But to his surprise, Mom was home."

Gannon pounded on the door. "Open up! Police."

"Yeah," I muttered in that direction. "Don't get your T-shirt in a wad." For a split second, thinking about him without that T-shirt on distracted me. I refocused. "Aunt Alicia, Mom will not take the fall for this."

Blaze punched the air. "Damned straight."

"You wanted Dad, well, you got him. Dead. D-E-A-D, which is what you should be for betraying your sister. As far as I'm concerned, my mother opened the door. A strange man barged in, gun in hand, and she swung. She didn't have time to register who it was."

Gannon rammed the door. The lock gave way. The door flew open. Out of the corner of my eye, I saw him barge into the foyer, register the body, and then make a beeline into the living room, his weapon drawn. "Care to tell me what's going on?"

"Care to tell me why you followed me?" I countered.

"The man on the floor is your father."

"How did you—"

"For twenty-three years, my dad waited for yours to reappear. On his deathbed, two years ago, my dad informed me it was now my fight. So I bought the house next to yours. I watched. I waited. I got a vibe today when you dashed off."

"Why was your dad after him?"

"Because your father was a dirty cop." Gannon's father had been a policeman, too. Internal Affairs.

I swung my gaze to my mother. "Did you know?"

"I had an inkling."

I regarded Gannon again. "Why did it take so long to find him?"

"Because the day he left you and your mother, he quit the force. Changed his name. Changed his social security and passport. It was as if he'd never existed."

I couldn't believe my aunt had betrayed my mother. My shoulders sagged. My faith in humanity was rocked to the core.

Blaze put her arm around me. "Hang tough," she whispered. "I've got stories that will blow your mind."

I shrugged from her hold. "Declan...Officer Gannon, my mother didn't know it was him. He burst into the house, and she hit him with the bat. She didn't have a clue."

Gannon's gaze swung from my mother to my aunt. "Is that so?"

"That's a lie!" my aunt cried. "I hit him. I did it. My sister is innocent."

Well, well. She possessed an ounce of decency. But then she pulled something from the pocket of her dress and popped it into her mouth.

"What did you take?" I hurried to her and grasped her wrist.

She wrenched away. "If I can't be with him in life, I'll spend eternity with him in death." Her mouth started to foam. In seconds, she collapsed to the floor. Dead from cyanide.

Blaze laughed hysterically. My mother began to sob. I stood stock still realizing, my aunt's admission notwithstanding, that my mother would be tried for the crime. Luckily, she knew some good defense attorneys.

And Gannon?

He looked at me sadly. "I guess going on a date now is out of the question?"

The Slivered Princess
Don Magin

"Mr. McCrow, I'm going to need a lawyer."

The door to the sleazy office I lovingly call home flew open and slammed into the wall. I was afraid that the glass window with the fancy black lettering, **Blackie McCrow, Esq., Attorney-at-Law**, and the silhouette of a raven would shatter. Hell, I just paid a struggling artist fifty bucks to paint it on there. Designed it myself. Fifty bucks I really didn't have to spare.

The attractive young blond dish who burst into my office wasted no time. She crossed the ten feet between the door and my desk and leaned over, out of breath, and nearly out of her blouse.

"I'm pretty sure the police are tailing me, and they'll be here any minute," she continued. "They think I killed a princess."

Now I might be the cleverest attorney since P. Mason himself, but it's not often I get a client who is accused of killing royalty. "Sit down, Miss…" I said, pointing to the saggy sofa that did double duty as a place for clients to settle into, and my bed after hours.

"Gerta. Rosie Gerta." She remained standing and anxious to tell her story.

"OK, suppose you tell me your story, Miss Gerta, before the police get here."

"I rescued my boyfriend, and his abductor has turned up dead."

Before she could go any further, my old friend, Lt. Bull, strolled through my office door with a uniformed police woman. Ignoring me, he addressed himself to my would-be client. "Miss Rosie Gerta, you're under arrest for the murder of Princess Gloria White of Lepland."

Miss Gerta looked at me with eyes that would melt all of Lepland.

"Don't say anything or answer any questions unless I advise you to," I told her.

"So, she's your client, I take it," said Bull, indicating that the policewoman should handcuff Miss Gerta.

"Yes, she is," I said, not taking my eyes away from hers, which now showed some measure of relief.

"You can talk to her downtown," said my favorite flatfoot, and out they went.

*****

An hour later, I was ushered into a small private room at headquarters. My client was already there, seated in one of two chairs at a small table. "Suppose you tell me your story," I said, flipping the second chair around and straddling it like a cowboy on his trusty steed. I had practiced this maneuver enough that three out of four times I didn't hurt myself. This time was perfect; I think I impressed her.

"Well, my boyfriend and I began, as you might put it, playing house, about six months ago. Then one day, he disappeared. He went off in his 4-wheeler with some of his buddies for a day of 'mudding'. Do you know what that is?"

I did, so I motioned for her to continue.

"A couple of hours later, when he didn't come home, I went down to the Mud Bog, you know, that bar on Finn Street. Several of his friends were there, but K wasn't."

"This K, he's your boyfriend?

"Yeah. His name is Kenneth Hart, but he hates the name Kenneth, so he goes by K. Anyway, he wasn't there. His friends were too wasted to even notice, but one of them said they saw him pick up a chick in a white parka and drive away. Now, K isn't an angel, but he's been true to me since we moved in together, so the story sounded funny. But I couldn't get anything else coherent from those drunks.

"I left the Bog by the back door, and the first thing I noticed was K's 4-wheeler parked in the alley. I stormed back inside and began yelling. *'Where is K and why is his buggy out back?'* I guess I got a little rowdy, pouring beer after beer over the heads of each of his buddies in turn. Finally, one of them admitted that a girl in white had picked K up shortly after they started drinking. She called herself Princess. The last time any of them saw him, he was being led out the back door by Princess.

"Before I left, I swore that if I found this Princess, I would kill her for stealing my K. Unknown to me, the bartender had called the police when I started my antics, and at least ten people in the bar heard me threaten to kill her, not to mention the police operator on the phone."

"When did all this happen, and how did the Princess die?" I asked.

"A couple of weeks ago, and she was stabbed through the heart with a sliver of glass," she said, answering my questions in order.

"Details, please," I said.

"For several hours after I left the bar, I didn't know what to do. I rode around looking for some evidence of K or the Princess. Then I ran into Blackie at the 7-11. Blackie is an old boyfriend of mine from a couple of years ago. We still see each other occasionally, but not since I took up with K. Anyway, he tried to come on to me. I said, "Get away you jerk. You know I'm with K now.

"He backed off, and said he thought we weren't together anymore, since he saw K heading out of town with another babe."

"*What do mean?*" I grabbed him by the shirt and shoved my face in his. "*When and where?*" I shouted.

"The other night, outside the Mud Bog. K got into a fancy white Jeep with a doll in a white parka. She was a real looker; jet black hair, skin white as snow, lips red as blood. He followed her like he was hypnotized or drugged or something. She headed down highway 32, but turned off-road into that field down by Beggar's Stream."

I hopped back on my bike and headed for route 32. I knew the field by Beggar's Stream well. It's a good place to head into the woods. It leads to the bottom of Knapp's Hill, a common place to hill climb. I followed hundreds of tire tracks toward the hill, until I came to a place where one set veered to the left. Those tracks were fresh, probably not more than a couple of hours old. They led to an abandoned stone cabin about five miles away. Right away it hit me: that place was always referred to as 'the castle', and K went off with 'the Princess'. Makes crazy sense, doesn't it? Princess—castle. Naturally, I headed that way."

Just then, the jailer came to the door with a hulk of a man, who pushed his way in and ran toward Gerta. I discretely looked away while they greeted each other warmly.

"This K?" I asked.

"Yes I am," hulk announced. "Who are you?"

"My lawyer," answered Miss Gerta, saving me the trouble. "I'm telling him the story. I just got to where I pulled up outside the castle."

"I'll take it from there," K said. "I heard a trail bike coming. I tried to figure out what to do, but my head wasn't working right. Next thing I know, Rosie comes barging in and slaps me across the face—hard! I just look at her, all hurt and everything, and she suddenly realizes I ain't in my right mind.

"*Where's the Princess?* she yells, and I look around like a dummy. I vaguely remember being with a babe dressed all in white, but try as I might, I can't remember what went on between us. I did remember her talking to someone outside, but I was too foggy to recognize the voice."

Rosie picked the story up from there. "I grabbed K, dragged him outside and got him on my bike behind me. I wrapped his arms around me, and hung on to one of them. I didn't know if he was lucid enough to hang on by himself. Driving with one hand, I got us out of there as fast as I could. We went back to our place and didn't budge for a couple of days."

"Not quite true," interjected K. "We 'budged' quite a bit, we just didn't leave the apartment."

He picked up the story from there, "We heard about the Princess being murdered on the TV. They said her body was found in Beggar's Creek, the night after Rosie rescued me from the castle. They said there were reports of a woman matching Rosie's description that threatened to kill her over a man that matched me."

"A couple of weeks later, we heard sirens on the street in front. We panicked," said Rosie, "and ran out the back. We split up, I went east and K turned west. I headed straight for your office."

"Why me?" I asked, not sure why my reputation would extend to the bike-riding, mud bogging set.

"You probably don't remember, but you defended a friend of mine, Goldie North, who was charged with malicious wounding of her husband. You didn't win the case, but you got her off with domestic violence and ten days. I didn't have time to look for a better lawyer, so you were it."

"All right," I said after that glowing recommendation. "I've got some investigating to do."

Being only a moderately successful attorney, I don't have a lot of resources. Fortunately I'm pretty familiar with the streets and street people. My network led me to the alley behind the Mud Bog. K's 4-wheeler was still there. The whole front end was bashed in and it had a shattered windshield with lots of pieces missing. My sources told me who they saw driving it.

*****

At the preliminary hearing, the prosecution presented a circumstantial case. There were no witnesses that could place Miss Gerta and the Princess together. There were no fingerprints on the glass recovered from the Princess's heart, nor on any of her clothing. The only things tying my client to the murder were the threats in the barroom and Rosie's well-known violent temper.

The prosecution called witness after witness, beginning with the bartender and parading through eight or nine patrons. They all testified to the violent language and actions of my client. At each one, as the prosecutor finished with, "Your witness", I answered, "No questions." And at each one, Rosie's face dropped a little more. I was sure she was hoping that I could at least get her off on a lesser charge.

The last witness called was Blackie. He testified that he talked to the defendant and told her that he saw K and the Princess drive off together.

He also testified that he told her which way they went. "She was as mad as a wet rattlesnake," he said, "and full of as much venom."

I objected, saying that he was drawing a conclusion not supported by facts, but the judge dismissed my objection, saying he had the right to his opinion. At least my objection seemed to lift Rosie's spirits a little.

This time, at "Your witness," I approached the witness box. "Did you have a romantic relationship with Miss Gerta?"

"Objection!" shouted the prosecutor. "Irrelevant!"

"I assure the court I have a valid reason for this line of questioning," I said to the judge.

"Sustained, but get to your point quickly." Then, to the witness, the judge said, "Answer the question."

Blackie lowered his head and mumbled, "Yeah."

"Please raise your head and your voice and tell the court when your relationship ended with Miss Gerta."

"When she started up with K, that's when," he said, glaring at the defendant. "She threw me over for that bum!"

"Is it not true that you discovered K's 4-wheeler behind the Mud Bog, and you drove it away?"

"No," he shouted, half standing.

"I remind you that you are under oath. If need be, I can bring forth witnesses who saw you drive off in K's vehicle. So I ask you again, did you take K's 4-wheeler the day after he disappeared with the Princess?" Of course it was a bluff, but I hoped in his frenzied state he wouldn't call me on it.

"So what if I did! He left it there with the keys in it. Everyone knows it's the best mudding vehicle around. I just wanted to put it to the test."

"So you, as you say, 'put it to the test', along Beggar's Creek and up Knapp's Hill? How did it perform?"

"Great! Like I said, everyone knows it's the best for that kind of stuff," he blurted out.

My voice rose in timbre as I put on my best impression of a TV lawyer. "But first you took a little detour to the castle, didn't you? And you picked up the Princess, promising her the ride of her life, didn't you? Then you told her to get out and you showed her how a real man races through Beggar's Creek, didn't you. But somehow you crashed, smashing up the windshield and the whole front of the 4-wheeler! What did she do, mock you? Laugh at you? Make you feel like an inept jerk? Make you so mad you grabbed a piece of the glass and stabbed her?

I waved a piece of paper under Blackie's nose. "I have a report that the sliver of glass taken from the Princess's body matches the glass from K's 4-wheeler." The paper was another bluff, an overdue rent notice on my lovely office, but he was too far gone now to notice.

"No! No! That's not what happened! It was an accident. She fell out when I almost flipped over. Then when I spun around I did flip, and the windshield must have hit her."

By now he was sobbing like a spanked little boy. "I must have blacked out, 'cause when I came to, she was laying in the creek. I pulled the vehicle upright and got it started. I brought it back to the alley behind the Bog.

"I tell you, it was an accident! An accident!"

Man with a Limp
James Donzella

It was a hot morning in Los Angeles. Dixon Webb, Private Investigator, entered room 302 of the Continental Building at 11:46 a.m.

"I've been callin' you for the last half hour," Jill Devlin, Blackmoor Detective Bureau's secretary said with a frown.

"Sorry, sweetheart," Dix said, as he came around behind her desk.

"Don't sweetheart me!" Jill said shrugging off Dixon's hug. "I nearly starved to death waiting for you last night. Where were you?"

"Worked late."

"He wants to see you right away," she said pointing to the door behind her.

Faded gold letters on the glass windowed door read:
Alton J. Blackmoor

"Where the *hell* you been?!" Blackmoor said. "Callin' you for hours. We gotta client."

"Details," Dix said, flopping onto a couch with questionable stains.

"That's for *you* to find out. Sent over a check for two hundred dollars."

Dix pushed his fedora over his eyes, pretended to nap. "You still owe me for my last expense report."

"You'll get the money, as soon as I verify your expenses. The Las Palmas. Room 212. See Mr. Norman Reinhardt. Get goin'."

*****

Music from the radio came from room 212 as Dix tapped his knuckle against the door.

"Who is it?" a male voice called out.

"Dixon Webb, Blackmoor Detective Bureau."

"Just a minute," the voice replied.

Dix heard a rhythmic thumping sound from behind the door, followed by the removal of the security chain. The door opened.

"Come in, Mr. Webb."

Reinhardt, maybe an inch shorter than Webb, looked tired, his face a ruddy red.

"Have a seat," he said.

Dix moved to a stuffed chair in the corner of the room. Reinhardt moved to a chair at a small desk. He carried a cane and walked with a pronounced limp.

"Thank you for coming."

"It's your nickel," Dix said taking a seat. "What's the rundown?"

"I'm tryin' to find my brother, Michael. You see, he's been estranged from the family for several years. Our mother passed recently. We were unable to get in touch with him."

"He's here in LA?"

"That's where we last heard from him. I have his last known address. When I went there, they told me he left over a month ago."

Dix rubbed the scar that ran from the cleft in the center of his chin along his jaw line. He'd acquired it from a Japanese mortar during the Battle of Okinawa. "Whaddya want me to do?"

"Find out where he is, if he's still in Los Angeles. I want to tell him about our mother in person, you understand. There was a falling out and if he knows I'm lookin' for him, he may disappear again."

"Describe him," Dix said opening his notebook.

"He's five-ten. Maybe five-eleven. Brown eyes. Curly brown hair. Fair complexion. Scar on the right side of his forehead. About an inch long. Medium build."

"I'll call as soon as I get somethin' solid," he said as he slipped the notebook in his jacket pocket.

*****

Michael Reinhardt's last known address was a hotel on Selma. Kind of joint where an extra five bucks a month gets you a room without cockroaches. A small man, looked to be in his late forties, sat behind the reception desk reading the Daily News. Dix sidled up to the counter.

"Two dollars a day," the man said without looking up from his paper. "Eleven bucks a week—in advance! No cookin' in da room."

"Thanks for the commercial. I'm not lookin' for a room."

The man looked up. Pinched his eyebrows together, said. "Whateva youz lookin' for, we ain't got it."

"I need some information on one of your tenants."

The clerk looked down at his paper again.

"Name's Reinhardt. Michael," Dix said as he slipped a ten spot from his pocket.

He put the bill on the counter, slid it toward the clerk then covered it with his hand. The clerk stood. Dix lifted his hand. The clerk reached for the bill but with an index finger Dix pulled it back.

"Michael Reinhardt. Probably moved out a coupla months ago."

"You a cop?"

"Private," Dix said as he moved the bill forward and back with his finger.

"Kinda tall guy?" the clerk said.

"Yeah. Curly brown hair."

"I remember the guy."

"What can ya tell me about him? Any idea where he went when he left the hotel?"

"Work, I guess."

"What kinda work?"

"Restaurant I think."

"How so?" Dix said.

"Left early in the mornin'. Came back around four o'clock smellin' like he worked in a kitchen," the clerk said. "You know? Greasy kinda smell."

"You know what restaurant?"

"Dunno."

"You cash a paycheck?"

"Nah! Paid rent in cash."

"Bus stop is right out front. You see him take a bus to work?"

"Nope. Walked."

"Which way?" Dix said with a tinge of excitement.

"Turned right."

"You've been very helpful," Dix said sliding the bill toward the clerk.

*****

Dix figured if Reinhardt didn't ride the bus, he must've worked at a joint that was a ten to fifteen-minute walk from his residence. Dix started visiting all the eateries west of the hotel, skipping establishments that didn't serve breakfast. On the corner of Gower and Sunset sat Mother's Cupboard, a busy little café. Dix took a seat at the lunch counter. Waitress approached. Mid-forties with red hair and dark penetrating eyes. Name tag attached to her apron strap read *Ellen*.

"Whatcha havin', sport?" she said magically producing a pencil from behind her ear.

"Just coffee."

"Apple pie's fresh, just outta the oven?"

"Just coffee."

In an instant she had a cup on a saucer and the hot brew pouring from a ten-gallon urn.

"Cream?" she said over her shoulder.

"Black."

"That'll be ten cents."

Dix tossed a dollar on the counter. Ellen picked up the bill.

"Mind if I, ask ya a question, Ellen?"

"If it ain't too personal."

"I'm lookin' for someone. Name's Michael Reinhardt. Supposed to have work at a restaurant 'round here."

"Yeah, he worked here for a few months."

"Maybe I will have that slice of pie."

"Comin' right up," she said.

*****

After a second cup of coffee and a generous wedge of hot apple pie, Dix got the rundown from the owner Vic Shanks.

"We get lots of breakfast trade durin' the week," Vic, said wiping his large hands on his greasy apron.

Shanks stood about five-foot-eight. Round in the belly. U.S. Navy globe and anchor tattoo on his muscular left forearm. Shanks was the cook on a Destroyer during the war.

"Customers want their food hot and fast," he said. "I needed a second pair of hands. This guy comes in lookin' for work on a busy mornin'. I tells him to put on an apron. He knew nothin' about workin' in a kitchen but he knew how to follow orders. Fast learner. Know what I mean?"

"He only worked for you a coupla months?" Dix said.

"Yeah. Comes in one mornin' says he's movin'. Gotta new job. Swing shift at a factory."

"Need a meatloaf 'n mash, Vic," Ellen called.

"Comin' up," Vic called back.

"He tell ya where he was movin'?"

"A place on Regent. I remember the address was five-hundred somethin'. Had to send him a check for the days he worked." Vic said as he dashed back into the kitchen.

*****

Detective work seems to always come down to one thing. Wearing out shoe leather. Dix started on the odd number addresses working his way up on Regent Street in Inglewood. Knocking on doors and checking mail boxes. Finishing with the odd numbers he crossed the street to the evens working his way back down. Dix checked the mailboxes of a small apartment building. 512 Regent. There was no listing for Reinhardt. He found the manager's door and leaned against the buzzer. A moment later, he pressed it again.

A woman's voice from the back of the apartment sounded like a dump truck grinding its gears on a steep grade.

"All right, all right, I'm comin'! Hold yer water. *Whaddya want?!*" she barked as she opened the door.

"You got a Michael Reinhardt living here?"

"Who wants to know?"

"Webb, Blackmoor Detective Bureau."

"What's he done?"

"His family's tryin to get in touch with him."

"Moved out a week ago," she said.

"Leave a forwarding address?"

"Nah, just up and left. Still owes me ten bucks on his rent."

Dix peeled off a ten spot, said. "Can I take a look at his room?"

She took the money, retrieved a key from a rack next to the door.

"Follow me."

Reinhardt rented apartment D. Dix surveyed the place on entering. It was a small, furnished apartment. Living room, kitchenette, bedroom with attached bath. Dix noticed a book of matches in an ashtray on an end table from the Starlight Lounge, Hollywood.

"These yours?" Dix said.

"Left 'em here."

"He get any visitors?"

"Girlfriend a few times. I tol 'em keep his door open. Ain't gonna have no hanky-panky in my house."

"Yeah," Dix said. "You run a respectable joint."

"It ain't easy, I'll tell ya that. People thinkin' they can play the radio at all hours."

The landlady was a talker.

"You get a name?"

"Huh?"

"The girlfriend? You get a name?"

"We was never introduced."

"You saw her a few times. I'd expect you kept a close eye on who was comin' an' goin'?"

"That's for dang sure," she said pompously. "I run a—"

"Respectable joint, I know. So, you got a good look at this girlfriend, right?"

"I did!"

"What'd she look like?"

"On the tall side. Red hair. She wore lotsa make-up. Like a floozy. Hair all up, lips red as can be. She comes by one time all dressed up in a short skirt, like she was goin' to some kinda party in the middle of the day."

"She ever come around at night?"

"Nah! He worked the night shift."

*****

Dix thought he had it figured. Back in his car he made his way to La Brea. Turned north toward Hollywood. West of La Brea on Sunset stood a single-story building. Neon sign across the façade read in bright orange, Starlight Lounge. One of those dime-a-dance venues that customers could spend three minutes dancing with a beautiful woman. He entered the establishment with the hope that Reinholdt's girlfriend worked there as a taxi dancer. He checked his hat with the girl in the cloakroom. Moved to a gallery where the male customers would gather to view the women. Off to one side, the dancers sat on couches in a bullpen, waiting for customers. None of the women in the bullpen matched the girlfriend's description.

He scanned the dancefloor. Band played *I'm in the Mood for Love*. There were ten—maybe eleven couples on the floor. Three of the male customers were in uniform. Two sailors and a marine. Rest of the male customers were in suits. As they moved around the dance floor, he made note of the female dancers. Two blonds, one dance with the marine the other the sailor. The second sailor danced with a brunette. As he continued to scan the floor, the band ended the song. Several of the girls made their way to the bullpen. One of them a rather tall redhead. Reinhardt's girl. Her dress, tight as a tourniquet showed off every curve. The kind of girl you'd see riding around Hollywood in a Cadillac Convertible. Some handsome movie idol mug behind the wheel.

With five dollars' worth of dance tickets, Dix made his way to the bullpen. The band began to play *Blue Moon*. He reached for the redhead's hand.

"What's your name?" he said.

"Crystal."

They stepped onto the dance floor.

"What's yours?" she said.

"Dixon. Everyone calls me Dix."

"You're a good dancer, Dix."

"Practice."

He handed her his tickets. "Here."

"What's this for?"

"I need some information. I'm lookin' for Michael."

"So that's it. Get outta here *mister*!" she said pushing him away. "You can tell that ex-wife of his she's not gettin' another dime!

"Listen," Dix said. "I don't know nothin' about—"

A round man, fiftyish pushed himself between Dix and Crystal.

"What's the trouble here?" he said a cigar clinched between his teeth.

"This mug's takin' liberties, Al!" she said.

"We don't allow any of that in this place, buster!" he said taking the cigar out of his mouth and waving it in the air.

"Now hold on," Dix said. "I was just askin'—"

He felt two sets of hands grab him from behind. One set belonged to a broad-shouldered gorilla. The other, short mug with a pointed nose.

"Git rid of 'im," Al said. "Make sure he understands we don't want him comin' back."

"Listen!" Dix said. "You got this all *wrong*!"

The two bouncers bum rushed him out the backdoor into the alley.

"Listen guys. I'm a private detective workin' a case. I don't want any trouble."

"Too late, pilgrim. You already got trouble," the big gorilla said as he punched Dix in the solar plexus. He dropped to the ground like a pile of wet laundry. The short weasel nosed mug kicked him in the ribs. Dix rolled over on his back.

"Now shove off 'n don't come back. *Understand*?!" the big gorilla said.

Dix struggled to his feet. The two hoods stood there staring at him.

"I said, shove off. Whadaya waitin' for?"

"I had a hat when I came in."

"Get his hat, Eddie," the big gorilla said.

"Number twenty-six," Dix said as he brushed himself off.

A few moments later Eddie returned to the alley tossed him the hat

"You guys gonna pay for this."

"Send us a bill," Eddie said with a laugh.

"Yeah! A bill," the gorilla said. "We'll send ya a check."

The two men laughed as they entered the building.

*****

"Blackmoor Detective Bureau," Jill said.

"Listen, honey," Dix groaned. "I want you to do me a favor."

"You don't sound so good. You okay?"

"Had a little trouble trackin' down this Reinholdt character."

"Boss says he wants to talk to ya."

The phone clicked in his ear. A moment later Blackmoor was on the line.

"What's this trouble you've been havin'?" Blackmoor said.

"Coupla goons at the Starlight gave me a work over."

"What the hell you doin' at the *Starlight*! You're not gettin' paid to dance with girls."

"I've located the girlfriend."

"The girlfriend?"

"Yeah," Dix said. "She'll lead me to Reinholdt."

"Now we're getting' somewhere," Blackmoor said with satisfaction.

"There's somthin' fishy about this case."

"Fishy or not," Blackmoor said. "You find this Reinholdt and call me as soon as you do. Savvy."

"Put Jill back on the line."

"Yeah, Dix?"

"Here's what I want you to do. Call Starlight Lounge. Ask for Crystal.

Tell her Michael's been hurt. She needs to come right away."

"Okay, Dix."

After hanging up with Jill, he sat in his car watching the Starlight. Less than five minutes passed when Crystal darted out of there and hailed a cab. She was let out at an apartment building on Gower. Dix checked the mailboxes. C. Malone: APT 12. He used the payphone across the street to called Blackmoor with the address.

As he hung up the phone, he saw Crystal leave with a man carrying a satchel. They drove off in a green coupe. Dix followed. They stopped at a small hotel on Argyle. The man got out. Crystal drove off. Dix entered the establishment and approached the desk clerk.

"The man who just checked in? Left an envelope in my cab."

"Room 15," the clerk said.

*****

"Who are you?" Reinhardt said as he opened the door.

"I'm a detective. Your brother just wants to talk to you."

"Brother? I don't have a brother."

"*What?!*"

"Someone called my girl. Said I was hurt. She said some shamus was lookin' for me, hired by my ex."

"Yeah. That was me. This mug hired me. Said he was your brother. Wanted to inform you of your mother's death."

"My mother passed, ten years ago," Reinhardt said.

"Somethin' told me this case was screwy. We'd better get over to Crystal's apartment. I've got a bad feelin'."

*****

Crystal's apartment was dark when they entered. Shades had all be drawn.

"I've been waiting," a male voice said.

Dix recognized the voice. A lamp switched on. Standing next to an end-table, .45 in his hand, the man who called himself Norman Reinholdt. Crystal sat on the couch bound and gagged.

"Who *are* you?" Michael asked.

"Norman Stone. Don't remember me? Stalag 19?" He moved closer, dragging his lame foot.

"I was there, but I don't—"

"You were the one workin' with the Nazis. You informed on our escape plan."

"You got the wrong man," Michael said.

"Don't do it, Stone," Dix commanded.

"It's because of you, I have this," Stone said, indicating his foot and holding out an equally-deformed right hand. "The Germans did this. I used to make watches. Now you're gonna pay."

Stone leveled the gun at Michael, Dix whipped out his revolver as Stone fired. Stone's shot missed. Dix's didn't. Two shots hit Stone dropping him to the floor like a sack of cement.

Michael rushed to Crystal, removed her gag.

"Oh, Michael, he was waiting in the dark," Crystal sobbed.

"It's okay, baby."

"What the *hell* was that about?!" said Dix.

"I remember now. One of the prisoners. Named Rein*hart*. He *was* a camp spy. I guess Stone made a mistake."

"You might say that."

✳✳✳✳✳

"Blackmoor Detective—"

"Jill! It's Dix. Put the boss on."

"What is it?" Blackmoor said answering the line.

"Our client's dead. He tried to murder Michael Reinholdt."

"Good lord!"

"It gets worse."

"Huh!"

"There's no such person as Norman Reinholdt. The checks a phony."

"Damnit, Webb! I've already sent that check to the—"

Dix left the phone booth with the receiver hanging from its cord.

"Another scotch 'n' soda, Louie," Dix said to the bartender.

What's in a Name?
J. T. Seate

Sometimes investigations start out as one thing and mutate into something else entirely. My name is Sam Mackintosh. I was a pretty good cop once. After that, I was a decent PI, but I'm not sure what I'm best at these days. There's an old saying, *misery loves company*, so I agreed to meet Charlie at Faye's Diner—a little joint filled with the ghosts of dead cigarettes and bacon grease, and was dark enough to fit my mood. The waitress's smile had all the warmth of a hacksaw, but anything to get out of the sleazy room where I always seemed to end up between wives.

Charlie was a fast talker with brisk gestures and a puss that resembled a mackerel. "Sam-O, you've got to quit hooking up with women whose names start with M," he advised.

"Tell me something I don't know."

"What? Marsha, Martha, Myrtle, how many has it been?"

"Luck of the draw," I told Charlie.

"What was this last one's name?"

"Maxine."

"She shoved you out the door with nothing but an empty wallet, right? Probably got the keys to your beloved '47 Buick, too?"

I didn't dignify the questions with an answer.

"Sure she did. Dames always leave a guy high and dry. At first, they act like you're Errol Flynn. They light up like a jukebox, but the light always dims, doesn't it, pal?"

I wanted to tell Charlie, *Fuck you and the hook that snagged you*, but he was having a good time.

"They laugh at your jokes and, in the end, the joke is on you. They make you feel like a bull with a rope around its balls." A conspiratorial chuckle. "Into everyone's life a little rain must fall. That's love for you."

More like a flood for me with the ink on my divorce papers barely dry, but I still had my trusty friend that promised to never let me down in a pinch. She was strapped to my right ankle.

Charlie continued, "My old lady was a doozey. I cut her loose. Kissed her fanny goodbye on the Fourth of July. Independence Day all year round. I've sworn off broads like an alcoholic taking the pledge, brother. You should try it."

Charlie was beginning to get on my nerves. I shot back, "So to what do I owe the pleasure?"

"This is your lucky day, old stick. I can give you a sweet payday if you'll follow a broad for one of my clients."

I tossed down the contents of my coffee cup wishing it was a shot glass. "If you expect me to wear out shoe leather on some skirt, you're thinking of some other chump. I've got a couple of bail-skips to track down."

"You're developing a nice pain-in-the-ass attitude, partner."

"But it comes from the heart."

"Since when did you get one of those?"

"Why don't *you* tail her?"

"I'm snowed under. Thought I'd toss you a bone, try to help out an old buddy." His fishy grin reminded me of a snake-oil salesman. "At least it's better than bail-skips, or getting a snapshot of some schlemiel wallowing his wife's best friend."

I figured this "help" was something more dangerous than *he* wanted to pursue.

When I said as much, Charlie replied, "Naw, a piece of cake for an old shamus like you. A woman is supposed to meet some pug down by the waterfront tomorrow. Her old man got wind of it and figures she might have a thing going. You got some other big deal at present?"

He had me there. My last job concluded abruptly when the guy I was tracking ended up face down sprawled in a mess of blood, mustard, and pickle relish on the sidewalk in front of a hotdog stand. He'd taken a bullet from a passing car. Apparently I hadn't been the only one on his trail, but it didn't help my reputation for a mark to wind up in the city morgue wearing a toe tag.

It was also true beggars couldn't be choosers, so in the end, money spoke louder than doubt. "She got a name?"

"Mrs. Dunwich."

"First name."

"Maggie," he said.

Sweet Jesus. "Swell," I said and took the donation.

*****

I was a Depression-era kid who thought he had it made as a cop, but an indiscretion moved me along to my current métier. Would've been fine if I had shown more sense when it came to the opposite sex. I once thought love happened in capital letters, but my marriages taught me it was mostly fine print. Thought I'd learned to read my latest wife like a Superman comic book, thought we were working it out, until I caught her with another guy. Apparently, we were reading different kinds of literature.

Why was *I* the one who got the boot from our love cottage? Maxine spent money like a cotton-picker on payday, and I'd never been a guy who could afford ten-dollar ties made in China, or imported cigars, or fancy restaurants with one-word names, but I managed to keep a roof over our heads. This weasel had been grazing in her pasture while yours truly had been beating the bushes as a private snoop. The two of them were probably drinking wine and carving me up like a roast. Still, I had to smile when I thought about this little creep getting involved with Maxine. It made about as much sense as hijacking a rollercoaster.

The two-timing dame was taking me for everything but my PI identification. My blue-worsted pinstripe suit was tossed out with the cat litter. Would she try for alimony? Hell yes, she would. She'd sink her fangs in as deeply as possible.

I happened to run across my 1933 high school yearbook among the items Maxine was trashing. I came to the page with hearts drawn around a picture and signed by Marsha. She'd been the first M girl to sugar me up. Certain women have the ability to reach down inside you and twist something. My M's had been like that. Charming fellow though I was, the Raymond Chandler baloney only held its glamour for so long. Not Marsha, nor those who followed, chose to be a permanent passenger aboard the SS Mackintosh as it sailed across the ocean of life, swimming away instead to calmer seas.

My reverie about the past, along with Charlie's fresh cash injection, kept me in Faye's far too long. After he left, I reminisced with some rummy about the war.

"The barrel of a gun is the blackest hole you can look into," he slurred in the course of our conversation. I wasn't so sure considering all the rabbit holes I'd fallen into chasing dames. Pondering my misfortunes, I hung around the diner until Faye turned off the lights.

*****

The physicality of my liaisons varied in size and shape from the petite to medium, from button noses to veritable ski slopes, but my passion was ankles, the kind Maggie Dunwich possessed.

She appeared mid-afternoon, and some dame she was. Eye-balling her from across the street, I could tell she was well-tended and had developed some class. My gaze eased over her frame as she walked along the street in a swaying, four-alarm glide. Her ensemble clung snuggly to her curves with a lover's touch highlighting an hour-glass figure. The luscious ankles turned into good-looking gams. Her look screamed *Femme Fatale*, high-octane all the way. Why the hell did her name have to be Maggie?

I trailed her in a cab and then on foot to a salty district along the waterfront. It was one hell of a place for a classy trick to be meeting whoever she was meeting, but nothing could truly surprise me after years of digging up dirt on people who preferred to keep their secrets buried. She knocked on the door of what looked like an office next to a warehouse. A man's hand and arm appeared, pushing the door open.

Normally, I heeded the adage of two being company and three being you-know-what. I hid nearby and waited, planning to brace her when she came out. Catching her off-guard might uncover the particulars for the lowbrow slumming. That was the plan, until I heard a scream.

There was nothing I hated worse than complications on a "piece of cake" job. I trotted to a greasy window next to the office door and tried to see in. A man stood with his back to the door. Maggie sat in a chair in front of him shivering like a frightened dog. The man's trousers were around his ankles. As a rule, I didn't trust men with their pants down.

I heard the man utter the distinctly unfriendly phrase. "Cooperate or I'll knock your teeth out."

Maggie shook her head. The fear on her face sent a rush of blood speeding through my arteries. In spite of my shortcomings, I didn't approve of violence toward women. As an ex-cop, I'd seen every kind of sadism from beatings with leather gloves so as not to cut flesh, to a woman hung from a hook and tortured mercilessly. But this scene proved to be something different.

On this occasion, I was packing my trusty .32 underneath my only good coat. I stormed into the room, weapon drawn. The man in front of Maggie turned abruptly. The venom in his ice cold stare threatened to peel away my skin. He was an ugly cuss with a shaved head, beady eyes, and an aggressive nose. His angry countenance held all the elements of a cave man who'd done some time in the stir. He leered at me with white-hot anger set in his scarred face. Since I was as gun-shy as a traveling salesman who had known too many farmers' daughters, I was glad that the scoundrel wasn't packing his own heater.

"What the hell?" he asked in a steely voice that matched his appearance.

"Sounds like the lady would prefer some other form of recreation," I offered.

"Lady?" he said with a snarl and started toward me.

"My weapon's not friendly," I said, referring to my pistol. "Another step and you're Swiss Cheese."

Maggie remained seated, not sure what to do.

"Get up and move away from him," I told her.

"This bimbo thinks she's something special now." He spat the words. "But she's no different than all the other broads that troll the coast."

"You're going to shut your yap while the lady and I walk out of here," I told the man I believed to be a merchant sailor along with being a thug. "I'll be contacting the cops about an attempted rape, so maybe you want to sail off into the sunset."

He looked at Maggie. Her eyes were as blue and wild as a Siamese cat's. "I'll catch up with you, bitch." He looked at me. "And you, too, good buddy."

His comments tweaked the funny monkey in my brain. My cop side kicked in. I took a step forward and landed a hard pistol whip against the brute's temple. He went down like a pile of fresh mush.

"You best take your ship out to sea and keep it there," I said. "*Hasta la cucaracha, hombre.*"

"Who are you?" Maggie managed to squeak out.

"For now, your white knight in shining armor," I said.

I loaded Maggie into a cab. Her only reaction to her near-miss was a tilt of her head to one side so she could massage the back of her neck. I would have bet my last clean pair of skivvies that baldy had a record. Some hard cases found Jesus inside the clink, but I would have laid odds *he* hadn't looked for Him, let alone found Him.

We saved our conversation until we found a lounge back on her end of town. Maggie sat primly on a barstool next to me while we sipped java that wasn't warm enough. Then those blue eyes looked at me, now resembling storm clouds over the ocean. I told myself to demonstrate medieval stoicism and remain emotionally detached as I looked at her, trying not to get carried away by her pouting mouth red with lipstick and practically begging to be kissed. I wondered how many schleps had been up close and personal with those lips.

To look at her was to be swept onto a current of desire. Her profile was classic, feminine, and bosomy. She might have modeled for the prow of a ship back in the day when seafarers believed such a sculpture had the power to ward off the whims of fate. When she crossed her legs, I took notice of the ankle nearest my pant leg. It twisted tantalizingly. She probably knew I was aching to put a lip-lock on her ruby-reds. The smell of her expensive perfume hit me like a punch in the nose. It was the kind of bug juice out of my price range. My nostrils flared as I sniffed.

Most all women with a checkered past know their drill, but Maggie had perfected hers. Images of us in sexual scenarios flitted through my mind, making my body restless. It hadn't taken much time alone to crave a woman's touch. That was me, ole cravin' Sam who wouldn't mind getting jake with Mrs. Dunwich. I wanted to touch as much as to be touched. I could imagine spending a torrid week on some island next to this package of delights. She generated the kind of primal urges that kept reproduction in vogue. Would've been better off to play Russian roulette than to let another female play games with my head, and yet, I wanted to kiss her like some kid panting over a dime lollypop.

It finally occurred to her to thank me. "You're not a cop."

"Used to be. Not anymore."

"Peeked through one keyhole too many?" she said with the slightest of smiles as her dangling leg swung to and fro.

She wasn't far off base. There had been a little issue between me and the chief's wife. Her name was Mary Jo, and it hastened my fall from grace and sudden career change.

"So, now you're a private dick."

I didn't like to be interrogated. "Your friend on the waterfront's the kinda guy who gives crime a bad name. Life has enough excitement without a pig like him adding to the drama," I said, volleying back into her court. In spite of her classy calm, I figured it was a cover. She had to be a little shaken and maybe even feeling fragile from her near miss. I tried to remain detached. "So, give me the story. It's bound to be better than what I'm thinking."

"Can I bum a cigarette?" If aged whiskey could generate sound, it would have sounded like her voice.

I asked the waitress for a fresh pack of Luckies, tapped one out, and lit it for her. She took a long drag and let the smoke slip out one side of her mouth, making somewhat of a performance of it. The interlude was followed by a heavy sigh. As if summoning strength to continue, a second cloud of languid smoke escaped sensually from Maggie's near flawless lips.

"I used to work at a dockside drinking joint called Davy Jones's Locker. A woman named Lillian McConnell owns it. After being there a while, I was as close to some security as I'd ever been, and my job was respectable. I was Lil's bookkeeper and a part-time waitress, the latter only when one of the regular girls didn't show." Maggie cleared her throat like she had a piece of rust caught in it. "Doing the bar-shift could be rough in The Locker. I hated cocktailing the floor."

Bad choices in wives notwithstanding, I wasn't carved out of a wet mouse turd yesterday. "Don't red-apple me, blue eyes." I sounded like a PI in a detective story. "I know the place. The barmaids wear G-strings and bras to keep them out of trouble with the law. But, for a price, a little action can be found around the fringes of the barroom. You play that game?"

"We all do what we must to survive." She took another long drag. Her bosom heaved admirably. "Then one day Lil sets me up with this high-roller."

"Mr. Dunwich, I presume." I heard the sarcasm in my voice and wished it wasn't there.

Maggie looked at me, her suspicions about her husband putting the tail on her confirmed. "Yeah, Mr. Dunwich. You can probably figure it. We have a date. He tells me I'm the most wonderful woman in the world. I see my chance to get away from the life once and for all, and I take it."

"Rags to riches. How's it working out?"

"Fine, until this creep who knew me before chases me down. I didn't strip or hook, but Jerome could say I did and he wanted money to keep quiet."

"Jerome? That slick-headed so-and-so's name is Jerome?"

Maggie shrugged. "A name's a name. What's yours?"

"Sam."

"Sam," she repeated, tasting it.

I'd known my share of women like Maggie, ones without the luxury of being born uptown; ones who had to struggle. Sometimes their only chance was to take advantage of their looks and hook up with some swell. I could picture the tawdry life Maggie lived before she got lucky. The cheap boarding-house rooms, adrift slobs coming and going on ancient staircases. I knew this because I'd lived in several of those places.

"I'm not passing judgment, Maggie, but I have to report to the guy who hired me. How did Jerome hook up with you?"

"I told Lil I wanted to be the place's bookkeeper, nothing more. She balked. 'You're sassy, girl. Your street-wise-smarts brings in customers,' she says to me, so I work the floor. Jerome sees me at The Locker. He makes a few passes, doesn't like me turning him down. Soon afterward, I get the rock on my finger and quit once and for all. Then one day, Jerome spots me, says he wants fifty Gs to keep quiet. I didn't think he knew about me, but there he was. You know the rest."

I whistled at the amount. The ostentatious rock on her finger could have been a nice down payment. Most of my exes liked their rocks, so I knew my way around carets. "Surely Dunwich knew your past."

"Only part of it. Not about me moonlighting while working for Lil. Only *she* knows about that...and Jerome."

"What about today?"

"We were going to arrange the pay-off. I'd met with him once before, but this was the first time he tried to take advantage. You'd think the money would be enough." She stubbed her cigarette butt into a glass ashtray. "So, what happens now? I guess you'll tell my husband I'm still held hostage by the life I've tried to escape?"

Ugly wouldn't let his fish off the hook just because I happened to inconveniently show up. Next time it would take more than knocking Jerome's face into the following week. It was only a matter of time before he either exposed her, or harmed her, and I didn't expect him to be patient. "There are other solutions, Maggie," I said with a slight smile.

"You mean you'll help me out of this?"

The lingering smoke cloud from our cigarettes had created a cocoon-like veil around us. She watched me carefully waiting for an answer.

"It all depends."

She took an inflating breath and leaned forward, placing her hand upon mine. Her blouse was straining to contain its cargo. I didn't know if her hopeful look was sincere or not, and I didn't much care. Okay, so maybe I was more interested in helping the damsel in distress who looked like Maggie Dunwich than reporting the setup back to Charlie, at least for the time being.

"Nice little scar through your right eyebrow. Adds character," she told me. "The war?"

"Ex-wife."

"You have one of *those*?"

"Doesn't everybody?"

Maggie couldn't squelch a laugh. Any ice between the two of us had melted. There was a woman for you. One minute they were helpless and the next, they were psychologically bending you to their will like a piece of sheet metal being riveted onto the belly of a B-29.

"Most men are asses," she offered, "but fortunately, not all."

I took a final gander at Maggie's breastworks before sliding off my stool. "Some days you get up in the morning and say, 'screw it,' and start from scratch," I said. "I have several ideas."

And our dance with the devil began.

*****

Confucius said, *"Before you embark on a journey of retribution, dig two graves,"* or something similar. Davy Jones's Locker was in a part of town that came alive when darkness descended, ready to savor the promise of the night like some great beast. The following Friday night, I told Maggie to do something with her hubby to provide both of them with an alibi. I planned to go to the Locker myself.

A cloud of blue smoke already hung suspended just above the milling throng by the time I arrived. The joint was jumping with swearing sailors, Marines, and dockworkers with pockets full of singles and bodies full of juice. From behind the Locker's bar, Harvey, the barkeep, held his own against the drunker-by-the-minute crowd, and Lillian was somewhere in the back room probably helping one of her girls into a skimpy outfit. Waitresses wound their way around the boisterous tables ignoring the cat-calls and fanny-feelers. It was payday for the motley crew of servicemen and Lillian had installed custom-made foam-rubber beer taps in the shape of breasts. Five kegs bore the creative spouts. For a buck, customers could nurse on beer straight from the tap for fifteen seconds; a unique gimmick and beyond popular.

Around ten o'clock, the bar's secondary attraction appeared to a cacophony of shouts and applause. She was called China Doll and emerged from a back room wearing a bright red, dragon-embroidered Kimono. She mingled with the rowdy crowd on her perilous way to the small stage tucked in the corner of the smoke-filled room. China Doll stood five-feet nothing, even in high-heels. When she ascended the platform, a boozy cheer went up from the drunks and soon-to-be-drunk.

Everyone admired China Doll's petite figure and exquisitely proportioned body as she slipped out of her Kimono. Music blasted from a bad sound system. As she turned, her devotion for the men in bell-bottoms was evident. She'd dedicated her derriere to the cause. Ship anchors were tattooed on each diminutive buttock. China Doll shimmied and shook. The anchors danced.

"You're an angel," a sailor called out as the crowd wolf-whistled and pounded on tables.

"You're breakin' my heart," another shouted.

"Lemme kiss those anchors, sweetie," a third voice bellowed through the dense, blue fog of dust and smoke.

As a second tune exploded above the den of voices, China Doll removed her flimsy top and wiggled her perky breasts toward her inebriated audience. Foot-stomping had the floor shaking.

Then the inevitable happened. A sailor, not much bigger than China Doll, leaped onto the stage and bit her on the butt. She yelped. She tried to shake free of the land-shark, but the little guy's choppers hung on like a dog to a trouser leg.

Another swabbie jumped onstage in a rescue attempt. He pounded his fist into the offender's right ear until China Doll was free. A blood-red circle now surrounded the anchor on her left cheek. She grabbed her Kimono, clutched it between her breasts, and headed for the relative security of a back room.

"Let's tear up that swabbie," someone suggested concerning the sailor who had disrupted the party.

"Can't even act civilized," a marine hollered from the bar. "Screw all you anchor-clankers!"

The slight wasn't about to go unnoticed. As jarheads and sailors positioned themselves for impending combat, Harvey stood on the bar and shouted, "Free beer for one minute," as loud as he could.

There was a hesitation and then everyone in the room tore toward one of the five beckoning foam-rubber attachments, exchanging one kind of free-for-all for another. The onslaught on the kegs was so great the bartender was knocked off balance and fell into the rampaging herd. The crush of bodies caused one of the tap handles to break off its keg. Beer blew the rubber breast aside and gushed in a white cascade, washing over a dozen sailors who began to batter one another into insensibility. I knew Harvey wouldn't keep his cool if the free-for-all went on for very long. Maggie had told me old Harv had pulled a Section Eight in the service for nearly beating the brains out of a barracks-mate with a chair leg.

As the battle for beer raged, I saw what I'd been hoping for. Maggie said Jerome usually dropped in on Friday nights. And there he was, eye-balling the battle, but staying out of its center, throwing a random punch at anyone who ventured within his reach.

Several sailors were on their hands and knees either looking for an available nozzle or trying to crawl their way out of the growing fray. The vastly outnumbered Marines had formed a flying wedge to break through the sailors who were grappling around the beer kegs. When they charged, the room became a patchwork of blue-jackets and bell-bottoms against a smaller contingent of olive-drab uniforms. Sixty some-odd drunkerds kicked, clawed, and bellowed loudly. All five taps now shot out cold liquid geysers soaking everyone with the frothy brew.

Outside, sirens approached the Locker. "The cops are here, you assholes!" Harvey wailed, knocking bodies aside so he could get to his feet.

The Shore Patrol and local police burst into the dive. With the help of their night sticks, they restored some semblance of order. Jerome had quietly disappeared into the back where the girls were. I slipped out the front door and moved to the alleyway leading to the side of the building where I believed Maggie's blackmailer would eventually exit.

Before long, the side door swung open. Jerome's shape filled the doorway. He was yelling at one of the girls, calling her names, demonstrating his low opinion of women in general. This time, I carried a sap in my pocket to go along with my hardware, but before I could get as close as I wanted, he spotted me. His reactions were quicker than I'd anticipated. He flew from the threshold of the door, knocked me down. His chin jutted forward. His ugly, vengeful mug set in Gestapo stone except for a mocking grin.

"Hello, sweetheart," he said with a world of insolence. "So you want to play again."

He pulled a hunting knife from his jacket, a vengeful man about to launch his rage with extreme prejudice. The knife glinted in his hand like a silver tooth. As I tried to reach for my .32, his grin widened victoriously, planning to gut me.

Then I saw the silver flash of a bracelet and a baseball bat swinging through space. It crashed into the side of Jerome's head. The knife flew from his hand, but the blow didn't bring him down. He staggered sideways.

Standing defiantly behind my assailant was China Doll, now covered by a short robe. With the fury of a Samurai warrior, she raised one foot and planted it squarely into the offender's groin. That brought him to his knees, pronto.

"You little piece of—"

With a look that would curdle milk, China Doll spun around and delivered another swift kick to Jerome's face. His words became gobbledy-gook as he pitched to one side and toppled over. There was someone else with her. It was Lillian. Maggie's tormentor lay on the dirty pavement, too out of it to cradle his wounded face or kicked crotch.

"Not a copper in sight," Lillian said. "All of 'em busy with our juice-headed service boys inside."

I got to my feet. China's Doll's quick actions had caused her robe to pull up to her waist, allowing a private viewing of those charming little anchors. I could picture the Doll married to a marine and kicking the stuffing out of him regularly.

Jerome moaned unintelligibly. China Doll looked down at her prey. "You were born a bad guy, and you go out same way," she said.

"I'll kill all you bitches," the man spat through a mouthful of blood.

China Doll lifted the bat and brought it crashing down on the man's skull. He jerked and popped a few red spit-bubbles. She cracked the bat against his head once more. He twitched again, but didn't move after that. Then he stopped breathing. Nothing but the fresh stench of soiled trousers remained. China Doll was one hard-boiled little dame. It wouldn't have surprised me if she'd reached in Jerome's pants, sliced off his Johnson, and kept it as a souvenir.

"What would have happened after the police took him?" Lil asked me, her eyes implacable. "He would get out of jail and come after us, and you, and Maggie. Now you won't have to worry about him. I'll say someone from the fight inside bashed his brains out and took a powder."

The script played like a cheap novel.

China Doll chimed in. "Now *this* peckerwood is going to be dead long time. Harv will be happy how I use his prize possession."

"Thank you for saving my ass. I owe both of you."

Lillian spoke up again, "Won't be no mourning over this scumbag. The Chamber of Commerce would be proud of us."

I agreed that a cold slab in the morgue was a righteous ending for Jerome. The little three-way love-fest we were having was grand, but the need to get my tail out of the alley and back to my low-rent Shangra-La got me moving.

*****

Since the Bogart movie called *The Big Sleep*, street cops and private dicks liked to use the phrase when referring to *corpus delicti*. Jerome's big sleep led me to a big awakening—women were inherently dangerous. They could change the truth quicker than I could change expressions. Maggie's new lease on life went as follows:

She wanted out from under her husband's thumb. When she saw how simple it was to remove hubby's money from the bank to pay off Jerome, she went back for more, a whole lot more. I explained that theft was a serious crime, even if it was taken from a spouse. Getting caught could lead to a prison full of bull-guards and half-crazed females. I came on as the gallant hero offering to protect a helpless woman against the hands of justice, all the while knowing Maggie was anything but helpless.

I chose to go for a better deal than Charlie had offered. I told Maggie, "You can take all your dough and go wherever you choose on one condition. You take *me* with you." I paused a moment for drama. "You and me to the end of the line."

Her eyelids fluttered. She claimed she'd had an epiphany after I'd been instrumental in getting Jerome out of the picture, so she agreed. Our unholy alliance was sealed when I pulled Maggie against me. Then

I kissed her. A surge of triumph rushed through me like it was D-Day. A person is lucky to experience such a kiss once in a lifetime, the kind that makes you feel both alive and ultimately doomed at the same time. We broke apart long enough to tear at each other's clothes and wound up writhing on the floor of my soon to be departed room-for-rent.

Ahhh, the rotten sweetness of corruption. My reaction must have been something akin to Captain Ahab's first sighting of the great white whale. When the event reached its zenith, she nearly swooned like a dewy heroine in a romance novel. Maybe she thought she owed me, but if Maggie's proclamation of pleasure was an act, her performance achieved award-winning status.

"*Of all the lives in all the towns in the entire world, you walk into mine,*" she murmured.

I appreciated the film reference, but I would rather have had Maggie Dunwich than any of Bogey's brooding damsels. She was sexy, she was there, and she'd just come into a nice piece of change.

Truth isn't absolute. It's a wardrobe to be changed as we see fit. But there *were* things that could eat at a man's integrity, a place where the unrighteous path begins. This deal with the devil would remain lodged into my psyche like an impacted wisdom tooth. Yeah, I got a nasty feeling about turning Charlie and Mr. Dunwich into chumps…for a while, but the swindle appealed to some devil on my shoulder. Ingratiating myself with both loot and a new squeeze could have gotten me in more hot water than boiling tea bags for this complicit and consensual extortion, but I was willing to take the chance.

The two of us skipped town. Maggie had given Dunwich the gate, hinges and all, and bounced back like a rubber ball. And my alimony payments had become a thing of the past.

"It's not like we're bank robbers or politicians," she said. Somewhere, Sherlock Holmes must be rolling over in his fictional grave.

So, here we are. Salt in the air. Salt on our skin. Salt on the rim of our margaritas, bathed in a radiant sunset that could be mistaken for salvation from a god neither of us believe in. But, to be honest, I miss

Faye's unattractive diner while on the lam in this place where I have turquoise water and Mrs. Dunwich. Maggie strikes poses intended to be appreciated. She especially likes to dance, so we dance. When she puts her mind to it, she can out-dance and out-love all my former M's. I can almost hear Charlie crying in his beer about the private dick for whom he'd done a favor taking off with a client's dame and his bank account. I actually called Charlie once to tell him what a grand time I was having. He began ranting about my ethics. I hung up softly hoping he might bellow for several minutes before he realized he was raving into a dead line. Back in the States, Ms. M and I could wind up in the slammer, but here, our love nest is warm and safe, set to the music of the islands, at least until the money runs out.

One thing you can't buy is time, and I sometimes wonder how much of it Maggie and I have before we start to look askance at one another, suspicious of motives lying beneath the surface of our capriciousness. Maggie isn't only the most recent specimen bearing the initial M, she is also the most mysterious. Did I really save her? Might *I* merely be the latest in a string of lovers, the newest piece in a chess game she's playing until she can figure how to make a better move? Suppose the con is on *me*. Suppose the whole thing was orchestrated, Jerome first, the husband second, and me third.

Do I expect a dish like Maggie to stay with a slug like me forever? The odds are against it. There are a thousand ways to end a relationship. The possibilities gnaw at my gut, trying to figure out what such an elaborate charade might accomplish while her body touches mine with untrustworthy warmth.

Our affair is like a jigsaw puzzle with a few pieces missing. I hope Maggie doesn't turn out to be yet another wrong woman who soon tires of the game like a cat with a mouse. Some men stick to a dame like gum on the bottom of a theater seat. I can't swear off of them either, but if there is another one after Maggie, I'll ask her name before I even say, "Hello."

The Five Cent Detective
S. B. Watson

The passer-by dropped the coins into the bum's tin cup and kept walking, hunched back and fedora disappearing into the neon-mizzle. The bum was quick to act, snatching the coins from the cup and hurling them after the disappearing overcoat. They tinkled across the cement into the gutter.

"What you think I'm doin' here?" the bum hacked into the rain. "Think I'm some fuckin' charity case? I'm running a *business* here, you jerk, don't go wastin' my time with your spare pocket change!"

Portland's Japantown lay silent in the mists. Dark figures huddled beneath the eaves of the New Meyer Hotel a block away. The bum sat back into the shelter of the recessed porch next to his cardboard sign, and watched them from the shadows. They'd come from the Blanchett House, the only free dinner in Portland for children of the street. But they hadn't stayed, and now they were locked outside after curfew. In the rain.

The bum sipped cold coffee from a lidless paper cup. He took an old commando stiletto—long and pointed into a dagger tip—from beneath his torn coat and began to dig at the dirt under his fingernails. He sat in the moist dark, breathing the Portland rain and listening to the traffic sounds from Burnside, a few blocks away.

"Your sign for real, mister?" the boy asked.

The bum glanced up from his fingernails, slipping the dagger back beneath his coat.

"Where the hell'd you come from?"

The kid was tall for his age, with a gangly sort of austerity. He swallowed, and pushed his horn-rimmed glasses higher on the bridge of his nose. "Your sign," he repeated, hair stringing across his forehead. "It's on the legit?"

"You see," the bum said, "I wrote this sign so smart people—unlike yourself—could read it and understand it, without having to ask. I wrote it so's I wouldn't have to explain it every time some dumb kid came and started to gawk. It means what it says." He turned to the sign and read it aloud. "'Any mystery solved, five cents. Satisfaction guaranteed or money back.'"

"I can pay," the kid said, holding out a shiny coin.

The bum took it and held it up to the watery glare of the streetlamp. It glimmered in the wet, a newly minted 1954 Jefferson nickel.

"What's the mystery, kid, other than how you could have grown up so dumb?"

The kid frowned, and shuffled back a step. "I think my dad wants to kill my mom."

"That's not a mystery. That's nine out of ten households. God himself couldn't solve that puzzle, so he created divorce and gave it to old Moses along with the ten commandments and a bunch of other crap. I can't help you." He handed the nickel back; the kid didn't take it. "Look, you don't really want me to answer that question," he growled. "You want me to make sure it doesn't happen. That's muscle stuff, kid. You need a bodyguard. Or a hitman. Someone with knuckles. I'm just a nickel detective. Here, take it."

The kid couldn't have been more than eleven or twelve. He stood in the rain, dressed in little else than a shabby coat, pants, and tattered lace-up boots. "Please, mister," he said.

When the lip started to quiver the bum grunted and pulled the nickel back. "Ok," he said, "Here's what I'll do. Hey, stop crying—that's dumb, kid. Crying won't get you nowhere. I'll take the nickel, and I'll look into it. But if I don't like what I see, I'm gonna come and give it back, and you're not gonna stop me. Deal?"

The kid sniffed aggressively, pushing the glasses back again, and nodded his head. "Deal."

"What's your name?"

"Peter Verratti."

"What's your mom's name?"

"Rita Verratti. And my dad's Carlo."

"Italian?"

The kid nodded.

"I killed your kind in the war, kid."

The boy shrugged. "So?"

The bum grinned. "That's more like it, Pete. Keep that chin up, and don't take shit from nobody. Where you live?"

The boy gave his address. It was a run-down tenement, a few blocks north, on the edge of Japantown.

"Now, why you think your dad's got it out for Rita?"

"Last few weeks, Mom started coming home late from work."

"Where's she work?"

"Sullivan's Café."

The bum raised his eyebrows. "Ritzy."

"She comes home late, every night. Dad's started yelling at her, and throwing things. He says, if she's stepping out with another guy, he'll kill her."

"You think she is?"

The boy started to quiver. "No. Maybe. I don't know. That's why…" He nodded to the cardboard sign.

"When's your mom get off, Pete?"

"Nine."

The bum pulled the mud-stained sleeve of his overcoat back from his wrist, revealing a scuffed steel watch with a cracked bezel. "That's thirty minutes from now."

"But she won't get home till late."

"And you don't know why?"

The boy shook his head.

"Alright," the bum said, reaching for the cardboard sign and the tin cup. "Get home. Listen to your dad howl."

"How long will it take you?" Peter asked as the bum stuffed his sign into the old military backpack and smashed a garrison cap onto his head.

"It'll take me as long as it takes me," the bum snarled, slinging the pack over one shoulder. "I'll find you when I'm satisfied with my answer. Or," he said, stopping and turning back towards Peter, "if I come to give that nickel back."

"What's your name?" Peter called after the quickly disappearing shadow.

"Ed Bent."

*****

Bent watched from the darkened alley as the lights clicked off inside Sullivan's. One by one, the tall, lean woman with dark red hair in the pencil skirt and white dress shirt moved between the dining rooms. Room by room, darkness followed her, until she disappeared into the kitchens. A few moments after the kitchen lights darked, Bent heard the clatter of a side door, around the corner on 6th. A gangly man in a tall overcoat, hiding his maître d' togs, turned the corner and moved up the boulevard.

After a lonely moment, Bent stepped from his hiding spot in a crevasse between two buildings and crossed the street to the corner.

Rita was moving away from him, a block in the lead, up 6th. Towards Japantown. She wore a grey peacoat beneath a khaki umbrella, opened against the rain. Bent followed, slowly ambling beneath the tattered backpack, damp overcoat flapping against stained trouser legs.

When Rita reached Burnside—the southern border of Japantown— she stopped, and turned, scanning back down the street.

It was too late to hide, so Bent continued shambling forward. Rita glanced at him a moment before looking on. The frantic traffic behind her lit the wet night like a revolving carousel; she stood darkly before it, under the shadow of the umbrella. Then she turned and threaded between the cars. Bent quickened his pace.

When he reached the other side of Burnside, he thought he'd lost her. The khaki umbrella and peacoat were nowhere to be seen.

Muttering under his breath, Bent pulled his backpack around and moved beneath the hanging arches of the old Apostolic Church building, on the corner of Burnside and 6th. He pulled a half-empty bottle of brandy from his pack and raised it to drink, but stopped just as the spiced liquid touched his lips.

The khaki umbrella was perched beside a doorway, halfway down the opposite block.

Bent stowed the brandy and hid in the low, dense shrubs bordering the church. Rita emerged moments later. Bent watched as she raised the umbrella and stepped back into the rain, walking deeper into Japantown. When she crossed out of sight he slipped out of his shrub and peered after her.

Two blocks down, she crossed to Bent's side of 6th and took a cross street. Heading east, towards the river. Bent turned and ran back to Burnside, mirroring her movements two blocks to the south, darting a block down the hill. He peered down 5th when he reached it. Rita was halfway across, still moving east. Bent crossed as well and ran to 4th.

Rita didn't appear on 4th.

Bent waited a few minutes before stepping out and leaving Burnside, walking into the slums. He crossed Couch. Still, Rita didn't appear on the cross street. He slowed as he neared Davis, the street she'd been using. There wasn't any place to go between 5th and 4th on Davis. Bent had moved quicker than Rita, so she *must* have stopped between the two numbered streets.

At Davis, he again peered around the corner. And again, halfway up the street, the khaki umbrella stood wedged in the unlit entryway of a tall, brick building.

Bent reached back and pulled a tattered notepad from his trouser pocket. A half-broken pencil came from beneath the folds of his overcoat. He remembered the first address, and wrote that down. Then he looked up to write down the current resting place of the umbrella just as Rita came out the door. She took the umbrella, without looking around, and moved up Davis, away from Bent.

For two hours, Bent trudged up side streets, darted through alleys, dodged behind rubbish bins and crawled through wet bushes and puddles of mud-water, trying to stay one step behind Rita without being spotted. The woman moved quickly, but without haste. She knew where she was going. Bent never saw her reference a map or notes on her journey; she never stopped to speak to passers-by. Once, as her meandering path neared the Union Depot by the river, she stopped, and peered back, poised beneath the umbrella like a startled deer in a wet forest. Her gaze passed Bent, unseeing, where he stood in the shallow entrance to a boarded-up building.

Every few blocks Rita stopped. Sometimes at a small tenement, sometimes at the back entrance to a business—barber shop, hardware store, hair salon, tavern. Every time, her practice was the same. She lowered the umbrella, glanced up and down the street, then rapped at the door. It opened. The room would be dimly lit. She entered. She never spent more than five minutes inside before reemerging, and hurrying on her way.

Rita was nervous. That much was obvious. Anxious and unprofessional. Bent followed her well, but even so he made some errors. She spotted him twice—a careless oversight on his part. A professional would have remembered the frowzy man in the garrison cap, stooped beneath his tattered backpack in the rain; Rita didn't.

Rita's path wound back and forth through Japantown, eventually twisting up the hill, past the railroad yards. As Rita neared 16th street, she began to check her wristwatch. At the corner of 16th and Lovejoy, she stopped.

Sixteenth was double-wide. A small patch of trees and poorly maintained parkland ran down its center. Bent slipped silently closer, into the park, and pressed into a copse of bushy pines until he was fifteen feet behind Rita. The sounds of his movement were masked by the rain.

At eleven on the dot a yellow sedan turned onto Lovejoy and pulled to the curb beside Rita. The window lowered. Music wafted through the falling rain. A low voice spoke. Rita answered. Bent couldn't hear what they said. Rita took a thick envelope from her purse and passed it forward, into the cab. Then the car drove away.

When the car turned the corner, Rita dropped the umbrella and put her face up to the drizzle. She stood like that, open to the rain, for a minute or two before hefting her head back to its proper position and lifting the umbrella. As she walked away, it seemed to Bent each step looked heavier than the last; whatever tension had driven her for the last two hours was lifted, but it had been replaced by something else… Something worse. Dread? Loathing? Fear? There was weight to those steps.

He let her walk and pulled out his notebook. It only took a second to write down the license of the sedan. Then he took a pink square of paper, torn at the bottom, and began to scribble a message—in Bent's professional opinion, dealing with this would require… assistance.

*****

Lamar Bonniface placed the slim cigarillo into the slotted ashtray on the marble fireplace mantle, and frowned at the slip of pink paper in his hand that he'd found, dropped through his mail slot, that morning. The last embers of the morning fire glowed with fuzzy warmth against his pant legs, where they were exposed beneath the hem of his smoking jacket. In the corner of the sprawling flat a grandmother clock struck the half-hour after six. Lacy ribbons of Egyptian tobacco smoke curled into the air from the ashtray.

With a sigh, Lamar tossed the pink note to the mantle and turned his back to the last heat of the fire, facing the long windows that bordered the outer wall of his rooms. The morning sun broke through the great stretch of paned glass, painting the long ambling flat in watery light. Through the windows, the distant hills rose above the borders of Portland, loping up into softly clouded skies. Lower, the city glittered in the morning shadows, not yet lit by the rising sun, gridlines of metal-grey streets and squat, blocky buildings running down beneath the hills to the river.

When the clock struck seven and the fire felt cold behind his heels, Lamar slipped from the smoking jacket, tossed it across the lounge to an Adirondack easy chair by the window, and turned into the entryway behind the fireplace. Overcoat, chocolate-brown fedora, calfskin gloves, and ebony cane were outfitted quickly from a narrow hutch. He opened the oak front door and slipped into the hall.

"Lamar," the woman's voice purred the moment he stepped out.

"Morning, Marigold," Lamar said, without looking up. He locked the door to his half of the apartment penthouse, and turned towards the elevators. By the sound of her heels against the carpeted floor, she was following him.

"Did you find the time to consider—"

Lamar slung the elevator cage open and stepped inside, turning as he closed it behind him.

Marigold stood on the other side of the cage. She was tall and lanky, with rusty-blond hair, her overcoat slung across her shoulders, arms crossed disapprovingly beneath it. Red sweater, brown tweed skirt, nude stockings, black pumps. He grinned at her and punched the button; she frowned, dark blue eyes gaining a murderous depth.

"I'll get back to you," Lamar called as he dropped below the floor.

Outside, he found his olive-green two-door Chevy Deluxe in the apartment parking lot, and climbed in. After fiddling with the choke, and pumping the gas a few times, the inline-six thrummed to life and Lamar pulled the green beast out into the street.

Portland was waking up beneath the cool morning sunlight. As Lamar cruised the streets towards the city center, running down the hill to the riverbanks, shop windows were being opened, blinds raised. Neon open-signs buzzed in the morning gloom; steam rose from café kitchen vents. Shop owners swept clean sidewalks, cigarettes glowing in their set jaws. He lowered his window and heard distant car horns and motors. The bellow of an ocean tanker called across the valley from the northern ports.

He pulled up beside Rucker's Cup, and parked beneath the steaming coffee-cup sign that jutted from the corner of the building, advertising on both Broadway and Park.

Lamar switched the engine off and stepped from the car, stepping blithely into the shop.

"Oh, for the love of Pete," the trim police officer groaned when he saw Lamar approaching, "what do you want *this* time?"

Lamar grinned, slipping into the seat beside the officer, dropping his fedora onto the counter. "Got a license plate for you," he said, pulling out a small notepad from the breast pocket of his overcoat. He ripped the top sheet from it, and placed it on the counter between them.

The officer shook his head, and put down his cup. "Man, when I said I owed you a few, you took that liberally."

"I'm not above granting favors myself, friend."

The cop grimaced.

"Hey, money does things. Moves and shakes. Sometime, when you need a rich SOB to bail you out of trouble…" Lamar raised both hands to frame his Rudolph Valentino face. "You can call me."

The cop sighed. "Oh, lay off it." He took the slip of paper and stuffed it into his breast pocket. "Come by the station later."

"One more thing," Lamar said, "before I go."

"Yeah?" The cop took a hot gulp. The steam rode his breath as he put the cup back down and turned his glare to Lamar.

"A list of addresses…"

*****

The evening light cast long shadows down the street as Ed Bent turned the corner. Firebird Heights rose up into the sky, blocky and angular, pitted recesses for dome lights studding the brown-brick façade all the way up between the room windows.

The streetlamp flickered as he walked under it, and went out. Above him, the clouds had cleared, leaving only the darkened bowl of the sky, ringed by the glow of the sunken sun.

Bent shuffled up the center of the street towards the apartments, pausing only to take the last sip of brandy from his bottle. He tossed it into the gutter when he finished. It shattered as he walked up the apartment steps.

The entryway was lit well. Bent put his face against the double doors and peered inside. Paisley carpeting ran the length of the hallway. Stairs climbed up on either side. He didn't see a doorman, so he pulled on the door handle. It was locked. Bent shrugged and turned to the intercom board, bolted to the side of the porch. He put a grimy finger up and ran slowly over the names.

"Gozzi," he said, stopping over a name halfway down the board.

Without hesitating he punched the button, then waited. A moment later a deep voice growled through the intercom, in a panting Italian accent. "Who's there? I'm not expecting nobody."

Bent turned and walked down the steps. The voice growled again behind him, but he ignored it, slipping along the side of the building.

Around back, a private parking lot sprawled, bordered by tottering chain link fences. Bent dropped his backpack and deftly leapt upon the fence. He was over in a moment, and moving silently between the cars, hunched below the level of the roofs. He worked quickly and methodically, running a swerving pattern along the edges of the lot, then winding inward. It took less than five minutes to locate the car he'd seen the night before, stopping for Rita on 16th and Lovejoy.

Lamar's information had been accurate.

The Pontiac Chieftan sat long and wide beneath the dim lights of the lot. Bent briefly rose up to peer towards the apartments—no movement, no sounds from the looming building. He ducked back down and pulled a long, thin metal strip from his coat and fit it between the window and the window-seal. After a few failed attempts, he felt the lock disengage. He pulled the Slim Jim out and opened the door.

Ashtrays. Door pockets. Console cubbies. Glove box. Beneath the seats. Quickly, Bent rifled through the front of the car. He found registration papers. Receipts from the Pago Pago, the Star Theatre, the Desert Room, Mary's Club. A strange leather pocket was half-sewn into the drivers'-side door. Bent had seen this before—a quick release holster. By the size of it, probably for a snubby revolver.

He closed the door and moved to the back. A few cigarette-burns on the upholstery. A New Testament in the footwell. A sports paper lay folded on the back seat. Bent picked it up—it was opened to yesterday's horse races, in Kentucky. He dropped it back to the seat and climbed out.

There was nothing concrete in Gozzi's car, and yet an indelible picture had formed in Bent's mind. Gozzi bet on the horses, ate at the best clubs, enjoyed the dancing women. Smoked, cruised, drank, and kept his gun where he could reach it. Gozzi was organized crime.

Bent stooped beside the car, thinking quickly. Was the mob above his pay grade? Hell, *everything* was above his pay grade, at five cents a pop. So, what did it really matter if Gozzi was a powder keg? Five cents was… well, it was five cents. He could always return it. He'd told the kid as much when he took the job. Bent had dealt with mob before. In Vegas, a few years back, when Bugsy Siegel was running *The Flamingo*. One mob run-in was plenty for a hard-up war vet. But then again…

Bent slipped out of the lot as quietly as he had entered, barely rattling the fence on his way.

*****

Rita was not an effortless server.

Lamar watched as she moved between the tables at Sullivan's. She walked flat-footed, the sway of her hips dangerously close to the corners of the white-clothed tables. She'd already spilled his own coffee when she delivered it. He cut a bite from the lemon chiffon pie in front of him, and held it on the edge of his fork, watching her as she disappeared around a corner into the adjoining room.

The door jingled as someone entered. Lamar ate the spongy bite of pie, half turning as a man in a heavy peacoat rustled past him. Rita came back just then, and had to wait for the newcomer to move before she could carry a tray of empty plates back to the kitchen.

Lamar's fork poised over the chiffon, his eyes darting after Rita, then back to the man.

He'd seen something. There had been an exchange. They'd acknowledged each other, during their sudden convergence, then tried to hide it.

Had he imagined it?

Lamar sipped his coffee, eyes narrowing on the man as he removed his coat and slung it across a chair at a table for two. He was tall and lean. Middle-aged, with a pencil mustache. The man scanned the room briefly, then sat, back towards Lamar.

A different server returned to take the man's order—they were brief. He was a regular, then. As she left, the man rose and walked to the back of the room, towards the restrooms.

Lamar relaxed slightly and looked back to the pie.

Before he could fork another bite, the man returned. He'd only been gone a few seconds. Lamar put the fork down… That hadn't been long enough.

Lamar looked towards the restrooms. The signs pointed down a hall, disappearing back into the building adjacent to the kitchens. He looked at the man; his back was still turned.

With a sigh, Lamar put his napkin down on his plate, rising silently from his seat. The man didn't turn. Lamar slipped quickly out of the seating area into the hallway. The restrooms opened to his left. A door opened to the right, towards the kitchens.

Lamar pushed the door and stepped into a small lounge. Employee lockers sat in boxed cubbies on one wall. A chair and table sat opposite, covered in ashtrays and newspapers, glamour magazines and cigarette butts. The room smelled of hairspray and tobacco. Behind the door hung coats and purses. Lamar lifted a slim leather handbag from the rest. It was Rita's.

For a moment he hesitated. This was crazy. No… not *crazy*, per se. This was the sort of thing Bent would do. A sly smile curled Lamar's lip. He opened the purse. Inside, just beneath the zipper, was a banded pack of envelopes. He took them out, pulled off the band, and looked inside the first one.

Pills. At least ten pills, of uniform color, shape, and size. Lamar checked the next one. Different pills. He closed and re-banded the envelopes, placed them back in Rita's purse, and stepped out.

When Lamar returned to his seat, the man with the peacoat was leaving. Lamar paid his check and ran to the door, grabbing his overcoat from the rack behind the front counter, but by the time he reached the street the man was gone, absorbed into the cool Portland night.

*****

It was a quarter till eleven. The night was dry. Leaves rustled beneath a restless wind that swept the dark alleys and scoured the pavement.

Bent watched from the shadows of the alley as Rita Veratti moved up the street, towards him. He shrank deeper into the darkness. A dry lump sat in the pit of his throat. He tried to swallow it down, but it stayed. He could hear the *tick-tock* of her heels against the sidewalk.

He checked his watch, reading the hands through the cracked bezel in the darkness with some difficulty. She'd finished her stops, by now. All that was left was the rendezvous with Gozzi at 16th and Lovejoy. Unfortunately for Rita, her night was about to become more complicated.

The clacking heels drew near.

Bent flattened himself against the alley wall. Her shadow rose beside him, looming across the sidewalk. He could hear the scuffing of her heels. It sounded like she was already there, and yet the long shadow continued to stretch down the pavement.

And then she appeared, right beside him, khaki umbrella in the crook of her arm, red hair tied back in a bandana, overcoat open to the clement night.

Bent leapt from the alley, slamming into her with the edge of his shoulder.

The force knocked Rita sideways, sprawling through the air into the street. Bent was upon her as she fell. She tried to scream; he held her face to the gritty asphalt, pressing against the side of her neck to occlude the vocal chords. She twisted beneath him but he smashed her down, pinning her against the ground with one knee.

One hand on her neck, a knee in her back; the other hand stayed free, scrabbled for her purse. Thankfully, she hadn't lost it when she'd sprawled. It was still hooked to her shoulder.

He ripped it open, dragging the contents out onto the street. The envelopes were still there, but fattened. Single-handedly, he fumbled them open. Green bills tumbled out. One after the other, all were stuffed with money. No pills—just money.

"Damn," he muttered, looking down at the woman beneath his knee.

The sound of soft shoe-soles slipped across the cement behind him. Bent leapt over Rita, scrambling forward into the street and clamoring to his feet. Without turning, he sprinted for a crevice between two brick buildings. When he reached it, he hurled himself through, only then turning his head to glance behind him.

Rita was sitting on her legs under the streetlamp, a hand to her face. Money scattered across the street, carried by the night's wild winds; a broad-shouldered man in dark trousers and a heavy overcoat scrambled after it. A second man was rushing towards Bent.

Bent pressed deeper into the crevice. It was narrow; he had to run sideways, stumbling over cans and plumbing pipes. The shadow of his pursuer darkened the pathway behind him. Bent could hear the man's breath panting, thick and hoarse, as he struggled to follow the scrawny bum.

Bent broke free and bolted obliquely across the street for another alleyway. When he reached the darkness he dropped, shuffling down beneath a pile of empty beer crates, and fell silent.

Blood pumped in Bent's ears, rushing like the gallop of wild horses. He closed his eyes, forcing his breathing to slow, deepening his quiet gulps of air as the pursuer's heavy steps crashed into the alley and swept past.

Carefully, Bent pulled his head up and peered down the alley. The man was tall and wide, outlined by a sharp fedora. As he broke the next street Bent saw the glint of brass knuckledusters on his right hand. Then the man was gone.

Bent rose from the crates, silently sheathing his stiletto dagger into the leather scabbard on his hip.

The Pontiac Chieftan cruised the streets for hours afterwards, slowly crisscrossing the alleys, moving up and down Japantown. Bent watched from the rooftop of a derelict building, sipping a bottle of brandy and picking his fingernails with the point of his dagger until the pale-yellow car turned a corner for the last time and the thrum of its engine died into the collective traffic-rumble of a city that never really slept.

*****

The next evening, Bent watched the mousy safecracker round the corner by the Blanchett house and stalk up the street. Harry walked with his back bowed, hands thrust in the pockets of his fur-lined jacket, head bobbing side-to-side.

"Ok, smartass," the little man grumbled as he stepped near enough to be heard, "you wanted information, you're gonna get it. Follow me."

Harry the Safecracker turned and walked away. Bent collected his backpack and stumbled up from the sidewalk. He left the cold coffee where it was and jogged to catch up with the little weasel of a man.

Harry led him out to Burnside, then up the thoroughfare a few blocks, where the buildings rose taller above the honking, jostling cars. Harry never looked back as he walked, just kept plodding up Burnside, hands in his pockets.

After walking ten blocks, Harry turned and crossed the street, threading between the cars. Bent paused before following, waiting for an opening before he leapt. Traffic pitched and roiled around him, horns blaring, and then he was through. Harry stood waiting beneath the awning for the Desert Room. Neon lights buzzed above the awning, glowing up into the dusk.

"This way," Harry mumbled, disappearing into the windowless brown door.

Inside was darkness, smoke rolling in thick billows, jazz drums rambling around the beat of a wandering trumpet and bass, laughter, shadowy motion, the tang of spilled beer, the moist expectancy of sex and fear and risk and reward.

Bent angled through the milling crowd of beat kids and winos towards the dancefloor, shortcutting the path Harry made to the back rooms. The music rattled his brain as he passed beneath the stage. A short blond wearing a tight black dress smeared against him, vibrating to the drums. He pushed her off, and slipped down the stairwell to the basements.

Harry opened a heavy red door, and pointed inside.

Inside, the music died away. The clatter fell. Folds of cigar smoke rolled languidly beneath an overhead lamp that cast a dome of light across a felt-green poker table.

"Sit, Bent," the old man across the table said, gesturing to an empty seat.

Harry slunk around the table in the shadows. Bent counted three other men in the room. One sitting beside the old man—a big guy, with a thick neck and broad shoulders. The other two stood in the back, with Harry. Stood still, like specters at a funeral.

The old man leaned into the light and took the cigar from his mouth. He had a thin, hawk-like face, a sharp nose, and hard eyes like stream-pebbles. "Ed Bent," he said, pulling a pink slip of paper from his pocket, torn at the bottom, and reading it beneath the light. "You sent my man this, a few days ago. Why?"

Bent shrugged, and flipped the chair around, leaning forward against the backrest as he sat. "I wanted information," he said. "You know, Harry owes me at minimum three favors. I figured it was the least he could do."

The old man's eyes narrowed. "You know who I am?" he asked.

"Big Jim Elkins," Bent said, scratching under his chin with a dirty fingernail.

Elkins nodded. "Then you've got *me* at a disadvantage," he said. "I don't like that. You know who I am, but I don't know you."

"You already said. I'm Ed Bent."

Elkins shook his head. "Harry's told me about you," he said. "Devil's Brigade, he said." Elkins grunted. "Weren't no 'Ed Bent' in the Devil's Brigade. I looked. And the only 'Ed Bents' in the city I could find are all accounted for. Which makes me wonder who the hell you really are, and what the hell you really want."

Bent smiled through the smoke. "I don't like your tone, Jim," he said, "and I don't think you're in a position to get lippy with me."

The shadows behind Elkins loomed closer, but Elkins gruffly shook his head. They stopped. "I'll give you a chance to define that statement, sir," Elkins growled, "before I have you killed and dumped in the river."

"I won't define jack-shit unless I want to," Bent snapped, leveling a finger at Elkins. "But I'll tell you what you're gonna do, for me. Cut off Rita Verratti."

Elkins took a grim draw off the cigar. "Who?"

Bent grinned. "Don't play dumb, old man. Your bag man," he said. "Or, bag *woman*. The little Italian gal you've got distributing prescription drugs to under-the-table dealers."

Elkins hissed, slamming his cigar hand against the poker table, scattering ash across the felt. "You just sealed your death, you jerk. Sealed your death and wasted my time."

"Kill me," Bent snapped, "and every detail about Verratti's route gets fed to the cops."

"And what makes you think they don't already know? I pay off most of the cops in this godforsaken burg, Bent."

"I checked with my guy on the force," Bent said. "None of those locations give payoffs. Veratti's not on the cop's radar. Sullivan's isn't known to be an Elkins' dive. What you're doing, Elkins, is distributing prescription drugs to your junkies without cutting the cops in for a take. You cobbled together a sweet little side ring, my man, without getting Carl Crisp from Vice, or Diamond Jim Purcell, that phony chief of police, or Mayor Peterson, or any of the others involved. So, if you so much as put a finger on me…" Bent smiled, and leaned back out of the light. "I have a friend," he said. "Knows it all. Has proof. I go down the river? He spills his guts. I know you've been having trouble, this year. Wanna give Crisp and Diamond Jim, and your crooked DA, and the Mayor, and all the rest, *another* reason to make you just a part of Old Town history?"

Elkins put the cigar between his teeth and chewed it slowly. The smoke curled from his tight, pinched lips as he thought, misting across his hard eyes. "What's your proposal?" he asked, at last.

"I don't care about your drugs. Do what you want. Just cut Rita out of it, like I said. Simple as that."

"You think that'll solve this impasse we got? Just letting the woman roam loose, with all that information?"

"I do. Know why I think it'll work?"

"Enlighten me."

"It'll work cuz if you so much as touch a hair on her head, I'll find out, and I'll snitch. And if you put me in the river, then my friend will find out, and *he'll* snitch."

"And if Rita snitches? What then?"

Bent shrugged. "Risk you'll have to take, I guess. Shoot her. At that point, I've done all I can. But even so, you'd be fucked. I suggest, then, that your boys explain to her, diplomatically, why it's in her best interest to keep her mouth shut." Bent rose from the chair. "Now, if you'll excuse me, gentlemen, I think I'll be going."

As Bent slipped from the door, he caught a final glimpse of Elkins. The man rolled the pink slip of paper furiously between his hands and hurled it angrily into the shadows.

*****

They met him outside, a few blocks into the neighborhoods. Bent reeled as Gozzi's calloused knuckles slammed into his gut, sending him tumbling backwards, deeper into the shadows of the alley, away from the brightness of the thoroughfare, the milling cars, the passersby.

"Lousy deal stinks," the massive, hulking shadow grunted over him, voice accented heavily with Italian. "I just wanted to let you know how *I* felt about it, Bent. Make a fool of me, on my route, will you?"

Gozzi lifted Bent up and threw him forward, into a metal dumpster. Bent slid to the ground. He caught sight of a second figure, arched over him, before Gozzi's steel-tipped shoes slammed into his side again and rolled him over. He felt the ribs crack and grind. Gozzi kicked him repeatedly, then.

"You'll kill 'im, Goz," the other man wheezed. "Lay off a bit."

"Kill him nothing. He ain't learned the meaning of pain yet."

The brass knuckledusters glinted. Bent curled into a ball against the ground. Not thirty feet away, the cars trundled past the alley, unaware of the struggle within.

Gozzi's hefty fist whipped upwards, but the other man caught it, and yanked it back. "Next time, Goz," he hissed. "Next time we kill him. You put him out now and Big Jim'll do you too. Wait your time, brother. Wait…"

They slipped away, on the edge of the breeze, disappearing back into the nighttime energy from which their kind was born.

Bent coughed in the dirt and rolled over. The stiletto dagger glinted in the shifting lights from the traffic, tip poised just beneath the hem of his jacket. It was a pity—he'd hoped Goz would punch. Give him something to sink his little companion into. It had been years…

Slowly, Bent dragged himself to his knees, then pulled himself to his feet, leaning against the dumpster like a trash-damsel against a rubbish-bin knight. Blood drooled from his nose and mouth. His eye felt like a golf-ball in a squeaky socket.

He'd planned to stop by Pete's. Tell him he'd be keeping the nickel. But after Goz, he wasn't sure he had the stomach for Japantown. Pete was smart enough. He'd figure it out on his own.

Bent sheathed the stiletto and stumbled off the dumpster to where his backpack lay. Hefting it up ground the broken ribs. The strap stung on his shoulder. Wincing, Bent stumbled down the alley.

✶✶✶✶✶

The Bonneville Apartments loomed against the dusk-blue sky as Bent skirted their perimeter, working around towards the private lot in back. Halfway round he reached up, gripping the nearly invisible tail of a rope that hung in the darkness.

The fire escape lowered silently; Lamar kept it well-greased.

Steeling himself to the effort, Bent grunted up onto the iron ladder and painfully climbed the side of the building. Portland fell below him, like a writhing jewel in the night. A cool wind, full of the scent of ripe trash, and spring flowers, and automobile exhaust, and yesterday's midnight rain blustered against him as he opened the window to the top-floor penthouse and climbed inside.

He closed the window and walked across the richly furnished bedroom to a small on-suite. He threw the overcoat across the bed on the way, and put the backpack on the floor beside the dresser.

His face in the mirror was cadaverous. A red welt surrounded his right eye. His mouth and chin were crusted in blood. Painfully, he stripped his shirt and kicked off his shoes, turned on the water in the sink and waited for it to get hot. When the steam rose from the white porcelain, Bent wet his hands to wash his face, but paused—he'd heard something. A distant sound, somewhere in the flat.

With a grunt he lowered his face to the water and washed the grime and the blood. Soaped the dirt beneath his fingernails. Rinsed his hair. Then he toweled off, doused with aftershave, combed the hair back, and stalked back to the bedroom where he exchanged the soiled trousers for starched slacks and a crisp white shirt. As he donned the plush smoking-jacket he heard the sound again, from the other room.

He tied the jacket, and pushed open the door to the lounge.

Marigold sat in his Adirondack chair by the fire, legs tucked beneath her, head bowed as she poured over a scattered mess of handwritten notes. She didn't look up as he came in.

"Hello, Lamar," she said. "Good of you to drop in."

Lamar sighed, and turned to the mantelpiece for his cigarette holder. "I see you found the key," he said as he lit an Egyptian.

Marigold looked up at him then. She paused for a moment, before fixing him under an arch gaze. "Bent fared well today?"

Lamar shrugged and grinned through the cigarillo. "You could say that." From his pocket he took the shining nickel.

Marigold sniffed.

Lamar turned back to the mantle and pulled an old Mason jar, half-full of dirty coins, closer to him. He considered the coin a moment, turning it in his fingers, and then dropped it into the jar with the rest.

"What are you planning on buying?" Marigold drawled, behind him.

"Don't know," said Lamar. "Haven't decided yet."

"Why do you do it?"

"What do you mean?" Lamar turned to the woman sitting in his chair.

Marigold lifted two fistfuls of notes. "All this," she said. "I still don't understand. You sneak out, every few weeks, in that dingy alter ego of yours, and panhandle the worst cases you can find. For a nickel. Honey, we don't need the money, you or I. We're relics of a social class that died out in the war. We're the rich dinosaurs that survived. So… Why?"

Lamar grinned. "How many times have you asked me this?"

"At least as many times as you have nickels in that jar."

Lamar shrugged, and sipped on the cigarillo. "Well, when the jar is full, maybe I'll tell you."

After a moment, Marigold looked back to the notes spread across her lap. "So," she said, "is this case finished? Are you ready to add your meticulous little journal to the rest?" She waved a dismissive hand at the bookshelf beside the fireplace, full of folio-sized, leather-bound albums.

"I'm satisfied with it," Lamar said.

"What happens to Rita?"

"Nothing."

"You really think your hollow bluff can protect her?"

"It's not hollow," Lamar growled. "And anyway, Elkins' connections are wearing thin, Goldi. He's running afoul of the local powers that be.

I doubt he'll have the luxury to afford her a second thought in a month's time."

Marigold shook her head, dismissively dropping papers to the floor beside her as she finished skimming them. "How did you know to contact Harry?" she asked. "You write, here, you contacted him straight away." She looked up. "But you only earmarked Elkins as being involved yesterday."

"I didn't *know* Elkins was involved when I contacted Harry," Lamar said. "But Rita's movements were suspicious, and indicative. Whatever she was working on, it seemed centered around Japantown. Stan Terry operates more in the south and the city center; the Teamsters specialize in racketeering; Tom Johnson rules the Avenue, across the river. That only left Elkins. So, I wrote to Harry, who I knew was Elkins' favorite little pusher, and who incidentally owed me a favor, and filled in the blanks later. The hunch paid off."

Marigold's eyes narrowed. She lifted a pen-scrabbled sheet of paper. "So, this was the solution Bent chose, then, after all? Warning Elkins about your 'friend' with dirt?"

Lamar nodded his head.

"Even though Bent's friend is, of course, Lamar, who's you?"

"What Big Jim doesn't know won't hurt him."

"Elkins beat you?"

"Elkins' men. But it's alright. They were working on their own time."

With a sigh, Marigold dropped the rest of the papers and rose from the chair. "That's not the old soldier I knew," she said, stepping close to him and stretching an arm over his shoulder.

Lamar raised an eyebrow. She stood inches from his face, dark eyes peering into his. "What would your commanding officer say?" he murmured.

"I'm not in the USO anymore, Sergeant," Marigold whispered, "I don't care."

She hovered there for a moment, before drawing back the wandering arm—the pink slip of Bonneville Apartments paper he'd left on the mantle twirled deftly between her fingers. "I see you kept my note safe," she said. "So how about it? Drinks? Tonight? Tomorrow? You name the time."

"I don't drink," Lamar said.

"Oh, that's right," Marigold laughed. "Bent drinks; Lamar smokes. I forgot. Most men came back from the war half the men they once were; you came back doubled. What a strange group of men you are, Lamar. Anyway, let's go. Bring that bruised eye of yours out for some dinner with another wealthy dinosaur. Couldn't hurt, could it?"

Lamar frowned at the smoldering cigarillo in his fingers. The broken ribs ached beneath his smoking jacket, radiating a heavy pain that probed sharply up into his shoulder. Marigold leaned closer. He could feel the warmth from her body, the soft perfume of her breath against his battered cheek.

"Actually, I think I have a broken rib, Goldi," he said. "Maybe a few."

"Oh well," she said, her voice close in his ear, "ribs heal, darling. Just ask Adam."

Cracker Jacks and the Granny Cases
A J and L Detective Agency Mystery
Wil A. Emerson

"Jimmy, there's a gal on the stoop. Looking at our sign. You up for dealing with her?" It wasn't the first time Larry had asked the question. When the phone started ringing at nine, Larry asked his brother every time, ten times total, if he was up to taking the call.

Jimmy had another sore throat but insisted on coming to the office. Larry figured if he felt good enough to come in, he might as well take over the lesser chores. Larry, in a deep dive, fingers on his forehead, was trying to figure out when to pay the rent but first had to tally up who owed them money, how much and when. Then he could juggle the deposits against the withdrawals and decide what day gave him an advantage. After the diabolic Kaminski affair, he kept better records. A dead man's wife didn't pay debts well.

The new job that needed their attention and would net them a few big bucks had to be put on hold. Their client, Booster Kramer, a hard nose gambler who had a player run out on him with a pocket of Booster's money, had a bad habit of driving after happy hour. He now sat in jail for the unrelated minor offense. So, at the moment, there wasn't any good reason for either brother to be out of the office. Time to do paper work whether interested or not.

"I got the walk-in, Larry. Good as gold."

Larry wished it were true but waved off the comment. Jimmy's aches and pains had increased. Vitamins and chicken soup weren't cutting it. As he thumped his pen on the table, the young woman he saw on the stoop entered the small vestibule leading to the office. Larry held his breath, waiting for her to put her umbrella in the stand before she entered their domain. Odds where she'd bring it in, shake the hell out of it while Jimmy asked if she needed help. Maybe it would help if he put a sign out front that stated umbrellas would be replaced if stolen. The downside was a new customer might take it as a warning they weren't in a safe area and turn away.

As it were, Larry figured he'd wipe up the rain residuals if the gal followed the unwelcome tradition. His brother, with a headache, shouldn't do the bending, wiping task. Dang how he could survive Vietnam and then come home with a slew of aggravating problems. Larry had his hands full keeping worries in check.

Jimmy eyed the door, too, waiting for the woman's approach. He set aside his coffee cup and adjusted the back of his desk chair. No need to look like he'd been taking a nap even if it were so.

A double tap on the door and in walked a demure female. Jimmy guessed she was not far from being a teenager. Reddish blond tresses hung half way past her chest, a beige mid-thigh raincoat over blue jeans. Left hand held a tote bag, yellow and purple, that looked like it outweighed her trim body. The other hand gripped a large green and pink umbrella, point down and dripping heavily.

Jimmy watched the large umbrella unleash its load. A waterfall, drops the size of marbles, landed on the wood floor. He shot a glance at Larry and knew he'd stew about the wet floor. Larry had this thing about the parquet flooring. Original wood, he wouldn't alter it even with a rug. The wood couldn't breathe. Mildew didn't grow in a flash but Larry reacted as if it would. Add a little moisture and a fungus would invade the office and fill Jimmy's lungs, too.

Jimmy decided he better deal with this gal as fast as possible. Best to keep Larry's day on the right track, mainly because he needed to concentrate. It was the end of the month, and bills were piled high. Jimmy would listen to whatever the woman/child had to say and usher her out. Even if the sore throat and a headache had a grip on him, he'd wipe up the floor to reduce Larry's anxieties.

"What can I do for you, Miss?" Jimmy stood and extended his hand.

"I see you don't have a secretary." The umbrella continued to waddle from her wrist action, shedding a hidden collection. "Nasty weather. They say it won't end for three more hours."

"Spring. That time of year," Jimmy replied.

"I noticed your sign. J and L Agency? What? Johnson and Larson, James and Luddington?" The woman jutted her chin forward.

"Lafferty. Jim and Larry Lafferty. We're a private investigative firm." "Oh, that I know. But why don't you use full names? Seems odd to me. But in the scheme of things, it doesn't really matter, does it? I'm not interested in being a partner."

Larry raised his chin. Partner? Jimmy better handle this gal. No need to intervene. However, never one to curb impulses, Larry said, "We're not looking for an employee."

Jimmy darted a dark eye at his brother. "Just exactly what can I do for you, Miss?" Jimmy motioned to the chair closest to his desk.

"Well, it's simple. I've got two cases I need help with. I'm overloaded. Can't tell the clients I don't have time for them and certainly don't want to give up retainer fees." She dug into the tote bag and pulled out a box of Cracker Jacks. "Don't mind? I haven't eaten since yesterday."

Jimmy nodded. "Be my guest. Two cases you said? You're a—what, a social worker?" He almost blurted 'child' but caught himself.

"Social workers aren't paid by clients." The Cracker Jacks cracked, one fell on her lap and she popped it back in her mouth. "I have a license. Just like you two. But I use my last name. Bethany Roberts."

"Bethany Roberts? You're a P.I.?" Jimmy eased back in his chair. "Not local. From the suburbs?"

"We're not hiring another investigator." Larry interjected. He wouldn't be unkind and say that P.I. work wasn't a woman's job. Not with all the hoopla in the papers about the Betty Friedan group, but the thought was hard to put aside. Times may be changing, but a messy world awaited anyone in the business. Larry couldn't justify a young woman entering this back alley, cheaters world. However, it was her next remark that made Larry blink twice, then return a soft growl.

"I don't intend to hire you, either." She nodded to Larry and turned her attention back to Jimmy. "My proposal is we work together on two cases. Share expenses and profits. Business deal, nothing more." She crunched another handful of the sweet-smelling snack.

"Well," Jimmy said, and paused long enough to grab a throat lozenge and pop it in his mouth, "this is unusual. Never considered an option like that before. Don't see how it would benefit us." The gal must be on the wrong side of almost broke. Then reconsidered. No longer a matter of almost.

Why not help her out? He mentally ran through the projects they were working on. Divorce cases—that neither he or Larry liked but they paid the utilities. Perhaps this gal would be better suited for broken hearted wives chasing down cheating husbands. Wouldn't give her the missing uncle case. Too much risk involved. Uncle Louie, a Hamtramck loafer, did a stint in Jackson prison for armed robbery before he heisted the family bankroll. Too many connections with the hardcore element. If anyone found him, Louie might call in a favor for an act of revenge. Of course, J and L had several insurance cases that netted enough cash for a few month's incidentals. He could relinquish one to this gal if she was really down on her luck.

Yet, should he ignore the goals he and his brother had set? Why relinquish any case when it's a dog fight for everyone? They needed better transportation, maybe even buy a brand-new car.

"Two elderly women. Unrelated." The rain spattered woman said. "Looking for grandchildren. One coughed up a five grand retainer. The other granny, a little tight on cash she said. Four grand even. Both accepted the hourly rate and all expenses. I couldn't resist. Signed and sealed. Need help. Figure two no names might want to work with me. Think about it."

Two *no names*? Larry and Jimmy eyed each other. Tennis ball style, back, forth. The woman in the middle. Who had the advantage?

She stood, fished in her tote bag and pulled out a white and pink business card. "Bethany Roberts, Licensed Private Investigator. Licensed in Chicago. Didn't like their politics. Detroit's not much better but it's familiar territory. All I need is a contract. Full names, etc. And we can get busy."

"The hourly rate? We don't jump into something on the blind." Jimmy felt confident she couldn't match their usual rate. Then studied the card again.

"Mr. Lafayette," and then a quick turn to Larry, "Mr. Lafayette, I don't mind you calling me Bethany, but since you are my elders, I'll use your surnames."

Jimmy and Larry couldn't help but shrug. Elders? That bothered them more than her mispronouncing their surname.

"Let's keep this professional and extend our best front to our clients." She leaned across Jimmy's desk, grabbed his note pad and wrote on it.

Jimmy lifted his chin, read it and showed the note to his brother. Larry nodded in agreement.

However unsure they were of this young woman, they were eager to meet client number one, Mrs. Clarice Bernstein and client number 2, Laura Rayburn. They weren't about to rock the boat on a hundred dollar a day gig.

Later, Jimmy poked Larry in the ribs and grinned. They hadn't jumped in feet first; they'd gone head over heels to take this Bethany Roberts gal up on her offer.

*****

The next morning, with the rain in remission, Bethany beeped the horn in front of Jimmy and Larry's office. "We'll go straight to number one, Bernstein. Unless you want to buy breakfast. I'm really hungry."

"Ate two hours ago. No need to stop." Larry shifted in the back seat. Already the gal expected them to spend their share of the fees on her empty stomach.

Bethany's eyes darted to Jimmy but he didn't respond.

Clarice Bernstein lived in a two-story clapboard house in Royal Oak. A mere three miles from the infamous Eight Mile Road marker that defined Detroit's struggle with the northern, more prosperous suburban cities. A quaint house, middle-income neighborhood. A driveway lined with red maples and the porch decorated with several pots of colorful flowers and flowing ferns.

Larry whispered to Jimmy, "Did you take your allergy meds? Those yellow flowers look like Goldenrod."

Bethany shook her head and said, "No, those are Marigolds. No problem." Then rapped on the bright green painted door.

Jimmy promptly sneezed. Larry handed him a handkerchief.

The door opened and a well-kept woman in a blue skirt and white blouse greeted them. There were streaks of white in her light brown hair and the cut fell in a modern style to her shoulders. Although Bethany referred to her as the grandmotherly type, she didn't appear to be the kind that spent the day knitting.

"Come in, please. It's such a relief to know you'll find Melissa. Please, take a seat." She stepped back in the foyer and pointed to the living room on the left. "It's comfortable in here. I'll bring tea for everyone." And she departed to the back of the house.

When Mrs. Bernstein returned with a silver tray, Larry rose and offered to carry it. "No, you're my guest. Please, just relax and enjoy my favorite tea."

As they sipped on the warm brew, Larry and Jimmy scanned the pages of a high-school year book Mrs. Bernstein offered them. She filled the conversation gap with stories about her granddaughter's young life, moving in with her after the girl's parents were in a fatal car accident. They'd made plans for her future and adjustments for needs and wants.

"Melissa was very active in high school as you can see. A cheerleader, honor student. Even the choir. I was so proud of her."

"You have every reason to be," Jimmy said with a smile. "It's strange that such a successful girl, with such a bright future, would leave, not have any contact with someone who loves her. You mentioned college in the fall. Michigan State. Was it her choice?"

"Definitely. She wasn't the kind of girl who could be persuaded to do something she didn't want to do. It's a mystery to me why she left so abruptly. Other than, well, embarrassed."

"Embarrassed," Larry asked. "Could it be she was involved with a young man?"

"Could be. I certainly didn't think any of her dates were serious, though. One day here and the next day gone. It's been ten days and I'm so disturbed by her disappearance."

"When did you report the disappearance to the police?"

"Oh heavens, utterly impossible." She placed her hand on her chest, as though to stop a heart attack.

"You didn't get the police involved? That's a big mistake. What if…" But Larry didn't get to finish his comment.

"I've gone over everything about Mrs. Bernstein's granddaughter's disappearance," Bethany said. "This is a personal matter. Confidential. What we need to do is start our search."

"It's irresponsible to not include the police. A young girl's disappearance is a serious matter." Jimmy said. Larry shook his head in agreement.

"Let's make one thing clear. I don't want my granddaughter chased by the police. I don't have to tell you why. Just bring her back home."

"Mind if we search her bedroom?"

"Yes, I mind. There's nothing in it that has anything to do with her disappearance."

Bethany jumped in, "I went through every drawer, the closet, bedside table. She cleared it out. A well-planned departure, I'd say."

Mrs. Bernstein stood, "It's nice meeting you, gentlemen." She pulled out a check book from the table drawer next to her chair. "Bethany assured me she deposited the retainer fee in her account. I'll give her another check for two eight-hour days. If you need to extend your search, just call and I'll pay for two more days. That's enough time to get the results I want."

Larry and Jimmy did their best not to react but Larry caught Jimmy's fingers moving like he was drumming a jazz piece. His blood pressure for sure at its higher limit.

Jimmy, as serious as he could get, said, "Can we take the Royal Oak

High School year book with us? There's valuable information in it. Talk to friends, teachers. No doubt someone knows her whereabouts. Kids don't run away without telling someone. And we need family photos." His voice strained, insistent.

"Don't bother the administrators at school. I've had copies made of pertinent photos. Bethany, be a doll and convince these boys the photos you have are enough. I don't want to go to the photo shop again. Nerves, too depressing."

"I understand, Mrs. Bernstein. No more stress. We've got what we need." Bethany touched her client's hand.

A show of sympathy or agreement? Neither of which Larry or Jimmy understood. This woman wasn't making good decisions.

*****

Bethany jumped behind the wheel again. Larry sat in the back seat only to prevent Jimmy from a bad case of car sickness. He'd be green if they went more than a half block. As Bethany merged her car into traffic, she said, "It won't take but ten minutes to get to our next client. She's expecting us at eleven."

"Is there somewhere we can stop for coffee? I can't handle another cup of fruited tea," Larry said with a grimace.

"You could have said no thanks." Bethany jerked her head around at Larry. "You don't like blueberry tea? My favorite. It was great."

"What's wrong with the client, that's what I want to know," Jimmy said. "Who doesn't want the police in on a missing kid case? Sounds fishy to me."

Larry added, "If this was our client's kid, guaranteed the cops would be involved. One hundred percent. On our side of the city, folks go a little crazy when a kid is missing. Geez, I don't understand women."

"All of them?" Bethany asked. "Or just a woman who wants to protect her granddaughter's future? It's bad enough she's missing out on normal activities but her grandmother's jewelry is..." Bethany twisted the steering wheel and came to an abrupt stop at the curb.

"Hey, are you trying to kill us? What's with the reckless driving?"

Then Jimmy paused. "Jewelry…did you say jewelry?"

Larry leaned toward the front seat. "Why didn't you tell us?"

"Oh hell, that just slipped out." Bethany's brow creased. "If Clarice finds out I told you, she'll take back the retainer. I swore I wouldn't reveal what the kid stole. Damn it, you can't let this influence you. I need this money. Need it bad." Tears rolled down her face, she rested her head on the steering wheel.

"Darn, don't cry. Hell, it's no big deal. You can count on us to keep a secret." Jimmy handed Bethany a wad of tissues.

"Used?" Bethany drew back. She brushed her eyes with the back of her hand. "Okay, I'm not moving an inch until you swear you won't repeat what I said."

"Not to be repeated in public," Larry said. "But something about this case stinks. I mean, why did 'granny' keep saying *was*…about her granddaughter, as in the past?"

*****

"If Mrs. Rayburn doesn't come to the door, she's in the back yard. We'll give her a few seconds." Bethany hit the screen door a little harder.

"Maybe this granny is a little hard of hearing." Larry scratched his head and looked at his watch. "You said eleven, we've been here five minutes."

"*Patience, Mr. Latimer.*" She rapped again and then backed away, leapt off the corner of the stoop. "Back yard. Yes, she knew we were coming." Bethany waved for the brothers to follow.

A cyclone fence separated the front from the back and the neighboring houses. Similar in style to Mrs. Bernstein's, this home, though, needed a little more repair. White paint flaking off the clapboard siding, a window screen torn but gray tape over it.

Jimmy reached out to open the fence, "She doesn't have a dog, does she?"

"Not presently," Bethany replied. She unleashed the clasp and held the gate open. "Mrs. Rayburn, it's Bethany."

A voice came from the far corner where a large patch of grass had been turned over, a mound of fresh black soil piled next to it. A stout woman about five-ten stepped from behind a strand of thick golden arborvitae. She wore a Detroit Tigers baseball cap, long jeans and a sleeveless tee-shirt. Fresh soil covered her feet and pant legs up to her knees as though she'd been standing in a deep hole. What struck Larry odd was the long-handled shovel at her side, held like a weapon.

She startled back. "What the hell!" The alarm in her voice was heightened by her wide, dark eyes. Eyeing Bethany, she tossed the shovel aside and brushed off the top of her bibbed blue jeans. "You said twelve. Early is not what I expected." She waved, a back hand to motion for them to leave the yard. "Wait in the front."

"Good thing she didn't throw the shovel at us. She's a match for an Olympic javelin thrower." Larry said as he scurried past Bethany and Jimmy to the front yard. "No contest for me."

"I'm sure she said eleven. Worked with my overall plan. First one, then the other, the rest of the day we could check out phone records, the bank. Go to the bus station. Damn, I'm sure she said eleven."

"All I want to know is what's being buried in the yard. Looked long and deep to me." Jimmy shook his head.

"Women. Who knows what's going on with them." Larry shook his head.

Bethany's lips tightened and her face grew red. "It's just a little misunderstanding. One hour. Let's get our info and get out of here."

Laura Rayburn had the same thought on her mind. She opened the door and handed Bethany a brown envelope. The crack was small, but wide enough for the brothers to see a long blue sofa, papers scattered on the floor and a couple boxes of Cracker Jacks on a coffee table. A manila envelope was passed through the opening.

"All you need to know is in this envelope. Name, dates, pictures, a couple of friends. One phone number. Shouldn't take long to find Rebecca. She's got bright yellow hair. Like her mother. Same attitude. Give me a written report in three days. Signed, dated. And call, damn it, before you arrive."

*****

"Where's a hardened criminal when you want one? Let's get on the phone and get Mitty Jackson out of jail so we can work on his case." Larry two-handed his hamburger and took a large bite.

"Two missing girls. Don't call the police and don't go to Royal Oak High School. What do you make of that?" Jimmy eyed Bethany while he sipped his chicken noodle soup.

"Can't we finish lunch and talk about the cases later? I haven't eaten since yesterday."

"Looked like your client had your favorite Cracker Jacks. Maybe if we got there at twelve, she would have shared them." Larry then eyed the receipt the waitress put on the table.

It didn't matter if he or Jimmy grabbed it. Same expense account. He paused long enough to give Bethany a chance to contribute her fair share, but when it was obvious she had no intention of going Dutch, he gritted his teeth and put ten dollars on the table. Partners? Or was this going to be her routine as long as they worked these two cases.

"We can go back to your office, make some plans. Maybe work through dinner." Bethany took the lead to her car. A beat-up green Chevy, one taillight missing and a large dent in the passenger door.

"Not a good idea," Larry blurted. "We've got other work to finish up. Then make a few calls for the grannies." It was more of an excuse to avoid buying another meal than to be alone.

Bethany stopped the car at the corner of John R and Meyers Road, "Easier to stop here."

They got out and started walking. Ferndale Police Department on the corner, a squad car peeled out in front of them.

"I think you got under her skin when you nixed the afternoon session. Something bothering you about the two cases or is it Bethany?" Jimmy asked Larry.

"She bothers me. As though she's got everything under control. And we're just convenient. A meal ticket. Not my style, brother."

The two-block walk gave Larry time to work off his anger and by the time he sat behind his desk his mood had leveled out.

Jimmy spread the school pictures of the two girls on Larry's desk.

"Let's go over what we know. Both girls are eighteen. The 'grannys' deny they were in deep with boyfriends."

Larry picked up the phone. After a lengthy exchange, he said to Jimmy, "Well, wouldn't you know. They aren't on the record books, never attended Royal Oak High School."

"Yet the 'grannies' say otherwise."

"Did you notice pages in the year book had been replaced?" Jimmy said.

"Kids get nasty and rip them out…especially if it's about competition. Girls are so jealous at that age. Remember the Dorsey sisters. Wow, we dodged bullets by breaking up with them."

"I liked Beverly, she liked you." Jimmy laughed. "Pages missing? You sure."

"Two or three, but then a few pages later, one or two added. Didn't you see them? Nice, fine tape job. Took it for granted, you did." Larry looked hard at Jimmy.

An hour later Larry called Bethany but didn't report their findings. "We need to get our hands on another year book. Not just pictures of pictures. Can you go get them? The grannies favor you. At least Bernstein does. Hard to tell about the javelin thrower."

"Don't misjudge her. Probably distraught that her granddaughter betrayed her, too. Antique brooches and necklaces worth—oh heavens, I did it again. Damn, it just slipped out."

"Are we looking for the girls or jewelry? What's the point of keeping this info to yourself? Might be helpful to know the facts." Larry held the phone out so Jimmy could hear, too.

"Well, it seems we have different values. I say the girls are all that matters."

"Did you ever date Cezary Kaminski? He had a knack for attracting women like you." Larry didn't think Bethany could have known Kaminski but they both didn't operate on logic.

"Kaminski? Sounds Polish. I'd did date a Polish guy one time. Had a big family. I'm sort of gun shy when it comes to big families."

"He was too…about big families. Not gun shy," Larry said. "Notice how I used *was*. Like in past tense. Can't help but thinking 'was' is a key word with the grannies case, too."

"So, what does your Polish guy have to do with the granny's problems?"

"Nothing except a good lesson. Kaminski got caught in the crossfire. He made bad choices. Jealous, flighty women. But, chasing down the bad guy in that particular case had its merits. I have a feeling we're butting heads with the 'grannys'. Something stinks in Royal Oak and it ain't old fish."

"Well, I'm going ahead with the case and your names are on the dotted lines. We settle this for Bernstein and Rayburn, take the money and run. I'll call you tomorrow. If it's raining, don't expect me to drive out your way."

"Well, if you're walking in the rain, don't come in. I don't want my floor ruined." Larry hung up.

"Not smart getting on her bad side. She hasn't given us our share of the retainer, yet. Three-way split. Goes a long way getting that car we want. I saw the new Fairlanes…they're beautiful. Sleek lines. Large back seat."

"Jimmy, you can't use the back seat. And I wouldn't want to be in the front if you did. One time was enough."

"Kid stuff. I ate too much candy and popcorn. Sorry you got the residuals. Dad just didn't pull over fast enough."

"He should have taken lessons from Bethany. I've got a neck sprain from that wild move she made."

"So, let's talk about the car. A sedan is roomy. Could use it for, you know, double dates."

"Neither one of us is dating now. Rethink the reason for a big car." Larry continued to look at the pictures that supposedly had been copied from the Royal Oak year book.

"There's something about Bethany. Attractive. I kind'a like her." Jimmy fingered the matte picture.

Larry pushed his chair back. "You've got to be kidding. She's the Izzy kind, and his latest gal shot him. Those kind always get caught up with the wrong people. Roberts may have a license but that doesn't mean she's…well, girlfriend material, up to snuff."

As he gazed at the only information they had, Jimmy pouted. It wasn't the first time his brother dashed his plans about dating a woman who caught his attention. Granted, he'd been spared a few problems because of Larry's broad sweep. But considering the type of work Bethany did, it seemed reasonable to believe she was on the up and up. What the heck? One date. If Jimmy had a chance to be alone with her, he'd ask her to go to a movie. Larry could stew by himself. And then he went back to the pictures.

"Larry, something bugs me. Doesn't the print seem sort'a old?"

"Old? Could be. Take a harder look at the hair style? See any young girls today with those curly bangs, waves on the sides?"

"Can't say I have but then again, I don't pay much attention to high school girls. Blonds, Polaroid girls, more my style," Jimmy grinned.

"I say we crank up the old Fairlane and drive up to the high school. Ask a few questions on the grounds. See if any kids in the neighborhood recognize these gals. Don't need any help from you know who. And when we get done there, let's scan the grannies' areas again. See what's smoking in Royal Oak."

Jimmy reached for his old Stetson, slapped it on his head and said, "Let's go by the camera shop first. Ralph Wingates' good at this stuff. Let's see if he thinks they've been rigged."

It took all of five minutes for their friend Ralph to add clarity to the scenario. "See the grainy texture?" He held a magnifying glass over each picture. "These were duplicated, not once but several times. And my guess is the originals are probably from the 30's. If these high school *girls* ran away, they'd be in their fifties or sixties by now."

Larry slapped the hood of the car as he got in the driver's seat. "Damn, someone's trying to pull one over on us. My gut says this is all about jewelry, not girls. Bethany's secrets? Part of the plan? Something else comes to mind. Where do you take jewelry when you need money?"

"Back to the shop you bought if from? I don't know," Jimmy said. "Only jewelry I have is my Timex watch. Cost twenty-four dollars. But I wouldn't mind buying a nice bracelet or necklace for a sweet girl someday."

"It won't be today. Guaranteed. So, let's back track. Do a little drive by. Client 1, then client 2 and then a big loop around the Roberts' office. A P.I.? Hard to imagine. You still have her card, right? Address…we need it."

"Times changing, Larry. Women aren't like our mother anymore. Except war time. Boy, they took over the factory jobs, then. Even Vietnam, a lot of gals doing men's work. Got to say, I admire them for their courage." Jimmy closed his eyes for a moment and remembered the gal he dated before he entered the army. When he came home, she was on the other side of the world taking care of those too sick to return.

"Reminiscing doesn't help, Jimmy. That was then, this is now."

*****

They found a parking area in the strip mall on Ten Mile Road, 1020 on the building's front. Bethany Roberts' Agency, per the business card, was in building 1022.

"Maybe in the back," Larry pointed to the side alley.

"The pawn shop," Jimmy pointed. "…Can hardly read the numbers. Is that 1022? A mistake? I feel a headache coming on."

"I'll buy you aspirin for lunch. Let's stop looking for Bethany. I want to pawn my watch."

A barrel-chested guy greeted them from behind a counter. A wall of beaded board held shelves with two long rows of small guns, rifles and knives. Below the black Formica counter, behind glass doors, were several rows of jewelry. Rings, necklaces, brooches, earrings. Gold, silver and various shades of gray metal and bright stones.

"Selling or buying?" The man asked. His tone not friendly, more matter of fact.

Larry took the lead, "If I want top dollar for a good Sieko, how do I get it?" Larry toyed with his watch underneath his shirt cuff.

"If you paid five hundred for it, call your insurance company, claim it stolen. If you want me to buy it, I'll give you fifty." He grunted then rested his elbows on the counter.

"Same kind of deal for my ex-wife's engagement ring?"

"Less, I'm overloaded with ex-wife's rings. All types. How desperate are you?" He flexed his muscular arms.

Jimmy looked at Larry's wrist, wondering when he'd bought a Seiko, then another thought struck him. "By any chance do you know a gal that works around here. Small, but wired. I mean not one to back off. Bright hair, reddish-blond? Heard she worked on this block."

The pawn guy broadened his shoulders, raised off the counter. "Hey, I've got a legit pawn shop here. Don't offer information. Are you selling or buying? If neither, take a hike."

Back in the Fairlane, Larry took the wheel again, "Okay, I think I know what we've got into."

They cruised around the first granny's block. This time a green, hard driven Chevy was parked in the drive way. "Want'a bet we locate the missing girls today?"

Jimmy sat high in the seat. "I was hoping it would take four days. Split three ways, nine grand, plus thirty-two hundred. A big pay day."

"You can't find what isn't missing. Not unless you bury it. We'll park down the block, take the alley. Let's see if we can get a look inside a window."

"Well, it's safer than chasing down gun dealers but I still don't like getting caught in someone's back yard. Scare a woman, she might shoot us."

Luck on their side, Larry and Jimmy found easy access into Clarice Bernstein's back yard. She had a broad porch on the back with a sliding glass window, six feet wide and a sheer curtain covering only one section. Even from behind a row of burning bushes, three women were clearly visible. Client 1, client 2 and Bethany. Glasses in front of them, a plate of sandwiches on the table, Bethany holding a box of Cracker Jacks. Broad smiles, as if sharing good times together.

Larry pointed and then whispered, "Off to the hiding hole. Get our proof. Then we go home. We're still entitled to the retainer fee."

Laura Rayburn's house wasn't set on a street with an alley so Larry and Jimmy snuck in the back yard of a neighbor who didn't have a car parked in the drive. When they reached the cyclone fence, they heard a growl followed by a series of barks.

"Bethany said she didn't have a dog." Larry startled back.

"I remember. Exact words 'didn't have one presently'. Struck me odd, just like *was,* past tense, got under your skin."

They watched as the black mutt raced back and forth along the fence. No bared teeth but a couple of angry growls and more yapping and barking.

"If it doesn't stop barking, it'll attract attention. Neighbors will call the cops."

"Burger joint down the block. Let's go."

When they returned, it didn't take but a few moments for the large watch dog to calm down. By the time they climbed over the fence, the mutt was chomping away, spread out on the grass, eyeing Jimmy as he dug into the fresh hole behind the row of waxy bushes. After the work was completed, they patted the dog's head, gave it the other half of the hamburger, cheese, pickle included, and climbed back over the fence.

*****

"Two ways to do this, ladies. We collect the retainer fee now. Or we take this nice heavy treasure trove to the cops and report your little scam. Signed and sealed, remember."

"Isn't that blackmail," Bethany asked as she dipped her hand into another box of Cracker Jacks. She munched and talked, "If they report the jewelry as missing and investigators can't find the jewels or the thief, then the insurance company pays. Simple." It didn't take long for her to squeal. Leaking information seemed to be her specialty.

"A simple case of insurance fraud," Larry replied.

"We don't want the damn jewelry. My sister and I have been burdened by it forever. Family treasures, everyone said. Who'd wear this gaudy stuff?" Laura, in sweat pants and a dark black tee shirt, explained. "Now tell me, do you think I'd look grand wearing brooches and earrings?"

Clarice nodded as she spoke. "And I only wear simple gold or silver. No ornaments."

"Sisters?" Larry and Jimmy exchanged glances again. Opposites in style and looks, but just like the brothers where in their own fashion.

"They can't be charged with fraud. You've got the goods in your hands, Larry *Lasiter*. Jimmy has dirt on his shoes. Maybe we should report a robbery. Add trespassing. Isn't that intent to commit…a…something? Something worse than fraud." Bethany seemed triumphant as she stood in front of the Lafferty brothers.

"Nice try, Bethany. How about impersonating a licensed private investigator, entrapment, accomplice to a fraud? Criminal activity written all over those fake contracts. If you ever had plans to become a P.I., you've blown it. You pulled a bad stunt that will keep you out of business forever."

"Why didn't you take these to an antiques dealer? Sell them," Jimmy asked.

"Would never get what they're worth. And the pawn guy would only give us pennies. Insurance pays much better. And we could still sell them later. More bang for our buck." Granny Laura said.

Granted, the women weren't hard-core criminals. Bernstein, the blueberry tea drinker or Rayburn, the javelin thrower, weren't your typical grannies, either.

Clarice said in a smug voice, "Why should we leave the family keepsakes in a drawer for someone else to steal?"

It all made sense in its convoluted way.

Jimmy asked, "So why not give them to another family member? Cousin, aunts, uncles."

"There's just three of us left."

"Another relative?" Larry said. "So, let whoever the third one is, have them."

"Not suitable for that *relative* either. A matter of needing the cold cash. Then pawn all of it after the insurance paid off." Laura Rayburn glanced toward Bethany.

Jimmy nodded, as if he understood, then said, "Let sleeping dogs lie."

"But there is the matter of the retainer fee. Contract, remember." Larry pressed forward.

"Gentleman, as hard as it is to say, with all due respect for your service, we don't have any money to pay the retainer. If the insurance came through…we…" Clarice Bernstein looked at Larry, then at Jimmy. "Can I offer you a cup of tea? Bethany will get it for you. I'm much too stressed to be of service right now." Tears ran down her face.

"Not a good time for tea, Granny." Then Bethany quickly covered her mouth.

Jimmy and Larry snapped back their heads.

"Okay, I wasn't about to let my grandmother and aunt be made fools of by that damn pawn store thief. I came up with the insurance angle."

*****

"At least we didn't waste four days chasing down two gals that weren't missing." Larry stuffed his hands in his pockets.

"Only a few hours," Jimmy said. "Not bad. Amusing if nothing else."

"Not as exciting as dodging gun dealers or trailing Kaminski's girlfriends."

"Maybe Booster Kramer got bailed out. Can get back to finding out who's been tapping into his bank account. He gave access to three different women."

"Women, can't trust them," Larry groaned.

"Pretty dull life without them," Jimmy said with a smile as he eyed the business card Bethany had given them. "Bethany got our name right on the way out. Waved at me. Said see you around, Mr. Lafferty."

Twink
Michael Bracken

The sun died a quick death, leaving the city awash in neon and shadow. The slender blond in the front office of a second-floor walk-up toyed with the banker's lamp on his desk before switching it off and rising. He opened the door separating the agency's two rooms and said to the stocky man in the back office, "It's been a long day."

Alex Walker looked up from his desk. Almost ten years separated him from the younger man standing in the open doorway.

"I need a drink," the blond said. "What do you need?"

"Clients," Walker said. "If we don't catch a break soon, you'll be filing for unemployment."

Charles Gifford said, "Now I really need that drink."

Walker stood, adjusted his shoulder holster and the .38 it contained, and pulled on a gray suit jacket. His receptionist's chinos and polo shirt cost more than the suit he had purchased off the rack at a men's discount clothing store. "Woody's?"

The blond shrugged. "I'm easy."

After they cut off the lights, Walker locked the outer door, and the two men walked downstairs and a block-and-a-half to Woody's Woodpecker. A long, narrow establishment, the place was just wide enough for a bar on one side and a row of darkened booths on the other. A dozen men lined the bar. Another dozen had paired off and they occupied six of the eight booths.

Walker and Gifford settled into the empty booth nearest the entrance. When the lone waiter stopped at their table, Walker ordered Jack-and-Coke. Gifford ordered pinot noir.

After their drinks arrived, Walker said, "I don't know when you'll see your next paycheck."

"I haven't cashed my first one, yet."

"Then why are you still here?"

The blond said, "You."

"Me?" Walker spun his glass in a circle without looking at it. "Why me?"

"I saw the look in your eye when I walked into your office the first day," Gifford explained. He slipped off one loafer and ran his foot up the inside of Walker's thigh. "You wanted me. You still want me, but you just won't admit it."

Walker reached between his thighs and grabbed his receptionist's foot before it reached his crotch. Lifting his glass with his other hand, he downed his drink and motioned to the waiter for a refill. "And if I said I wanted you now?"

"Do, and find out." Gifford sipped from his wine glass but left his foot where it was.

Walker's second drink arrived. He downed it as quickly as he had downed the first. Then he released his grip on the blond's foot and said, "Let's go."

Gifford finished his pinot noir, slipped his foot back into his loafer, and waited until his employer paid for their drinks before rising from the booth. He hooked his arm in Walker's when they stepped outside, and they walked together toward the parking garage where Walker kept his black SUV.

As they passed the building that housed Walker Private Investigations, Gifford said, "We're being followed."

"Over my left shoulder, face like a pug," Walker said. "I spotted him when we left the bar."

"Why would someone follow us?"

"I don't know, but I plan to ask."

"When? How?"

Walker didn't answer directly. "Let me put you into a cab."

"But—"

Walker stepped off the curb between two parked hybrids and flagged down a Yellow Cab. After he put his receptionist in the back seat, he pressed a folded twenty and a key into Gifford's hand. Then he gave the driver his address and closed the door.

*****

Gifford was waiting in Walker's apartment when his employer arrived an hour later. The knuckles of Walker's right hand were bloody, but it wasn't his blood. Gifford followed Walker to the bathroom and stood in the open doorway. "What happened?"

"The guy was following me, not us," Walker explained as he washed his hands. "I caught him inside the parking garage stairwell and asked him a question with this." He held up his right fist. "I had to repeat my question a few times before he answered."

"Why was he following you?"

"He said Bradford Johnson sent him to find out why I came back."

"Johnson?" Gifford asked. "Who's Johnson?"

"We were partners, once, working Vice. We had steady hours and earned a little extra money on weekends handling security for a certain private drinking establishment."

Gifford followed Walker to the kitchen, where Walker retrieved a beer. He offered one to his receptionist, but Gifford shook his head.

Walker opened the beer and took a long swallow. "Someone started shaking down the bar's patrons—a preacher, a couple of family values politicians, and other men in the closet who couldn't afford to come out. One of them was related to a guy in the police chief's office, so there was an investigation. Before long it centered on us. No one would testify against us, and Internal Affairs never proved a thing, but Johnson and I were encouraged to retire. They wanted us to take our pensions and disappear."

"And?"

"We did," Walker said. "We both retired, and we both disappeared. At least, I did. I went to Mexico for four years—four years spent sitting on a beach with a beer in my hand and sand in my ass. I came back because I ran out of money, and I missed the city."

"So, why would your partner care that you came back?"

"The statute of limitations hasn't expired," Walker said. "I can still testify against him."

"You think he did it?"

Walker shrugged. "Johnson was always looking for an angle, a way to get ahead."

He drew a fresh beer from the fridge, and they returned to the living room. The twenty Walker had given Gifford earlier that evening lay on the coffee table. Walker picked it up. "What's this?"

Gifford said, "I don't need the money."

Walker's eyes narrowed as he stared at his receptionist. Then he pocketed the twenty.

*****

Gifford returned to his own apartment a few hours later—a three-bedroom in a high-rise paid for by a trust fund—and he was first into the office the following morning. When Walker arrived, Gifford said, "I found your former partner."

"Where?"

"He does some work for Edwin Cathcart—the philanthropist—but I can't tell what, exactly." The Cathcart Foundation supported several non-profit arts organizations about town, from art museums to the symphony orchestra, and Cathcart was the family face seen most often at charity events. "Cathcart was in the paper just last week."

Gifford motioned Walker around to his side of the desk and showed him photos of the sixty-nine-year-old philanthropist taken at a ballet fund-raiser that the local newspaper had posted on its website. He clicked through the photos one at a time until Walker stopped him and tapped a finger against the screen.

"There, in the background," Walker said, his finger covering the face of a man that could have been his body-double—tall, broad-shouldered, and thick-chested—but wearing a far more expensive suit and with his short hair colored and salon-styled, not cut into a salt-and-pepper flat-top. Unlike Walker, the man in the photograph had not spent the previous four years sitting on a beach and his boyish face had not aged into the texture of a catcher's mitt. "That's Johnson."

Gifford enlarged the photograph so that it filled the computer screen.

Walker asked, "Who're these other people?"

Gifford named three people visible in the background with Johnson, all patrons of the arts. Then he identified the aging twink hanging from Cathcart's arm as David Lang. "I used to see Lang at the clubs. He was always more interested in Sugar Daddies than in anyone his own age."

"Looks like he hooked a big one."

*****

They took a break mid-day and walked to Dick's Diner for lunch. Over open-faced roast beef sandwiches and greasy French fries, the two men danced around recent events.

"Last night," Walker said. "What's that mean?"

"What do you want it to mean?"

"I'm not certain," Walker said. "You're my employee."

"Only if you pay me."

"What? You want to be a partner?"

"I certainly don't need the money."

"Because there isn't any," Walker said. "Not yet anyhow."

"I'm not interested in answering phones and filing paperwork, if the phone ever rang and we had anything to file," Gifford said. "I want to be involved in the rough stuff."

Walker stared across the table at the slender blond he'd hired a month earlier. "Have you ever been in a fight?"

"I've bitch slapped a few lovers."

Walker snorted. "A real fight, with your fists."

Gifford shook his head.

"Ever fire a gun?"

"I shot skeet with my grandfather."

"Ever shot anything living—a whacked out drug addict charging you with a knife or maybe just a squirrel?”

Gifford shook his head.

“You’re not ready for the rough stuff.”

“So, teach me.” Gifford reached across the table and covered Walker’s meaty fist with his slim-fingered hand as he stared into his employer’s eyes.

A pair of plainclothes detectives walked in and eyeballed the diners. One found an empty table and settled there. The other, a slender man the age Walker had been when he’d been encouraged to retire, bee-lined it to the table Walker and Gifford shared.

Walker saw him approaching and pulled back his hand.

“What rock did you crawl out from under?” Sgt. Greg Hampton asked.

“A Mexican rock.” Walker stood and shook the other man’s hand. “I’ve been back about a month.”

“I’ve seen your partner around. He resurfaced a couple of years ago, doing some kind of security work for rich people.”

“I heard,” Walker said. “You still in Vice?”

“Homicide,” Hampton said. “I transferred eighteen months ago.”

“You like it?”

“It’s a living,” Hampton said as he shrugged. He glanced over his shoulder. “I need to get back to my partner.”

“Thanks for coming over,” Walker said. “A lot of the other guys treat me like I’m a pariah.”

“What they said about you,” the homicide detective said. “I never believed a word of it.”

“Thanks,” Walker said. “I appreciate it.”

“You ever need anything, let me know.”

“Any idea where Johnson’s hanging his hat these days?”

“Haven’t heard.”

The men shook hands again and then Hampton returned to the table where his current partner sat.

“You finished?” Walker asked his receptionist. When Gifford

nodded, he said, "Let's go."

*****

Walker had not kept up with social media during the four years he sat on a Mexican beach, but Gifford was adept with several applications, from Facebook to Grindr to LinkedIn. Once back in the office, each sat at his desk and began a search for Walker's former partner.

Walker kept the landline busy as he called former associates on both sides of the law who couldn't or wouldn't tell him where Johnson received his mail. Gifford approached his search from the other end of the social strata, working top down in an effort to locate someone other than Edwin Cathcart who had hired Johnson at any time in the recent past or anyone from his clubbing days who knew of any connection between David Lang and Bradford Johnson other than Cathcart.

They compared notes a few hours later.

"I've had three people tell me Johnson's living on the Upper East Side," Walker said. "None of them could tell me exactly where."

Gifford slid a piece of paper onto the desk in front of his employer, an address neatly penned in blue ink in the center of it. "I don't know what hold he has on the Remingtons, but Johnson's been living in their rent-controlled apartment for more than a year while they're in London. Percival Remington introduced him to Edwin Cathcart before he left the country, and Johnson's been employed by the Cathcart Foundation ever since."

"Doing what?"

"Probably doing Cathcart's twink," Gifford said. "Johnson's supposed to provide protection for the old man, but he's been seen on several occasions with David Lang but without Cathcart."

*****

Walker pushed the address around on his desk for the next few hours. After Gifford left for the evening, he walked down to Woody's Woodpecker, fended off the advances of two rent boys, and downed three Jack-and-Cokes. Then he drove to the address Gifford had given him.

Bradford Johnson opened the apartment door and his eyes widened in surprise. Walker didn't wait for an invitation. He pushed the door open wider and stepped past Johnson into a living room filled with expensive furnishings. The couch alone would have set Walker back half a year's pension.

"You've moved up in the world."

"I have a good thing going," Johnson said. "Don't mess it up."

"That why you sent a guy to follow me?"

"I didn't send anyone to follow you," Johnson insisted. "I didn't even know you were back in the country."

"You got away with it four years ago," Walker said, "and left me with nothing."

"You got exactly what you deserved. You were planning to rat me out."

"I should have," Walker said. "I should have let you twist in the wind."

"That why you came back? You looking for a little taste of the good life and think you can put the squeeze on me to get it?"

"I hadn't given you a second thought until you set that pug-faced guy on my tail," Walker said. "Now you're all I think about."

"You can go pound sand," Johnson said. He grabbed Walker's arm and tried to twist the other man toward the door. "Time for you to leave."

Walker pulled away and the sleeve of his cheap suit jacket tore open at the shoulder seam. Johnson grabbed him again. Walker swung his right fist and planted it in the middle of his former partner's face. Johnson's nose erupted in a fountain of blood, spraying both of them.

Johnson stepped backward and fell over the coffee table, pulling Walker down with him. They rolled across the floor trading punches until Walker pushed himself to his feet and looked down at his former partner.

"You put your bloodhound on a short leash," Walker insisted. "I see him sniffing around again and I'll pay a visit to Internal Affairs, maybe even put them onto whatever scam you're running now."

Walker slammed the door on his way out.

*****

"Your ex-partner is leading the news," Gifford said as he showed Walker the local newspaper's website the next morning. "Someone shot him."

Walker wore a different suit that morning, a blue pinstripe purchased at the same time as the damaged gray suit as part of a two-for-one special, and he told his receptionist about his confrontation with Johnson the previous evening. "I smashed his nose and his blood's on my other suit."

"Did you—?"

"No," Walker insisted. "I knocked him around, but he was alive when I left."

"The newspaper says he was likely killed sometime after midnight," Gifford said. "What time did you leave?"

"Nine, maybe nine-thirty," Walker said, "but his blood's not all I have to worry about. I lost my .38 in the scuffle."

Gifford stared a question at his boss.

"Someone else was there," Walker said. "There were two wine glasses on the coffee table and the bedroom door was closed. Whoever was there must have overheard everything."

"What did you do after you left Johnson's apartment?"

"I went home."

"Alone?"

Walker nodded.

"No, you didn't," Gifford said. "I was there waiting for you. You arrived around ten. We had drinks before bed. I spent the night."

"What's in it for you?"

"You," Gifford said. "I told you that's why I hang around."

"You don't owe me anything," Walker said. "Hell, you barely know me."

"I know you better than you think," Gifford explained. "Four years ago, I was a regular at the private drinking establishment where you and Johnson provided security."

"That's an exclusive club. How—?"

Gifford didn't let his employer finish. "My family has quiet money. We don't flash it around like the Cathcarts, and we keep our name out of the news."

"You walked in here five weeks ago looking for a job. How did you know I was hiring?"

"I didn't, but I've seen all the old movies. I knew you needed a hot blond at the front desk."

Walker eyed his receptionist and did not disagree.

Gifford continued. "I set up a Google Alert for your name four years ago. I had forgotten all about it until I received an alert when you received your private investigator's license and another when you applied for your business permit. Once I knew you were back in the city, I tracked you down."

Walker shook his head and turned as if to walk into his office.

His receptionist stopped him. "There's more news," he said. "Someone was killed breaking into the Cathcart mansion this morning."

Gifford clicked through to the article about the home invasion and subsequent shooting. A photograph of the dead man accompanied the article. "Recognize him?"

"That's the man who was following us the other night."

"His name's Fred Tate."

*****

Walker settled into the chair behind his desk and phoned Sgt. Hampton. After he identified himself, Walker asked, "What can you tell me about Fred Tate, the man killed at the Cathcart Mansion early this morning?"

"That isn't the first question I expected to come out of your mouth," Hampton said. "You heard your former partner got iced last night, didn't you?"

"He probably deserved it."

"Johnson was killed with a .38," Hampton said. "There's a .38 registered in your name. You want to let us take a look at it?"

"You think I'm stupid enough to kill someone using a registered weapon?" Walker asked. "I was on the force long enough to know when to use a throwdown."

"Maybe you didn't plan to shoot him," Hampton said. "Maybe he was shot in a moment of anger. Somebody beat the crap out of him before he died."

"Wasn't me," Walker said.

"So, you'll let us take a look at your .38?"

"I'll stop by the next time I'm in your neighborhood," Walker promised. "What about Tate?"

"He has a sheet. Assault mostly, but he's a person of interest in two unsolved homicides. What's he got to do with you?"

"When I figure it out, I'll let you know."

After he ended the call, Walker exited his office and told his receptionist, "Shut everything down. We need to get out of here before the place is crawling with cops."

*****

They holed up in a cheap motel where they paid for their room with cash, and the dwarf working the front desk didn't bat an eye when two men let a room mid-morning.

"As best I can figure, I'm what ties Johnson's murder to Tate's death," Walker said.

"You think Tate was Johnson's visitor last night?"

"I doubt it. Johnson always preferred twinks."

"Can the police tie you to Tate?"

"I doubt they'd have a reason to try," Walker said. "There won't be much of an investigation. When a rich man kills an intruder like Tate, the D.A. is unlikely to prosecute. If there's even a suggestion that he might, the rich guy's lawyers will smother the D.A. in paperwork and bury the case. I've seen too many blue bloods get out of too many scrapes just by tossing their money around." He looked at his receptionist. "No offense."

The two men stared at one another for a moment before Gifford asked another question. "Johnson hires Tate to follow you, maybe rough you up a bit, but you spot him and turn the play around," Gifford said. "So why does he break into Cathcart's place?"

"Let's find out."

Gifford only had his iPhone, but it gave him access to the Internet and to social media. Cathcart's contemporaries were silent on that morning's shootings, but throughout the day David Lang's former friends tweeted several crude comments about the old man's ability to fire his gun. Some of the tweets expressed jealousy that Lang had leeched onto the philanthropist while they were still turning tricks, and a few pondered what might have happened to Lang if the intruder had killed Cathcart.

"What would happen?" Walker asked.

"They married in a private ceremony six months ago," Gifford said. "There's probably a pre-nup to protect Cathcart's money in case of divorce, but Cathcart never had children and Lang would be his rightful heir. Cathcart still controls the Foundation's money, which is why he appears at all the fundraisers, but rumors are floating around that his personal fortune's dwindling. That can't make Lang happy."

Walker said, "The only way to know for certain what's going on is to confront Cathcart."

*****

Shortly after sunset, Walker and Gifford drove to the Cathcart mansion. Security was lax, despite that morning's incident, and no police vehicles were in sight as Walker pointed his SUV up the long drive. He parked, the only vehicle in the circular drive, and told Gifford to wait for his return.

Walker took the front steps two at a time, crossed the wide porch, and leaned into the bell. Cathcart opened the door a moment later.

"You another cop?"

Walker did not deny it as he stepped through the open doorway. "Just a few more questions, if you have the time."

The philanthropist swung the door closed. Neither of them noticed that it failed to latch. Then Cathcart turned and led Walker across the marble-floored foyer to the library, a room where no actual reading ever took place. The smell of dusty tomes and aged leather permeated the room, and the bookshelves had gaps where volumes had been removed and never returned. As he followed the philanthropist, Walker passed three large, leather-bound books stacked neatly on a small table.

"I was surprised you answered the door," Walker said to Cathcart's back. "Where's your staff?"

"I explained all this to the other officers this morning."

"So, explain it to me."

"There's just the one—the cook. He's been with me as far back as I can remember," Cathcart said as he settled into a leather wingback chair, leaving the private detective standing with his back to the door. "I had to let the others go."

"When?"

The philanthropist shrugged. "Various times. There's been a slow attrition."

"So, it's just you and the cook here now?"

"No," said a voice from behind Walker. "The cook's gone home for the day."

Walker turned. David Lang stood in the doorway, wearing chinos and an untucked polo shirt. Much younger than either of the other men in the room, his face showed signs of aging that were not visible in the newspaper photo Gifford had shown Walker the day before.

"You're the man who killed Brad," Lang accused. "I was there when you assaulted him."

"If you were there," Walker said, defending himself against the accusation, "then you know I didn't kill Johnson. He was fine, just a little worse for wear, when I left."

"You must have come back later."

Cathcart glared at his much-younger spouse, "You were with Brad last night?"

"He wanted me to go away with him," Lang explained. "He knew things about my past and he threatened to tell you about them if I didn't. He said I had to leave with him today or his first stop this morning would be here to see you. I believed him. Brad seemed to know everybody's secrets and he used them to get his way. He always got his way."

Cathcart said, "I knew he was putting pressure on you, but I didn't think you would leave me."

"How could you stop us?" Lang asked. Then his eyes narrowed, and he made his second accusation. "It was you, then. You killed Brad."

"I did no such thing."

"You had him killed," Walker interjected as he tried to put the pieces together. "Then you killed the man you hired to kill Brad."

"Why would I do that?"

"Your lover was leaving you for someone else, someone younger, more virile, more—"

"David isn't worth the effort," Cathcart said. His eyes said something different. "I can buy a dozen to replace him."

"You can't even afford to retain household staff," Walker said. "You had Fred Tate following me. After he killed Brad, he came here. What did he want from you? What did he ask for before you shot him?"

Again, Cathcart denied involvement in Johnson's death. "I never saw that man before in my life."

"You got it all wrong," Lang told Walker as he pulled the private investigator's missing .38 from his waistband. He squeezed the trigger and a blood blossom erupted from Cathcart's chest. Without a change of expression, Lang said, "Tate came to see me."

Walker didn't blink as he turned to the aging twink holding his revolver. "Why?"

"I knew him from the clubs, and he owed me a favor. He was supposed to make you think Brad was gunning for you, and he did. He wasn't happy with the beatdown you put on him and thought he could play the angle. He went to see Brad, but it was too late, Brad was already dead. He came here to see if I had jammed him up somehow, and he was putting the squeeze on me when Edwin came downstairs. I didn't even know Edwin owned a gun, but when he saw what was happening, he shot Tate."

"And solved all your problems," Walker said. He nodded at the body in the wingback chair. "Until now."

"This'll work out even better," Lang said, "both of them dead and you in the frame."

Gifford stepped into the room behind Lang, but Lang didn't hear him, and Walker didn't take his eyes off the gun pointed at his gut. He asked, "Why me?"

"Brad told me about the scheme you two had going before you left the force."

"I wasn't part of that."

Lang continued talking, his voice masking whatever small sounds Gifford made behind him. "You're the only person who had something on Brad, and he said you could ruin everything for him. I had you located in Mexico, so I knew when you returned to the city last month, and I counted on you to make him sweat."

Gifford lifted one of the leather-bound books from the table nearest the door and approached Lang from behind.

"I wasn't about to leave Edwin, not now that we're married and what's left of his money is mine. Brad wouldn't believe me. He was going to confront Edwin, make him believe I wanted Brad to kill him," Lang explained. "But Brad wouldn't do it because he didn't have the balls. When you lost your gun last night, everything fell into place. I could have my cake and eat it, too."

"So, what will you do now?"

"Kill you. Tell the police you came in here and killed Edwin. Then tell them the gun went off when I tried to wrestle it away from you."

"You'll have to be much closer for the powder burns to be

believable." Walker stepped toward Lang.

Lang raised the gun. As he squeezed the trigger, Gifford bitch-slapped him with the leather-bound book. Lang collapsed and the shot went wide.

*****

Walker used Gifford's iPhone to call Sgt. Greg Hampton, and they waited with the dead man and his unconscious twink until the police arrived.

The private detective and his receptionist walked Sgt. Hampton through everything that had happened, and, when they finished, the homicide detective told them to go home.

"I think you're ready for the rough stuff, partner," Walker said as he and Gifford crossed the foyer, "but we won't be able to keep your name out of the news."

"A little publicity won't hurt," Gifford replied. "It might even bring in a few clients."

Walker pulled open the door, and they faced a sunrise not quite bright enough to destroy the shadows of the night.

Eddie's Girl
Glenn Francis Faelnar

Joseph Trent stared out of his window on a hot afternoon in the middle of July, hoping to get a whiff of air from the world outside. The heat was relentless that afternoon. The air conditioner in his office was nothing more than a display. It'd been out of commission since the first day he moved into his office. He never met the previous owners but the broken air conditioner probably wasn't something that convinced them to stay. Or maybe they'd broken the air conditioner and refused to replace it, that's why the landlord of the building kicked them out. The charming landlord was a fellow in his fifties who wasn't shy about being the building's resident asshole. The landlord wore it like it was a suit for church on Sunday. Suffice to say, nobody wanted to rent the office because of the landlord's pleasing personality, except for him, because he's had plenty of experience dealing with assholes. When you're kind of an asshole yourself, you get pretty good at dealing with other assholes.

That afternoon was just like any other day in the office. It was dull and the clients were scarce. Half the time, Joe wonders where he was going to find rent for the next month. Luckily, a few blessings drop in every now and again. A lot of those blessings came from cheating husbands and wives. Those were the regular clientele of a private investigator and he thanks the world for it. When the world has made cheating a hobby, then there's bound to be some money to be made from it. Despite that, he often wondered why his office wasn't overflowing with clients on a regular basis. Thoughts of him not being good at his job often came to mind but he brushed them off because he believed that wasn't true. He'd only been operating for about a year and a half, so it was unfair for him to look to bigger competition for comparison. He took out a cigarette from the pack on his table and began smoking. In the line of job that he was in, waiting was always the worst part.

He was half done with his cigarette when someone came knocking on his door. He wondered whether it was a client or his fun landlord, who dropped by his office once a week to remind him that his rent was still due. Sometimes he stayed quiet, waiting until his landlord stopped knocking and eventually went away. He heard two more knocks from the door but held off on answering. That was until he heard the voice on the other side of the door.

"Hello, is anyone there?" From what he could tell, it sounded like an old lady—and he was hard-pressed to believe that his landlord had suddenly learned the art of doing voices. So by reason of deduction, it was probably a client outside his door.

He took a last puff from his cigarette and rubbed what remained of it against the inside of his ashtray. He waved the smoke out of the air and comically directed it outside his window. He straightened his tie and, as he mustered his most welcoming voice, said:

"Please, come in."

He was devastated when his door opened and revealed his landlord with a typical sour look on his face.

"Fuck, Jimmy," Joe said.

"You can curse at me all you want Trent, you're rent still due for next month. Hell, you can curse at me all you want if it helps you pay your rent."

"Do you really have to knock on my door once a week to remind me?"

"Hey, it's my building so I can do whatever the fuck I want," Jimmy said.

"Look, I'll pay rent next month. You can tattoo that on your forehead so you won't forget."

"No delays this time?" Jimmy said.

"Yes. No delays this time. Now, can you please go? I'm still a little freaked out that you resorted to sounding like an old woman just to trick me into believing you were a client."

"I wouldn't have to if you'd pay your rent on time."

"Just go away, Jimmy."

"Don't forget. No delays, all right?"

"All right already. Just close the door behind you," Joe said.

"Oh, and this old woman wanted to see you." Jimmy got out of the way to reveal an old lady who had been standing behind him all the time.

"Fuck you very much Jimmy," Joe said as he watched Jimmy leave. "I'm really sorry about that ma'am. Please, come in."

The bespectacled old lady slowly made her way inside Joe's office. Her purse hung on her right arm while she held her umbrella in her left hand. In her right hand she held what appeared to be a newspaper clipping.

Joe half stood. "Do you need any help ma'am?"

"Oh, no young man, I'll get there. Just give me a minute."

He sat back down and waited for the old woman to get to the chair across from his desk. As it was she moved at a turtle's pace. He understood that she was old and her motor functions weren't what they used to be. Still, if she was in a race with a rabbit to see who would get to the chair first, the rabbit would've lapped her ten times before she could even make it on her first. But she was the only client he'd had in weeks, so patience was a necessity.

When she was finally settled, Joe sighed in relief before saying, "So, what can I do for you this afternoon, Mrs.—"

"Field, Dolores Field."

"It's nice to meet you, Mrs. Field. I'm Joe Trent."

Dolores smiled politely. "I saw the Limelight Investigations advertisement in the newspaper and I decided to bring my case to you. The man you were just speaking to was kind enough to direct me here."

"I'm sure he was," Joe said, sarcastically. "What can I do for you this afternoon Mrs. Field?"

"I was hoping you could help me find my husband. His name is

Eddie."

Dolores Field took out a photo from her purse and gave it to Joe. It was of her and her husband, Eddie, with the Statue of Liberty in the background.

"How long has Eddie been missing?"

"He's been missing since this morning," Dolores Field said. "He went out to buy diapers and some milk but never came back."

"Are you sure he's missing, Mrs. Field?" Joe said. "Maybe he just made another stop somewhere. I mean, the day's not over yet. It's still four in the afternoon."

"Oh, I know my Eddie. He never goes anywhere in the afternoon. He leaves in the morning and he always comes back."

"Have you called the cops yet?"

"Oh no, I didn't," Dolores Field said.

"Why not?" Joe said.

"I don't believe he's in any real danger."

"What makes you say that?"

"Because I think my Eddie is having an affair."

And there it was.

The words that came out of Dolores Field's mouth were the same words uttered by almost every client who hires a private investigator.

"Mrs. Field, if you don't mind, can I ask how old you are?"

"I'm seventy-one years old."

"And what about your husband?"

"My Eddie was seventy-five years old last May," Dolores Field said.

Joe was a little puzzled because part of him couldn't believe that old people like Dolores and Eddie could have affairs. But if cheating was almost the norm in society, then age wouldn't be a factor.

He sat back in his chair and considered smoking another cigarette. "Mrs. Field, what makes you think your husband is cheating?" He played with the packet, but didn't take one out.

Dolores leaned forward. "Well, he's been going to the convenience store lately. I thought it was just a memory thing given that we are at that age and he always brought back milk from the store. Then one day, he went to the store but didn't buy any milk."

"Maybe your husband remembered you still had milk when he got to the store."

"But he would come home with a huge grin on his face. He never did that before."

The cigarette was still looking good. "Okay, Mrs. Field. Let's say your husband was having an affair, do you have any idea who the other woman could be?"

"Sarah Covington," Dolores Field said, without any hesitation.

"Oh, and who is Sarah Covington?"

Dolores sat back in her chair again. "She was my best friend."

"Was? I'm assuming she isn't anymore?"

She looked around the office, avoiding eye contact. "Not after what she did."

"What did she do, if I may ask?"

"She sent a letter to my Eddie saying she was going to wait for him no matter how long it took. Like she was hoping that I would be on my way to heaven sooner or later."

"So, you think that Mr. Field finally gave in and went with Ms. Covington?"

"My Eddie never liked Sarah. That was something he always made clear to me. But I think that snake took him from me."

Joe felt a little sad hearing the tragic tale of a friendship ending over a person they loved at the same time. And their age just magnified the tragedy.

He tried to sound sympathetic. "Do you have an address for this Sarah Covington?"

"Oh, yes. I'm sure she still lives in the same place. I know she wasn't going to leave without taking my Eddie with her."

Dolores Field wrote down the address on the piece of paper Joe gave her. Her hands shook as she wrote. The stroke of your wrist and your penmanship changes at a certain age and it showed with Dolores Field's shaky letters. She gave the piece paper back to Joe as soon as she finished.

"I'll visit Ms. Covington's residence as soon as I can," Joe said.

"Does that mean you'll take my case and bring back my Eddie?"

"Well…" Joe purposely left a long pause after what he said and looked at Dolores Field with every intention of reminding her that his services weren't free.

"Oh, right," Dolores Field said, as she remembered that the only thing that was free in this world was the air you breathe.

She rifled through her purse and took out her wallet. She sifted through her cash then looked up at Joe and said "How much was your fee?"

Joe felt a little conscientious that he was billing this old lady who probably only has a limited amount of cash. So he said "Well, any amount is fine Mrs. Field."

Dolores Field took out half the cash she had in her wallet and gave it to Joe. As she did, she blanketed his hands and said, "Thank you so much for your help, Mr. Trent."

"No thanks necessary, Mrs. Field."

Joe watched as Mrs. Field left his office. He still had the cash in his hands when she closed the door behind her, and then he counted it. He was hoping there was enough—or close to—the amount that was due next month. To his disappointment, it was short by a mile. He convinced himself not to dwell on it at his office and decided to dwell on it at the bar a few blocks away. Mr. Field had been missing for a few hours and was probably at his lover's house. He would go to Sarah Covington's house tomorrow and fetch Mrs. Field's husband, Eddie. It was the easiest job he'd ever been given, and he left his office, ready for a drink.

*****

Joe let out a disappointing sigh as he stood a few inches from where Sarah Covington was laid to rest. Her tombstone said that she had taken up residence at the North Park Cemetery two years before. Unless she rose from the dead to fulfill her unrequited love, the possibility of her taking Eddie Field dissipated. Her daughter, Sophie, was kind enough to let him tag along while she and her kids visited her mother. Sophie went by Lindel now instead of Covington. She saw the disappointment in his eyes and said "Is everything alright Mr. Trent?"

Joe realized the rudeness of sporting a disappointing look in front of a dead lead's daughter, so he wiped it away with a smile and said "Yes. Everything's fine Mrs. Lindel."

"Were you a student of my mother's at the University?" Sophie Lindel asked.

"No. I'm actually a private investigator. I was hired to find someone who was an acquaintance of your mother."

"Who was it?" Sophie Lindel said.

"I can't really disclose my client's information. But seeing as your mother died two years ago, that kind of puts an end to the single lead I had," Joe said.

"Well, I'm sorry my mother died."

"No apologies necessary. People die all the time. Sometimes even horribly which makes you wonder if there's a god out there."

Joe saw the horrified look on her face, and realized that he'd said something inappropriate to her in front of her children at her mother's grave.

"I'm going to go."

"Yes, I think you should."

"Thank you for your time and I'm sorry that your mom died." He cringed when he said that last part but it was too late to take it back. All he could do was walk away and save himself from any more embarrassment.

Joe got in his car and dialed Dolores Field's number on his phone. She was probably going to expect some good news so the phone call he was about to make was going to be unpleasant.

"Hello, Mrs. Field. Good morning."

"Mr. Trent, I didn't expect your call this early. Were you able to find my Eddie? Did Sarah put up a fight?" Dolores Field said.

"Well, she didn't put up a fight because she couldn't," Joe said.

"Oh, so my Eddie saw some sense and remembered who he really loved?" Dolores Field said.

"Uh, that's not exactly what happened either."

"What do you mean Mr. Trent?" Dolores Field said.

"Um, how do I say this? Mrs. Field, your husband isn't with Sarah Covington because Mrs. Covington has been dead for two years now."

"Oh my Lord, that sounds awful," Dolores Field said.

"I know. I guess you'd feel that way considering she was your best friend for years," Joe said.

"No, I meant it's awful that my Eddie is still out there missing and I don't have the slightest idea where he is."

"Oh, I thought you were distraught by the news that your old best friend has been dead for two years now."

"When you get to my age, Mr. Trent, you understand that death is just around the corner," Dolores Field said. "I haven't been friends with Sarah for a really long time. I won't deny that there were times that I prayed that she get hit by a car or get eaten by lions after she went after my Eddie even though she knew he and I were already married."

"Mrs. Field, I think we should focus on finding Eddie," Joe said. He felt guilty hearing Dolores Field talk about Sarah Covington who was deceased.

"Oh, yes, of course."

"Which store does he frequently buy milk?"

"He usually goes to the convenience store at the gas stop beside Edna's Diner," Dolores Field said.

"Alright Mrs. Field, I'll go there and ask around. I'll call when I have some better news."

Joe hung up and placed his phone back in his pocket. He woke his car up and made his way to Edna's Diner. He hasn't had breakfast yet so it was a lucky coincidence that there was a diner there because he was famished.

*****

After Joe wolfed down a pair of pancakes with some eggs and bacon, he paid his bill and left the diner—making his way to the convenience store at the gas station. Inside he headed straight for the cashier. There was a line so he had to wait. He looked around and decided to get a can of coke before getting back in line, waiting for his turn.

When he finally made it to the front, the cashier scanned it as he took a $10 bill from his wallet. Smiling, the cashier handed him his change and told him to "Have a nice day."

"Hey, is it okay if I asked you something?" Joe said.

The cashier tilted his head to the side to see if there were other customers behind Joe. There weren't any. "Okay, shoot."

"Have you seen this guy?" Joe handed the cashier, who had Mack written on his nametag, and waited for his response.

Mack took one look at it and immediately recognized the man in the picture.

"Yes. That's Mister E."

"Does he come here often?"

"He came here to buy milk for three days straight which was weird," Mack said.

"Why was it weird?"

"I mean, I get that he was old but no one drinks milk that fast. Heck, I still have milk in my fridge from two days ago," Mack said.

"Has he been coming here more frequently than usual?"

"He came here so often that I started calling him Mr. E." Mack said. "He was cool old guy."

"Was there anyone with him, or was he alone?"

"No, he was alone. I always got a sense, though, that he was waiting for someone."

"What made you think that?"

"He was always looking out the store window with a huge grin on his face," Mack said.

"You didn't see anyone waiting for him outside?"

"No, no one at all."

"Was he here yesterday?" Joe said.

"Yes but here's the odd thing, he never came inside," Mack said. "He stood outside for a while then just disappeared."

"Did you see where he went?"

"No, it was busy."

"You didn't go outside to check?" Joe said.

"No. My shift had already started. I'm only allowed to leave my station for bathroom breaks and lunch."

"Okay. Thanks anyway."

Joe picked up the can of soda and started to leave when the cashier asked: "Hey, why are you asking about Mister E? Is everything okay with him?"

"I'm just looking for him. He hasn't been home since yesterday."

"Shit. Are you his grandson or something?"

Joe was about to tell Mack that he was a private investigator hired by Eddie Field's wife to find him but he decided to go with it. It wasn't going to hurt anybody anyway.

"Yes, I'm his grandson," Joe said.

"Fuck. Sorry about your grandfather man. I mean, my grandfather died so I never really got to meet him."

"I'm sorry to hear that."

"It's alright. My dad said that my grandmother found him in bed with another woman, so she shot him with his own shotgun."

"Okay. Thanks Mack."

"Good luck finding Mister E."

Joe left the convenience store and hoped that he wouldn't find Eddie Field in bed with another woman. He'll probably have nightmares if he ever saw that.

He made his way to the parking lot, but before he got inside his car, he took one last look at the diner which gave him an idea to ask around inside. He figured that maybe Eddie Field got hungry at some point.

He went back inside the diner and went up to the cashier. She had just finished billing one of the tables and handed it to one of the waitresses. She didn't notice him as he stood there so he had to call out to her.

"Excuse me." She failed to notice so he tried again, waving his hand in her line of sight for good measure.

The cashier turned her gaze to him, clearly annoyed, and said, "There are plenty of tables, sir. If you can kindly sit at one then someone will be over to take your order."

He tried to smile. "Oh no, I just ate here earlier."

"So what do you want?"

"I was wondering if this guy came in here yesterday." He handed her Eddie Field's photo. She took it, letting out a sigh when she did.

The cashier stared at the photo for a few seconds then gave the photo back to Joe.

"No, I've never seen this old man here."

"Are you sure?"

The cashier, who has had enough of Joe's shit, called out to one of the waitresses. "Anna, come here for a sec."

Anna came over with a smile on her face at first, but when she saw Joe, her smile disappeared. Joe saw this and wasn't surprised. He knew he wasn't a looker by society's standards, and he had since accepted that. But it stung a little, by his own admission.

"Are you here to give me my tip?" Anna asked, hopefully.

"Sorry?"

"You forgot to leave a tip for me when you left."

"You forgot to tip her?" The cashier chimed in.

Joe got startled. "Shit. I'm sorry."

He checked his wallet and realized that he was about to use some of the cash from Dolores Field which was intended for part of his rent.

"Are you sure I forgot to tip you?" Joe said. Anna raised her eyebrow and angrily crossed her arms. He tried to sound apologetic. "I'm sorry."

He took out enough for the tip, then shook his head in disappointment.

As she handed it over to the cashier, she asked, "Is there anything you wanted me for, Margie?"

"This man's looking for some old guy," Margie said.

Joe handed Anna the picture. "Have you seen him around? Maybe he got a bite to eat here."

"Yes, I've seen him. He was here yesterday," Anna said.

"Was he with somebody?" Joe said.

"He was with a blonde woman. It seemed like they were together." Anna gave a slight chuckle. "There was no way they were related, given the way she kept rubbing his arm."

"How come I never saw them?" Margie said.

"I think you were in the bathroom."

"Oh, right," Margie said.

Joe tried not to sound too impatient. "Did you happen to see where they went afterwards?"

"They probably went to the motel up towards the highway. They were clearly ready to jump each other's bones. The woman even gave me the stink eye, as if I had some desire to steal her man—which was fucked up."

Anna gave the photo back to Joe. "Was he your dad or something?"

Joe was presented with another opportunity to tell someone that he was a private investigator that was hired by the old man's wife to track him down but he ignored that and decided to keep up his charade. He wouldn't be seeing any of them again anyway.

"Yes. We're really worried about him."

"You should definitely check the motel down the road. It's pretty hard to miss."

"I will. Thank you."

It was the only major building along the strip, and went by the name of *Heavenly Suites Motel*. It made him wonder why the owner landed on that name and what made him decide it was the best one for his business. He was never good at picking names as evidenced by the name of his own business, *Limelight Investigations*. But he decided it was best not to dwell too long on unanswerable questions He got out of car and headed straight for the front desk.

At the front desk were two clerks, a man and a woman. The man was reading a copy of Playboy magazine with unwavering focus—his hand occasionally disappearing below the Registration desk counter. The woman was filing her nails while she chewed gum. She made a bubble then popped it right away. She used her tongue to fish back some of the gum that stuck to the side of her lips, pulling it back inside her mouth for chewing. Joe walked up to the desk and said "Uh, hi."

The woman glanced up with only her eyes while her face remained tilted to the side as she continued to chew her gum. Joe gave her an awkward smile. She pointed to the poster on the left side of the wall that said "$45 per night."

He shook his head a couple of times. "I'm not here to check in. I'm looking for someone, and was hoping you could help me."

The woman tilted her head straight and slapped the man beside her who was still mesmerized by the one of the models in the magazine.

"What the fuck, Aya?" The man said.

"Shut the fuck up, Cole," Aya said. "Stop fiddling yourself while you read that magazine in broad daylight, you disgusting pervert."

"Fuck you. Maybe I wouldn't have to fiddle myself in broad daylight if we were fucking every night like married couples are supposed to."

"We can fuck every night when you learn how to do dirty talk properly."

"Hey, I can talk dirty. I'm good at that."

"But you always take it too far."

"When have I ever taken it too far?"

"Last time we fucked, I was about to get where I'm supposed to until you said that Hitler was probably in the bathroom listening to us fuck." She looked directly at Joe. "Who says something like that in the middle of sex?"

"I already apologized for that," Cole said. "I was watching some shit about Hitler on the History Channel and that got me thinking."

"Watching that made you think that the man was in our bathroom?"

"He could've been. You and I can't see ghosts so we can't prove that he wasn't," Cole said. "He was probably into some weird shit on account of how messed up he was."

The whole conversation between the married couple was getting a little too personal. Before Aya was able to respond to her husband, Joe cut her off. "Um, excuse me."

Both Aya and Cole turned their attention to Joe. Cole said, "What do you want?"

"He's looking for someone. That's why I called your attention, you fucking idiot," Aya said.

"Fuck you. I didn't know that," Cole said. "Who are you looking for?"

"I'm looking for this man." Joe handed over the photo of Eddie Field. "I was wondering if he checked in to your motel."

Aya looked at the photo first then showed to Cole. Cole leaned in and got a closer look. Then Aya looked at Joe and said "Is this old man your dad?"

This was another opportunity for Joe to tell both owners of the motel that he was a private investigator who was hired by the old man's wife to find him. But instead, he kept his lie going and said "Yes, that's my dad." He even said it convincingly.

Cole and Aya looked at each other like they were trying to decide who was going to tell Joe, then Cole nodded and turned his attention back to Joe. His expression changed to one that was riddled with sadness.

"I don't know how to say this man, but your dad is, you know, cheating on your mom." Joe felt that Cole seemed to be more upset by what he'd said.

Then Aya said, "Your dad checked in last night with a blonde with fake breasts."

"Oh." Joe managed to look surprised, in order to keep up the charade of familial relation to Eddie Field.

"Wait, hold on a minute Aya. How the fuck do you know she had a fake pair of tits?"

"You telling me those tits looked natural to you?"

"They did from where I was standing."

"Well, that just proves you're as dumb as they come," Aya said.

"Hey, don't call me dumb. I told you that I didn't like it when my Mom called me that," Cole said.

"Okay. I'm sorry."

"Have they checked out yet?" Joe said.

Aya asked Cole to get the log book from the drawer under the table. Cole fished it out then handed it to her. She opened the log book and flipped to the most recent page, then scanned the entries with her finger. Then her eyes went from left to right.

"No. They haven't checked out yet."

"Can you tell me which room they checked in to?"

"I'm afraid I can't do that," Aya said.

"Why?"

"It's motel policy," Cole said. "Only motel tenants can get access to that information."

"But I don't need to check in. I just need to find my dad," Joe said, fully convinced of his lie.

"Well, that's a damn shame," Cole said.

"You can come back tomorrow if you want," Aya said.

Joe checked his watch and saw that it was almost noon. This was his only chance to get Eddie Field back to his wife and close this case.

Joe sighed and said, "Fuck it. Give me a room key."

Aya and Cole both shared a grin as Joe gave them a fifty in exchange for a key.

"What room are they in?" Joe said.

"They're in Room 501," Aya said.

"You can't miss it. It's by the vending machine below the stairs," Cole said.

"Thanks."

Before he was fully out the door, he heard Cole tell Aya that the thought of Eddie with the blonde got him horny. He shook his head as both husband and wife staggered off to the office in the back.

On his way to Room 501 he stopped by the vending machine to buy some chips. The money he got from Dolores Field was almost out, but he still had enough change.

He knocked on the door to 501and waited for it open. When it didn't, he knocked on it again and said "Eddie Field, are you in there?" There was no answer. He tried the doorknob, and fortunately it was open.

The room was in a state—pillows and cushions were scattered on the floor, and the bathroom door was open. Then he saw Eddie Field, alone on the bed, fully clothed.

"Hey Mr. Field, my name is Joseph Trent from Limelight Investigations. I was hired by your wife, Dolores, to find you and bring you back home."

Eddie Field didn't respond and remained stationary on the bed as if Joe wasn't there. Joe shook his leg but still there was no response. Two thoughts immediately came to mind. Either Eddie Field'd had a hell of a night and was now sleeping like a log. Or he wasn't moving because he was dead. Joe checked his pulse and to his disappointment, it was the latter. Eddie Field was dead.

Joe stared at the lifeless body then decided to check Eddie's wallet for cash.

He wasn't proud of what he did, but he wasn't sorry either. Eddie Field was dead and wasn't going to miss the money.

He took out his handkerchief and checked Eddie's pockets. When he pulled Eddie's wallet out, something else fell out as well. He picked it up. It was a lottery ticket. He stuck the ticket in his jacket pocket, then turned his focus onto Eddie's wallet.

To be honest, there wasn't much. He took out a few bills but left $5 in as a thank you to Eddie. He put the wallet back in Eddie's pocket, then checked the body for a phone. No such luck. Maybe Eddie had left it in his car.

He went outside the room and made his way back to the front desk. He hoped that Aya and Cole were done fornicating so that he could use their phone to call the cops. He was curious as to how they would react when they heard the news that they had a dead tenant in one of their rooms.

Thankfully, Cole was back in the front desk with a satisfied look on his face. Joe found it unnerving the way Cole looked.

"Hey, I need to use your phone," Joe said.

"What do you need a phone for?"

"I need to call the cops."

"Why the fuck do you need to call the cops?" Cole said. "Wait, did you see the packet of coke earlier?"

"What?" Joe was surprised because he hadn't seen anything.

"I can't let you use our phone man. I don't care who you are. You're not going to rat me out to the cops. I shoot snitches motherfucker."

"Calm down, okay?" Joe said. "I'm not here to rat you out."

"You said you needed to use our phone to call the cops."

"I need to call the cops because there's a dead old man in one of your rooms."

"Shit. Wait," Cole said. "Was it your dad?"

Joe decided to keep up his lie one last time.

"Yes, it was."

Cole handed the phone over to him and said "I need to go and tell my wife."

Joe nodded and watched Cole disappear into the backroom again.

*****

Joe made a stop by the liquor store and bought a six-pack. He needed a drink after the conversation he just had with Dolores Field. It was hard telling her that her husband was dead.

He kept some of the details to himself and didn't mention that her husband was with another woman, much younger than her probably, when he died. And about the fake tits. She was already crying so much when he broke the news, if he'd told her about her husband's infidelity, it would've devastated her even more, and ruin the good memories she had of him. He told her that the police had her husband's body and that he was sorry.

On his way back to his office, he stumbled onto a newsstand. He saw the newspaper display and remembered the lottery ticket that fallen out of Eddie's pocket. He bought a copy so as to check the results from yesterday. He wasn't hoping for anything, but it didn't hurt to try. He folded the newspaper and made his way to his office.

As he arrived in his office he checked his watch—7:30pm.

He placed the beer in his fridge and checked if there was anything to eat. Some takeout Chinese food left over from a while back. He took it, along with a bottle of beer, and sat behind his desk. But when he opened the plastic bag he had to pull his head back from the smell. It was spoiled. He threw it in the trash and decided to just have beer for dinner instead.

He picked up the newspaper and unfolded it flat on his desk— flipping through the pages while taking little sips of his beer.

There was news about a man from a part of the world he'd never set foot in, who wanted to divorce his wife because he wanted to marry his dog. He wasn't sure if that was real, or just mere fiction. It was too weird to be true. He moved on and flipped to another page.

When he finally got to the page where the lottery result were printed, he took out Eddie's ticket from his pocket and checked the numbers.

He carefully checked each number, and froze when he made it to the last digit. Then he fell back in his chair and took a large gulp from his bottle when he realized that Eddie had just won the lottery.

He paused for a moment and took in the sheer overwhelming feeling of elation at winning the lottery. Okay, so the ticket wasn't originally his, but he had it and he was the only one who knew that it had been a winner.

Just to make sure, he checked the numbers in the newspaper again and made sure his eyes weren't deceiving him. He scanned the winning numbers three times before accepting that it was real. He then checked how much the winning prize was. It was at $23 million.

The words "Holy fucking shit" immediately went out of his mouth.

However, Joe was faced with a moral dilemma. Should he claim the winnings and give Dolores Field a cut? Or should he give the ticket to Dolores Field, let her claim the winnings, and hope that she would be kind enough to give him a share?

He knew what the easy decision was, but he knew that it would only satisfy his inner asshole. So he set the ticket on the table, and began smoking while he contemplated on what to do with all that cash.

Joe's deep contemplation of his current dilemma was halted by the unexpected knock on his door. He hid the beer bottle under his desk before he sat up, not wanting to look unprofessional to any potential client. He was about to open the door when he realized that Eddie's lottery ticket was still on the table. He quickly ran back and hid it in his pocket, running his fingers through his hair as he returned to open the door.

A woman with blonde hair was on the other side. She gave him a warm smile and he smile back at her in kind. He invited her in and closed the door behind them.

"Hi," Joe said.

"Hello," The woman replied.

"I have to say, I don't usually have clients come in this late."

"Oh, I'm really sorry."

"That's alright," Joe said.

The woman smiled.

Joe moved toward his desk and invited the woman to take a seat. Before he sat down, he said "So, what can I do for you, miss—"

"Oh, it's Loren. Betty Loren."

"How can I be of service, Miss Loren?"

"Well, you can start by handing over the lottery ticket." Betty Loren took out a revolver from her purse and pointed it at Joe.

He threw up his hands while he feigned ignorance. "I don't know what you're talking about."

"Bullshit. I know you have the ticket."

"I swear to God. I don't know what you're talking about."

"Stop fucking around, okay?" Betty Loren said. "I know you have it with you. I checked Eddie's pockets earlier and it wasn't there."

"Wait, how do you know Eddie?" Then he realized that the woman with the gun pointed at him was the blonde woman with Eddie at the motel. He suddenly remembered what Aya said back at the motel and his eyes slowly shifted their focus to her chest.

"Hey, eyes up mister!"

Joe immediately shifted his focus and said "What?"

"Fuck you. You were clearly eyeing my tits just now."

"Sorry. I just—" Joe said.

"What?" Betty Loren said.

"I didn't mean to stare. It's just that the girl at the motel said you had fake breasts," Joe said.

Betty Loren was clearly insulted. "Fuck you."

"She said it, not me," Joe said.

"Well, fuck that bitch. She clearly doesn't know what she's talking about."

"You're probably right."

"Of course I am." Betty Loren cupped one of her breasts with her free hand. "This is probably more real than her flat chest."

"I mean, if she has a flat chest, then it's probably real," Joe said.

"Shut the fuck up!" Betty Loren said. "Now, hand over the lottery ticket."

"Let me ask you this first. Did you kill Eddie?"

"What? No. No I didn't."

"Are you sure? He was pretty dead when I found him in his room."

"I said I didn't fucking kill him. It was an accident."

"How about we make a deal? You tell me what really happened between you and Eddie and I'll tell you where the ticket is."

"Why do you want to know? Are you his son or something?"

This was the actual last time, Joe promised himself, that he would lie about being Eddie's son.

"That's right. He was my dad."

Betty Loren paused for a moment. She finally relented and said "Fine. But you better have that ticket ready."

"Sure," Joe said.

Betty Loren then proceeded to tell the tale of how she got together with Eddie Field. They met at the store he frequented one morning when he was making one of his milk runs. Eddie had approached her and told her that he was smitten by her beauty. She was taken aback by his frankness but she figured that his age factored in greatly when it came to courage. Most men she'd had experience with had simply clammed up and shrunk before they could even say a word. But not Eddie Field. His courage and honesty worked like a charm. They began meeting each other there for three days straight. On the third day, Eddie Field expressed his desire to run away with her. Her excitement overwhelmed her hesitation and she had agreed to Eddie's proposal.

They had then met up yesterday and left in Eddie's car after they ate at the nearby diner. They were not far along the road when Eddie decided he'd changed his mind. Eddie felt guilty for leaving his wife, Dolores. He'd even cried as he'd apologized to Betty. She was slightly annoyed but understood. They had eventually stopped at the motel because Eddie found it hard to drive in the dark, and Betty refused point blank to drive him back to his wife.

"Wait, so how did Eddie die?"

"I was getting to that."

"Oh, sorry. Go ahead."

"So, we were at the motel room and I felt bad for him." Betty Loren said. "He kept apologizing to me which was getting annoying. And I was mad at him for getting my hopes up of experiencing something I've only read in romance novels. It was the part of the story where the young maiden gets whisked away by the older gentlemen on his white horse or in a carriage or even on a motorcycle."

"I barely have time to read so I wouldn't know any of that." It was a lie, because he did have time to read, but he refused to pick up a book. "But that does sound romantic, in a creepy way, I guess."

"Anyway," Betty Loren said, not minding the comment about it being creepy. "I decided to do something for him that he probably hasn't experienced in a long time. I was going to rub his dick with my tits."

"Well, at least he died happy."

"It, kind of, didn't happen."

"What do you mean?"

"I took off my bra and gave him a little show. Then all of a sudden, he started to stiffen up."

"Okay, I think we can skip that part. Though I am impressed with how you managed to get him up without him taking a pill first. You must've gotten him really excited."

"Why would he need a pill?" Then Betty Loren gave Joe a disgusted look. "I wasn't talking about his dick, you fucking perv."

"You said he stiffened up."

"I meant his whole body. His whole body stiffened up," Betty Loren said.

"Oh," Joe said, finally realizing Eddie's cause of death.

"I checked his pulse and it was gone. I panicked so I got in his car and left."

"Wait, so how did you know about the lottery ticket?" Joe said.

"He bought that ticket when we stopped by a little store on our way back. He said he was feeling lucky. I remembered he'd bought one when I got home late last night and thought it could be a winning ticket. You never know. So, I came back for it this morning, and that's when I saw you there."

"And you went into the room when I went to the lobby to call the cops?"

Betty Loren nodded.

"Shit."

"Now, hand over the ticket or I swear to God I'll shoot you in the dick." Betty Loren lowered her aim to where she had a clear shot of Joe's goods.

"Okay. Jesus Christ," Joe said. "Can you please just aim it a little higher first? You're freaking me out."

"I'll do that after you give me the ticket," Betty Loren said.

Joe reached into his pocket, but before he could pull out the ticket, there was a knock on his door.

"Fuck." Joe immediately thought that Jimmy, his obnoxious landlord, was at the other side of the door. Jimmy was probably back to remind him that rent was due. Though, twice in one day was a rarity, he wouldn't put it past him, given how much of an asshole he was.

But even he didn't want Jimmy to get shot.

"Are you expecting someone?" Betty Loren said.

"No," Joe said. "But let me get the door and I'll send whoever it is on their way."

"Give me the ticket first." Betty Loren said.

"If I don't answer the door now, whoever is on the other side might get suspicious. You don't want the cops coming in, don't you?"

"Go get fucking the door. But hurry up. And no funny business or I'll shoot you in the asshole."

Joe walked to the door as calmly as he could, opened it, and found that the man on the other side wasn't his landlord. It was someone else. Before he could ask who the man was, he was met with a fist to his face.

Joe held his right cheek as he stumbled backwards into the room.

"What the fuck?"

"What the hell are you doing here, Nolan?" Betty Loren said.

Joe regained his balance and looked at Betty Loren with his eyebrow raised.

"You know this guy?"

"Of course she does, you asshole," Nolan Loren said. "I'm the man who's going to beat the living shit out of you."

"That still doesn't explain who you are," Joe said.

"He's my husband," Betty Loren said.

"What?"

"So, this is the asshole you've been fucking." Nolan Loren said. "I can't believe you would do this to me, Betty."

Nolan Loren charged at Joe and held him up by the front of his shirt. "Did you enjoy getting to fuck my wife? I'm going to rip off your dick and feed it to your dog."

"I don't have a dog." Joe said.

"I'll feed it to your cat then."

"I don't have a cat either."

"Well, then what do you have?" Nolan Loren appeared to be genuinely curious.

"I don't have any pets. Well, there might be a rat in the room but it comes and goes."

"Then I'll feed it to the rat!" Nolan Loren said.

"For God's sake, I'm not fucking your wife!" Joe said.

"Like I'll fucking believe you," Nolan Loren said.

"We're not fucking, you idiot," Betty Loren said.

"What?" Nolan Loren turned his attention to his wife.

"I'm not fucking him," Betty Loren said. "I would never fuck a guy like him."

"Thanks, I guess."

Nolan Loren let go of Joe and went up to Betty. "I don't understand. Are you in love with him?"

"I just said I'm not fucking him, you dipshit."

"People can be in love and not fuck. I'm still in love with you after all this time. and we hardly ever fuck like we did back then. There again, Father Dave told me that's true for all marriages."

"I keep telling you to stop listening to Father Dave. He doesn't know anything about marriage. He's priest for God's sake."

Joe felt sorry for Nolan Loren, seemingly trapped in a sexless marriage.

"Your wife's right. We're not fucking and she's not in love with me."

"But I saw you at the motel," Nolan Loren said. "You left after he did."

"Wait, you were following me?" Betty Loren said.

"I had to. You were acting strange all week, then you came home late last night. So, tell me, is he the guy you've been fucking?"

"I swear to God, Nolan, if you keep insinuating that I'm fucking this asshole, I'm going to shoot you first." Betty Loren turned her gun towards her husband. Joe had completely forgotten about the gun after he got hit in the face.

"Jesus Christ, Betty. Why do you have a gun?" Nolan Loren immediately put his hands up.

"Can you please just tell him why you're here?" Joe said.

"Yeah Betty, why are you here?" Nolan Loren said. Betty Loren wasn't a fan of her husband's accusing tone.

"I'm here because that fucking asshole has my lottery ticket." Betty Logan said.

"Well, it was Eddie's ticket." Joe said.

"It was our ticket." Betty Loren said.

"What the fuck? Who the hell is Eddie?"

"He's the old guy your wife accidentally killed when she showed him her breasts." Joe said.

"Why would you do that?" Nolan Loren said. He was completely heartbroken.

"Both of you just shut the fuck up," Betty Loren said. "Hand over the ticket, now."

"Wait, did you win?" Nolan Loren looked at Joe with curiosity.

"Well..." Joe wanted to lie but Betty Loren pointed her gun at his crotch again. "Yes. Eddie bought a winning ticket."

Betty Loren's eyes lit up as she said "I knew it."

"Baby, does that mean we're rich?" Nolan Loren said.

"No, it doesn't," Betty Loren said.

"What?" Nolan Loren said.

"Nolan, I'm leaving you," Betty Loren said.

"Why the fuck would you do that?"

"Let's be honest Nolan, we've hardly been a couple for years now."

Betty Loren said. "I mean, we haven't even fucked in years."

"That's because you keep pushing me away whenever I try to get intimate with you."

"Why do you think that is, Nolan?"

Neither of them knew the answer to her question.

"It doesn't matter now. Just give me the ticket so I can leave and never come back."

"But, Baby, please. We can work this out." Nolan Loren took a few steps forward then Betty Loren shot him in the leg.

"What the fuck?" Joe said.

"You fucking shot me." Nolan said, as he fell to the floor, clutching his wounded leg.

"Shut the fuck up." Betty Loren turned to Joe. "Now, give me the ticket or I'll shoot you in the dick next."

"Jesus Christ, fine."

Joe reached for the ticket in his pocket again but before he took it out, he said "Can you at least promise me something, please?"

"What?" Betty Loren said.

"Can you give some of the money to Eddie's wife, Dolores? You kind of owe her for stealing and killing her husband."

"I didn't steal Eddie. He was the one who came to me. And I already told you, I did not fucking kill him."

"Well, your breasts did." Joe said.

"Oh, fuck off." Betty Loren said.

"Just give her some of the money, okay?"

"I think you should do it, Babe," Nolan Loren said.

"Shut the fuck up, Nolan," Betty Loren said. "Alright, I'll give her some of the money. Now, where's my ticket?"

Joe took the ticket from his pocket and handed it over to Betty Loren, who took the ticket and hid it inside her blouse. She slowly walked toward the door, with her gun still pointed at Joe's crotch, then out of the room, closing the door behind her and then disappearing to places unknown.

Joe breathed a sigh of relief, knowing that his crotch was no longer in danger. Nolan Loren was still on the floor, writhing in agony from getting shot in the leg.

"Hey, can you please help me?" Nolan Loren said.

Joe thought about letting Nolan Loren bleed out, especially after Nolan had sucker punched him in his face. But having a dead body in his room would freak Jimmy out, and he'd probably get kicked out immediately.

"Sit tight, buddy," Joe said.

✶✶✶✶✶

Six months later, Joe got a knock on his door. He was fresh from his afternoon nap, where he dreamed about the winning ticket that would've solved all of his problems. He rubbed his face with his hands then straightened his tie. He let out a deep sigh then stood up. He opened the door and found someone familiar was on the other side.

"Nolan. It's been a long time," Joe said.

"Yes, it has," Nolan Loren said.

"Please, come in."

Nolan Loren still had a clear limp from the bullet wound as he walked to the chair across from Joe's desk. Joe waited for him to sit down and get settled. Joe sat down afterwards.

"How are you doing, Nolan?"

"I'm doing fine, thanks. I've been volunteering more at my church."

"That's great, I guess," Joe said. "Have you heard from Betty?"

"No." He still felt a little pain at the mention of his wife's name. "She's probably somewhere far away."

"Sorry about that, man," Joe said. "But at least she kept her promise. Dolores Field called me a few days after Betty left with the ticket and said that someone left a suitcase full of cash by her door. She was convinced that it was from Eddie. Well, I guess in a way, it was."

"That's great," Nolan Loren said.

"So, what brings you here?"

"I want to hire you. I saw the Limelight Investigations ad in the newspaper and remembered that I came here last time."

"Under very different circumstances though," Joe said.

"I'm really sorry I punched you in the face. I really thought you were fucking Betty."

Joe waved it off and said "It's all water under the bridge."

Nolan Loren chuckled. There was something on his mind that he needed to ask. "By the way, how did you come up with the name Limelight Investigations?"

"Well, another company was renting this place before I did," Joe said. "I guess it was named Limelight. It had the name on the door, I was strapped for cash, so I figured I'd just put investigations below it."

Joe saw the gears in Nolan's head turning.

"Oh. That's smart."

"So, who do you want me to find?"

"I want you to find my wife."

"You're fucking with me right?"

"What makes you say that?"

"Nolan, you just said that Betty's probably somewhere far away. Plus, I wouldn't want to find her anyway because I don't want to give her another chance to shoot my dick."

"True, she did say that she was going to shoot you in the dick."

"You'll have to find someone else to find your crazy wife," Joe said.

"But I don't want you to find Betty," Nolan Loren said.

"You said you wanted me to find your wife."

"Yes," Nolan Loren said. "I want you to find my other wife, the new one."

"You have another wife?"

"Yes. I got married three months ago," Nolan Loren said.

"And she just disappeared, all of a sudden?" Joe said.

"I mean, yes," Nolan Loren said.

Joe thought that it would be hilarious if Nolan's new wife had run off with an old man. He let out a heavy sigh and said "Alright. I'll give you my rates, then ask you a few questions. It's payment first, by the way."

"Yes, of course."

"Great." Joe got out his notebook and pen. "Before we start, can I ask you something?"

"Sure. Go ahead."

"And I mean this without offense. Have you tried asking your priest why your wives keep leaving you?"

Nolan Loren took no offense to the question and merely shrugged it off. "No idea, man."

"Okay. Let's get started then."

Joe charged Nolan Loren more than his usual rate. It was for punching him in the face. It was petty, sure. But at least Joe had money for next month's rent with a few extra dollars for beer.

Bear and Bird in the Snow
Michael Thomét

The ice on the asphalt of the mountain road made the maroon car difficult to control as it climbed ever upward. Snow billowed about, reducing visibility to a distressing closeness, and the guardrail that lined the edge of the road was the only protection against the hundred-foot drop. Compared to the bulk and momentum of the old Malibu, the guardrail seemed flimsy at best.

The road led farther and farther up and into the crevice that made up Juniper Gorge, a luxury resort for those who wanted rustic privacy but still wanted full-service kitchens. The junipers from the name crowded the road from above and below, clinging to the earth and rock. Their bent and twisted trunks rocked and roiled, the only shelter from the wind zipping down the curves of the mountain. The car skidded left and right, trying to gain traction against the buffeting gusts which threatened to deliver it into oblivion.

Ahead, finally, the building rose into view. Lodge 87. A giant log cabin nestled against the rock, red paint covering decades-old logs juxtaposed with modern glass facades. The flurries made it hard to see, but it looked to be at least two stories with a pitched roof and lights glittering out into the darkness of the overcast evening. Streams of white smoke rose from pipes across the roof, settling over the top of the lodge like a cloud.

The breaks whined from too many missed service appointments as the car came to a stop at the end of the drive. Andrew Bear stepped out of the driver's side and beamed in the crispness of the air. He wore a light jacket over a plaid, cotton shirt and black trousers that didn't do one bit to keep out the cold. The air stung at his cheeks, leaving them red along with the tip of his nose. He didn't mind.

"Isn't it wonderful up here, Zachary? Clean air, cool breeze, snow falling all about. Wonderful!" He made a frame with his thumb and fingers. "Man, if we have time, I'd love to get some landscape shots. Everything's so raw up here."

The passenger door opened and a bundle of fleece stepped out. Zachary Bird looked like a plump, grey sheep with light brown poking out wherever skin escaped the warm coat and crinkly snow pants. "Cool breeze? It must be single digits out here. I can't tell because my phone can't connect to the weather service. I can't believe you agreed to this."

"We agreed, both of us, remember?" Andrew waltzed over to the trunk and opened it. Inside were two gigantic black duffel bags, a pair of tripods, and snow chains. "We can't turn away a good client!"

Zachary joined him and hoisted a bag over his shoulder by the strap. Voice lowered, he said, "I just couldn't get over how terrified she sounded over the threat. Have you read it yet?"

"The book?" Andrew grabbed the other bag and thumped one of its pockets. "I thought you were doing that."

"What?" With a shimmy of his neck, Zachary poked his face out of the furry hood he'd ensconced himself in. "God, it's cold!" The snow immediately caught in the fine strands of his brown hair, which was getting long. "You grabbed the book and hid it away somewhere!"

"It was on my desk! You could have grabbed it any time!"

"Your desk? Might as well been tossed out with the state of that." Zachary grabbed a tripod. "How are we supposed to investigate—"

"Uhh, who are you?"

The voice cut through the crisp air like a hammer, practically shouted over the wind. It belonged to a blond woman in a bright-red parka with a martini glass in a hand as pale as the snow itself. She looked like a raspberry balanced on the end of a twig. Behind her, a group assembled at the end of the short walk that ran along the side of the lodge.

"Photographers!" Andrew slammed the trunk closed with a sidelong glance at his companion. "Andrew Bear Photography Studio." He stepped out from behind the car and extended a hand. "I'm Andrew, and this is my assistant Zachary Bird. We're here to shoot the weekend festivities?"

"Assistant?" The blond raspberry shook her head. "Photographers? Does anyone know about this?"

A tumble of brown curls in a long, blue sweater-dress jogged up the pavement and slid to a stop. "Kris, I…" She took a long gulp of air. "I told you, didn't I?"

The woman with the curls was Roxie Schomer, a three-time published author and the reason Andrew had braved the icy roads with a car clearly not made for such travel.

"Told me? Oh, is this the surprise?" The blonde raised her almost imperceptible eyebrows. "Photographers, really?"

"You said…" Roxie gulped for more air. "You said it would be memorable."

"Roxie…" A tall, man stepped forward and turned toward her. His handsome face was shaped perfectly for the bald look he sported, and he wore a grey suit relaxed and open. His loosened tie fluttered in the wind. "You should have asked. I don't want some photographers watching me the whole weekend. I don't even know if we have a bed for anyone."

"But… but it's your present!" Roxie turned and smiled at the two photographers. "Hi Andy, and Zach."

Andrew put on a wide smile, though a bristle shot down his spine. There was only one woman who was allowed to call him Andy, and she was nestled away in her office back in Allston. "Miss Schomer here asked us to come up and take pictures of the birthday weekend. We won't get in your way, I promise!"

"We don't want to make you uncomfortable," Zachary said, joining Andrew by his side.

"They're cute! Let them take pictures." The singsong voice came from a tall, muscular form bedecked in a cotton-candy overcoat. A porcelain face poked out under a ginger faux hawk.

"Yeah, bet you don't mind, Ever. Always in front of cameras." The speaker, a short man in a baggy hoodie and grey sweatpants, looked drab in comparison.

"Wait, Ever? You're Everest Hopper, aren't you?" Andrew walked forward, hands outstretched, a grin on his face. "I watched your runway last season! One model for an entire line. Amazing!"

Of course, Roxie had told him a bit about each guest, but Andrew would have recognized Everest Hopper, Ever to their friends. They were the enby face of James Bao, the hottest new designer in fashion. As for the others, Andrew had to play dumb, at least for a while.

The man in the suit was Braxton Lambert, the birthday boy, and the reason for the gathering. He ran Brax, a financial app worth several millions that had made it big with the younger Gen Z kids. Kris, the woman in the red parka, was Kristen Stevenson, some meteorologist that Zachary had gotten excited about. Then there was Ty Dunlap, the short guy in the sweats. He was the odd one out, having never made a name for himself.

Braxton stepped forward, putting himself between the group and Andrew. "Sorry, Mr. Bear was it? Look, I'd rather not have you all here. It's supposed to be a weekend with friends. Not…"

"Strange photographers prying into the details of your life, I get it." Andrew dusted the snow from his swept-back, black hair. "If you don't want us here, we aren't going to impose." He turned to Zachary and handed him the keys and the other bag. "Go ahead and put the bags back. I need to discuss our cancellation fee with Miss Schomer."

Zachary hoisted the second bag, took a deep breath, and marched back towards the trunk. Then, he yelped and his feet flew out from under him. The bags skidded along the icy pavement as Zachary crashed to the ground with a thunk.

"Zach, you ok?" Andrew jumped over to his friend, scrambling to find purchase with his feet. Helping the round, padded man up proved difficult.

Once up, Zachary shouted, "I'm fine. Fine! Just slipped on a bit of ice, I think."

The crowd had gathered closer. Kris looked out over the descending road. "Guys, I don't know. The road looks pretty bad." She glanced at the sky. "I don't think that's getting better."

"You got chains?" Ty walked over and kicked the car's tires. "These ain't snow tires like ours. How'd you even get up here?"

"Chains?" Andrew accompanied the question with a raise of one eyebrow. "Am I supposed to have chains? I've never driven in the mountains before, barely ever been out of Allston."

"You've driven a lot of mountain roads," Roxie said, looking at Ty. "You think they'd be ok?"

"Naw." He shook his head. "They'd crash for sure."

Kris shifted the martini to her other hand and pawed at Braxton. "We can't do that to them, can we?"

"No, no." He sighed and held a hand out to Andrew and Zachary. "Come on. We'll see if we can make room and call roadside or something."

With folded arms and a quavering voice, Ever said, "It's about time! I swear it's getting colder by the minute out here!"

With that, the group drifted down the walkway towards a door. Andrew turned to face Zachary and walked backwards. In a low voice he said, "You really ok? That looked convincing!"

"Padded head to toe." He rubbed the back of his head and grinned ear to ear.

"Real proud of your performance, aren't you? I told you it would work!" Wrapping an arm around Zachary's shoulders, Andrew faced himself forward.

Roxie held the front door of the lodge open for the two of them. Her eyes traced the arm along Zachary's shoulder. "Oh," she said, "are you two like, master and apprentice, to use a euphemism?"

A laugh bubbled up from Andrew's stomach. "What, me and Zachary? He wishes! He's just a bit dizzy from the fall."

Just under his breath, Zachary added, "Not this time, at least." He winced as Andrew's grip tightened, finding shoulder under all that padding. Zachary cleared his throat. "I'll be ok, just tell me where to sit."

Hot air met the two as they shimmied awkwardly through the door and sidestepped the stairs that greeted them just inside. The crackling of fire filled the room, joined by the sounds of the guests arranging themselves on a gigantic burgundy-leather sectional. It could seat the five party guests with ease, and the two extras if needed.

A fireplace with a real log fire roared from beneath a stone mantle. The room seemed to go on forever, merging seamlessly with a black-and-white kitchen, full by Andrew's standards. An alcove, with its own seating area and huge windows, served as a walkway for a separate dining area. It had seating for eight, twelve if pressed. The wall between the dining area and the kitchen had a small serving window with cabinets on either side.

"This room alone is bigger than our studio," Andrew said under his breath. He imagined what he could do with the space. Shaking the idea from his mind, he considered the absolute decadence of it all. Sure, most of the guests were pretty successful, but Andrew was sure one look at the bill for the place would have told him just how upper crust they were.

"Sit next to me, poor thing." Ever patted a bit of couch and smiled a half smile at Zachary.

Guided by Andrew into the indicated spot, Zachary sank into the plush sofa and leaned back, closing his eyes. He hadn't actually been hurt, Andrew knew, but he sure was playing the part. A couple of the others—Kris and Braxton—took seats in the chairs opposite. Braxton had shed his suit jacket and tie somewhere out of sight. Andrew found it interesting they avoided the couch altogether, as if presiding like a king and queen. The nearly empty sectional made Zachary and Ever look tiny and a bit too close together for casual company.

"Anybody got a signal?" Leaning against the banister, Ty held his phone up into the air.

As if in response, the front door slammed open, almost knocking Roxie to her feet. A bluster of cold air whipped through the room as she struggled against the wood to close it. "Kris, the key?"

Fishing the key from her parka, the blond woman stood up and jaunted over to the door. She sighed after the deadbolt fell into place with a thunk. Then Kris pocketed the key once more and walked over to the alcove.

"Guys, it's really bad out there," Kris said. She stared out the gigantic windows, which some designer had decided to use instead of timber for that side of the room. A few treetops were visible through the glass, but most of the view faded into white. The sound of wind whistled through the building, finding gaps between the wood that no human ever could.

Pulling his phone out and scanning the screen, Andrew announced, "I don't have any bars, and I've got the best coverage for the state. Zachary was saying his wasn't connecting on the drive up."

"It's the mountain and the snow blocking signals," Zachary said, finally opening his eyes. Ever was pouting at him, but the emotion didn't seem to reach their eyes.

Standing up and loosening the top button of his shirt, Braxton sighed. "It won't be long before it gets dark, and I'm not sending you down the mountain at night. You're not together, but could you share? I'm not sure we can find any beds, let alone two."

"I guess…" Roxie shrugged. "I could room with someone and they could take my room?" There was some general ascent, but no one offered their bed for her.

Ty rapped his knuckles idly on the wood. "What about the room downstairs? The one that's locked?"

"Oh, the storage?" Kris fumbled in the pocket of her parka and produced the key again. "The resort said it was stuff left over from a renovation, but you can try." She tossed the key at Ty who caught it deftly. "Woah! Bet you're still king of the court, huh?"

The corner of Ty's mouth twitched, wavering between grin and frown. "Too slow to ball anymore," he said and motioned to Andrew. "Come on, picture man."

Andrew took a step, and Zachary struggled to get up. "I'm feeling better, don't worry," he said in response to Ever's fussing. Zachary and Andrew followed Ty down the stairs.

As it turned out, the "storage room" had once been some kind of bedroom. Dust lined everything in the small space, but they'd unearthed a bunk bed, probably intended for sleeping children as far away from the parents as possible. Boxes containing old linens served as furniture. There was a sealed door that clearly once led into the neighboring bathroom, before the bathroom had been expanded into a full bath with general floor access.

As Andrew inspected the camera equipment he'd pulled from his bag, Zachary asked, "Top or bottom?"

"Either's fine," Andrew said offhandedly. "Prefer top, but I can do either. Why? Did you notice something?"

He looked up to find Zachary, unbundled from his fleece coat. His face had taken on a red undertone. "For the bunks…"

"Oh, right." A wide grin bubbled up onto Andrew's face. "You should be bottom, anyway, since you're injured, right?" He mimed air quotes around the word injured.

Zachary turned away, clearly hiding his face. Andrew chuckled to himself and returned to his camera.

There was a knock, and Roxie's voice floated through the door. "Hey, Kris is making food if you want to come up." She smiled when Andrew opened the door, and she added in a low voice, "Everything ok?"

Andrew shrugged. "Seems fine. Lucky this was here." He indicated the bunk bed. "How are you holding up?"

Her smile faltered. "I am a bundle of nerves. Everyone's on edge a little. It's going to boil over during dinner."

"We're here, and you'll be safe," Andrew said. He gave her that soft smile he knew most people liked. "Zachary's great at social observation, aren't you?"

"Uh, yeah!" Zachary faced Roxie with wide eyes and a thin smile betraying gritted teeth. He gave a thumbs up.

Andrew gave a bit of a laugh. "That's a joke, Roxie. I'm the people guy."

Roxie turned up her palms. "Yeah, anyone could see that! Anyway, come on up before they get suspicious."

Andrew motioned for Zachary to follow them. He mused to himself: maybe someone already was.

*****

The sound of knives scraping plates punctuated the conversation over dinner. Dinner was a makeshift chicken piccata that was a bit too sour for Zach's taste. He liked lemon and chicken together, and capers were ok, but he suspected that nationally recognized meteorologist Kris Stevenson didn't spend as much time in the kitchen as she let on.

Zach wondered when he would be able to mention that he knew who she was and the work she had done. It was easy for Andrew to recognize an international fashion model, but it would have been strange for Zach to mention anyone, even if he'd known them before. He didn't use Braxton's app, but he'd heard of it being popular with people in college.

So he sat and watched. Zach didn't much enjoy eating in large groups. It reminded him too much of his days working at the diner and the whole situation that happened there. In a way, he was grateful, because it had pulled him away from a dead-end life, and because of Andrew. Zach just wished that it was easier work that had brought them together.

A chill radiated from the glass of the double-paned window in the alcove off the main room. The snowstorm raged outside, blanketing everything in white and grey. Even with night descending, the snow that came down shone blinding white, reflecting the light from the lodge.

Wind rippled past the building, rocking and whistling in an unsteady reminder of the porous nature of log construction and the diminutive width of glass. The burgundy leather of the loveseat had finally warmed up from Zach sitting there. If it weren't for the roaring fire and what was likely a complicated vent system, Zach knew he'd be shivering.

The others had chosen the social thing and sat in the sectional and chairs in front of the fireplace. Both Zach and Andrew had been invited, but Zach didn't feel quite so comfortable crammed so close to everyone. Besides, from the side he could observe them. And he was avoiding Ever, because frankly the model intimidated Zach. He'd never met someone quite so forward, though Zach thought it likely some kind of public persona.

Andrew, of course, ever the social butterfly, sat right in the center of things. He laughed along at stories, commented on the food, and probably had charmed them all. But Zach noted that Andrew wasn't giving anything away, nor was he leading the conversation.

Ever reached up a hand and beckoned. "Why don't you join us, Zach?"

"Oh, don't mind him," Andrew said with that sly smile of his. "Zachary gets a bit anxious around people. Good assistant, takes orders well, but he doesn't meet the clients, you know?"

"Oh, he takes orders, does he?" The group burst into laughter as Ever nibbled on their lower lip. It was in that way that's supposed to entice people, but their eyes glanced a little to the left, rather than directly at Zach.

When the laughter had stopped, Zach said, "I'm used to sitting on the side, it's fine." He took a bite of the chicken piccata, and the conversation continued without him.

Kris had taken a seat in one of the free-standing chairs, completely engulfed by the lawn-furniture padding strapped to the wooden slats of the chair. Her voice floated through the conversation that began again, but Zach didn't like that she was so obscured. All Zach could see of her was a pale hand resting on one of the chair's arms. A martini glass seemed to be welded to her fingers.

Braxton, had taken the other chair. His frame had no hope of being contained though, and his shiny, bald head encroached the back of the chair. Given the height of the sectional, though, the chair probably offered the best support for one of his stature. He'd kicked his shoes off to the side, and the bottom of his button-up shirt showed through the gap in the back of the chair.

"Ahem," Kris said after a lull in the conversation. She stood up from her chair. Everyone still eating put their plates to the side. "I know that this weekend hasn't been quite to plan, but I am glad you all could come." She smiled and passed a glance between Zach and Andrew. "Yes, I know you two don't really know us, but we're always glad to make new friends!"

She paused, and Andrew took the moment to be his charming self. "We're most thankful for you to include us. You could have kept us downstairs, but you invited us to eat with you and share your stories. Zachary and I are very appreciative." He nodded and Zach followed, putting on his most grateful smile.

The smile on Kris's face stretched wide and a wrinkle formed under her left eye. "Yes, well, it would have been rude for us to lock you downstairs, wouldn't it?" She took a moment to sip from her martini. "I hope that we can all come together and celebrate the reason for our gathering. Braxton, the big 4-0!"

Sparse claps and snaps circled the room as Kris sat down. She urged the guest of honor to stand. "Speech!" Roxie called out.

Shuffling out of the chair, Braxton scanned the room. The top three buttons of his shirt had come undone sometime during the night. "Thank you, thank you! Even though my actual birthday was last week, I am so happy to get together with all of you and celebrate it. Thank you Kris for organizing this. I haven't seen a lot of you in ages!"

"We didn't have a big to do for my 40th," Ever said with a pout. They had curled up in the corner, languishing over the back of the sofa and encroaching dangerously close to Andrew's personal space.

Braxton laughed and said, "Ever, you were in Malta for your 40th and couldn't be bothered with us peasants!" The room filled with chuckles. "Really, though, it warms my heart to see all of you. I know things have been hectic with our lives, and we're all off doing big things, so it means a lot that you'd want to spend the weekend with me."

Raising his tumbler of whiskey brought forth a bevy of cheers. Everyone seemed happy and smiling, except for one. Ty, who'd taken the corner wedge, clapped and cheered along with the others, but did so with a thin mouth and a roll of his eyes.

After basking in the celebration, Braxton sat back down. In a while, everything quieted down. Kris threw up her hands and said, "Oh! And I almost forgot to mention that in addition to Braxton's birthday, I wanted to congratulate Roxie on her third book!" She pulled a copy of *The Nobody's Club* from somewhere in her parka and held it up.

"Oh," Roxie said from the far end of the sofa. "You don't have to mention that. It's been out for a couple months already." She chuckled, and her face flushed.

There were a few sparse claps, but this time, Zach noticed, only Kris was smiling. Everyone else looked like they had swallowed a cockroach.

"Nonsense!" Kris put her hands out and wiggled her fingers in Roxie's direction. "I thought, maybe later in the weekend, you could sign a copy for each of us? I brought enough for, well, the people who were invited. Sorry Andy."

The way she called him Andy stuck in Zach's throat. He wanted to correct them, but he knew that it would look confrontational. And Zach had a part to play.

"It's fine," Andrew said. "Roxie, I didn't know you were a writer! What's the book about?"

The woman glanced over at Andrew, then Zach, those brown eyes wide like headlights, pleading. It was a question that had to be introduced, a topic that had to be raised. They were there to discover who might want to harm Roxie, after all, and the book was at the center of it. Eventually she said, "Uh, well it's about a group—"

"It's about us," Ty said through gritted teeth. "About the nobodies."

"It's not about—"

"Oh, darling, we're not stupid," Ever said with a catlike smile. They shifted in their seat like they were going to pounce. "You didn't even hide the names much. Emma and Emmett? Trace? Kat? That's me, Ty, and Kris."

"It's homage to my friends!" Roxie frantically looked from one person to the next. "I always have you guys represented in my stories!"

Braxton put his hand out, palm up towards Ever. "You didn't have to split Ever into a guy and a girl, though," he said. "That's a bit mean-spirited."

"Oh, isn't that…" Kris paused, the effort of thinking crossing her face. "I think that was so Roxie could give a good reason the love interest couldn't be with them."

"Yeah, that!" Roxie pointed at the chair where Kris sat.

"Better than the real story, I guess," Ever said. They turned their head away and scowled. "At least there's a good reason you can't stay with two people who are siblings.

"Hey, now," Braxton said. "That's uncalled for. We got through it and stayed friends."

"Yeah, you friends with a lot of your castoffs." Ty glanced around the room.

"Woah!" Kris stood up and waved her hands. "What is going on here? Why are we arguing over a book? Ok, sure, there's stuff taken from the club, but it's just a made up story. I mean, that ending isn't what happened, right? It's not us really!"

"It kind of happened," Ever muttered. "Not the part where Roxie and Braxton ride off into the sunset. The other part with the club ending."

"Ever!" Braxton leaned forward and snapped an angry look at them. "We don't have to talk about—"

"What?" Ever batted their eyelashes back at him. "Did you think that one was going to the grave?" They looked around at Kris, then Roxie, then Ty. "It's what happened. In case anybody needed clearing up."

Jumping to his feet, Ty lashed out, "Man I didn't even want to come. This is too much. Too much!" He stomped off, his heavy footfalls slamming against the steps as he ascended the stairs. All the way, he kept his face down and away from the others.

Roxie, the only one of the friends still sitting, burst into tears. "It's not—I didn't—I'm sorry!" She ran past the alcove where Zach sat and into the darkness and cold of the unused dining area. Choked sobs followed in her wake.

A glance from Andrew was all that Zach needed. He rose as quietly as he could on leather seating and slunk over to the woman. She had pulled her hair over her face and pressed herself against the frigid glass. The sounds of the argument continued, but muted just enough to alert Zach that he could talk freely as long as they kept quiet.

He reached an uncertain hand out an put it on Roxie's shoulder. "Hey—"

"Don't!" She jerked away. "Why? Why did he have to do that?"

"Andrew?" Zach's voice was barely a whisper. "We've got to see who's harboring what grudges."

"I told you all that!" A certain steel came over Roxie's voice, but she kept the volume low. "I told you that they'd be upset I'd used them and the club."

"Ok, but it's a big gap between anger and motive." Zach held up a finger and began counting. "Ever's clearly upset at being misrepresented. Ty's angry about how things ended. Braxton seems a bit on edge about a relationship he and Ever had? At least Kris doesn't seem angry about the book"

"Oh, she—I mean Kat—she's not a big part of the story." The sobs had slowed.

"Would she be angry about not getting her part?"

"Maybe, but it's really that I used some stuff from her and Braxton's relationship with the main romance between Rickie and Laura. Kris might not look it, but she's probably a bit upset at that. She always hid her anger well."

"Ok," Zach said. "So, you probably shared some intimate details that she's not happy with. Suffice it to say that everyone's angry about the book, but they don't seem… murderous."

The sobs stopped. Roxie pulled her hair back and looked at Zach. The trails from her tears glistened in the low light. "I thought Andy was the one good at social stuff."

"Andrew," Zach said, stressing the name, "likes people. It allows him to catch them off guard and ask questions people wouldn't normally answer. Me? People make me nervous, but that means I notice more about them. I don't think it's a big feat to notice what I've seen about the argument, though." He sighed. "I feel like I'm missing something, but there's nothing there."

"That doesn't make a girl feel safe."

"I wouldn't worry." Zach tried to give his best Andrew smile. "I always feel like I'm missing something."

A small laugh poked through the tears. Roxie pointed at Zach's face. "Don't do that. It's not cute like you think it is."

"I don't know how he does it," Zach said, glancing over his shoulder at Andrew.

"Walk me back out there before I fall apart again."

Rejoining the group held little fanfare. Ever had already gone upstairs, and it was just Kris and Braxton there with Andrew. Andrew opened his mouth to speak, but it was Braxton who said it first. "How are you feeling, Roxie?"

"Oh, I feel like a fool," Roxie said and slumped down on the couch. "I shouldn't have written it."

"Well, maybe," Braxton said. "But it's there and we'll get through it. We've done it before."

Kris put down her martini glass for the first time that night and reached down to Roxie. "We always get through it, don't we? Come. Let's go to bed. People will be alright in the morning. God, I might need a zolly tonight. You want one?"

Roxie shook her head and slid herself off the couch. She grabbed Kris around the shoulder. Her hair engulfed the two of them as they walked toward the stairs.

"Hey, uh, I know it's only nine," Braxton said. "But, I think it wouldn't be a bad idea for us all to turn in." He walked over to the door on the other side of the room. "I need to get out of this and maybe into a hot bath. I just hope there's hot water with all this shit coming down."

He turned back to the duo and gave a wave before walking into the room and closing the door behind him.

Back in the room downstairs, Zach let out a long sigh and collapsed on the bottom bunk. "How do you deal with people all the time?"

Andrew leaned against the frame. "Oh, I have a lot of practice. What have you got?"

"Nothing much," Zach said, kicking off his shoes. "I can tell you in the morning. When we don't have—"

There was the creak of wood, footsteps, and then a thunk from above. The sound of rushing water followed.

"Got it," Andrew said. "With the way these stairs bend, I didn't even realize his room was above us."

Zach leaned his head back into the uncased pillow they'd found in the dusty boxes earlier. "I hope he doesn't snore like you do."

Andrew kicked the bedframe. "You wouldn't even know if I snore!"

"You do it at your desk all the time!"

Andrew cackled and reached for the light switch.

*****

The early morning light filled the tiny room as Andrew awoke. The mattress in the top bunk felt thin and old, which it probably was, and the bunk itself was a bit short for Andrew's long legs. Crusts of sleep broke as Andrew rubbed his eyes and stretched, trying and failing to relieve him of the cramps left by the night.

He yawned as Zachary slipped into the room, towel over one shoulder, already dressed for the day in his usual polo and jeans. His brown hair looked black with the water, matching the darkness of his eyes that Andrew could see even across the room. "God," Andrew said, his voice hoarse. "What time is it? Did you sleep?"

Zachary closed the door behind him and held up the towel. "It's nine," he said and began to fold the towel into neat thirds. "I fell asleep for a while around midnight."

"I was out immediately, but I kept waking up." The ceiling loomed close as Andrew propped himself up on his elbows. "Was something going on?"

With a quick turn, Zachary stared out the window. "Braxton was pretty popular last night. I recorded the times until I fell asleep." There was a bit of hesitation in his voice. "Two visits. One around ten and the other at eleven-fifteen."

With all the strength he could muster, Andrew pushed himself over the edge and onto the thin, metal ladder. "You didn't stay up just to—"

"You should start getting ready before it gets too late." Remaining facing away, Zachary spoke over his shoulder.

The chill of the room swept through the exposed hairs on Andrew's chest and calves. "Ah," he said, feeling the grin bubble up to his face. He began retrieving clothes from his bag. "How's the water?"

"Not very warm," Zachary said. "Cold's good for you."

With a groan, Andrew shuffled over to the door. "Guess it can't be helped with all the snow and the amount of people." He opened the door and slipped through.

After a downright frigid shower and getting dressed, Andrew joined Zachary in the main room of the basement. It was filled with an accoutrement of gaming tables, including a green-felted, full sized pool table, and a smaller foozeball table off to the side. An entertainment nook had a pair of loveseats arranged toward a screen that would have taken up the entire back wall of the office at the studio.

Flipping through his phone with a flat expression on his face, Zachary faced the closed door that hid the stairs up to the ground floor. His lower lip quivered occasionally, and every now and then a tooth snagged a bit of loose skin there.

Taking up position next to his friend, Andrew said, "Any signal?"

"No." Zachary clicked the screen off and put his phone in his pocket. "There was some in the night, but we're not looking to leave, are we?"

With a shake of his head, Andrew grabbed the doorknob and gave it a turn. It didn't yield. "What?"

"Yeah, it's locked." Zachary got out of the doorway and leaned against the wall. "The door's got key locks on both sides. Did you notice that most of the doors are like that?"

"When did you have time to notice that?" The door was solid pine, from what Andrew could tell. Why would an inner door need a lock at all? "Guess they didn't want us snooping around at night. How long has it been since you knocked?"

"Knocked?" Zachary's brow furrowed and he glanced between the door and his hand.

Raising his hand to strike the door, Andrew said, "Oh, for crying out loud!" The sound of three sharp raps echoed through the room and reverberated into the cabin.

A short while later, a scuffle sounded down the wooden steps and stopped just on the other side. The door handle jiggled but didn't give way. A voice floated through, "Oh? It's locked? Hang on, I'll get the key."

"Sorry to be a bother," Andrew said as the footfalls receded. "Kris, I think?"

Zachary nodded. "She seems like someone who would be up early."

A few minutes later, the door swung open, nearly pinning Zachary to the wall. Kris stood on the other side, bundled in her red parka. "Sorry guys. Guess the door was already locked when we closed it last night."

"These things happen," Andrew said and gave Kris a big smile. "Hope there's enough food for us."

"Enough?" Kris gave out a laugh. "They overstocked the kitchen for me. Come on up!"

Shortly, Andrew had shooed Kris out of the kitchen and was preparing eggs and bacon on the stove. The popping sounds and rich aroma of the thick cuts of meat, accompanied by the smell of fresh coffee, drew groggy people down from upstairs. Taking orders as they came, Andrew eventually sat down to eat his own meal.

"Surprised the birthday boy isn't out yet," he said between bites of a well-peppered over-hard egg.

He looked over to the closed door, and then around at the listless guests. Roxie shivered in the loveseat by the glass, staring out at the blinding white flakes of the ever-present snowstorm. She had refused the eggs offered her and sat down with a mug of tea in hand. Kris and Ever were sprawled out on the floor in front of the fire talking over some family photos Kris had brought with her. Ty sat at the end of the counter with a plate and cup of orange juice, scraping a fork over the remainder of his bacon and eggs, long since devoured.

"He doesn't seem the type to sleep in very late," Zachary said. "Business types are usually early risers."

Ty looked up from his empty plate and stared at Zachary for a moment. "Up at ass-crack, usually." When Andrew glanced over and raised an eyebrow, Ty added, "Used to room with him in college. Woke me up every morning."

Trading a look with Zachary, Andrew announced to the room, "It's ten-thirty, I think, can someone who knows Braxton go wake him up? I'd like to go ham on making him breakfast for letting us stay with you all."

Kris handed Ever the stack of photos and said "My dad looks silly in this one." Then she stretched, stood up, and approached the door. "Braxton! You don't want to miss out on your breakfast, do you? You love bacon!" She knocked on the door a few times before pulling out her phone. "Damn, still no signal. He's in there right?" She tried the door, but it was locked. Turning to look at Andrew, she added, "Uh, he's not answering. Braxton?"

In a moment, Andrew was at the door, giving it a sterner knock. Zachary had popped off his chair and hovered next to the door. "You've got a key, right," he said, pointing to Kris.

"Oh, right." She reached into her pocket and produced the brass key. "Hey—"

Zachary had pulled it out of her hands and pushed Andrew out of the way. With a click, the lock turned and Zachary pushed the door open a crack. He poked a head in, stared for a moment, and then shut the door, wedging himself in front of it. His mouth drew to a thin line, and he gave Andrew a sharp nod before turning around.

The others had gathered round, confusion growing on one face, then the next. Kris held her mouth in a scowl as she tried to retrieve the key from Zachary.

Andrew cleared his throat. "I think it would be best if we stepped away from the door and sat down." He shifted his gaze over to Zachary. "You're sure?"

"If not, it's a convincing prank. And an awful one too."

Kris was the first to find her voice. "Wait, what does he mean?" It came out sharp and hooked, but held the slightest bit of panic.

"Please, let's step away." Andrew held out his arms and created a barrier between the group and Zachary. Over his shoulder, Andrew whispered, "You take a look. I'll deal with them."

Nodding, Zachary slipped into the room and an audible click sounded from the lock. The group rushed Andrew for the moment the door was open, shouting protests, but Andrew held them back. It was a tough task. Any longer and Ever, certainly, would have barreled him over.

"I demand to know what's going on!" Kris jabbed a finger into Andrew's chest.

Ever pulled at one of Andrew's arms. "Has something happened?"

"What do you think?" Sarcasm dripped in Ty's voice. "They doing this just for funzies?"

Roxie's voice was a tremble. "Zach's not… investigating, is he?"

Catching her eye, Andrew gave a quick nod. Her hands flew to her hair and pulled it in front of her face. A wail escaped her lips.

"Investigating?" Kris looked between Roxie and Andrew. "What does she mean by that?"

"Sorry," Andrew said, "I really am." He planted himself against the door. "I really am a photographer, honest, but Zachary and I are here on business as private investigators."

Kris advanced. "I didn't ask you who you were, asshole. I asked what she meant."

"I'm afraid," Andrew said, "and I am truly sorry, but Braxton has died in the night."

The questions and shouts came at once but Andrew waved his hands, managing to get them silenced. "I'll know more when Zachary's done looking around in there. But likely he was murdered. And one of you four did it."

*****

After turning the key, shouting assaulted Zach from the other side of the locked door. The tones of Andrew's voice, soft but firm, joined the shouts. He was handling the people, so Zach addressed the problem.

A coppery smell hung in the air and there was no question as to the source. The interior of the master suite, so Zach assumed, housed a gigantic bed, an open door to a bathroom, a reading nook in an alcove, and a full-sized tub, curiously in the main room. The tub was occupied.

Braxton's naked body lay face down, half submerged in a translucent red liquid—water and blood. A steak knife stuck out from his left shoulder. A streak of dried blood ran down into the liquid. Upon closer inspection, a sinister gash traced along the man's neck, likely killing the man in seconds. Since neither Zach nor Andrew had heard a scream in the night, it must have been swift.

Taking out his phone, Zach began compiling notes. Though he had no signal, he'd been sure to charge it the night before, after he'd marked the late night observations. For the first note, he took a picture of the body and noted the wounds and state of the tub. He was careful not to touch anything. The abrupt situation had left Zach without any of the gloves he'd packed in case there was something that needed careful handling. The edges of his coat would have to do.

Braxton lay draped over the tub, rather than sat in it. His feet were up in the air, knees submerged, along with his midsection. The man's head rested on the far corner, and one of his hands hung near the faucet and knobs. It was possible Braxton was reaching for the button further along the side, which Zach assumed operated jets, though the darkness of the water prevented verification. He wasn't about to reach into the water to find out, for several reasons.

A pair of overturned tumblers rested on the foam bath mat at the side of the tub, dried, dark trails leaking out and into the fibers. Above, on the squared-off stonework around the basin, a faint brown semicircle remained, joined by the bit of dark red stain that splattered the stone and porcelain lip of the tub. On the edge of one tumbler, a residue remained. The color was faint and indeterminate, or else there just wasn't enough to make a dark impression.

Turning away from the scene of the murder, Zach examined the rest of the room for signs of visits. There had been at least two, as Zach had recorded, but there might have been others still after he'd fallen asleep.

Braxton had moved in. His suitcase, empty, stood partially open in a corner. Carefully opening the closet near the door revealed he had unpacked his clothes and put them away. The grey suit he'd worn the previous day lay discarded next to the massive bed, wrinkled and haphazard. Either Braxton did not think about the care of his suits, or he had removed it in a hurry.

Atop the bed, the royal blue comforter bunched up here and there. Two pillows in brown cases lay strewn about. One perched precariously on the edge of the far side. The other sat crumpled up near the center, far from the black-painted headboard. Giant throw pillows had been tossed into the corner of the room.

The nook at the far end of the room felt frigid, surrounded on three sides by thin glass. Two of the windows were encrusted with snow, while the third looked in on a screened patio. There wasn't access to the patio from the room, just a window between, like a strange viewing area. With the glass, anything in the nook would be on display. It was a curious construction.

Two more tumblers graced the small, round table in the nook, filled with the dregs of a dark, red liquid that smelled heady and fruity. A fly hovered around the edge of one of the glasses. Probably wine, but there wasn't any trace of a bottle, save for a cork wedged in a cushion. In searching for the bottle, Zach discovered a small bottle of whiskey stashed in the cubbyhole of the right-side nightstand.

Between the glasses, a copy of Roxie's book sat open, flat against the table. Some pages had been torn out and were balled up the corner of the alcove. The pages that Zach could see were covered in pen and highlighter. The pages that remained in the book were heavily dogeared and the spine had been broken so badly that the paperback could lay flat without closing.

The rest of the room felt largely untouched. A thank you card from the property owner was on one nightstand, perfectly squared with the corner. The dresser under the mounted TV had dust on all of its handles. The remote for the TV itself remained atop the dresser, also covered in dust. It was unlikely that anything would come through on it anyway, with the weather.

The bathroom showed no signs of use. Even the toilet paper roll still had its first sheet glued to the roll. The shower looked dry, which was no surprise considering the bath was used at least once instead. Zach didn't dare inspect the tile with his hands, but he was certain there wouldn't be any damp.

The oddest thing about the bathroom was the window looking out into the front porch. Across the way, a bench was placed looking directly inside. Zach shuddered. Who decided that was a good place for a window, much less a bench?

After finishing taking pictures and notes of everything he found, Zach decided it was time to report to Andrew. He walked over to the door, turned the key as quiet as he could, and used his coat sleeve to grip the knob.

An oppressive tension met Zach on the other side of the door. Andrew guarded the door, stock still, while the others had arranged themselves in the vicinity. Roxie and Ty sat on stools at the kitchen island, both with lines across their foreheads and heavyset eyes. Ty had lost the weariness of the morning, but it had been replaced with a weightier, knowing exhaustion.

Opposite the door, Kris leaned against a post where the room transitioned from kitchen to seating. Though resting against the wood, she looked rigid and taller than she had before, as if no bone in her body were relaxed. Beside her on the sectional, Ever sat hunched over, knees under, with their elbows on the back of the sofa. One knuckle was wedged between their teeth.

When the door opened, all eyes locked on Zach. It felt like he'd been hit with a spotlight. Andrew turned his head to look into the room, blinked, and then turned back. "God, that's bad," he said under breath. "You ok?"

Nodding, Zach turned, closed and locked the door, and handed Andrew his phone. "It's a bit of a mess in there, but I think I saw everything that could be. I'd do better with gloves, but we can wait and see if we need more."

With the door closed, it was almost like nothing had happened, but there was no erasing the image from his mind. The others hadn't seen it at all, and that perhaps eased their grief. After all, to them, their friend still felt alive. They hadn't received the closure, the finality that Zach had. Well, one of them had, and Zach was going to find out who.

"Right." Andrew cleared his throat as he scrolled through the notes on the phone. He raised his voice. "Zachary has been very thorough and has been careful not to disturb the room." He brought the phone closer and enlarged a picture of the torn pages from Roxie's book. "When I'm done, I'm going to ask you all some questions. To figure out what happened."

"In the meantime," he said, holding up his hand before anyone could protest, "you all need to keep trying to get an emergency call out."

"Try even if you don't have bars," Zach added. "Try text messages. Emergency calls and texts can sometimes get through on other networks."

"It's my hope that once the storm falters, or someone decides to send help on their own, we'll have this wrapped up for the authorities." Andrew gave them all a slight smile. "We'll figure out who killed Braxton. That's a promise."

*****

"Who do you think you are," Ever said in a low growl. "You come up here, Braxton gets hurt, and you just act like nothing's happened! Like it's no big deal! Whoever did this… whoever hurt him… speak up. So I can take you out of this world myself!"

"Hey!" Andrew threw up a hand as he gave Zachary back his phone. "I get that you're upset. We all are, right? Yeah, sure, Zachary and I don't show it, but this is our job."

"I carry every death I've seen with me," Zachary said. He fixed Ever with a stare from his black eyes. "I never forget them, and I never forgive the ones who do it."

"I just can't believe it…" Although Roxie had cried herself out already, fresh tears welled at the top of her cheeks. "He can't be…"

"Please, just tell me this is some joke." Kris held her forehead up with tight fists. "He's in there, just fine and he's just messing with us. God! I should have just left the group alone. None of this would have happened if—"

"That's no way to think," Andrew said, cutting her off. "Every decision we make could lead to something bad happening. You can't blame yourself for wanting to get together with some old friends."

"All we can do now is figure out what happened," Zachary said. "Let's start with—"

"Seriously," Ty said, stomping a foot on the floor. "Who the fuck are you guys? What gives?"

Between sniffles, Roxie produced some folded paper from her pocket. "This explains who they are." She opened the paper up to reveal a few printed pages from a news site. She handed it to Ty.

Ty scanned the pages and gave a sidelong glance at Andrew. "So, spys, huh?" His eyes were bloodshot and seemed hollowed out from his grief. Kris reached out and he gave her the article.

"Private investigators," Andrew corrected.

Ty clicked his tongue. "Same difference."

Flipping through the pages, Kris said, "Oh, it says someone was murdered at a vineyard and you solved it." The words came out listless and dull. A second passed before she slumped down against the wall, shaking. "Murder… It's so easy to think that he's fine…"

After their anger earlier, Ever remained silent. They stared at the wall with two deep embers. It was as though they were trying to bore a hole through the wood to see Braxton where Zachary had found him. Their face had lost its porcelain sheen, replaced with an undertone of ash. If Andrew hadn't known better, he'd have swore they were dead.

Ty shifted in his seat and looked at the bundle of hair next to him. "Roxie, what gives, girl?"

"Uh, well, I received an email after Kris sent out the invites." Roxie reached into her pocket and pulled out a phone. "Oh, right, I can't get into my email, can I?"

"I have it here," Zachary said. "Any important notes I save offline." Zachary cleared his throat and read. "Roxie—How dare you write about us! Those were our lives! Our secrets! You show up, I'll make you wish you hadn't. This is a warning. A threat. A promise."

"It's unsigned," Roxie added. "And the email is a throwaway, right?"

"Temail is a disposable email domain," Andrew explained. "They deactivate as soon as the message is delivered. I've used it plenty of times."

Roxie sighed. "So, I was scared."

"She called me up and asked about it," Kris said. "I thought it was pretty nasty. You told me it wasn't like the rando hate mail you've gotten before."

"It was my private email!" Crossing her arms, Roxie huffed. "I only use it for close friends. I was actually annoyed you sent the invite there."

"Wait, so, who has it?" Ty looked around the room. "I don't."

"You all do," Zachary said. "All the emails are listed in the invite."

Andrew nodded and asked, "Roxie, you told us that you gave it to

Kris before, right?"

The woman grimaced and knotted her hands in her hair. "Yeah, well, I didn't mean to. I sent her something on accident from that inbox."

"Yeah, my discount for the book."

Ty squinted at Roxie. "A discount? I ain't get a discount."

"Well," Roxie said, pulling the hair in front of her face. "When I noticed I was in the wrong email… I had a moment of panic. Then I thought… maybe I shouldn't poke the bear, you know?"

"Ha! I knew it!" Ever sat up straight and pointed a long finger at Roxie. "You admitted it! You knew we'd be upset about the book!"

For a moment, the room filled with a back and forth of accusations and defenses between the two. Kris and Ty joined in, less emphatically than Ever, but the noise was getting out of control.

"Hey!" Andrew's shout was enough to get a strangled squeak out of Ever. "I get that the book made waves, but there's a dead guy, your friend, in the other room, and shouting's not going to get us closer to solving it."

Shock rippled through the room as Andrew's blunt words hung in the air.

Kris broke the silence. "Who said you're going to 'solve' anything?" Kris drew air quotes and stared Andrew down with her steel blue eyes. "There's going to be police, right? And what if you did it? You arrived, and suddenly someone's killed our friend."

"Hey, yeah!" Ever turned their accusing finger on Andrew. "You did it, didn't you? Or him! We loved Braxton too much to…" The rest of the sentence faded away as Ever vaulted over the back of the couch.

Before Ever could take two steps, Zachary said, "That would be impossible. We were locked downstairs." He nodded to Kris. "She let us out this morning. We had no way of locking it ourselves."

Ever snapped their head to Kris, who nodded. The anger on Ever's face sank back into cold sorrow, as they settled back down into the sectional.

"Besides," said Andrew, "Zachary and I are the only third party here.

We didn't know Braxton, so why would we do anything? Plus, we have experience investigating suspicious deaths."

"But you're just gonna let Roxie go free, ain't you?" After standing up, Ty inched away from the woman sitting next to him.

"It wasn't me! What? Ty! You know me better than that!"

"I assure you," Zachary said, "that I will let nothing come in the way of finding this killer."

Andrew cleared his throat. "I've seen firsthand that Zachary doesn't let client relationships, friendships, or even family cloud his judgment. He's burnt bridges in the aim of the truth, and I'm willing to do so as well."

All of them studied Zachary. He may have had a soft, round exterior, a pleasant face and warmth embedded in his skin. But in that moment, a hard line drew across his lips. His brown, bushy brows shaded his eyes, which themselves were dark, almost-black lasers that flitted from one suspect to the other.

Ever visibly gulped. "He looked so cute and cuddly yesterday, but now…"

"It's the quiet ones you have to watch out for," Kris added in a whisper.

Ty nodded and reached a hand around to scratch his back. "Guess if I'd been stuck I'd want him on my side."

"I really didn't do it," Roxie said. "Honest!"

Before the shouting began again, Andrew held up his hands. "So I'm going to ask some questions, like I said. Let's start with your relation to Braxton."

Kris pouted. "You don't know that already?"

Andrew shrugged. "I like to hear it from the horse's mouth."

Zachary pointed at Kris. "You first. To verify my notes, you're Kristen Stevenson with the National Weather Institute? I am sorry to meet under these circumstances."

Kris looked like she had swallowed a frog. "Oh, uh, you've heard of me?"

"I just read your SciNews interview about the new BRASS system."

A frown formed on Kris's face. "System is redundant. Barometric Residue Analytical Schedule System."

With a slight wave to get Kris's attention, Andrew asked, "What was your relationship with Braxton?"

"Nothing, now," Kris said. "We'd all drifted apart. That's why I set this up! But back in college we went out." She traded a glance with Roxie. "Not the only one, mind you."

Andrew furrowed his brow and diverted his attention to his client. "We know about that, at least that they were involved. Anything more to add?"

"You read it, didn't you?" With a nod, Ty indicated a copy of Roxie's book on the table in front of the sectional. "That thing says it all. Both her and Ever."

"At different times, of course." Roxie added quickly. "And Kris too. The book isn't what went on, anyway."

"Well, yeah," Kris said. "You cut me almost clean out of it. Roxie was the rebound girl, after I called it quits with him."

"Bullshit." Ever got back to their feet. They stood taller than anyone in the room, an imposing figure if there was any in the room. "Hate to break it to you both, but he was never into you. You just looked good on his arm to his business contacts."

A gasp rose up from Roxie's chest, but Kris laughed it off. "Of course. That's why I broke it off. Roxie, you didn't think that… Oh, poor thing!" Kris walked over and put her arm around Roxie's shoulders.

Tears had already started to well in Roxie's eyes. "I… I know he had all that baggage, but… He really seemed to care."

Folding his arms, Ty said, "It don't matter now, do it? For the record, I was just his roommate. Saw more of him that I liked, though."

Ever gave a clipped laugh. "Oh, yeah, he hated wearing clothes, but he always had to keep up appearances. Braxton shed them at every chance he could."

Without looking Andrew in the eye, Ty mumbled. "Not really… into people, you know?"

Kris scrunched up her nose like she'd eaten a raw lemon. "Ty, that sounds vile!"

"That didn't come out right. Like relationships, you know? Hate them."

"You studied them too much," Kris said and looked at Andrew. "Ty's into psych. Or was back then. We had a few classes together. Well, until…" She trailed off.

Ty finished the suggestion. "Until my scholarship ran out."

Kris tilted her head left and right as she considered it. "Yeah, that, I guess."

After jotting down a note, Zachary asked, "What happened?"

"The club. Ty here. Certified nobody." He held his hand up, making the letter O, and shook it once in the air. Kris and Ever followed suit, while Roxie just tossed a listless hand out in front of her.

Andrew looked from one to the other. "A nobody?"

Between quiet sobs, Roxie said, "You really didn't read the book, did you?"

"Ah, well, Zachary was supposed to—"

"He hid the book from me." The glance Zachary gave Andrew would have slain a less-confident person. "It doesn't matter. I skimmed it last night."

"It was the Club for Nobodies," Ever said. "Me and Braxton started it. We were angry at the Greek system for failing us, and decided to fight back."

"That's why it started?" Kris raised her free hand, palm up. "So weird. I didn't join until Braxton and I started dating. It was supposed to be… how to put it?"

Ty raised his head. "We weren't nobody. A promise to become somebody." Heavy lines crossed his face.

"Yeah. Like when we graduated, we'd graduate from 'being nobodies' at the same time." Kris smiled for a moment, then glanced over to Ty. "Sorry, Ty, I didn't mean…"

"You meant it." Ty took a step away from Kris. "I'm still a nobody. I didn't graduate."

"Ty…" Roxie looked up and at the man.

"Club folded, hun." Ever walked across the room and attempted to trap Ty in their arms. "None of us are nobodies anymore."

Shrugging the embrace off, Ty said, "Yeah, whatever. Heard you had to cancel a vacation to Ibiza for this."

"That?" Ever swirled around to look at Kris. "That's because Miss Planner had to move the weekend last minute."

Kris dislodged herself from Roxie and held up her hands. "I had my interview last week, sorry! TWI doesn't get a lot of press, and BRASS is my baby."

"Whatever you say." Ever walked back over to the couch and sat on the back of it. "Awful weekend for it. I gave up warm sands for a snowstorm and—" Their hand flew to their mouth. "God, I almost forgot about it…"

A silence fell over the room as several pairs of eyes drifted over to the door that Andrew still guarded.

"Ok, let's go through everyone's night," Andrew said, nodding at Zachary. "Zachary will take notes."

"I'll go because I'm pretty simple," Kris said. "I took Roxie up like you know, and I put her in her room. Then I went to bed myself. I took a zolly and was out as soon as I hit the pillow."

"A zolly?" Andrew shook his head at the word.

Roxie answered for Kris. "Sleeping pills she gets for her insomnia that she absolutely has and isn't faking at all." Kris shot her a dirty look.

Zachary noted it all down. "You were up first?"

Kris shrugged. "As far as I know? Not long before you two, but you saw no one was here when you started breakfast."

"Ok, Roxie," Andrew said. "What happened after Kris left?"

"I moped. Cried a little. Fell asleep." She twirled her hair in her hand. "I woke up around three and used the bathroom, but I was so tired after that."

Andrew frowned. "You weren't scared?"

"Why would I—Oh, the threat?" She thought about it for a moment. "Do you think someone would have? While I was sleeping?"

"Honestly," Zachary said, "When you took a while to come down, I got worried."

"That's such an ugly thought," Ever said.

Andrew cleared his throat. "And what about you, Ever? What was your night like?"

"Oh, uh, well I just went to bed." They curled their fingers, suddenly interested in studying their nails. "Ty blew up and Roxie was crying in the dark, so I got bored and went up."

Zachary tapped something into his phone. "You didn't leave your room all night?"

"Why would I?" Ever spied something under their fingernail and picked at it. "We've all got bathrooms. I wanted a bath, but only the two bathrooms have a tub."

Roxie blinked. "The double bath upstairs has a tub? Oh that would have been so nice."

"You didn't look?" Ever squinted at the woman. "First thing I did."

"Well, I didn't want to go into Kris and Ty's rooms."

"To get us back on track," Andrew said. "Ever, you contemplated a bath and then…?"

"Oh, I just went to bed." Ever resumed inspecting their nails. "What else was I going to do?"

Andrew had a few ideas, but he kept them to himself. "Ok, so Ty, you were the last one down this morning. Are you usually a late riser?"

Clearing his throat, Ty said, "Work nights, so yeah."

"And you were pretty angry last night," Zachary said.

"Yeah, so? I got pissed." Ty folded his arms. "Everybody fighting and all."

"I think," Zachary said, "that you were angry about how the club ended."

"I—" Ty stopped himself and thought about it for a moment. "I've had that a long time. How I ruined the club."

Zachary stopped taking notes and looked up. "You said you ruined it?"

"Ancient history, man," Ty said. "Pulled a stunt and dean shut us down."

"Ty…" Roxie took a step closer but Ty stopped her with a cold stare.

"But," Zachary said, "that's not what the book said, is it?"

"Can't trust what you read," Ty said.

Ever laughed. "You can trust that! Braxton shut the club down Ty. Well, he botched a meeting with the dean. Bad. You just don't want to admit it."

"Man, why's everyone dogpiling me?"

"Not a man," Ever said. A scowl had formed on their face.

Before it turned into a shouting match, Andrew clapped once, loud and short. "Let's focus. Ty, you went up first and came down last. What were you doing last night?"

"Ok, so yeah." Ty turned his face to the floor. "I was mad. 'Bout the book, the club, all of it. Tried to sleep, but I can't stop thinking. So I get up. Decide to yell at someone. Go to knock on Roxie's door, but… she ain't there."

Zachary asked, "Could she have been asleep?"

"Naw. I looked in." His face darkened. "Sorry. Door was unlocked and I was mad."

"Ew," Roxie said and shuddered. "I would have locked it if I could."

"But," Andrew said, "that raises the question. Roxie, where were you?"

"Huh?" A blank expression fell over Roxie's face. After a moment, she reddened. "Oh, I guess if I wasn't in my room…"

"…then you were somewhere else," Zachary finished for her. "I suspect you were downstairs in Braxton's room."

Shouts assaulted Roxie who shielded herself with her hair. She squealed something in defense, but it came out as a sound more than words. Eventually, a yell from Andrew startled them enough to make sense of what she was saying.

"He was fine when I left him!"

"Roxie," Andrew said, "you went to meet someone in the middle of the night when your life had been threatened?"

"I—" The group watched as Roxie formed her words. Her sentence came out very deliberately. "Well, it was Braxton. He wouldn't hurt me. Even Zach said so."

All eyes turned to the shorter of the private detectives. "I said that no one seemed to harbor a motive big enough for murder, yet." He swallowed. "Clearly I was wrong."

"So?" Andrew turned his gaze upon Roxie. "Tell us what happened."

"I wanted to talk about the book. To talk about him and me. You know? It's really not a stretch to see that the girl in the novel gets the guy in the end, but that's not how it happened in real life. Readers want a happily-ever-after, so I changed a bunch of stuff from real life to make it work. Like making the old flame into a brother and sister. That way he couldn't be with them even if he wanted to."

With a roll of their eyes, Ever said, "Did you have to split me up into the gender binary?"

Roxie sighed. "Ever, the characters aren't even like you! Emma's this prim and proper girl and Emmett's got a whole personality around his motorcycle. I just used E names because I like to put you all in my books."

"I could ride a bike, you don't know," Ever said with a pout.

Andrew ignored the statement and moved on. "How'd Braxton react?"

"Fine, I guess." Hiding her face, Roxie elaborated. "Like, he was fine with the book. He knew it didn't really mean anything. He thought I should have talked with everyone first. He's seen people sue for less. When I asked about the ending, about how they got together, he was pretty ambivalent about it all."

Zachary raised a hand. "What do you mean?"

"Oh, I guess, I was asking him if it could have worked out like that.

I don't know if he got it or not. He just kept saying that it was a story. That it wasn't how life happened. That it wasn't real. I think he missed what I was asking."

"Oh, Roxie, no…" Kris put her arm back around the woman and bumped her forehead against Roxie's temple. "Roxie… he was never going to… He compared everyone to Ever. None of us were going to beat that." She pressed her lips into a thin line. "At least he didn't entirely abandon you but…"

With a sigh, Roxie pushed Kris away. "Yeah, I get that. I do. I just… wanted one last try. Yeah, so, we finished talking and I went back upstairs. I wasn't feeling great about myself, you know? So I just kind of laid in bed listening to the wind until I passed out."

Andrew asked, "Why didn't you mention the meeting before?"

"Huh?" Roxie thought it over for a moment, playing with a stray curl. "I guess it didn't seem important. He was fine and I was a bit embarrassed. Crawling back to your college love? Not a great look."

Zachary looked up from his notes. "Did you discuss it over a book?"

"What?" Roxie scrunched up her nose. "We talked about the book, but I didn't bring one in, if that's what you mean? I didn't bring one on the trip."

"And nobody else had any late night rendezvous?" Andrew tried to look each one of them in the eye, but couldn't. Roxie and Ty were both studying the floor. Kris had her eyes on Roxie. Ever had turned their back and was looking out the window into the white nothingness beyond.

After a moment, Zachary announced, "At least one of you is lying."

*****

Zach looked up from his notes and laid out the information he was willing to share. "There were two sets of glasses in the room, both used by very different people, so there were at least two meetings last night. One at ten, the other at eleven-fifteen."

"Oh," Roxie said. "It was around ten, I think, for me."

"That leaves eleven fifteen," Zach said. "Of the two, I'm most interested in the wine drinkers. Some kind of red wine, I believe."

"Oh, that leaves Roxie out," Kris said.

"What?" Roxie straightened up and looked at the woman next to her. "Why would that leave me out?"

"I read somewhere," Kris said, "that you can't have wine, right? Like you're forbidden or something?"

"What are you talking about?" Roxie took a big breath and let it out, practiced and slow. "Of course I can have wine. It's about moderation. Anyway, I'm secular, so it doesn't matter."

Zach prepared to take down a note. "So, you were the one drinking wine?"

The slightest of grins came over Roxie's face. "What? No. Can't stand the stuff." She cleared her throat. "I didn't see any glasses out when I was there. Braxton and I didn't drink anything. We didn't have time to, really. I wasn't in there very long."

Forestalling the note, Zach checked his notes about the timings he'd heard in the night. "That seems right for that first visit. It only lasted a couple minutes."

"So," Andrew said, "who drank the wine?"

The room remained quiet. Zach was surprised that no one else denied liking wine, particularly Ty, who didn't seem the type. Then again, Andrew was nothing like Zach's father, and they both enjoyed gin. Switching tactics, Zach asked, "Where would someone get a bottle of wine in this lodge?"

"There's one in the cabinet," Kris said, walking over to the black cabinets on the back wall of the kitchen. "Right… here." She opened the cabinet in the corner, revealing a variety of spirits and bottles, but no wine. "That's odd. It was there when I made my last martini." She moved to the refrigerator and opened it up. "Oh, here it is…"

"Don't pick it up!" Andrew moved to intercept Kris, but it was too late.

Kris looked down at the bottle and then flinched and carefully set it on the island like it was a gun. "I'm sorry, I didn't think about it. I've already touched it. I moved it looking for gin yesterday."

The Cabernet was nestled in a slender, green bottle with a simple, white label. The seal was missing and the cork had been replaced by a topper of some sort. Zach still didn't know wine, even after the affair with the vineyard. The bottle was about half full.

"That wasn't in there when I made breakfast," Andrew announced. "I only saw the bottle of vermouth in there."

Ty looked around the room. "Who got into the fridge this morning? I got some juice. I didn't notice it."

"I helped you get the food," Kris said to Andrew. "Oh, and Ever, you grabbed some cream, right?"

Ever gave her a sour look. "That's because you made the coffee too strong! I didn't notice, though. The cream was right in the door."

Everyone glanced at Roxie. After looking around for a moment, she pointed to a mug over on the table in the alcove. "I made myself some tea up in my room. I… decided it was better to stay away from everyone today."

Zach nodded and noted it down. How could he have missed someone carrying a big bottle and hiding it in the refrigerator? Looking around at the guests gave him the answer. Everyone was wearing something long or baggy. Kris's red parka could hide anything. Ty's baggy hoodie could easily conceal a bottle, and so could Ever's bright overcoat. Roxie hadn't been near the refrigerator, he remembered, she had brought the tea down with her in the morning.

Breaking Zach's train of thought, Ever said, "Ok, so I was the eleven-fifteen. We drank whiskey from a bottle Braxton had, not wine."

The silence lasted for a moment before accusations flew. Roxie seemed shocked while Kris looked ready to deck Ever. Ty yelled. Andrew tried to get it under control, to little effect. Ever ignored it all and kept talking.

Eventually, everyone quieted down enough to hear Ever. "As I was saying, there weren't any wine glasses or anything like that. I'd have noticed and made a stink. Braxton hated what red wine did to him in the morning."

Lines appeared on Andrew's forehead, which meant he was trying to wrap his head around something. "So, he drinks whiskey instead? That doesn't make any sense to me."

The guests shrugged, having apparently already forgotten the importance of Ever's statement.

Zach was determined not to let it go. "So, tell us about what happened."

"Oh, well, there's no avoiding it, I suppose. I was trying to spare you all some hurt." Ever glanced to Roxie and Kris. "Uh, you see, Braxton and I got together last night."

"What?" The word hung on Roxie's lips, barely even expressed.

Kris looked doubtful. "You mean you and he…"

"We had sex. I'm not ashamed of it." Ever ignored Roxie's choking sobs and kept talking. "We hadn't seen each other in a while, and he'd been giving me that look all evening. He's been single for a year, you know? He told me. He gave up trying to find anyone better than me. Like he could."

"So he never… he wouldn't…" Roxie could barely hold it together.

Kris returned to comforting her friend. "Shh. You know he was always hung up on Ever. That wasn't going to change. We were just stepping stones, you know?"

It didn't seem to help. Roxie's sobs chunked louder. Deciding to let Andrew deal with emotional people, Zach walked over to Ever. "Ok, so, you came down at eleven fifteen and he let you in. Tell me exactly what happened." He poised to take notes.

"Exactly? If you say so." Ever grinned for just a moment before their expression soured. "I keep thinking he's going to come out that door. You won't let us see him?"

"Trust me when I say you don't want to." Impatience crept into Zach's voice. "So the meeting?"

"Meeting nothing! I came down, knocked on the door and he opened it. He had this smile, ear to ear. Here he was, admitting that he wanted me back, that he was ready to tell the world. He wasn't wearing a thing, and I couldn't help myself. I kissed him, and he returned it, just like the old days. I got him on the bed, ass down on the pillow and—"

"Ok, maybe not that much detail." Zach felt the heat in his cheeks already.

"I love making boys squirm! Adorable!" The grin came back, but there was a sadness to Ever's eyes that somewhat confirmed what Zach had considered the day before. Ever's over-the-top personality was largely for show.

"After the…?"

"The sex. After we had sex, Braxton pulled out a bottle of whiskey, and we relaxed in the tub for, oh, an hour."

At about eleven-forty, Zach remembered, the bathtub had filled up for the second time of the night. Braxton had used the tub just before Zach had settled into bed, which was what had prompted him to stay up and record what he noticed. Zach had fallen asleep before the second visitor, evidently Ever, had left.

"An hour?" Zach made a note of it. "Didn't the water get cold?"

"Nope! There were these jets, you know?" Ever mimed the shape of the tub. "I don't know how they did it, but those things always had hot water. Kept us warm and toasty!"

"What did you talk about?"

"Oh, that…" Ever frowned. "You know, he was ready. He was going to come out here and tell everyone about us. And I wanted it. I'd waited so long for it. I'm my own person, and he'd hurt me bad back at school, but I was ready too. He said he couldn't live without me, and—"

For the first time, Ever's façade cracked and tears came to their clear blue eyes. "And I guess he really couldn't."

Ty called across the room. "Hey, what'd you say to make Ever cry?"

Ever's dam broke. They whirled and pointed a finger towards the group. "Which one of you did this? Which one? He was ready! Finally ready!"

The room fell silent. Zach wanted to get the last bit of the story, but he knew when to keep his mouth shut and just watch.

Kris was the first to speak. "Ever, no, you didn't want him back, did you? After how he left you?"

"Whatever!" The words came amid thick tears. "We were kids then! Everybody was telling him what he should look like or how he should act. We made it! We didn't have to be other people anymore!"

At some point, while Zach had been questioning Ever, Roxie had dried up and her face had grown long with the exhaustion finally settling in. "Ever," she said, "you've never been anyone other than you."

"Yeah, sure, but it was hard for Braxton." Ever's tears had stopped and their voice had taken on an edge. "It took twenty years, but he finally got it. Then one of you assholes took him from me! I waited so long!"

It seemed overwrought, but Zach wondered if that was just who Ever was. Underneath the flippancy and the flirting, there was a scared person who had been waiting their whole life for one domino to fall. Or was the sorrow the act, put on for the benefit of two investigators?

When no one could find something to say to Ever, Zach decided it was his time. "Ever, one last thing. What happened when you left?"

The question threw them off. "When I left? I got out of the tub and dried off, put on my clothes and left. Braxton thought it would be too shocking for me to stay the night. Oh, I wanted to, but he said no! So I left him in the bath. I was getting wrinkly anyway."

Andrew cleared his throat. "Why didn't you mention this earlier?"

"I…" Once again, Ever's façade faltered and tears rolled gently down their cheeks. "I didn't think it was right. He'd promised to tell everyone today, and then he couldn't. So… I didn't. I was going to carry it in my heart forever."

Zach made his final notes and handed his phone to Andrew. He blinked several times, hands together against his mouth, thinking it over.

"I think I know who killed Braxton," he said eventually. He kept his voice low so everyone would have to lean in to hear him. "But I need something to tie it together. A key to this mystery."

"Zachary, that's it!" Andrew strode over to Zach and patted him on the back. "A key! The door was locked, just like the door downstairs. These doors don't have turn locks on the inside."

Roxie shot Ty a deadly look. "Don't I know it."

"So, the killer is the one with the key," Andrew said. He pointed at Kris. "You're the one who unlocked the door earlier!"

Kris took a step back and a confused look came over her. "I—what?"

"No," Zach said. His voice was clear and solid. "You had to get the key from someone else. You gave it to someone yesterday." He turned, looking the culprit straight in the eye. "You had the key, didn't you, Ty?"

The man jumped and turned to run, but he'd cornered himself in the kitchen. On one side stood Roxie and Kris. The other had Andrew and Zach. There was nowhere to run. He hung his head and slid down the wall onto the floor. A wail rose from somewhere deep inside him.

"I already knew it," Zach said, "before the key came up, because when we first discussed the murder, you said 'Guess if I'd been stuck' and scratched your back. No one had seen how Braxton had died except me. So I knew back then."

Ever launched at Ty as the truth apparently finally sunk in. "Why'd you do it? Why? Tell me!" Andrew, always stronger than he looked, managed to hold the model back, though it looked like a losing battle.

Ty didn't answer, so Zach answered for him. "The book set it off. It was too close to the truth. And it had something in it that Ty had blamed himself for. The club got shut down because of him, or so he'd thought, but the book told a different story. That's why you came, right Ty? To determine if it was true? And Ever here—"

"I told him." Shakes overcame Ever's body. "I… I said it was the truth. I… Braxton is dead because…"

Kris shook her head slowly. "Ever, he was going to figure it out eventually."

"So," Roxie said, "it had nothing to do with any relationship?"

"Naw." Ty glanced up. His voice came out like a croak. "It's not always some romance shit Roxie. He ruined me. I took leave, lost my scholarship, quit school, all because I thought I'd messed up the club and all our futures. Then you all blasted up and I… I'm still working retail. And I did the shitty job, cause I knew it was my fault. But then, the book comes out and… well you know the rest."

The confession hung in the air like a gun had gone off. Then, something broke, and people began to move. Kris brandished the key and suggested locking Ty up until they could get a signal through. They settled on an upstairs bathroom. The man was a shell of his former rage, barely responding as the group pulled him up the steps, through his own room, and locked him in. The idea there was that he was out of the way, but he could get water from the tap if he needed it.

That settled, the group got working on trying to contact anyone from down the mountain.

*****

"I hate phones!" For the fifth time, Kris grumbled from the bottom of the stairs where she had perched. She had discarded her parka, complaining that it was too warm. She later complained that the wind was too loud, the steps were too hard, and that she was too cold. She had a headache, and had been vocal about how staring at a screen trying to get a call or a message through had caused it, and that, of course, was all Andrew's fault.

He did his best to ignore her. In fact, he had positioned himself at the kitchen island so that he didn't have to see all the scowls, sighs, and stretching she did pointedly in his direction. It was unwarranted, anyway. Zachary had been the one to give out the instructions, but for some reason, she was annoyed with Andrew.

She had a point. Phones were annoying. Someday, Andrew hoped, they would replace phones with something more reliable, but he knew it was just wishful thinking from a bad situation. Phones were fine. He used phones often to trawl news sites for cases that he and Zachary might take. And to look for news about *her*, but thinking about her was worse than thinking about the dead body putrefying in a bath not twenty feet away.

Andrew assumed that most of the others had driven it from their minds, like Kris apparently had. Roxie had taken back her spot in the alcove where she'd started the morning. Ever sprawled out on the leather sectional, holding a phone above them as they tapped the screen. Zachary looked lost in thought, leaning against the far end of the island.

Then again, Zachary could compartmentalize anything and focus on a task that needed doing. Almost too well. His laser focus was a great boon in investigating mysteries, but it also made him forget about everything else around him. It had gotten him in trouble a few times. Once, Zachary had almost been lost. The sight of him nearly shunted over the brink had stuck with Andrew. If anything had actually happened, Andrew would have quit the whole thing, stuck to photography, actual photography, and never put someone in danger again.

But Zachary hadn't let it get to him. He had learned from the experience and he kept going. The man had a great sense of justice. Andrew wondered if it could ever be shaken. He doubted it.

Since he had been just sitting there watching Zachary for uncountable minutes, Andrew decided on a break. He shifted over to the stool closest to Zachary and peeked at the man's phone. He was writing something in his notes app, probably what he was going to present to the police when, if, they ever arrived.

"Hey slacker," Andrew said and gave Zachary a pat on the back.

The man jumped and nearly dropped the phone. "Don't—You made me write 'contortionist' into the report!" He hastily replaced the word with "confabulated" and turned the screen off. "Anyway, I'm writing a report on the investigation. Someone has to."

"Just say 'lied' instead of that two-dollar word," Andrew suggested. Before Zachary could explain why confabulated was the right word, Andrew asked, "What part are you on?"

"The wine in the refrigerator."

"Oh, that, yeah." Andrew glanced at the bottle still sitting nearby, untouched since earlier. "You know, I don't get that."

"What about it?"

"Well, what was his game plan there?" Andrew shrugged. "He wasn't wearing gloves. Didn't see any yesterday, or in his room. So… how was he going to get away with it?"

"People aren't perfect, Andrew." Even still, a frown came over Zachary's face. "It does seem particularly short-sighted, though. That bottle hasn't been wiped down. I doubt the knife has either. Though the knife could be explained since we all had one last night."

"Yeah," Andrew said. "So what was he planning? Or, maybe it wasn't planned at all."

"Huh? What do you mean?" Whenever Zachary got caught off-guard, he squinted. "It was clearly planned. He'd gone through that book with ink and highlighter."

"Ok, so, yeah, he wanted to have it out with Braxton, but kill him?" Andrew shrugged. "I don't think he decided that until last night."

"You mean when the argument happened?" Zachary turned his screen on and looked through his notes. "Not until Ever mentioned the truth about the ending, right?"

Andrew nodded, but something seemed off about that. "Was it Ever who mention that? The ending?"

"Well, they confirmed that the ending was mostly true," Zachary said. "But that doesn't feel right, either."

Silence filled the air between them. Andrew could feel the heat radiating off his fellow investigator. The man always heated up like an engine when he was in work mode.

"I got it! I got through!" The shout came from the alcove.

Abandoning their discussion, Andrew rushed over to Roxie. "What? Finally!"

Roxie shied away from the crowd gathering around her. "It's just a text message, but it went through and didn't turn red for a whole minute."

She held up the phone so they could see. It read, "Send help. Lodge 87. Snowed in. Send police. One man dead." Simple and to the point, just like Zachary had instructed.

A minute passed before a new text bubble appeared. "Clearing the road now. Police alerted. They're sending officers via chopper. Is everyone else ok?"

A cheer erupted from the group as they stared at the tiny message. Something had finally gone right. When the high from the relief began to wear off several minutes later, Andrew slid into the seat next to Roxie.

She laughed. "I'm glad you two were here! I wasn't going to call anyone, but when I talked to Kris about it, I got so nervous that I decided to do it anyway."

Zachary, from the chair across, shook his head. "We really didn't do much. The police would have figured it out."

"Yeah, Ty wasn't very careful," Andrew said.

"What do you mean?" Ever settled into the seat next to Zachary. For a moment, it looked like Zachary was going to be engulfed by a cotton-candy serpent, but Ever relented at the last moment.

"Oh, fingerprints," Zachary said. "He would have been caught easily."

The thought from earlier came back to Andrew. "Ever, why'd you mention the ending like you did? Last night I mean."

"Of the book?" Ever thought for a moment. "I don't know. We were talking about it already, weren't we?"

"Oh, yeah," Roxie said. "That was Braxton, wasn't it?"

"No." Zachary had opened his notes again. "I remember him trying to steer the conversation away from the ending."

"Kris, was it you?" Roxie looked around to find her friend. "Oh, where's Kris?"

The group looked around for her but she was nowhere to be found. The howling wind was the only sound, and that, too, abated. Then something floated down from above them. Voices.

Andrew held a finger to his lips and crept toward the stairs. The wind whipped up again, drowning out the sound of the voice, but also muffling footfalls as he carefully climbed, step by step.

The upper landing had a circular layout with four doors right at the top of the stairs. The voices, somewhat clearer now, came through the crack under the door to Kris's room. Andrew glanced back to find that Zachary, quiet as a mouse, had followed, the others still downstairs.

Leaning low over the crack, Andrew listened.

"What do you think is going to happen?" The voice was low, but unmistakably belonging to Kris. "They're going to let you go? Look, I helped you out with the bottle, but they've got you dead to rights."

There was a pause. Another voice, more muffled, floated through. It was too garbled to hear, but along with it came the sounds of sobbing. Ty must have been upset, but crying? Something about that worried Andrew.

Kris answered the voice. "Yeah, I got what I wanted, but I can't help you."

After a short pause, Kris gave a single, short laugh. "I'd like to see you prove it. You killed him, and that's all they care about. Just because I pushed you doesn't mean anything."

There was silence for a moment, then a quiet sound that Andrew couldn't make out. From the other side of the door, Kris sighed. "I can't help you. You're the only one who can help you now. Like I said before. I mean, what will it matter? You lost everything when you dropped out. You're working a dead-end job. You don't even own a house. You're 39 Ty. It's too late for you! Now you're going to spend the rest of your life in jail. There's really only one option."

A long, chopping sob came from the other side of the door. No, that was wrong. It wasn't a sob, but it was water. Andrew's mind raced. The bedroom connected to a bathroom. Where they had locked Ty. The long bathroom. For the bathtub. The tub!

Andrew barreled through the door. Kris knelt by the door, head bent low, and she jumped to her feet at the sound of Andrew's entrance. She blocked the door. Andrew shoved her out of the way. He produced the key. In seconds, Andrew flung the bathroom door open and leapt to the tub.

Ty's head lolled just under the water. His eyes were open but drooped in a tiredness that Andrew had seen only a few times before. The water soaked through Andrew's shirt as he reached in the tub and pulled Ty from the depths. The sound of dripping water cascaded on the tile, accompanied by the raking sounds escaping Ty's mouth.

Andrew's put his hands on the center of Ty's chest and compressed again and again. Some water trickled out of the dazed man's mouth, but it wasn't enough. Bending low over Ty's mouth, Andrew pinched the man's nose and forced air into his lungs. Twice.

After a few more compressions, a gout of water escaped Ty's lips, along with sputtering and gasping. His eyes didn't open much, still lazy and drooping, but the water looked better on the floor than inside Ty. Andrew tilted the man on his side and more water drained out, along with a little bit of yellow foam. Something small and white drifted out and mixed with the water and bile.

On the floor was an orange bottle of white pills marked zolpidem. Kris had mentioned taking a "zolly" the night before. A sigh escaped his lips as he noticed the bottle was still mostly full. Ty hadn't taken very many.

Already, Ty seemed a little more awake, the shock perhaps taking its toll. Andrew pulled the man up into a seated position. "Hey, Ty," he said. "Stay with me here."

Andrew looked back into the room. With the commotion, Roxie and Ever had joined Zachary, and the three of them had latched onto Kris. She sat on the floor, back against the bed, with her hands restrained on either side.

The minutes seemed to go on for hours, but eventually Ty leaned over and vomited in the nearby toilet. Amid the stinking bile, more half-digested pills sank into the muck. After, his eyes stopped fluttering closed. Dark circles lined his eyes, and every part of his face sagged, but he was going to pull through.

Andrew turned his attention on Kris, who sat there looking smug. He nodded at her. "What's got you so high on your horse?"

She shook her head and widened her eyes. "Oh, I'm just glad you got there in time. I didn't have the key, and I was so concerned! That's what I'm going to say at least. And they'll believe me. I'm a respected scientist."

A tin voice floated into the room. "Yeah, I got what I wanted, but I can't help you."

Kris snapped a sour scowl to the side where Zachary sat holding up his phone. "Miss Stevenson," he said, "you may be a scientist, but surely you haven't forgotten that phones can record without a connection, right?"

The scowl became a yell as Kris's face turned red and shook. "You give that! Erase it! Let me go!" She pulled at her hands, forming claws as she did. Ever flexed and yanked a hand down, showcasing the strength of their toned model muscles, eliciting a yelp from Kris. She struggled again, but her mouth closed into a thin, neutral line, then she slumped her shoulders and stared off into space.

Roxie was the first to break the silence? "Why Kris?"

"Why? Why?! Because of you! Because of me! Because of all the women he threw away so he didn't have to admit it to himself. He used you. He used me. Then he ran away! He even ran away from Ever!"

"Shut up," Ever said. "You know how hard it was for him. The pressures people put on him. Hell, you knew when you got together he wasn't over me. You tried to do it anyway."

"It didn't stop at college, you know." Kris spat the words rather than spoke them. "After he dropped you, Roxie, he went from one woman to the next. I kept tabs on it over the years. Twelve women. He ruined them, because he was so kind, so good, so driven, so perfect. Then he left. Broke their hearts. He was a flawed little boy scared and running away. And he knew it! I couldn't let another man get away with it!"

"Another man?" The words came out of Roxie's mouth slow. "Are you talking about your dad? Kris, he died in the Gulf War."

Kris yanked against the hands restraining her. "No, he didn't! He can't have! He was at school, watching me. You wrote about him in the book! I don't know why I didn't realize before."

A growl issued from Roxie's throat. "I keep telling everyone. The book isn't real! I made people up! Maybe I made someone who looks like your dad, I don't know. You were always showing me photos."

Zachary's voice came out slow and even. "So, because Braxton ruined you, like your father did by dying in that war, you decided to ruin him?" Andrew could only half see the man, and didn't want to leave Ty alone, but he could feel the look on Zachary's face. It was the same look he got when he'd discovered a killer. That round, light brown face with narrowed, black eyes that could pierce through you like blades.

Kris only stared through into empty space. Zachary continued. "You don't get it, do you? You made your choices and tried to steer him away from his heart. But in the end, you decided to become exactly what you hated about him. Abandoning people? You abandoned every one of your friends the moment you planned this. Making sure the storm would hit on the right weekend? Getting Roxie to bring along someone to blame Ty with authority? Destroying any amount of happiness that Ever could have had? You didn't just abandon them. You used them. Then you were ready to throw Ty away like he was garbage!"

A stillness fell over them as the words sunk in, but Zachary wasn't done. "And it was all pointless anyway! Braxton had reconciled. He realized what he'd done. He was ready to admit the wrongs he'd done. But you're not able to admit your wrongs, are you? So are you any worse than the demon you've created in your own mind? If I'd only realized it last night, how you pulled the strings like some puppeteer!"

Kris only stared off into space. Her eyes bored holes in Andrew, deep as bullet wounds, but there was no emotion there anymore. She had lost, she had failed, and she had given up.

A great whooshing overcame the sound of wind and snow that still swirled outside. Andrew let his shoulders relax as he recognized the sound of a helicopter's blades. Zachary stood and looked out the window of the bedroom, which faced the drive. "The police. There's just enough space there to land, thank goodness."

Andrew looked between Ty and Kris. It was going to be hard to get Ty any consolation for his role in the night's proceedings, but he was going to try. The man was a weapon, not a killer, and the true mastermind was caught.

Even still. There was a lot of explaining ahead of Andrew, and it wasn't going to be easy. He looked at Zachary. The man stood there, staring at the woman, and his eyes were hollow. Even harder than telling the police, Andrew realized, would be convincing Zachary it wasn't his fault.

Memindip and the Persian Poet
Jay Andrew Connor
1

As my on-again off-again friend, Adagouti, will readily tell you, Life can become very complex. Especially the second time around, as a Private Investigator.

— Death still has her eyes on you. She is like a leopard who hasn't eaten for a week. She's hungry for you.

— But I still have the good favour of Be'kal?

— For the moment. But he won't protect you forever. You need to prove yourself worthy of this opportunity—that you are still a righter of wrongs, a voice for the innocent, an avenger for justice. You just have to keep doing that in order to keep the Higher Powers appeased.

— But apart from having Tomaso Akriki's body and odd memories, I am still Memindip, of the Lazera tribe, a noble North African offshoot of the Psylli.

Adagouti glares at me like a lioness defending her kill.

— No. You are the late Memindip, of the long departed Lazera, who was caught trying to cheat a Portuguese trader by selling him quartz instead of diamonds. The fact that he killed you with an ornate bejewelled dagger in 1701 is a moot, albeit understandable, point. The fact that the wandering remains of your tribe buried you without correct ritual and ceremony, creating your corporeal presence, is not a moot point but the bane of my very existence!

Adagouti has never forgiven me for the mistakes he made during my rebirth. His wrinkled, tortoise-like head bobs up and down several times, then he says:

— As you are now an investigator, you'll need to find a new cause to champion. It's the only choice you have if you wish to keep this second life of yours for as long as you can.

I'm about to ask where I would find such a thing, when the ringing of my alarm clock on the nightstand brings me back from my dream land.

Background noise from the city street mixes with that from inside my 4th floor manzil, which means Marzouk is already preparing breakfast.

I wash the sleep from my body then offer up a short prayer to Opoula, the water goddess, before adding a small drop of my blood to the water. In doing so I return to her the two fluids of life as I empty the bowl.

So far this second life has been good. But as Adagouti knows, the money left in the back of the sleeping room closet by the late Tomaso Akriki will not last indefinitely. And without that, how will I afford such things as my weekly housekeeper? Or Marzouk, come to that?

As I walk into the kitchen and dining area, I am still amazed by what I've been told is a calendar, hanging on the wall. Marzouk has crossed off another square, indicating that today is Tuesday, March 4th, 1969.

He greets me with, "Good morning, Sayidi." Then puts a bowl of fresh cut bread on the table, followed by two plates of khlea and eggs, scrambled the American way, or so he assures me. I sip my tea, take a piece of bread, and start to eat.

After a silent five minutes, Marzouk asks, "Forgive me, but is everything okay with you, Sayidi? You appear tense—stressed even. I take it you slept well?"

"I slept. But all it confirmed was that I should be wary of a nearby leopard."

Marzouk becomes slightly agitated. "You are talking about a dream, aren't you, Sayidi? As far as I know, Ekpe has been outlawed for some time."

I look up from my breakfast. "I'm talking about Death herself, alsinijab alsaghir. What is this Ekpe?"

"A disbanded and condemned secret leopard cult that practiced murder, so it could indulge in cannibalism, Sayidi."

I smile and take another piece of bread. "Sadly, that might be preferable to wondering when Death will strike her bargain with the Gods, then take me by surprise."

Marzouk takes another piece of bread before casually continuing the conversation.

"To be forever looking over your shoulder cannot be good for your health. What you need, Sayidi, is a relaxing shave and a haircut—20 fils."

"And for that price the service is good?"

"The place I always recommended to my passengers is in the Turkish district. Mehmet Jakar is the finest barber, shaver, and Indian head masseuse, in the whole of this city."

"And you use him yourself?"

"Alas Sayidi, would that I could afford such a regular luxury. But if I could, then most certainly I'd visit him should I have need of his services."

I look closely at Marzouk, unable to tell if he speaks the truth, or lies as fluently as a member of the city's legal profession. I say, "Would I be able to get an appointment to be ministered to by one so famous?"

Marzouk smiles, "A word from me and he would refuse the king himself."

2

After a 20 minute journey of barely missed collisions and several hand gestures I've not seen before, Marzouk parks up alongside a single storey barber's shop in what appears to be a backstreet, off the main souk, in the Turkish district of the city. As he drives off in a haze of exhaust smoke, he calls out, "I'll be back in an hour, Sayidi."

Five minutes later I am in the large chrome and black leather chair, tilted backwards, face wrapped in hot towels. The air smells of bay rum, cloves, cigars and pomade. On one side I can hear Mehmet as he strops a razor. From the other the noise of the street outside through the open doorway. A brown Bakelite radio on the windowsill is powered from the same light socket as the hair clippers. From the speaker comes the BBC World Service at a low volume.

Behind me I hear a rustle as someone enters and sits on one of several chairs against the back wall. Moments later a woman's voice asks, "Are you Tomaso Memindip, the private detective who was in the newspapers recently? You solved a murder before the police did."

Mehmet removes the towel covering my mouth, then goes back to slowly stropping the razor.

Cautious, I say, "Yes, I am that Tomaso Memindip."

After a decision-making hesitation, she continues with the conversation. "My name is Anita Purkell. I believe my brother, Dante, is missing. I want you to find him."

I fold the towel away from my eyes. The large mirror in front of me reflects a young woman—maybe 25 or 26—light brown hair and European complexion rather than Afrikaans, her accent tinged with Northern Italian. She's wearing a silk headscarf of watercolour poppies on a milk cream background, the design out-shining her light cotton dress—though her eyes are hidden behind round blind-beggar sunglasses.

Mehmet removes the remaining towels, and before he coats my face with shaving soap, I ask, "How do you know he's missing? Have you talked to the police? Hospitals? Other members of your family? Has he perhaps been declared a dissident and is hiding from the militia?"

Having worked the soap up into a lather, Mehmet deftly coats my cheeks, chin and neck with foam, before picking up the cutthroat razor and scraping it off with the newly honed blade.

As he shaves me, Ms Purkell continues, "I've already checked the hospitals for the last week. The police? They've shown no interest in looking into his disappearance. So when a taxi driver handed me your card, I decided to see if you could help. To answer your last question, my brother isn't an activist. He has no interest in politics."

"A taxi driver?" As best I remember, Marzouk had retired his permit when he became my assistant.

"Yes, White Knight Cabs. He said he worked for a member of your agency. Marzouk something-or-other."

"So how did you know where to find me?"

"The driver said you'd be here before ten today for your regular hot towel and massage. If I needed something solving, then I should talk to you. I visited the library first thing this morning, read about you in the newspapers, and thought you might be able to help me." She pauses and wrinkles her nose. "If you're not interested then I'll try and find someone else."

As she starts to leave, I remember Adagouti's words about staying in the favour of the Gods. "I haven't said I'll not take your case."

"So you will?"

"I'll need more details before I decide. And we need to discuss my fee…."

She sits back down again. "I'm not sure what happened. We used to be so close, but something's changed. He became furtive—secretive—and nervous. Then I received a letter saying he needed to go away for a while—some kind of large project that required his full attention. But to just leave without talking to me first is something he'd never do. That's how I knew something was wrong."

"Did the letter say where he was going?"

"No. Just that the only way he could concentrate was through total isolation."

Mehmet finishes my shave, wipes away the excess soap, then picks up the electric clippers. "Trim? It's an all in price."

"No, this is more than enough." I get up and look directly at Ms Purkell. "You have the card from the taxi driver?" She nods, and hands it to me. It looks almost identical to the ones I carry—except in place of my name is *The Fourth Floor Detective Agency*. I hand it back to her. "If you could visit my, er, office? Say 3pm this afternoon?"

"Whatever. I just want to find Dante. Or at least know he's safe and well."

I watch her go, then turn to Mehmet. "I understand you do the relaxing head massage?"

The barber nods and smiles, flexing and cracking his fingers.

I get back in the chair. "Ten minutes. Then I have a little squirrel to skin."

3

Across the dining table, Marzouk says, "But, Sayidi, how are we going to get people to come to us if we don't advertise?" He has a point, but I don't want to concede it.

I look at the clock—ten minutes to 3—then at Marzouk. "We'll discuss this matter later, but for now what've you learned about this Anita Purkell?"

"She works for Laverne and Maples, a legal firm dealing exclusively with International import and export. She's their translator—Arabic, French, English—contracts, licences, that sort of thing."

"So she is someone of importance?"

"You'd think, as their chief translator and transcriber, but her clothing says otherwise. Not short of money, but frugal."

I remember her appearance earlier. Quality silk headscarf, but cheaper cotton frock. "And her brother?"

"Alas, Sayidi, none of the drivers know anything about him. If he takes taxis then they're not from the White Knight Company."

I look at Marzouk incredulously. "They're your source of information?"

"A very reliable source. People talk to drivers, and drivers remember details that passengers believe to be inconsequential."

"And do you gossip about me?"

"Sayidi, please. We are the Fourth Floor Detective Agency. Information is our business."

"Which is another thing—" There is a knock on the door "—that we will need to discuss later. Go, welcome Miss Purkell to our manzil."

4

Anita Purkell sits back in the Colonial club style chair. "No, I didn't save the envelope, so I've no idea what the postmark was."

We're in the living room at the back of the apartment. Large sliding glass doors leading out onto the balcony face two comfortable chairs and a sofa, so occupants can see across part of the city. While Marzouk prepares tea, I sit in the other single chair and ask some questions.

"The letter mentions a project? What does your brother do?"

"He's a printer and book binder by trade. Sometimes he helps with restoration and preservation projects for libraries and the like. That's when his assistant takes over, so he can concentrate on whatever he needs to. But when I asked, Constantine says he had no idea that Dante had taken on another contract. He'd found a note two weeks ago, pushed under the shop door. It was similar to the letter. An additional contract that would take up all of his time, and that he trusted Constantine to complete and finish off any outstanding work on the order book. That's why the police are disinterested. They took the letter and note at face value, which is why they don't believe me."

I make a pretence of mulling things over, then, "Okay, 500 dirham a week, plus expenses. And that doesn't guarantee success. I'll also need the address of your brother's business."

She opens her shoulder bag and removes 5 notes from a small roll. "I just want to know he's safe and well." Small notebook and slim gold pencil provides the address. "Constantine lives above the shop and often works late to clear any backlog." She looks at me as Marzouk brings tea. Once poured, she asks, "Do you need anything else?"

"Only a photograph of your brother."

She delves back into her bag and presents me with a passport and an expired travel document. "These are the best I could find at short notice."

She sips tea as I look at the small monochrome picture stapled to the visa before passing the paperwork over to Marzouk. A young man, early 30s, dark black hair, bright intelligent eyes, goatee beard. Marzouk carefully removes the staples. "This should be adequate for our purposes. I assume he still has the beard?"

Ms Purkell smiles. "Yes. Despite my comments, he's still kept it."

Then we both rise and go to the front door, which Marzouk opens ahead of us. As she leaves, she turns. "I have a terrible feeling he's in some kind of trouble."

I smile to try and calm her. "We shall see what we shall see."

<h1 style="text-align:center">5</h1>

The following day, after breakfast and an unnervingly uneventful journey across the city, Marzouk drops me off at *Kitab Tabiea*, Dante's business address. I tell Marzouk to wait, and when I enter the print shop I'm greeted by tall, stocky Constantine. He is an old Greek in his fifties—neck like a bull and dark eyes, deeper than a man's soul. His hands look like they have splashes of black ink forever ingrained under the skin.

I shake his hand, saying, "I am Tomaso Memindip," as I pass him one of my cards.

"Coffee?" He indicates a stainless steel electric percolator to the side of an old floor standing printing press.

"Thank you, yes."

As he pours two cups I move a pile of untrimmed handbills from a chair seat and sit by his workbench-cum-desk.

He adds sugar and as he brings it over, I say, "I'm searching for Dante Purkell. I've been asked to look into his disappearance."

"I know. Anita told me last night. But according to the police he's not missing."

"And you?"

"Maybe. Maybe not. The letter and note could be forged, or he just had a bad day working on some difficult engraving, or woodcut, and his hands were hurting from too much tool work."

I look over the workbench. "So if he has a new job, where does he work? Obviously not here."

"We can't store chemicals in the shop—not even in a locked cabinet. The city's worried in case they can be used for bomb making. Maybe, if you were a knowledgeable chemist and had a secret laboratory." He shakes his head dismissively. "The gendarmes search us regularly. They also check everything we print, in case we're stupid enough to run off a thousand copies of some political manifesto, and keep them here on show. Dante has his own workshop, about half way between here and Fehmal. Head towards there and you can't miss it. It's built out of the remains of the old Legion outpost. Dante has it on a long term lease."

I look at him and take a gamble. "And did you find anything when you were last there?"

He smiles. "You're sharp. After Anita visited a week ago I took a trip up there. It looked like it had been searched, but whoever had done the searching had been careful not to leave the workshop in a state. Dante is very particular about his tools, and to me it was obvious they had been disturbed. I could tell as someone had put them back in the wrong order. Plus," He opens a drawer in the bench. "There were these papers in a makeshift fire. Dante would never burn anything in the workshop in case the smoke got into the book he was working on."

Constantine hands me several pieces of quality writing paper, one with a printed ornate letterhead above a typewritten letter—the address, scorched, but unburned, *The Museum of Antiquities*. Some of the pieces have large smears of what looks like a heavy yellowish oil— slightly sticky, and not absorbed well by the paper.

He goes back to the percolator and refills his cup. "I've told no one about them. After I took them I thought better of it, but didn't want to be caught putting them back. You can keep them, if you think they'll do you any good. Oh, and when you find Dante? Tell him he now owes me for six weeks work."

I pick up an envelope from the bench and slip the half burned pieces into it. As I start to leave, I ask, "Do I need a key?"

"Side windowsill, third flowerpot from the left."

Back in the Chrysler, Marzouk is eager for excitement. "Where to now, Sayidi?"

I pause, then decide that Dante's workshop can wait. "I need to go to the Museum of Antiquities. How soon do you think you can get us there?"

Marzouk looks at his newly purchased wristwatch, and I wonder if 100 dirham a month is perhaps an overly generous salary. "Ten, maybe fifteen minutes."

"Then let's get going before the sun becomes unbearable."

"Right, Sayidi, the museum it is!" And with a twist of the steering wheel we are back into the chaos that is the city's traffic system.

6

The Museum is an oasis of cool marble and overhead fans—several Egyptian statues grace the sides of the double height entrance hall, which is busy with tourists sightseeing and workmen putting up large pin boards and posters advertising an upcoming exhibition. Central to the area is a large circular desk with *Information* written on a sign hanging above it.

As I step up to the counter, an attentive young woman smiles, and asks, "How can we help you today?" Definitely not a local official.

"I'd like to see," I look at the name I've written on the back of the envelope—silently blaming Marzouk's driving for my inabilities with writing implements. "Doctor Keyatta. I'm trying to trace someone he wrote to recently."

She turns and points to a tall man standing near a set of stairs leading to the next floor. "He's over there, organising the new display. On Saturday an original copy of the Shahnameh will be on view. It's one of only five copies known to have survived from the 11th Century."

I head towards the person indicated, saying, "Thank you, I'll endeavour to ask of it when we speak."

Engrossed in his work, Keyatta's dark skin is emphasised by his white shirt and light fawn trousers—and he appears overly tall to those around him. Zulu origins perhaps?

Keyatta looks up as I approach. "I need more pin boards. We're trying to make this an event not to be missed, but…." His voice tails off as he realises his mistake.

I clear my throat. "I am the detective Tomaso Memindip, and I'd like to discuss the disappearance of Dante Purkell," I hold up the envelope, "And why someone would wish to burn a letter with your signature on it."

"Disappearance? We still need two more posters for the Shahnameh display." He takes the envelope from me, lifts the flap and looks at the half burned papers. "This is the work order for those pieces. Six large black and white posters of the Shahnameh, open at an illuminated page, and the artwork hand coloured so that it stands out. Eye catching." He puts the damaged papers into the envelope and hands it back to me.

I push the conversation forward. "When did Dante deliver the last one?"

"The order is for six in total, but we only received the fourth one several days ago. Dante's helper—the Greek—he delivers them."

I look at the 4ft high poster to the side of a large empty glass cabinet. Soft focus black and white, with the pages of the open book a bright splash of multi-coloured detail. Across the top if it are the words:

The Persians — An Historical Retrospective

As I study it, impressed by the beauty of the artwork, Keyatta says:

"We took our copy of the Shahnameh to the National Museum in Cairo, and they verified my authentication as correct. It's from the original copy studio that Ferdowsi used to publish his epic poem. Fifty thousand distichs." He looks at me enquiringly, then adds "Couplets. Two line verses?"

I don't mention that I remember hearing a travelling Storyman recite sections of it, one evening, around a large fire which, according to Adagouti, was on the evening of June 18th, 1693. Instead I just nod and smile.

Keyatta continues, "The exhibition opens with a special preview on Friday, which gives us just today and tomorrow to get the posters and put them in the right places. At this rate we'll be working well into

Friday morning. Will you be coming to the opening?"

I shake my head. "I'm committed to this investigation."

Keyatta carefully looks about us, then says, "Would you care to see the Shahnameh before we put it into the display case?"

"Is such possible?"

"For a relatively small donation—to the Museum, of course."

I take a 20 dirham note from my wallet. Keyatta silently looks at it, then up at me, his hands still by his sides. I reach back in and add another 20, to which he smiles, folds the money into his trouser pocket, and leads the way back to his office.

Closing the door behind us, he moves to a large safe set in the back wall. As he spins the combination dial, he says, "I have it here. We needed it out of the vault so it could be photographed, and then taken to Cairo for authentication."

"But you were sure it was an original before then?"

"Of course. I authenticated it myself after I discovered it in one of the old vault storage boxes."

From inside the safe he takes out a pair of white cotton gloves and puts them on before removing the bound work. Carefully he places it on the blotter of his desk and starts opening it at various bookmarked pages.

The illustrations are breath-taking—their quality and colours powerful enough to snare the viewer into looking deeper, discovering detail that would be missed by a casual glance. Keyatta turns to another section, and we are transported from the court of Hushang to the exploits of Kai Khosrow.

Keyatta says, "The poet died almost penniless, having lost the support of his patron and benefactor over religious beliefs." He closes the book, puts it back in the safe along with the white gloves, and re-spins the dial. Security done, he escorts me back to the Information desk.

"Should you visit the museum on Friday for the preview opening, you'll find a lot more unique and wonderful items included in the exhibition. And if you cannot make it for the preview, then the pieces will be on show for the next 4 weeks."

"Thank you. I shall endeavour to visit if I can." Then I head out, passing between the giant Egyptian statues and into the late morning sunlight.

7

As I walk down the Museum steps towards Marzouk and his taxi, a booming voice behind me calls out, "Hey, Mr. Investigator, what are you doing here?"

Commandant Monnes, camel-coloured uniform sharply pressed, Sam Brown holster at his hip, comes down the steps towards me. "What are you and your little squirrel up to? And don't give me any of that righter of wrongs either. I now know all about the Fourth Floor Detective Agency."

I smile a greeting. "At present I am tasked to find a missing person. Dante Purkell." I pause to see if Monnes reacts to the name. He remains unresponsive, so I continue. "His sister has concerns about his welfare."

"And your business brought you here?"

I open the envelope and show him the oil-stained and charred remains of the letter. "His assistant found this partly burned when he was at their workshop near Fehmal. I wanted to talk to Doctor Keyatta about what the letter may have contained. He says it was for work printing and hand colouring posters for the upcoming display."

"The Shahnameh? My men and I have been run ragged checking and rechecking the security for this event."

"And you're sure the Shahnameh will be safe?"

Monnes glares at me. "Of course I'm sure." A short pause, then "Why? What do you know?"

I hold up my hands. "Nothing, I swear."

Monnes half smiles. "I doubt I'd believe you even if you did take an oath. Have you found anything else?"

"Nothing besides the half-burned letter."

"Well, it wasn't there when my gendarmes visited his workshop about two weeks ago."

I try not to sound surprised. "I was given it by Dante's assistant, Constantine. He said he found it the day after Dante's disappearance." I take a quick breath and see if he will talk more about the case. "His sister said you'd shown no interest."

"Actually she's his half-sister—different mothers. She came to us and when I found out about the Shahnameh connection I had two of my men do a discrete investigation. They found nothing untoward." Monnes holds out his hand, and I reluctantly give him the envelope as he asks, "Any more evidence you're withholding?"

I smile. "It's only evidence if there's been a crime committed." He glares at me, so I quickly add, "None as yet."

"Let's keep it that way." Then he carries on down the steps, pauses to glare at Marzouk in his taxi, before waving his arms and moving him on.

Two minutes later, after Marzouk has gone round the block, he parks back up alongside the museum steps.

"Where to now, Sayidi?"

"I think it's time to visit Dante's workshop."

8

The ride out is fairly uneventful, due to the lack of any oncoming traffic, and the fact it is getting too near midday to make long distance travel anything but uncomfortable. Down a dusty side road we come to what looks like an old single storey building of clay and daub—whitewashed walls and flat roof to keep the heat down. The wind powered water pump is static, but the sound of a generator at the back of the property is loud enough to indicate someone is at home. That, and the 1957 Ford pick-up truck parked outside.

Marzouk gets out, softly walks up to one of the front windows and takes a discrete look inside. Satisfied, he returns to the car.

"Well, Sayidi, it is not quite as we would've hoped."

"I take it Dante Purcell is not to be seen?"

"I saw only the big Greek. He seems to be working on something spread across a large draftsman's board. It looks like he's painting something."

"And no one else?"

"With the amount of benches and equipment, it would be hard for anyone not to be noticed."

"Still, let us both see what Constantine has to say for himself."

As quietly as possible I get out of the car and we walk up to the front door, Marzouk leading, his hand in his jacket pocket where I know he keeps a flick knife. When we reach the entrance, Marzouk moves to one side and I take hold of the door handle. I mentally prepare myself, then turn the handle. But instead of the expected resistance there isn't any, and I stumble through the doorway, almost tripping over the threshold board.

Startled by our entrance, Constantine exclaims, "Chazos!" before catching his breath, then adds, "Why couldn't you just knock like normal people?" He waves a hand at the massive black and white poster he's been working on. "Now I've got to clean the oil paint off and re-do that section. It's bad enough I'm having to finish these two and get them dried before tomorrow morning, without the likes of you and your sidekick scaring the Devil out of me. What do you want anyway?"

Marzouk remains silent while I explain. "We have come from the Museum of Antiquities, so we know you've been delivering the posters to Doctor Keyatta. But when I spoke to you at the shop in the city, you said Dante had taken the project on himself, using this workshop to complete the order. And here we are, finding that it's you who has been doing the work all along."

Constantine sits back on the draftsman's high stool, and puts the fine haired brush to one side. "Dante did the original research. He took all the photos, sourced the pigments and researched the old Persian methods for creating inks and illustration techniques. Me? I'm the one who gets dressed in leather aprons and heavy rubber gloves when it comes to developing photographic negatives and creating the metal etchings. Only in this case I didn't have to. Multiple screen prints, various coloured layers from black, through grey, to a very thin white overlay."

It's clear he's a craftsman who is passionate about his skills.

"So what happened to Dante?"

The Greek sighs. "I told you, I don't know. One day he's here discussing the project. Then he talks to his sister, and the next thing I know he's nowhere to be found."

"Do you know what they talked about? Did they quarrel?"

He sucks on a tooth, then, "I'm not really sure. They both went down into the cellar—it's where we keep acids, thinners, base paint oils—so I didn't hear anything. And when they came back up they were both silent. She left immediately. Dante showed me some of the photographs he'd taken at the museum, said he intended to colour the posters using oils, then left without saying where he was going."

"So who tried to burn the letter?"

"No idea. I locked up one evening, came back two days later and the half burned papers were on top of the carving bench, scattered with wood shavings and a pool of boiled linseed oil, all stone cold. Dante would never damage the bench doing something like that, plus boiled oil rarely ignites without some considerable heating first."

"And the spare key?"

"Still under the plant pot on the sill. It's not exactly a secret hiding place."

"And does Doctor Keyatta know it's you completing the work?"

"Probably not. All he cares about is the up-coming exhibition." He looks up at the clock on the far wall. "Now, if you're done, I've this poster to fix and spread on the drying frame outside. The midday sun gives the work the appearance of age—which is what Keyatta wants."

Marzouk is already heading towards the car when I turn and ask Constantine, "With Dante missing, who will Keyatta pay for the work?"

"Anita. She deals with that side of the business."

"So she has more concerns than just a missing brother?"

"Maybe. But that's a question you're going to have to ask her yourself. Now, if you don't mind?"

I nod my goodbye, and once in the back of the car I tell Marzouk, "Head back to the manzil. The sun is at midday, and neither of us are English."

He throws the car into gear, stamps down on the accelerator, and leaving a cloud of dust and the rattle of small stones behind us, we depart.

Back on the main road again, he asks, "What are your feelings about all of this, Sayidi?"

"I think something isn't right when Constantine is completing work and Dante is nowhere to be seen. I think it's time to talk to Ms Purkell again—but that will be after the heat is out of the day."

9

After a restful, Adagouti-free nap, I eventually retire to the living room. Looking out across part of the city, I am sitting with the telephone handset pressed against my ear. The secretary at Laverne & Maples has gone to check on whether Ms Purkell is at her desk, or away somewhere, though not before telling me that:

"She is an important person. She's always very busy and might not want to be disturbed." Then she adds, emphatically, "By anyone."

After several minutes, the secretary's voice comes back on the line. "Please wait while I connect you."

There is a loud click, an insistent buzzing like an angry bee, then Ms Purkell picks up the receiver.

"You have news?" Her voice sounds cold, though I've yet to get used to this impersonal form of communication.

"Not in regard to Dante, but I do have some questions that require answering." There's silence in my ear, so I continue. "Why didn't you tell me Dante is your step-brother?"

"Would it have made any difference?"

"No. But it would have been nice if you'd been honest with me from the start. Especially when I find out it's you who issues and clears the invoices for your brother's company."

"I don't see—"

I cut her off. "I'm assuming you need him to countersign bank drafts and cheques?"

"Yes, but—"

"So this is about Constantine's back wages?"

"No. I mean yes. Sort of. I need to transfer some funds in regard to several items Dante was commissioned to create and export. If they're stuck in the Freeport holding area then the buyers will demand their money back."

"And these items are?"

She hesitates, then says, "They are two facsimiles of the Shahnameh. Dante was allowed to take photographs of the original, but instead of taking a few, he took photographs of every page. He wasn't intending to sell the facsimiles as originals. He just created three. One for the Museum of Antiquities, and two others for private collectors of Persian literature. Those are the two which are held in the Freeport warehouse, in storage, waiting for him to sign the release papers."

"Who else knows about the copies?"

"Just us, as far as I know. The museum wouldn't be at all happy knowing what Dante's done. They've had their copy authenticated, but if word were to get out that it was their copy that's been copied, then I don't think they'd look to employ him on any more of their projects."

"And the buyers know they're purchasing copies, and not the real thing?"

She doesn't hesitate this time. "Yes! They knew from the start, when they commissioned them. I made sure that Dante had paperwork to that effect, just in case something went wrong and he was accused of forgery."

"And the copies? They're still in the holding shed?"

"Why shouldn't they be? No one has paid for their release or onward delivery. Until that's done then they're stuck there."

"And you still have no idea of where your stepbrother might be?"

She pauses, and when she speaks I can hear the emotion in her voice rather than the cold anger of frustration.

"Despite our differences he is still family. And that is something which is important to me."

"Above all else?"

There's another few seconds of thoughtful hesitation, then, "Yes. I cannot think of anything that would make me believe otherwise."

I say "Thank you," then put the handset back in its cradle, all the time trying to work out why I now feel uneasy at the way things are progressing.

10

As the Greenwich Time Signal peeps its last 'peeeeeep' from the speaker of the radiogram—indicating that it is now 10am, local time, Thursday March 6th, precisely—there is a knock at the front door of the manzil.

I wait for Marzouk to answer it, but on the third, more insistent series of thumps, I realise that Marzouk is still out on an errand.

I turn off the radio, calling out "I'm coming! Akbh jamah nafsak!" And when I open the front door, I'm greeted by the young gendarme I now know is called Nadeem Maleek. He smiles a weary smile.

"If I had any horses to hold, Mr Investigator, then I would hope they'd all be thoroughbreds."

I smile. Despite the young man's chosen profession, I still find myself liking him. Nodding a greeting, I ask, "I have tea on the stove, or is this more a business call?"

"Alas it is all business these days. Commandant Monnes requests the displeasure of your company in regard to a matter you are apparently involved in."

"Dante Purkell?"

He holds his hands up. "I am but the messenger, recounting words and instructions that were passed on to me." He purses his lips, then continues, "Needless to say he is not best pleased." He looks over my shoulder—both the left and then the right—before observing: "I'm assuming you'll require transport? I have a car waiting in the street below."

I write a quick message for Marzouk to read on his return, then accompany gendarme Maleek to the police station—a car journey remarkable for its total lack of any interruption or confrontational incident. So remarkable is it that, as we pull up outside Police HQ, I make a mental note to ask Marzouk about getting his car fitted with a siren and flashing lights—an addition I truly believe would be life-saving. Namely my own.

Inside I barely have time to announce myself "Tomaso Memindip, to see—" before the desk sergeant cuts me off with a curt "You. Wait. Over there." He then picks up the telephone, presses a button on the console below, waits, then says, "Your suspect is here, Commandant. Do you want to interview him in your office or in the cells?"

Before I have a chance to splutter my indignation, the sergeant says, "Very good, sir." He puts the phone down and points to me again. "You. Commandant's office. Third door down. You can count that far, can't you?"

I smile politely, enquire in old Berber Tamazight if he is the result of his father having had congress with livestock rather than one of his wives, and then proceed quickly down the passageway until I am in front of Commandant Monnes' office door. Before I can respectfully knock, I hear a shouted, "Get in here!"

I open the office door, dreading the fires of damnation, and am ordered to "Sit!" It appears there is a moratorium on the police speaking words of more than one syllable.

On his desk, illuminated by the large, brass, swan neck desk lamp, is an open folder. Inside its covers are the pieces of the partially burned letter from Doctor Keyatta.

Without looking at me, Monnes asks, "Is the blood on this anything to do with you?"

Caught by surprise I answer honestly, "No. Why should I have bled on it and not mentioned the fact when I handed the pieces over?"

Monnes looks up at me and I hold his stare unblinkingly, as I would when facing down a cobra. Eventually he looks away.

"My forensic team found traces of blood preserved under the linseed oil. The only thing they can deduce is that it's blood. The damage from the oil is pretty extensive, but they're sure it's blood."

"Has Doctor Keyatta claimed ownership?" Clearly not, otherwise why call me to his office.

"Nobody is claiming it as theirs. Not the Doctor or his secretary, nor the Greek, and now you."

"So you're concluding that it belongs to Dante Purkell?"

"I conclude nothing until I have hard evidence—or at least a body, and a suspect to match it to. However, my instincts tell me that the blood may well be that of Dante Purkell, and the letter was set alight by his killer."

"That then asks the question; why add linseed oil?"

Monnes rubs at his eyes with the knuckles of his index fingers. "I think the plan was to burn the workshop to the ground. Only whoever attempted to do it was too stupid to know that boiled Linseed oil needs to be heated to a high temperature before it will catch alight. That rules out Dante himself and the Greek as well."

Monnes looks at me sharply. "You don't happen to know what the properties of linseed oil are, do you?"

I adopt my cobra killing stare once more. "Actually I do," but leave out the part about only recently learning it from Constantine the Greek. "But that aside, why would Dante Purkell, or Constantine, want to burn down their only source of income?"

Monnes barks a short "Ha!" followed by, "Not for the insurance, that's for sure. They don't have any."

"And you think the blood is from Dante Purkell's death?"

"No body, no murder. And no murderer either. I'm waiting to see if they still have the corpse dog over at the station in Rondehal. I think the Red Cross left one the last time they had a bomb take out a building. There again, the gendarmes may well have sold the poor animal for all I know. Regardless, I'll requisition it and have some of my men check out the ground around that desert workshop of theirs. Half the time the wind changes everything. Footprints disappear, sand covers stones, everything becomes as smooth and perfect as the skin of an apricot. But the scent of death is something else entirely."

"Be'kal's breath can be both a blessing, and a curse at times."

Commandant Monnes looks at me sharply. "You don't strike me as a follower of the ancient beliefs."

"I, er… I've been researching my ancestral line. Psylli, I believe, before the time of the Muslim invasions. Be'kal is one of the Old Gods, from a time now lost and all but forgotten."

Monnes, still glaring at me, says, "Well, don't go muttering that sort of thing in public. There are imans and fanatics who don't take kindly to such. And the last thing I need is some kind of religious uprising. It's bad enough with all the Communists and politicos agitating things, but religion is something else entirely."

Monnes looks back down at the documents on his desk, and without looking up, says, "If you're not gone from this building in the next 60 seconds, I'll charge you with loitering."

Outside, and nearing midday, I'm thankful to see that Marzouk is parked as discretely as he can on the main road across from the police HQ, in the shade of the adjacent building.

As I settle in the back seat, I ask: "Did you get my message?"

"Yes, Sayidi. And I have news. There were originally two items crated up for export, as you rightly believed. However, three weeks ago one was removed and replaced by another of identical proportions, with no change to the despatch or delivery arrangements. The two crates are being held on one docket at the Departures warehouse until the administration fees and storage costs have been met. Until then they remain in bond, under lock and key."

"And if the fees are not paid on time?"

"Then the goods become forfeit, and will be disposed of via public auction at the end of the relevant month."

"Fine." I consider our next course of action, finally deciding, "It's too close to midday to worry about anything other than getting back to the manzil before the sun bakes us to a crisp. But first thing this afternoon I feel it would be prudent to talk to Doctor Keyatta once more."

11

"Doctor Keyatta is very, *very*, busy and cannot be disturbed." The receptionist is very insistent on the latter as she looks down her nose at me from the safety of her Information Desk barrier. Behind me a line of people has started to form, some checking their watches, others grumbling to themselves about this unexpected delay.

Unperturbed, I continue with my line of questioning. "So he is here?"

"Of course he's here. We are due to have the exhibition preview start at 6pm tomorrow, so these final 24 hours are vitally important in getting things perfect. We're expecting many civil dignitaries, plus the backers, obviously, and other very important people." Again she looks down her nose at me. "People who are more important than mere investigators."

"Perfectly understandable," I try and smile as sincerely as I can while wondering if another 20 dirham donation to Museum funds might be called for. Her stern expression dismisses the idea for me, so I resort to other tactics. Looking over her shoulder I smile and wave as if seeing someone I recognise, and when she turns to see who it might be, I slip around the desk and behind one of the Egyptian statues, heading into the inner sanctum of the Museum itself.

As she turns back she is confronted by the next angry person in search of an answer to their enquiry.

I carry on down the passageway until I locate Doctor Keyatta's office door. Without knocking I enter, surprising him sitting at his desk, safe open behind him, and with the copy of the Shahnameh open on his desk. The binding is of worn and cracked leather, most probably from an old and inconsequential volume picked up in a backstreet souk. The pages have been warped along their exposed edges, and coloured a light coffee brown. The Greek's words come back to me regarding the effects of the sun.

Keyatta stand up, obviously angry, but I pre-empt his protests by saying, "You must be disappointed that the posters have flaws in them."

"Flaws?" Thrown off guard, he sounds confused and indignant. "What flaws can there be? They look perfectly okay to a trained, as opposed to an uneducated, eye."

I shake my head. "No. The posters show the original damages caused by time. You can recreate the appearance of age, but you cannot replicate it completely. Plus I don't think it was Dante Purkell's intension to deceive, nor to steal the original. The breath of Be'kal may well smooth away imperfections in the sand, but it cannot replace photographic images." Without pausing, I then ask: "Where did you hide Dante Purkell's body?"

"What?"

"You had to move his body when the desert workshop didn't burn down. I'm assuming you panicked when the oil didn't catch alight, leaving you with all that mess."

Keyatta's expression becomes cold as he slowly sits back down again. "I should've persevered and gone looking for something more flammable. But the wind had started to get up and there had been warnings of a heavy sandstorm travelling southward. I didn't want to get caught in that. It would've choked the car's engine and left me stranded. But I'd already dragged his body from the drying racks out the back, so I was left with no other option but to change my plan."

"But why did you kill him? A falling out of thieves?"

Keyatta smiles. "Oh no, nothing as stupid as that. Dante was far too honest to be a thief. Proud and arrogant, yes. But greed certainly got the better of him. When I approached him to create a copy I used the excuse that the Museum would keep the original in the vault and display the copy, which is true—the insurance company would never allow the original to be displayed without armed guards protecting it. I'd even agreed to put a note beside it to that effect, and naming Dante as the creator of the facsimile. All good publicity." He picks up an ornate letter opener from the cluttered desktop blotter, turning it over in his hands and looking down at it as if fascinated by it. "But Dante didn't follow instructions. Instead of creating one he created three."

"Who were the other two copies for?"

"I don't know. From the addresses on the packing cases I assume they were for dealers or specific collectors. He'd even included some extra text at the bottom of the pages, close to the spine. It said something like 'This is a facsimile created with permission' then named me. The third copy had that text masked out—apparently something that's easy to do during the screen printing process."

"So you buried his body elsewhere?"

Keyatta sighs. "I didn't have time to create a funeral pyre. There's an old wadi on the way back to the city—usually full of scavengers. About a mile up it there's the remains of a cave. I dumped his body in that. When the waters come he'll be covered in silt. If not, then he's probably kept a Fennec or a sand cat and her cubs fed for several weeks."

As I see the flick of his wrist I'm already stepping to one side and the letter opener sticks firmly into the wood of the door frame with a thud barely audible above the outside noise.

Keyatta sighs again and shrugs his shoulders. "Well, you cannot blame a man for trying. So, where do we go from here? I assume you either want to be paid to keep quiet, or you're looking for a cut of the sale when I make it?"

"Is that what you would do if you were me?"

"No. If I were you, then I'd kill me and take 100 percent."

"But that only works if I already know where to sell it and what price I should be asking. You created a problem by killing Dante Purkell. You need his signature to release the two crates—one of which I'm sure now contains the museum's copy of the Shahnameh. I suspect you've been trying to practice his signature? It's a shame that his half-sister, Anita, completed and signed most of the letters and all of the invoices. I'm assuming it was you who forged the letter to her and the note pushed under the shop door?"

"I managed to razor a page of his handwriting from the front of his work book, which was all I could find after the fire didn't take. It was a rushed job, but it seemed to work after a fashion." Keyatta looks at the various ornaments and accessories on the desk that are within easy reach. Nothing with any point or blade, though a statue of a horned representation of the god, Isis, strikes me as having potential if used in close combat. Keyatta stands, snatches up a round glass paperweight and is about to throw it when the resonant voice and body of Commandant Monnes, barges through the half open door and I have to jump to one side to avoid being caught by the door handle.

"I wouldn't do that if I were you, Doctor. It'll only add to the already long list of charges you'll be facing in court."

Keyatta, looking crestfallen and dejected, sits back down before two burly gendarmes enter and drag him out of his office in handcuffs.

Monnes sits down in one of the comfortable chairs half facing the desk.

"Your little rat is a persistent creature, I'll give him that."

"You mean Marzouk?"

"How many other rodents do you have that do your bidding?"

"None. Marzouk is more than efficient to be sufficient."

"Whatever. I also sent two men down to the dockyard. Apparently the security guards were initially a little reluctant about letting them have the two cases until it was pointed out what they were involved in, albeit indirectly."

"So how much did you manage to hear?"

"Almost all, I think. At least the most important part, where he admitted to killing Dante Purkell and hiding his corpse up a wadi."

I look at the doorframe, still with the letter opener sticking from it. "Was that before or after the attempted murder?"

"Hard to tell. Probably after, I would say." He cocks his head a little to one side. "You may think it attempted murder. Others might believe it to be justifiable homicide." He stands, straightens his light brown uniform, and is about to leave when the noise from the corridor outside the office manifests itself in the form of the woman who was behind the

Information Desk in the foyer.

"Tell me what is going on! I've just seen Doctor Keyatta being escorted out of the building in handcuffs!"

Monnes glares her into silence. "He's being arrested and charged with murder, along with fraud and grand theft for good measure."

"But what do we do about the exhibition?"

Monnes impatiently adjusts the gun in its holster. "Madam, I wouldn't look on these events as some kind of loss. Take this as a promotional opportunity."

"What?"

"From now on you're in charge of it all." With that he departs the office, no doubt heading back to the Police HQ, leaving the poor woman even more confused. She turns to me, but all I can do is shrug my shoulders, smile, and make good my escape back out into the street.

12

As I put the telephone receiver back onto its cradle, Marzouk asks:

"It is never a pleasant task, Sayidi, to tell a person that a loved one is no more. How did Miss Purkell take the news of her stepbrother's death?"

The coldness in her voice had been obvious. I was simply confirming what she already believed to be true. The Commandant's gendarmes had still to locate Dante Purkell's remains, at which time they would inform her, and the world, of his official demise. But for now she had a chance to prepare herself for the inevitable onslaught of prying reporters and staff photographers. They'd already had the double feeding frenzy of both the attempted theft of an artefact of great importance, but also the downfall of a very prominent public official in the form of Doctor Keyatta. Now it was a case of which publication could out sensationalise the others, their front pages vying for public attention. Anything as long as it extracted the fils from the readers' pockets.

"She seems to be taking it very well, considering the circumstances."

Marzouk looks thoughtful for a moment. "So, with the original poems back at the Museum, what will happen to the copies?"

"No doubt they will be disputed over for some time to come, especially as the Museum didn't sanction them in the first place."

"Still, Sayidi, at least we were paid for our efforts this time."

I nod, though I know that money is no salve against the pain of personal loss.

13

The Sahara Bugle Gazette Tuesday 8th April 1969

Defendant Shot and Killed During Prominent Murder Trial

In a violent turn of events yesterday during the trial of disgraced head of the Museum of Antiquities, Doctor Marius J. Keyatta (the defendant), was shot and killed while giving evidence. The woman, Ms Anita Purkell, half-sister of the murdered Dante Purkell, waited until Doctor Keyatta had finished giving his account of the affair, before using a small automatic pistol to fire three shots. The first two hit Doctor Keyatta in the chest, while the third caught him in the head, from which he died instantly. Ms Purkell then proceeded to surrender herself to court officials, and was led from the court by two armed gendarmes.

Barely is Good Enough
Martin Zeigler

"Mom! What the hell?"

Look, it meant a lot, her coming all the way up to Northernmost State University for my graduation, but, holy crap, she was about to hit fifty, and here she was lugging my crate of LPs down three flights from my dorm room to her car.

Okay, my brother Harvey's car. And, yeah, maybe that should of meant something, him coming along. But right now, all I could think of was Mom dropping all them record albums on the pavement.

"Better let me have that," I said to her. "Your bones are gonna break in two."

"Here you go, Cooper, honey," she said. "I'll just drag my fragile old self upstairs and find a pair of socks to bring down."

I took the crate and put it in the trunk. "Good idea, Mom. By the way, where's Dad?"

"Working overtime, genius. Recouping all that tuition wasted on you over the past seven years."

That was Harvey, not my mom. She would never talk to nobody that way.

"That's hilarious, Harv," I said. "But I been going here only four years. Four. Freshman, softmore, and...and...whatever the other ones are. Just like everybody else does. Nice try, though. I didn't know private eyes did comedy."

"We investigators are a serious bunch, little brother. We avoid laughter like the plague. Unless someone happens along who can't tell a four from a seven."

"All right. That's enough, you two."

Now *that* was Mom.

"If your father were here, he'd have a word with each of you."

Harv gave me a smirk. "Not to worry, Coop. I'm sure he'd keep your word short."

Figuring this was some kind of dig, I said, "Harv, you drove all the way up here just to bust my balls?"

"Boys! That's enough!"

Mom looked ready to say a lot more, maybe about me using the word *balls*, but all she did was shake her head and go, "Forget it. Let's just finish up so we can get on our way."

Harv watched Mom climb the stairs to my room, then turned to me. "Why, Coop, the reason I drove all the way up here to the hallowed halls of NSU was not to bust the balls of my little brother, but rather to watch him, in his cap and gown, step up, as an alumnus of the class of seventy-six, and receive his well-deserved diploma, thereby assuring the audience, if not the entire world, that he is fully prepared to take on the challenges posed by modern society. So what was it you majored in?"

"General knowledge."

"Really? General knowledge?"

"That's what I said."

"You can actually get a degree in general knowledge?"

"Yeah, what of it?"

"Well, I suppose it beats a degree in a little bit of knowledge. Because you know what they say."

"No, what's that?"

"A little bit of knowledge is a dangerous thing."

"I never heard nobody say that. Uh...how dangerous?"

"No need to fret over it, little brother. You did the safe thing and went with general."

I stared hard at my big brother until I spotted Mom at the bottom of the stairs coming our way.

"Mom!" I cried out. "What the hell?"

Her face was bright red, and the veiny things in her neck was sticking out, all from hauling my two big huge suitcases, one in each hand. She set them down behind the car, then wiped her forehead with the back of her hand.

"Mom," I said, "you're gonna kill yourself."

I about killed myself sliding both suitcases into the trunk, alongside the crate of LPs.

"You told me you was just gonna get a couple socks," I said, "not a couple suitcases."

"Well, Cooper, honey. When I went back up to your room with the intent of getting that one pair of socks, I couldn't find any socks anywhere. Or any of your other clothes for that matter. Not in the drawers or in the closet or on any of the shelves. And then I spotted the one suitcase on your bed and thought to myself, 'Dear, sweet Cooper, bless his heart. He did the packing already.' And so, expecting to find all your clothes clean and nicely folded, ready to take home, I eagerly flipped open the suitcase and took a look inside. And what do you think I saw, Cooper, honey?"

"You saw what's in the suitcase."

"Can you elaborate?"

"What's *elaborate* mean?"

"It means can you tell me more?"

"Yeah, sure. You saw what's in the suitcase, and you're my mom."

She kind of smiled, like what I just said was some kind of joke, then smiled in a different way, like what she was about to say was a different kind of joke. "What I saw, honey, crammed in that suitcase, was a massive, sweaty lump of what at one time might have been the same nice shirts and slacks—and, yes, even socks—that I'd bought for you at the beginning of every year since you'd started college. All of it now ripped, wrinkled, and reeking."

"What's *reeking* mean?"

"Stinking to high heaven."

"Yeah, okay. That might be what's in the suitcase. You didn't take nothing out, did you?"

"Not on your life."

"Good. Because that suitcase is where I kept all my threads while I was at school."

"Kept your? Honey, that's what closets and dresser drawers are for."

"Suitcase is easier."

"And how often did you do your laundry?"

"What do you mean?"

"Washing your clothes. When was the last time you did that?"

"Haven't got around to it yet."

"Yet? What do you mean, *yet*?"

"I mean, the washer and drying machines are in the dorm's basement, and I haven't went down there yet."

Mom kind of looked at me. "Honey. Oh, honey."

"What?"

"Honey, how did you—I mean, what did you wear every day?"

"Simple, Mom. Whenever I needed anything, I just reached into the suitcase and yanked something out. And then shoved whatever I didn't need back in."

"That's it?" she said.

"Yeah. I told you it was simple."

"But no washing."

"No, not yet."

Mom didn't say nothing, but I could see the bulge in her neck getting bigger.

And Harv started shaking his head and doing the eye roll.

And I could hear myself saying, "Geez, come on, you guys."

We was still standing behind the car, staring into the open trunk, when Mom pointed to the other suitcase, the one she must of found under the bed. "What's in that one?"

"It's locked," I said. "But I got the key."

"I know it's locked, honey. But what's inside it?"

That's when Harv put a hand on her shoulder. "Ma," he said. "I have a feeling it's best we don't ask."

*****

With Harv at the wheel, Mom beside him, me in the backseat, and all my crap in the trunk, we left NSU behind, got on the freeway, and headed south.

At least I think it was south.

Anyway, getting my diploma and putting stuff in the trunk took a lot out of me, and all I wanted to do was catch a few Zs. But the second I closed my eyes, the sound of my dear brother's lovely voice popped them back open, and the first thing I seen was his eyes in the rearview mirror looking at me.

"So, Coop," he said. "General knowledge, right?"

"We gotta go through this again?" I said.

"Just one question. That's it."

"Okay. What."

"Who won the Revolutionary War?"

"Come on, Harv. I had a big final exam two days ago. I'm done with tests."

"A final exam in what?"

"Geez, I don't remember. World history, I think."

"World history, you said?"

"Yeah. I guess."

"Okay, then, here's a world history question. Who won the Revolutionary War?"

"For crap sakes. Mom, stop him."

"Okay, little brother, I'll word it more simply. A number of years ago, the American colonists and the British got themselves into a little pickle. Who won?"

"Mom!" I said, slapping the corner of her seat.

"All right. That's enough, you two."

"But, Ma," Harv said. "All I'm asking him to do is say either 'us' or 'them.'"

Mom turned in her seat as best she could. "Cooper, honey, please say either 'us' or 'them' so we can enjoy the rest of our two-and-a-half hour drive in peace and quiet."

I sucked in a deep breath and blew it right back out. "Okay, okay. *Them*. You satisfied?"

Did I guess right or not? I couldn't tell. Because, first off, Harv slapped the steering wheel and shouted out, all excited, "Holy cow! You know something? I never thought of it before, but my little brother's right!"

But then Mom said, "He is?

Then Harv said, "He sure is, Ma. The Brits did win! And do you know what that means?"

"I have no idea, Harvey."

"It means we're in deep, deep, deep, deep trouble!"

"We are?"

That's when Harv, who was in the far left aisle, took a quick look behind him, then cut across three aisles of traffic.

Okay, *lanes*. I think they're called lanes, not aisles, but whatever. We wound up in the lane at the far right, heading for the next exit.

"Harvey," Mom said. "What's going on?"

"This is serious, Ma."

"What is?" Mom sounded real scared now. And I was squeezing my door handle real tight.

"Everything, Ma!"

"Oh, Lord!" she said. "Oh, my Lord!" Her voice was all shaky. "We out of gas? We have a flat? There something wrong with the engine?"

"Worse than all of those combined!" Harv said. "The British won, which means we're driving home on the wrong side of the freeway!"

*****

Oh, boy, did Harv and Mom get a big laugh out of that one.

I got it finally. I wasn't stupid.

There was a TV show back in the sixties, around the time I started at NSU, about this British guy who became a prisoner in a village, and every episode begun with him racing down the road in a car, except the steering wheel was on the wrong side of the car and the car was on the wrong side of the road. And what Harv was saying was that if the British won, we'd still be British and doing everything the way that British guy done.

So, yeah, I got it.

"Cute, Harv," I said. "Real cute."

Harv skipped past the exit and went back to the aisle we was in to begin with, still laughing like one of them animals that sounds like they're laughing.

And Mom, who'd caught on right off because she's smart, calmed down from her own laughing to poke Harv in the shoulder and say, "Harvey, sweetheart, you're awful. And, Cooper, honey, don't you worry about it. We all make mistakes."

"Holy crap," I said. "I can't be expected to remember who won every goddamn war."

"Speaking of which, little brother, how did you do on that world history final?"

"I passed, if it's anything to you," I said. "With an A."

I figured they didn't need to know that the history class, like all classes at Northernmost State, was grade yourself, and only a moron would give himself an F.

*****

"Mom! What the hell?"

This was a good kind of what the hell, because as soon as we got home, Mom went to the fridge and pulled out a batch of homemade mac and cheese she must of whipped up earlier, before her and Harv took off for my graduation. And by the time Harv and me unloaded the car and quit arguing why I tossed all my textbooks out the dorm room window, the grub was all golden and baked and ready to eat.

"That sure looks good, Mom," I said.

"Wash your hands, you two," Mom said.

"She means with soap," Harv said.

Now that I was back home, I'd be staying in my old room. Harv had a place of his own, but he couldn't pass up the mac and cheese. And

Mom, of course, cooked the stuff. So soon all three of us were at the kitchen table, chowing down, raving how great it all tasted, when all of a sudden, out of the blue, Harv turned to me and said, "So, Mr. Magna Cum Laude, what do you plan to do in the way of work?"

"Magna cum what?" I said.

"A job. Have you applied for one yet?"

"I was at school, in case you forgot."

"You can actually write letters of application at a dormitory desk," Harv said.

"Not anymore I can't." And I thought I made a pretty good point.

"Then go get Dad's typewriter and give this kitchen table a try."

"With cheese and bits of macaroni all over?" I said. "No thanks. And anyway, I put in a lot of hard work at NSU, so I'm gonna take a well-deserted rest."

"In other words, stay in your room, listen to whatever new Simon and Garfunkel album is out, and mooch off Mom and Dad for the rest of your life."

"Simon and Garfunkel split up," I said.

The look of surprise on Harv's face told me I got him on that one. So much for him acting all know-it-all.

"All right, you two."

Mom put her fork down on her plate and touched her mouth with a napkin. "You know, Harvey," she said, "I've been giving this some thought for a while now, and I believe I've come up with an idea."

"What's that, Ma?"

"We all know real life is a bit different from college. It takes a little getting adjusted to."

"Not for me," Harv said.

Oh, boy, I thought. Here it comes. And sure enough, it did.

"I went to business school here in town," he said. "At the same time, I worked side jobs, earned my way. But I managed my time wisely and responsibly. And now I'm gainfully employed. Private detective work can actually be a lucrative occupation if you possess the skills and training and willingness to put in the effort that I do."

Not knowing what to say, I said something anyway. "Well, oooooh."

Harv did the eye roll. "No reason you can't do the same, little brother."

Mom said, "Well, Harvey, some people aren't as get-up-and-go as you. Cooper's a little shy, and—"

"Shy? Ma, is that what you call it? 'Who won the Revolutionary War?' 'Gee, I don't know. I'm shy.'"

"Okay! Okay!" I said. "We won! It was us, not them! You happy?"

"Water under the bridge," Harv said.

"All right, you two. Look, Harvey, what I was trying to get at is: why don't you take Cooper under your wing for a little while?"

The look that come over Harv's face was probably the same one that come over mine. It was like Mom'd asked if, next time around, we'd like the mac to be the same but the cheese to be moldy.

"What do you mean by 'a little while?'" Harv asked.

I was kind of wondering the same thing.

"I don't know," Mom said. "Just long enough for Cooper to get his foot in the door at a job. A real job."

"Doing what exactly? Ma, this is private investigative work. What would he do, follow me around wherever I go, carrying a giant magnifying glass?"

"Yeah, Mom," I said. "I don't want my foot in no door or my hand on some big huge thing that makes things bigger and huger."

Harv turned to me and kept looking at me when he said, "Ma, this is the way it has to be. Coop here has to go out and earn a living on his own. And he needs to do that now. Without help from anybody. Simple as that."

"Really, sweetheart?" Mom said. "Yes, you did go to business school. Yes, you worked several part-time jobs. Yes, you studied at all hours. But all the while, who cooked your meals? Who did your laundry the same way she did Cooper's and will probably continue to do Cooper's? And who let you live in this house entirely rent-free? Do you remember?"

Harv shrugged and mumbled something and then shut up.

Mom pointed to his plate. "More macaroni and cheese?"

*****

"Mom! What the hell?"

"Cooper, I wish you would stop saying that."

"But Mom. First you ask Harv if I can work for him. But turns out he doesn't want me working for him, and, what's more, I don't want me working for him. And all that should of told you something. And what it should of told you was we don't want to work with each other. But then what do you do? You go ahead with the big spoon and slap down a huge pile of mac and cheese on his plate, and all of a sudden he's all, 'Yeah, I guess I could give old Coop a try for a week or two.' And next second, after he sucks down the last macaroni, he's at the back door jabbing a finger at me and telling me to be at his office at eight in the morning or else. And all that because of mac and cheese."

Mom reached out and put her hand on mine. "Honey, we all have to work at some point. Harvey works. Your father works—and boy does he. And I work at the supermarket. Yes, I took the day off today to attend your graduation, but I'll have to go back tomorrow. That's part of life."

"But, Mom, you don't understand. I need to decompress."

"Decompress?"

"I don't know what it means. But I know I need to do it."

"Cooper, it's what professional scuba divers do. For their jobs. So if you need to decompress, you first need to get a job."

"You're making this complicated, Mom."

"I don't mean to. Look, if your father doesn't call about having to put in extra hours tonight, he'll be home in an hour. Maybe the three of us can then have a little discussion about this."

Hell no, I thought. I loved doing things with Dad when he was home. Going to the movies or sneaking in foot-long hot dogs at the drive-in. Even standing around telling stupid jokes, the kind I could get. But I didn't know and was afraid to find out what it'd be like sitting around the table with him and having a little discussion.

"You win, Mom," I said, throwing up my hands. "I'll meet up with Harv tomorrow morning."

"That's the spirit."

"Uh, can you drive me to his office?"

Mom smiled. "It's only three blocks from here, but, sure, I'll be glad to."

*****

*Superior Investigations * Private * Discreet*

That's what was painted on the window in gold letters. The window had blinds, but they were slanted, so I was able to peek through them and see Harv hunched over his desk like a good little private eye.

When I opened the door, a bell rung and he looked up. "Yes, sir, may I help you?"

"Funny, Harv."

"Say, you look and sound just like my little brother, except he never gets up this early."

"I'm here now, Harv. See?"

"*You* might be, but my brother isn't."

"I am so!"

"Yes, but my brother isn't."

"Yeah, well, right now I'd rather be where he is, but I made a promise to Mom."

"And I'd rather you and my brother both be somewhere else, but I made the same promise. So sit down. I have your first assignment."

Oh, goody, I thought.

There was a little card in front of him, and he slid it over. "Something I want you to pick up for me," he said. "I don't have time to do it myself."

The card had writing on it. "Notebooks?" I said. "You want notebooks?"

"Just like it says. The narrow, pocket-sized kind with the spiral at the top so they open that way."

"Why the hell does a private eye need a notebook?"

"Well, in my case I need them to take notes. But I can't speak for everyone in the profession."

"But a bunch of them? Says here you want a whole boxful."

"One notebook per client, and I have lots of clients."

"You write everything they say?"

Harv put up his hands. "Look, Coop. I suspect the concept of taking notes is foreign to you, so maybe someday I'll show you how you don't need to put down every single word. But right now, I'm busy with several cases. And so I'd appreciate it if you just went out and bought those spiral notebooks for me."

He took out his wallet and pulled out a couple twenty-dollar bills and set them in front of me. "This is for the notebooks and a day's work. That's right. You have the whole day to do this. All I want by tomorrow morning are the box of notebooks and a receipt for tax purposes. You keep the change. Fair enough?"

"Where do I get them, the notebooks?"

"Able Office Supply. The name and address are on the card. The one in your hand."

"I mean, where's the address?"

"Right there on the card."

"No, I mean where's this Able place at?"

"At the address. On the card. Holy cow, Coop."

"No, what I mean is, how do I get there?"

"Coop, by getting in a car and driving to Able Office Supply instead of sitting here driving me insane."

I know I'm lousy at making myself clear. A prof at NSU once asked me where I got my gift for explaining things. But when I tried to tell him I didn't know I could explain things, he asked me what I was talking about.

Anyway, with Harv I gave it one more try.

"Harv, what I'm saying is, I know the store's at this address on the card, but where in the city is the address?"

"Use a map for God's sake."

He must of saw the lost look on my face. "You do know what a map is, don't you?"

"Kind of. In world history, they had maps showing where all these armies were at. And you could tell they didn't have no problem getting around, because there was big red arrows everywhere."

Harv gave me a look like I just hatched out of an egg. "Coop, how in the world do you get around without a map? You bought all those records at NSU, for instance. How'd you find the record store? Or movie theaters? Or restaurants?"

"I walked around till I found them."

"Jesus. No wonder you worked up that giant tumor of sweat Ma found in your luggage."

"Giant what?"

Harv looked at his watch. "Never mind. Look. I don't have time to teach you how to read a map, so you'll just have to do that same sort of walking around thing today. Although I wouldn't recommend walking. It's a big city. Taking a car would be the way to do it."

"Do what?"

"Drive around until you accidentally come across Able Office Supply. You do have all day."

"The thing is, about driving..."

"Oh, that's right. You don't own a car. Well, take Ma's. As you know, the house key's under the doormat, and the car key's on the hook in the pantry."

"No, what I mean is—"

"Ma won't mind. She walks to work. In the meantime, I need to scoot. I'm tied up with a tricky case involving an embezzlement."

"What's an embezzlement?"

"It's almost like an embarrassment. Which you are rapidly becoming."

*****

The car key was exactly where Harv said it was, but I left it there and went to catch a bus instead.

I knew something about busses. I took them to the movies when I was in high school. What I mean is, I took them to the movies instead of high school. And I always caught them at the main station close to home.

The card Harv gave me said the notebook store was on the corner of Spruce Avenue and another street. Bus number 32 went along Spruce Avenue. So I got on bus number 32.

So there I was, on the number 32, on Spruce Avenue, a road that went on forever, listening to the driver shout out the cross streets as we come to them. "Twenty-fifth Street!" he'd yell. Or, later on, "A Hundred and Twenty-Fifth Street!" Or even later, "Three Hundred and Twenty-Fifth Street!" Like that.

I sat in my seat listening real careful for the right cross street, the one on the card, so I could pull the cord by my window and get off, but the driver just wouldn't call it out.

What he did, though, was call out, "Seven Hundred and Twenty-Fifth Street! End of the line! Everybody off!"

Well, crap. I mean, crap.

There was about five other people on the bus, and they all got off, and I got up out of my seat and went to the driver and I said, "Driver, this is Seven Hundred and Twenty-Fifth Street."

"That's what I said, young man. End of the line."

"But this isn't my street. And you haven't yet called out my street. My street is where Able Office Supply is at."

"Don't know anything about Able Office Supply."

"They sell the tiny notebooks with the spiral on top."

"Well, if it's on Spruce, you'll just have to get off here and walk a bit farther up the road, I'm afraid."

"Walk?" I said. I was all nervous and breaking out into a sweat. "Do you wanna know how far it is? I'll tell you how far it is. I just figured it out in my head. It's a hundred and eleven streets."

"Blocks, you mean?"

"Yeah, blocks. There's no other busses going that way?"

"This is it, I'm afraid. I'll be turning around here in a few minutes and heading back. If you want to stay on, you're welcome to. Your pass is still good."

So that's what I did. I sat back in my seat, and pretty soon the bus swung around, and the driver once again started belting out the street numbers. Only this time they kept getting smaller and smaller. Plus, it was getting later and later and darker and darker and the bus kept getting further and further away from Able Office Supply. And all of this kind of got me to thinking I was getting in deeper and deeper crap with my brother.

At last the bus pulled into the same station I started off from. "End of the line!" the driver yelled.

Just before getting off, I stopped by the driver and I said, "A hundred and eleven blocks I would of had to walk. That's unfair."

The driver looked up at me. "You know, it just hit me," he said. "That number doesn't sound right. What street did you say that office supply store is on? Spruce and what?"

"Seven hundred and Thirty-First," I said. "You stopped on Seven Hundred and Twenty-Fifth and shouted out end of the line."

"How do you figure a hundred and eleven blocks?"

"I subtracted one street from the other."

"Well, in my world that's six blocks."

"Bullcrap, six. I got a hundred and eleven."

"Son, you would have had to walk only six blocks, and they're short ones. Where'd you learn to subtract, young man?"

"Northernmost State University," I said, feeling kind of proud of my almer modder. "Basic Elementary Arithmetic for Beginners."

"What grade did you get, if you don't mind my asking? And tell the truth."

The more I stood there by the driver thinking I was right, the more I got to thinking maybe I should of paid more attention in Basic

Elementary Arithmetic for Beginners. But he wanted an honest answer, so I gave it.

"I got an A-plus," I said. "Cross my heart."

*****

First thing Harv said to me when I stepped into his office next morning was, "Let me guess. You didn't get the notebooks and you took a bus instead of Ma's car."

"How you figure all that?"

"Because, one, you don't have the notebooks, and, two, you smell like bus."

I sniffed my fingers. "I don't smell nothing. And I took a shower when I got up, and I put on clean threads. Just like Mom says she'll make me do every morning."

"Doesn't matter. Once you get that smell of bus on you, there's no getting rid of it. That's why no one rides them anymore."

"Plenty of riders on my bus."

"Yes, and I'm sure they smell like it."

"And I'm sure you smell like your desk," I said.

That stopped him for a second, maybe even made him smile a little. But in no time, Harv was back to being Harv. "But why a bus instead of Ma's car, Coop? And why didn't you get the notebooks?"

I figured it was time to confess to something, and it was probably better not knowing how to drive than not knowing how to subtract. So I stepped a little closer to Harv, but not too close, just in case he wanted to kill me. And I sort of whispered, "I took the bus, Harv, on account of I don't have a driver's license."

"Jesus!" Harv said, and he wasn't whispering. "No driver's license? How old are you, anyway? Six?"

That's how many blocks it was from the end of the line to the notebook store, and I hoped I wouldn't never ever hear that number again.

"Harv, I tried getting a license a couple years ago. Up in Northernmostville. That's the town where Northernmost State is at."

"I sort of gathered that, Coop."

"A guy I know at NSU drove me to the licensing place, and I used his car to take the test. But the test wasn't fair.

"What do you mean—wasn't fair?"

"When I accidentally went through a red light, the examiner told me the test was over."

"That's because you ran a red light! And I assume you failed?"

"Well, I'm not sure. You see, I accidentally went through another red light on our way back to the station."

"Jesus. What did the examiner say to that?"

"He didn't say nothing. We just sat there in the station parking lot. And when I let him know the score I deserved, he just shook his head and left. And that's the unfair part."

"Because he left?"

"No, because I never got a license, and the score I gave myself was a damn good one."

"Jesus," Harv said again. "Well, you're going to have to get a driver's license. And get one quick. Because I'll need you to be able to go anywhere at any time. Otherwise, I can't use you. There's only so much I can do for you, Coop, even if this is for Ma. Understand?"

"Yeah, I do."

He opened his wallet and pulled out a hundred-dollar bill.

"Do you know what this is?" he asked.

"Something to slip the examiner?"

"No, it's to pay for some driving lessons. And it's also a reminder."

"Of what?"

He snapped the bill. "That you only go through a traffic light when it's this color."

*****

A week later I marched into Harv's office and proudly flashed him my temporary license. "I get the permanent one in a couple weeks!"

"That's good, little brother. Whose car did you use this time?"

"Mom's. And she drove me to the station here in town, in case you're wondering. So you wanna know how I did?"

"You must have passed, since you have your license."

"Well, here's the funny part, Harv. Wanna hear the funny part?"

"No, I think I'm good."

"So, during the exam, I'm coming up to an intersection, and suddenly I remember you telling me what color the traffic light has to be. And seeing that the traffic light wasn't that color, I went and slammed the brakes hard. And I mean real hard. So hard, you could hear the tires squeal and feel the back end lift up."

"Sounds as if you got a little overanxious there, Coop."

"I sure did! Mom's car come to such a quick stop that when it did stop, everything inside the car kept going. Things like me and the examiner."

"Is this the funny part?"

"Kind of. What stopped me from going too far was my seatbelt. What *didn't* stop the examiner from going too far was *his* seatbelt. And what stopped the big huge truck from plowing into us from behind must of been good brakes. And his horn worked great too."

"Sounds like Ma needs to get that seatbelt checked."

"Yeah, and the front window, too, on account of the crack the examiner's head made before he went bouncing back into his seat."

"I bet Ma's insurance will love that. And by the way, it's a *windshield*, not a *window*. But, hey, at least you didn't run a red light this time."

"No, I didn't, Harv, because the light wasn't red. It was green. But not the same kind of green as the hundred-dollar bill you showed me. That green was darker. The traffic light's green was lighter, so I didn't know if I was supposed to stop or go right on through. So I figured better safe than sorry."

"A decision which no doubt stunned the examiner."

"Yeah, and not only that, but he was surprised as hell and he hurt like hell. But he'll be okay. And so will I. Because after we get back to the station, the first thing he done was rub his hand over his head and yell, 'God damn it!' And after that he says to me, 'Look. I don't know if you remember me, but I tested you back in Northernmostville. And what I should do is flunk you now just like I did back then. I would be perfectly justified in doing so, given that you don't belong behind anything resembling a steering wheel. But you know what? I won't flunk you. Why? Because if I did, I might end up having to test you a third time.'"

"Sounds like you both lucked out. That's great, Coop. Now maybe we can get down to business."

"Speaking of lucking out, Harv, wait'll you hear about the written part of the test."

"Maybe some other year, Coop, okay? Right now I have a couple of cases here that—"

"Okay, so the written part's about twenty questions, and they all come with five answers, and you have to pick the right one."

"Multiple choice, in other words."

"Yeah, that's right. So I take the pencil and fill in what I think are the right circles and take the answer sheet up to the front desk, and a lady there looks it over and tells me I passed."

"Which I figured, Coop, because, once again, here you are with your driver's license."

"Yeah, I passed, but just barely. She says if I'd of missed one more question, I'd of flunked big time."

"Maybe if you had studied the driver's manual more diligently you would have boosted your score to something more respectable than barely passing."

"Yeah, maybe, Harv. But that's not what our motto is all about."

"And what motto might that be?"

"The motto you would of saw in the gym lobby when you went to my graduation."

"I must have missed it."

"How could you of missed it? It's right there on the wall, in big huge letters."

"What is?"

"Our school motto, Harv! NSU's motto! A motto to live by till your dying day. 'DON'T LET OTHERS DEFINE YOUR SUCCESS. BARELY IS GOOD ENOUGH.'"

Harv did the eye roll. "Wow. That certainly sets high standards to a whole new level."

"That's for sure, whatever you said. And you wanna know something else, Harv?"

"No. What I want is to discuss two very important cases with you."

"Okay, but first I gotta tell you what sometimes happened at NSU when I went to the gym and passed by that motto."

Before, it was the eye roll. Now it was the big sigh. "Can't this wait, Coop?"

"What happened, Harv, was I'd look at that motto and see the word *barely* and sometimes think it was barley."

"Sounds like an easy mistake to make. Now if we could—"

"Remember the time Mom made that barley soup?"

"No, Coop, I don't. I honestly don't."

"Well, I do. She only made it once, but I remember it. And I gotta tell you something."

"And what's that?"

"It was like slurping spoon after spoon of tiny, slimy spitballs. But you know what?"

"Please tell me."

"It was good enough."

*****

I figured by the look on his face that Harv was ready to talk work. "So what about them cases?" I asked.

"You ready?" he said.

"Yeah, sure."

"You sure?"

"I just said 'yeah, sure.'"

"Okay," he said. "There are two of them. The one that's been keeping me busy and the one you'll be starting on this very afternoon."

"Me, a case? A real case?"

"That's right."

"But what about the notebooks?"

Harv sat back in his chair. "Oh, you'll still need to get those for me, but they can wait. These cases take priority, because cases are how I make my living."

"But if you're gonna put me on a case, what about *my* living?"

"Listen to you. Taking entire days off to ride the bus and run red lights and stop for green ones, and already you're demanding equal pay. What's next? Joining a union and going on strike?"

"Isn't that something that happens in baseball?"

"Coop, during the seven years you were going for your general knowledge degree, did you ever read a newspaper?"

"No, but I think a prof read part of a headline to us once."

Harv laughed at something—I don't know what—and then leaned forward. "Look, little brother, I'll pay you, okay? But before we get to your case, we need to talk about the one I'm on. Actually, I'm on several, but the one I want to talk over with you is the case involving embezzlement. Remember when I mentioned that before?"

"Yeah, it sounds like *embarrassment.* What about it?"

"Well, the two words might sound the same, but one's a crime and the other isn't."

"I hope it's not embarrassment."

"I hear you, little brother. I imagine you must have experienced that once or twice."

"I remember once. A prof asked me, in front of the whole class, what the capital of West Germany was, and I said I didn't know, I never took US geology. And all of a sudden him and everyone else broke out into hysterectomies."

"Hyster..."

"You know, like laughing real loud and slapping their knees."

And now Harv looked like he was about to do the same thing, but then he got all serious and started fiddling with his necktie. "Yes, well, embarrassing situations like that must be intimidating, all right. But embezzlement is a lot worse. Especially with the case I'm working."

"Why?"

"I'll be blunt, Coop. Without getting too deep into the specifics, a serious crime has been committed and I believe the mounting evidence points to one individual."

"Do I know him? I don't want to know nobody who's an embezzlement."

"As a matter of fact, little brother, you do know him. And so do I."

"Yeah? So who's the lucky guy?"

Harv aimed his eyes right at me. "It's Dad."

*****

I shot up out of my chair. "Dad—Dad committed a crime?"

Harv stood up, too. "Possibly several of them, Coop. Stealing from company accounts, even from subsidiaries."

"What's a subsidiary?"

"It doesn't matter. The point is, he's been pilfering large amounts of money for a long, long time, and he will likely go to prison for an even longer amount of time."

"Geez, Harv, why are you telling me all this?"

"Why not?"

"Here's why not. Dad don't hardly ever come home. But I figure he'll come home now and then. But if he's in jail, he won't never come home at all. But if I didn't know he was in jail, I could still figure he'll come home now and then. That's why I don't wanna hear none of this."

"But you'd only be deluding yourself, little brother."

"I'd only be what?"

"Kidding yourself. It's always better to know the truth."

"I don't know about that, Harv. I think there's stuff out there, it's better not knowing nothing about."

Harv sat back down, and I knew a big idea was coming.

"I disagree, Coop. I think we should strive to learn as much as we can about everything."

"Okay," I said. "How about I take some time off and teach myself all there's to know about embezzlement?"

"And then what?"

"And then what *what*?

"And then what will you do? I mean Dad learned a thing or two about embezzlement and ended up stealing vast fortunes. I learned a thing or two about embezzlement and caught him red-handed. What do you plan to do once you learn a thing or two?"

"Hell if I know. I haven't learned nothing yet."

"Maybe you won't do anything. Maybe you'll just end up knowing a thing or two more about embezzlement than you did before, and there's nothing wrong with that. Or maybe you'll use the thing or two to save a business or two, and that would be great. On the other hand, if you decide to cash in big on the first thing and even bigger on the second thing, you might just end up seeing Dad more often than you ever dreamed of."

"You know what, Harv? Forget embezzlement. I'll go learn something else."

Harv kind of nodded and sort of smiled. "That's a wise choice, little brother. The subject of embezzlement can get pretty involved. And if you actually want to get into the habit of learning, especially after all these years, I suggest you start small and build up from there."

"Start small? What's that mean?"

"Oh, learning the names of the fifty states, for example."

"There's fifty? I thought there was only three."

"You're thinking of the three states of matter. Solid, liquid, and gas."

"I heard about them, Harv, but I didn't know they was states. Anyway, who cares? Because I think I got a better idea."

"And what's that?"

Now it was my turn to sit down. "How about teaching me all you can about that case you want me on?"

"Now you're talking."

*****

So Harv talked and I listened, and when he was through he asked if we were good, and I said, yeah, we was good.

"Good," he said. "Now, as I mentioned, you'll be taking pictures on your assignment. I just want to ask you a few questions so I can feel comfortable lending you this equipment."

"Yeah, sure, ask," I said.

"Okay, here we go. Have you ever seen one of these before?"

"Yeah, sure."

"What is it?"

"It's a camera."

"Very good. And what about this?"

"It's a shutter button."

Harv's mouth dropped open and he gave me a look like I just solved one of them big huge math things with all the Xs and numbers.

"Wow, Coop," he said.

I kind of shrugged.

"And this right here," Harv said. "Do you know what it is and what to do with it?"

"It's a roll of film, and you load it into the camera so you can take pictures. If the camera don't have no film in it, you can't take no pictures. But before you take pictures, you gotta set the right film speed. And after you use up a roll, you gotta rewind the film back onto the roll and then send the roll in to get developed, unless you wanna go find a darkroom and develop the pictures yourself."

He clapped his hands together. "Little brother, I am truly impressed! As they say in court, no further questions. So here's the camera. It's already loaded. And here's an extra roll of film. Now have at it. And, oh, one more thing."

He reached into his pocket, and after staring at them for the longest time, like he was afraid he'd never see them again, he handed his car keys over to me. "Cooper, the lawyers working with me on the embezzlement case have provided me with a loaner car, so you can use mine. But before I let you do that, I just want to ask one thing."

Crap, I said to myself. He's gonna ask me a question out of the driver's manual. Like what aisle do I need to be in when I take a right turn.

"Can you please just make it multiple choice?" I said.

"Multiple what? Oh, no, nothing like that, Coop. All I ask is that you not wrap my car around a tree."

"Harv," I said, "I don't think I can turn that fast."

He chuckled and punched me in the shoulder. "Good one," he said.

I'm glad it was a good one because I didn't know what he meant by good one.

*****

Maybe I should of showed my brother the suitcase.

No, not the one with the crusty threads that Mom and me wound up taking to some stinky dump sixty miles out of town.

No, not that suitcase.

The other one. The one Harv told Mom, maybe it'd be best not asking what's inside it.

Yeah, that was Harv talking! Mister It's-Good-To-Know-Every-Single-Thing-About-Everything! Mister There-Should-Never-Be-No-Secrets! Him telling Mom: not only shouldn't they look inside that suitcase, they shouldn't even ask to look inside!

And that was okay by me, because I didn't want Harv or Mom or anyone else looking or asking. It was my suitcase. The one I kept under lock and key. The one with things inside I wanted kept inside, unless I took them out on my own.

Things like my single lens reflex camera. Like my extra lenses—the close-ups, wide angles, and telephotos. Like my filters, especially the polarizer that turned the sky a nice deep blue. Like my rolls and rolls of film with every ASA you can think of. And, most of all, like my boxes and boxes and more boxes of slides, of scenery and buildings and people, that showed I knew something about light and shadow and composition and color, all stuff I soaked up taking a ton of classes.

And by *ton*, I don't mean how much a big, huge thing weighs, because I don't know how much a big, huge thing weighs. I mean lots. Lots of classes. I mean every single photography class that NSU had to offer. I took them all. Classes where I actually sat and listened and done the work. And where I wound up giving myself an A. Or a B. Or sometimes a C or even a D when I thought I could of did a hell of a lot better.

So yeah, when Harv quizzed me on his photo stuff, maybe I should of brung my secret suitcase and opened it up and showed him a thing or two. Or better yet, a slide or two.

But then maybe that would of backfired. Maybe Harv would of held them slides up to the light and said, "You call this photography?" Or shook his head at all the pricey gear in that suitcase and said, "No wonder Dad had to turn to embezzlement."

So nope. Nothing doing. Harv was right. It was best him not knowing or asking. If I was gonna prove myself to my brother, it shouldn't be with the work I done but with the work he wanted done.

*****

It took three and a half hours of driving around, but I finally found Ballmore Park. It was a quarter to four, and the fun was supposed to start at exactly four, so it looked like I made it in the nick of time. All I had to do was back Harv's car off the curb and grab the camera from the trunk.

The way Harv told it, a Mrs Dalmont come to his office a week ago, all upset that her hubby was cheating on her. I thought "cheating" meant hiding playing cards up your sleeve, but Harv told me in this case it meant screwing. And I knew all about what that word meant except for the parts I wished I knew more about.

Mrs Dalmont—Gloria was her first name—said she had a plan on how to catch her hubby in the act, but she was ashamed to say what the plan was. And later Harv set me straight on what "in the act" meant. It meant screwing.

When Harv let Gloria know there was no reason to be ashamed and that his work was private and discreet, just like the sign in his window said, she let him know how much she appreciated that. And then she went on about how her and her hubby, Evan, used to celebrate his birthday every single year by going to Ballmore Park at exactly four o'clock in the afternoon and doing it in the bushes. And later Harv let me know what "doing it" meant. It meant screwing.

And, anyway, about the plan, Gloria said that maybe, just maybe, on Evan's next birthday, which was coming up real soon, Evan might just get it in his head to drive out to Ballmore Park at exactly four o'clock and do it in the bushes with someone other than Gloria. And what Harv later said to me was that "do it" wasn't any different than "doing it," and he saw no need to go over the same material twice.

Harv told Gloria her plan was perfect, and, what's more, since Ballmore was a public park, old Evan and his new lady friend couldn't very well squawk about their privacy being intruded on if someone just happened across them and begun snapping one photo after another.

And later, when Harv was about to explain to me what "just happened across them" meant, I raised my hand and gave him my guess.

And he was glad I finally caught on.

So there I was, at Ballmore Park on Evan Dalmont's birthday, at a little after four o'clock, walking the trails and looking for hidden spots where screwing might be going on.

And that's when I heard, from behind the bushes right next to me, a couple voices, a low one and a high one, with the low voice groaning, "Hold on! I'm trying, baby! I'm trying real hard!" and the high voice squealing, "Oh, Evan! Try harder! Do you hear me? Harder!"

And figuring this all had something to do with doing it, because what else could it be, I grabbed ahold of my camera and went tearing through them bushes, looking through the viewfinder and clicking away at the shutter button. And, on top of that, shouting out, loud and clear, "Happy birthday, Evan! Happy birthday to you!"

First, there was Evan's bare rear end in the frame. Click. And then him hearing happy birthday and spinning his head my way with his eyes all big. Click. And then him rolling his big, huge, flabby pink self onto a bunch of dead leaves. Click.

That left his lady friend all alone and naked on a patch of moss. Click. And her trying to cover every part of herself with some other part of herself. Click. Click. Click. And then her curling into a ball and crying out, but not squealing like she done before, "Oh, Lord! Oh, my Lord! Oh, my good and gracious Lord!"

But this time no click.

Because right then and there, I quit hitting the shutter button and quit looking through the viewfinder and begun to see what the real picture was.

And that's when I done a little crying out myself.

"Mom! What the hell?"

*****

What could I do but expose the whole roll of film to the sun, rewind it, and later say to my big brother, "These pics will turn out great! I just know it!"

Film Blank

From the Podcasts of Summer Cum Laude, College Detective

Michael J. Ciaraldi

"It's a rainy afternoon on campus. But on the top floor of Founders Hall, one young woman searches for answers." It was indeed a rainy afternoon on campus. In her dormitory room a young woman sat speaking into her recorder.

"She's ready for mystery," she continued. The phone on her desk rang. "She's ready for excitement." Another ring. "She's ready for *anything*!" Ring. "She's—"

Snatching up the phone, she spoke crisply into the receiver. "Summer Cum Laude, College Detective."

From the phone came a hesitant voice. "Hello, Gompei's? I'd like a pizza to go, and no anchovies."

"The name's not Gompei's, buster. You have to say my name 'Loud'"

"What? Gompei's?" he shouted.

"Idiot!" She slammed down the phone and resumed recording. "Where was I?"

The phone rang again. With a sigh, Summer picked it up. "Summer Cum Laude, College Detective."

A familiar anxious voice came from the phone. "Summer? I'm glad you're in. Any news?"

"I've been working on your case, Mr. President."

"Have you made any progress in finding the perpetrators of this vile deed?"

There was a knock on the door. "Excuse me." Summer covered the receiver with her hand and called, "Come in; it's unlocked."

A slim young woman bounced into the room and closed the door.

She was perky; there's no other way to describe her. "Hi, Summer," she said.

"Hi, Scooter. Hang on." Summer returned to speaking into the phone. "Sorry, Mr. President. I'm following up some leads, but nothing to report yet."

"Well, keep at it."

"Yes, sir, I'll be in touch. Bye."

An expression of astonishment appeared on Scooter's face. "The President is one of your clients? He called you from Washington?"

Patiently, Summer explained. "No, Scooter. Not the President in Washington; the President of the university."

Scooter's face fell, then brightened. "Oh. Still. With President Queeg on your side, maybe the residence hall people will finally let you put that glass panel in your door, with your name on it." Scooter jerked her thumb toward the door of the dorm room. "What's the case about?"

"Oh, he's convinced there's a scandal at Dining Services. It's probably nothing."

Another knock came on the door. "Come on in; it's unlocked!" Summer called.

A tall young man walked in with a briefcase in his hand. His jeans were dappled with chemical burns and had holes burned by dropped bits of solder; he wore a T-shirt with an unbuttoned flannel shirt over it. He looked back and forth between the two women and finally addressed Summer. "Ms. Lawdy?"

"'Loud'. You have to say my name '*Loud*'."

"*Lawdy?*"

"Oh, for heaven's sake! My name is pronounced 'Summer *Coom* Loud'. Got it? Just call me 'Summer', OK? This is my new assistant, Scooter. Who are you, and what do you want?" 30 seconds into a new case, and her patience was already wearing thin.

"My name is Harry Deighton, and I'm a graduate student here in the Physics Department."

Summer waved him toward a chair. He and Scooter both sat, then

Summer looked at him quizzically. "Aren't you a little young to be a graduate student?"

"I was only 15 when I graduated from high school."

"That's interesting. My parents used to remind me that kids as young as 12 have gone to college."

Scooter piped up. "My parents used to say that to my brother. But..." Realization started to dawn "...he never seemed to take the hint."

They all looked at each other thoughtfully for a few seconds. Summer finally broke the awkward silence. "Well, anyway, why are you here?"

Harry replied, "I'm doing research on radioactivity with Prof. Moreau, and something alarming happened this afternoon."

Scooter prompted him. "Go on."

Summer said to her, "You're the assistant, remember?"

"Sorry."

Summer turned back to Harry. "Go on."

"I'm studying a particular radioactive isotope. We shoot its emissions through a crystal and it produces a distinctive pattern on a sheet of photographic film."

Harry pulled a sheet of glossy white paper out of his briefcase and showed it to Summer and Scooter. "Here's the results from this afternoon's test."

Summer peered at it, then raised one eyebrow. "It's blank. So?"

Scooter piped up, "That must mean your sample isn't radioactive any more!"

"Right. And that means one of two things: Either, number one, I have inadvertently discovered a way to instantly make this isotope inert, in which case I will become the youngest person in history to win the Nobel Prize in Physics. Or..."

Summer prompted him. "Yes?"

"Or, number two, someone has stolen the real isotope and substituted a fake. If I don't get the real isotope back, this will be a health hazard for thousands of people, the university will lose its federal funding, and I'll be expelled!" He looked at her plaintively. "Help me,

Summer Cum Laude, you're my only hope."

Summer stood up. Briskly, she said, "Don't worry, Harry, we'll find your missing isotope!" She took her tan trench coat from the coat rack and donned it, then put on her fedora and tilted it down rakishly over one eye. "Or my name isn't—" A dramatic pause "—Summer Cum Laude, College Detective!"

*****

"After stopping at Scooter's room to pick up her new trench coat and fedora, and spending a few minutes discussing interrogation techniques, we started our investigation at the Physics Department, at the office of..." Summer peered at the sign. "Professor Thomas Oliver Moreau, Ph.D." She knocked. From inside came, "Come in."

Slipping the recorder into her coat pocket, Summer led Scooter into the office. They saw a distinguished-looking gentleman seated at his desk, wearing a tweed sport coat with leather patches on the elbows. "Prof. Moreau?"

"Yes. Sit down."

The two sleuths sat and removed their hats. Summer started the interrogation. "We have a few questions, Professor. Or should I say, 'Doctor'?"

"Either is fine." He examined their faces. "You're not my advisees, are you?"

"No, no. I'm Summer Cum Laude, and this is my assistant, Scooter."

Moreau looked at Scooter more intently. "*You* look familiar..."

"Last spring, before I graduated from high school, I sat in on your quantum electrodynamics course."

Summer looked at her in surprise, then recovered. "Anyway, we wanted to ask if you knew whether any radioactive isotopes were missing from the department."

Moreau answered quickly, "Oh, I wouldn't know anything about that."

Seeing an opening, Scooter asked, "But you're the Radiation Safety Officer for the Physics Department, aren't you?"

Moreau replied slowly, "Yes..."

Summer interrupted, "So you're in charge of the inventory of all radioactive materials in the department, right?"

"Yes..."

Scooter pounced. "So if any isotopes were missing, you're the one who would know, right?"

"Oh. Yes." A worried look crossed his face. "Well, what I meant to say is that, if any isotopes were missing I would know about it, but since there aren't, I don't. Wouldn't. Whatever." His look turned crafty. "Say, why should I answer your questions?"

Summer said, "Oh, President Queeg has asked me to look into some things around campus." Scooter shot Summer a surprised look. "Just one more question, Dr. Moreau. Were you on campus yesterday evening?"

"I stopped in for a minute when I returned to town."

"From where?"

"I spent the weekend in Maine. My family owns a small island off the coast there. We have a cottage."

Summer stood, and Scooter followed suit. "Thank you, sir. You've been very helpful. We'll be going now."

"Don't mention it."

*****

The next morning, Harry came to Summer's room. "So, how is the investigation going?" he asked.

"Making progress."

"Will Scooter be joining us?"

"No, she has class right now."

"I could come back later..."

"No, no, have a seat." Summer gestured toward her bed; with a bolster leaning against the wall, it doubled as a couch. They sat. "So, Harry, tell me about yourself. Why did you go into physics?"

"I guess I've always been interested in how things work. I took my mom's vacuum cleaner apart, I built my own ham radio equipment, that sort of thing."

Summer looked at him with growing interest. *He's cute, isn't he?* crossed her mind. "Hmm..." she prompted.

Harry warmed to his subject. "As I got more into it, I realized that physics is the study of how the universe works. On the most fundamental level."

"Wow...."

"So, Summer, how did you become a 'college detective'?"

Summer kept gazing into his eyes.

"Summer?"

Summer broke out of her reverie. "Oh. Well, I suppose it started when I was little. My parents had a complete set of Nancy Drew and Hardy Boys books, and a ton of comics. You know, they always call Batman 'The World's Greatest Detective'."

"Uh-huh."

"Then I moved up to Sherlock Holmes. But I really got interested when I got here to college and started taking popular culture courses. I felt such a kinship with the hard-boiled private eyes we studied: Sam Spade, Travis Magee, Guy Noir, Nick Danger..." Harry was starting to look dubious. "I studied their techniques, starting offering my services, set up my Web site, and one day I had my first case! Professor Ipcress asked me to find her missing files. I solved that one, and went on to others. There was the Anselmo pedagogy case, and that giant rat from Sumatra that escaped from the Biotechnology Department—"

"I didn't hear about that."

"Well, naturally they hushed it up to avoid panic."

"I see..." *Is this girl crazy, or what?* started to creep into his mind.

"But you know, what I really admired about these people was their sense of honor. They fight for the little guy, for justice, for freedom. And they don't quit. Look at Spider-Man: The public hates him; his aunt is always at death's door; his uncle, his parents, and his girlfriend Gwen got killed by villains, but he never gives up." Her face was lit up; this is what drives her. "He does the right thing because it's the right thing. He has a motto: 'With great power must come great responsibility.'"

Harry looked at her with new respect. "Wow…"

They gazed into each other's eyes for a long moment. They started to lean forward, their eyes closed, their lips parted…

Scooter knocked on the door. "Summer! Are you in?"

Summer and Harry sprang apart. "Come on in, it's unlocked," she called, then pulled out her recorder and muttered into it, "Note to self: Last time I make that mistake…"

Scooter entered. "Oh, hi, Harry."

"Scooter."

"If you're free, Scooter, we need to follow up some leads," said Summer.

"Should I come along?" Harry asked.

"No, this is a job for the pros."

"OK, then I'll be going."

As Harry left, Scooter asked, "So, what's up?"

The phone rang. As Summer picked it up, she said to Scooter, "Excuse me."

"Summer Cum Laude, College Detective."

From the phone came the anxious voice of the retired admiral. "Summer, what's the latest?"

"Oh, hello, President Queeg. Sorry, nothing new to report."

"Well, give it your highest priority. After your schoolwork, of course."

"I will, sir."

"Why, when I was in command of the fleet, if someone did this, I'd have him swabbing the decks for a month."

"I see."

"And no dessert for two months!"

"I can see how that would be appropriate."

"Too bad we don't have any yardarms at the university."

"Isn't that a little extreme, sir?"

"One has to maintain discipline in any organization."

"Oh, well, of course."

"You'll alert me of any developments?"

"Yes, Mr. President, I'll be in touch. Bye."

Barely waiting for Summer to put down her phone, Scooter burst out, "What was that all about?"

"Oh, President Queeg is being his usual paranoid self. You see, they served fresh strawberries at the annual Faculty Dinner last month at Caine Memorial Dining Hall. He saw the workers take the leftovers back into the kitchen, so he stopped in later that evening for a snack. There were no strawberries left, and he got upset."

"What happened to the strawberries?"

"Nothing sinister; the kitchen workers ate the leftovers. They were too embarrassed to tell the President that, so now he's convinced that someone is pilfering from the refrigerator in the dining hall."

"That's pretty weird."

"You're telling me. Now I'm supposed to be investigating a crime that didn't even occur. I don't know what I'm going to tell him." Summer sighed. "Oh, well, back to our real case. We need to find out if anything unusual is going on in the Physics Department. Something sinister. Something criminal."

"We've already talked with Prof. Moreau..."

"And got nowhere. We'll need to go to an underworld hangout to get more information."

"A wretched hive of scum and villainy?"

"Something like that. I was thinking of Moby Rick's. It's close to campus, it's pretty sleazy, and all kinds of disreputable characters hang out there. You know, students who never seem to graduate, adjunct faculty, theatre majors. And you know what they say, 'Everybody comes to Rick's.'"

"Moby Rick's. What else do they say about it? 'You'll have a whale of a time?' 'They wail all night'?"

"Look, Scooter, I know I told you that a private eye needs snappy patter, but you need to work on yours some more. Let's go."

*****

Summer and Scooter walked into Moby Rick's, a sleazy off-campus coffeehouse, looking cool in their trench coats and fedoras; Summer's was tan and Scooter's a deep brown. The counterman, Rocko, stood behind the bar, wiping it with a dirty rag. Various disreputable-looking customers were sitting at the mismatched tables, nursing cappuccinos and plotting nefarious deeds, no doubt. Summer addressed the counterman. "A triple espresso with a shot of hazelnut syrup and some skim milk." Then she looked at Scooter and jerked her head toward the counterman.

Scooter placed her order. "A grandé hot chocolate with whipped cream. Lots of it."

The counterman set their drinks on the bar and growled, "That'll be nine bucks. And fifty cents."

"Pay the man," snapped Summer.

Scooter took a plastic card out of her pocket and put it on the bar. The counterman picked it up, looked at it with disgust, and handed it back. "We don't accept University Dining Services cards here."

Scooter took the card back and handed him a bill. "Sorry. Here's ten. Keep the change."

"Thanks. Fifty cents. Now I can have that lobotomy I've been saving up for."

Summer and Scooter faced the rest of the room and leaned back against the bar. Summer took out her recorder and spoke into it. "One of the detective's most important obligations is training the next generation of crime fighters. I turned to Scooter and said: 'We need to find some physics majors. So, assistant, let's see your detective skills at work. Which one of these low-lifes is the physics major?'"

Scooter rotated her head from side to side, looking back and forth around the room. After a minute she looked back at Summer and shrugged. "Beats me."

"It's that fellow in the corner. But how did I know that?"

"Well, he's wearing glasses mended with tape."

"Good. How far does that narrow it down?"

"Hmmm. Based on the glasses, I would say that he is either a physics major, a computer science major, or..."

"Or?" Summer prompted.

"Harry Potter!"

"Good point, but I'd say we can eliminate Mr. Potter. So, you've narrowed it down to physics or CS. What's the one clue which enables us to decide?"

Scooter thought a while, then gave up. "I don't know, Summer."

"Observe the slide rule hanging from his belt. This is fine for the kinds of calculations a physics major would make. But a CS major needs an electronic calculator which can handle binary, octal, and hexadecimal numbers. Ergo, he is a physics major."

Scooter shook her head. "Summer, you amaze me."

"Hey, sometimes I amaze myself. Follow my lead."

Summer slipped the recorder into her coat pocket. They walked over to the corner table where the alleged physics major was sitting. He wore a faded T-shirt with a design factory-printed on it: a name tag which read:

HELLO

My name is

Inigo Montoya.

You killed my father.

Prepare to die.

All but the first four words of the legend were sloppily crossed out with fabric paint, and replaced by the word "Phil".

Summer smiled at him. "Mind if I sit here?"

Phil looked at Summer, then at all the empty tables, then back at Summer, then gestured at the chair opposite him. "Not at all."

Summer sat, saying, "Thanks, handsome."

"What about your friend?"

"She can stand."

Scooter took up a position behind Summer, a little off to the side.

Phil eyed her warily. "I see."

"So, how are things in the Physics Department?" asked Summer.

"How did you know I'm a physics major?"

"A girl can tell these things, if she knows what to look for."

"Are you interested in physics?"

"Yes, especially radioactive isotopes. I understand that security is very tight."

"I suppose."

"Suppose someone were stealing isotopes. Where would they hide them?"

"Why should I tell you?"

"Let's just say that my assistant here will get angry. You wouldn't like her if she got angry."

Phil sneered. "I don't think I like her now." He looked at Scooter appraisingly, thinking that she looked like she couldn't fight her way out of a wet paper bag. "Am I supposed to be scared?"

Summer went on. "Appearances can be deceiving, my friend." Scooter scowled and said nothing. "She knows jiu-jitsu." Scooter moved into a martial-arts crouch. Phil was starting to look worried. "Judo." Scooter shifted her stance and scowled even more fiercely. Phil was looking even more worried. "Karate..." Scooter started examining her hands intently, rubbing the edge of one against the palm of the other, as if checking the callus she had developed from breaking boards.

Phil was sweating now. He looked wildly around the room; all the other customers were pointedly looking the other way. "All right, all right. I guess the best place would be somewhere that the radiation wouldn't be noticed. Say, by the campus nuclear reactor. Or maybe an abandoned warehouse."

"We know where the reactor is. What's this about an abandoned warehouse?"

"Well, I remember hearing that Prof. Moreau owns one on Central Street."

"I know the one you mean. So Moreau owns it, does he?" She stood, then leaned over and patted Phil on the cheek. "Thanks, cutie." She gestured to Scooter. "Let's go."

As they headed toward the door, Summer turned to Scooter. "Good work."

"Thanks. But, Summer, I don't have any martial arts training."

"I never said you did. But it is true that you know jiu-jitsu, judo, karate, sushi, and several other Japanese words."

"It's a good thing we pulled that off. Or we might have become acquainted with another Japanese word."

"What's that?"

"Hara-kiri."

*****

Scooter and Harry emerged from between two campus buildings and started to walk across the quad. Harry asked, "So, why did you want to see me?"

"Summer wanted me to ask if we could borrow some equipment from your lab. Here's a list."

Harry looked it over quickly. "That shouldn't be a problem, especially if it will help solve the case. Let's go over to the physics building, and I'll show you how to use the stuff."

"Sounds good."

"How did you wind up as Summer's assistant, anyway?"

"I only met her a few weeks ago, shortly after I started here at the university. I was walking across the quad one day, right about here, in fact..."

Two students were tossing a Frisbee back and forth, Scooter said. *Beanie on my head, I looked around, admiring the campus buildings. The Frisbee landed near my feet. "Hey, frosh! Little help here!" yelled one of the throwers. I noticed the Frisbee, bent down to pick it up, straightened up, and tossed it to the other thrower, expertly, if I say so myself. "Here you go." "Thanks!"*

I saw an older student entering the quad, looking intently at the ground as she walked along. Oblivious, she walked right through the

Frisbee game. Then she knelt down and started examining the ground with a magnifying glass. I walked closer. The kneeling student muttered, "You're blocking the light." "Sorry." I moved aside, and then watched her for a while. "What are you doing?" "Investigating." "Huh?" "Aha!"

She picked a small glinting object off the ground, took a plastic evidence bag out of her pocket, and put it in the bag. I couldn't help myself. "What is it?" I asked. "Professor Ipcress' contact lens. One of the first rules of being a detective: you never know what your next case will be." "Detective?" I asked.

She straightened up, put her equipment away in the pockets of her trench coat, dusted off her hands, then took a business card out of her pocket, and handed it to me. I started reading it aloud. "'Summer Cum... Laude,'" I pronounced it 'Loud', of course... "'College Detective.' That's you?"

"In the flesh."

"Neat."

"I'm glad you think so," said Summer. "I'm looking for an assistant. Interested?" I thought for a second. "Maybe..." "Good, you're hired. Come to my office this evening around 7:00." "Office?" "OK, it's my dorm room, but I had to start somewhere. Are we on?"

The Frisbee landed at my feet just as I was saying, "Uh, sure." "Hey, frosh!" yelled one of the throwers. Summer extended her hand. "Great. Welcome to the world of detecting. Uh...what's your name, anyway?" The other thrower yelled, "Hey, frosh! Wake up!" "Oh, it's..." I started to say. The yell came again. "Hey, frosh! Grab that Frisbee and scoot 'er over here!" I realized I was the one being addressed, and blurted out, "Scoot 'er?"

"Scooter—I love it!" cried Summer. "A perfect name for a hard-boiled detective's young, innocent protégé." She grabbed my hand and shook it, saying, "See you at 7:00. Bye!" Then she hurried away. I just stood there, a little stunned.

"So that's how it happened," Scooter concluded.

"Cool. So when did you finally tell her your real name?"

"Hmm...Let's see..."

*****

That evening, Summer and Scooter entered the darkened warehouse, each carrying a flashlight. As they picked their way through the discarded pallets on the floor, ticking sounds came from the Geiger counter in Scooter's other hand.

"There's radiation, all right," Summer whispered. "What's the reading?"

Scooter shone her flashlight on the Geiger counter's dial and replied, "Based on the data Harry gave me when he lent us this Geiger counter, plus my own calculations, I would say that all the missing isotopes are here in this abandoned warehouse."

"Good work, Scooter! Now to find something linking them to Prof. Moreau."

Suddenly the lights snapped on full, revealing Moreau in the center of the room. "How about the fact that I am holding the container of isotopes in my hand?" he sneered, gesturing with the case he held.

"It's you!" Summer cried. "But you can get all the isotopes you need for your research. Why steal them?"

Scooter said, "I think I know. To obtain the isotopes legitimately, he would have to explain what he was going to do with them. And if he wanted to keep that a secret..."

"Right you are. Very useful things, isotopes. For example, you could use some to power a directed energy weapon."

"A what?" asked Summer.

"More popularly known as...a ray gun!" He shouted wildly. "This is the end for you, Ms. College Detective. Your meddling stops now!"

Prof. Moreau reached into his coat, pulling out a device of coils and wires. He shot at Summer and Scooter. They dodged out of the way as a blinding flash appeared and an explosion rocked the room.

Scooter looked back at where they had been standing a moment before. "My God! You've blown a hole in the wall!" she cried.

Prof. Moreau laughed maniacally as he shot at them again. Scooter crumbled to the floor as Summer dodged again. Another flash and explosion. "Scooter!" she cried, then, "Professor! Stop! You don't know what you're doing!"

Moreau's voice was deadly calm. "I know exactly what I'm doing."

"But you've destroyed two walls already. The building won't be able to take it!"

Prof. Moreau fired again at Summer as she dodged once more. Another flash and explosion.

Moreau calmly aimed the ray gun at Summer as she stood with her back against the only undamaged wall. "Professor!" she pleaded.

"Time to die..." He fired once more. The flash of the ray gun was followed by pitch darkness; the power had gone out. The entire building seemed to groan.

"Oh, no!" Summer cried. "You've broken down the fourth wall!"

With a deafening roar, the building collapsed.

*****

A flickering red light appeared, gradually brightening. The crackling sounds of a fire. The room started to fill with billowing smoke. The building was on fire, spreading toward the room where the two detectives lay. Summer was lying on the floor, face down, buried under a pile of wreckage, only her head and shoulders free. Scooter was lying on her back, covered from the waist down by debris.

Scooter coughed, then yelled, "Summer, wake up. Summer!"

"Huh?" Summer replied groggily.

"Summer! Wake up! You have to save us!"

"I'm awake! I'm awake! What's going on?"

Scooter tried to control her voice. "You want the long answer or the short answer?"

"Short."

"Well, the building fell on top of us, and it's on fire."

"OK," Summer said, still trying to wake up the rest of the way. "What's your status?"

"I'm buried under this rubble, I think my leg is broken, and I'm bleeding profusely. And, I'm on my back so I can't get any leverage. Other than that, things are pretty good if you don't consider the fire. How about you?"

"Let's see." She wiggled, tugged, then looked back at herself. "No broken bones as far as I can tell. Minor bleeding. Hold on." Summer tried to crawl out. No good. She tried to raise her torso using her arms. No good. "I'm stuck."

Scooter's voice turned icy calm. "Well, Summer, here's how I see the situation. We have three options: Number 1: You can fail to rescue us, in which case I bleed to death and you burn to death. Number 2: You can get yourself out, but you take so long that I bleed to death before then. Or Number 3: You can get your butt in gear..." Her control slipped as she shouted, "...and get us both out of here!"

Summer tried again. She collapsed and groaned. "No good."

Scooter tried another tack. "All right. Remember how you're always quoting Spider-Man?"

"'With great power must come great responsibility'?"

"Right. Can you apply that principle in this case?"

Summer tried unsuccessfully to rise yet again, then gasped, "It's backward. I have the responsibility; I need the power."

"Whatever," Scooter replied. "Remember issue 36? Doctor Doom knocked an entire building down on top of Spider-Man, but he found the strength to escape."

"Issue 36? That was Doctor Octopus, not Doctor Doom." Summer coughed as she gathered her thoughts. "Let's see. Spidey didn't meet Doctor Doom until years later—"

"Whatever! Get us out of here!"

"OK! OK!"

As the sound, light, and smoke from the fire increased, Summer struggled to lift the rubble enough to drag herself out. Once. Twice. On the third try, she succeeded, then limped to where Scooter was lying. With one motion she seized the beam lying across Scooter's legs and flung it aside. She scooped up Scooter and staggered out the door just as the fire reached a crescendo in the room.

*****

Moving quietly, Moreau entered the control room of the campus nuclear reactor building. He carried a parcel, which he set down on the floor. He started to manipulate the controls on the control panel. A few minutes later, he didn't notice as a figure entered slowly, wearing a tan trench coat, with a hat pulled down over the face and one hand in a coat pocket. From the figure came Summer's voice. "Step away from the reactor control panel, Doctor."

"You again? I thought I killed you."

"Some people are harder to kill than others."

"I can fix that," said Moreau. He drew a revolver and pointed it at her.

"You don't have to do this."

"Who's going to stop me?" He sneered. "Say, where's your insipid assistant?"

She started at this, then said, "Scooter's gone for help. She should be here any minute with Inspector Doppler and a squad of the Campus Police."

"Inspector Doppler? He's nothing but a stupid policeman. There's nothing he can do to prevent my turning this reactor into our campus' own little atomic bomb."

"Doctor, no! Harry assured me that there's not enough radioactive material in that reactor to explode."

"Not ordinarily. But since I have already added all the isotopes I stole, all that remains is to throw this switch and drain off the coolant. The core melts down and then boom! And just in case that doesn't work, this bomb will destroy the reactor and contaminate the entire city." He bent down and ripped open the parcel, revealing the mechanism inside. He straightened up, holding the detonator button on the end of a wire attached to the bomb.

"You won't get away with this."

"Who says I want to? When this reactor blows, you and I will be past caring, but the world will never forget Dr. Thomas Oliver Moreau. Now stay back."

She started to move slowly to the side, maintaining her distance but keeping Moreau's attention on her. Another figure entered from behind Moreau, this one in a brown trench coat and hat. She crept up behind him slowly and quietly. Slowly she started to pull a day-glo green baseball bat from behind her back.

Moreau continued to rave. "All I have to do is flick this switch to drain the coolant, and press the detonator as a backup. Either way, in a few seconds we'll both be dead." He heard a noise behind him and started to turn.

"Wait!" came Summer's voice. He turned back to the figure in front of him as she whipped off her hat and unbuttoned her coat, revealing Scooter on crutches.

"What? How?" sputtered Moreau.

Scooter pulled Summer's recorder out of her coat pocket and waved it. Summer's voice came from the recorder. "It's all a matter of being prepared."

"Then where's...?"

He started to turn. Summer, still wearing Scooter's coat and hat, cracked him on the head with the bat. Moreau wavered, then toppled over, dropping the detonator button, which Summer deftly caught in midair. "And that's that!" she cried with a big grin.

And from the recorder came Summer's voice. "And that's that!"

*****

Summer, Scooter, Harry, and President Queeg gathered in Summer's dorm room.

"You saved us, Summer. You saved us all. The University will always be grateful," said the retired admiral, looking very dapper in his business suit and gold-braided naval cap.

"Thank you, President Queeg," said Summer. "I couldn't have done it without Scooter and Harry."

"We're grateful to all of you. If you ever have any library fines or something like that, just let me know," Queeg replied. "Now, about those strawberries..."

"Oh," said Summer. "I'm sorry to have to tell you this, Mr. President, but, uh, Prof. Moreau stole those strawberries and ate them. With him in custody for trying to blow up the campus, it's not worth prosecuting him for the strawberries. At least that's what the, uh, district attorney told me."

"Moreau, eh? Was there no end to his villainy? Oh, well..."

Summer put her hand comfortingly on his arm. "There, there, Mr. President, there will be more strawberries."

"I suppose so. Well, thanks again to you all. Bye." With a tip of his cap he left.

Summer sat down in her desk chair. Scooter and Harry sat next to each other on the bed.

"Another case solved," said Summer. "So, Harry, how about you and I getting some dinner? I know a nice place with good food, candlelight, soft music..."

Harry looked embarrassed. "I'd like to, Summer, but Susan and I have plans."

"Susan? Who's Susan?"

"That's me, Summer," Scooter said gently. "'Susan' is my real name. You're the only one who calls me 'Scooter'"

Harry and Scooter clasped hands and looked at each other fondly.

Harry broke the silence. "Well, I guess we'd better get going. Thanks again, Summer." He and Scooter stood.

"I see," said Summer. "Well, you two kids have fun."

Summer stood. She exchanged a solemn handshake with Harry, then hugged Scooter. Scooter and Harry headed out to the corridor as Summer shook her head and smiled wryly. "They grow up so fast..."

She sat down again, then pulled out her pocket recorder and started to dictate. She sighed. "The life of a private eye is a lonely one." From outside came campus noises: bells chiming the hour, the patter of rain. "Sometimes there is triumph, and sometimes heartbreak. But on the top floor of Founders Hall, on a rainy evening, one young woman stands ready." Her voice rose dramatically. "She's ready for mystery."

The telephone on her desk rang.

"She's ready for excitement."

The phone rang again.

"She's ready for anything!"

The phone rang again.

"She's—"

The phone rang one more time, then cut off as Summer took the recorder from her mouth, picked up the phone, and crisply spoke into it. "Summer Cum Laude, College Detective."

Author's Note: This story is dedicated to all those who inspired it, including Murray Burnett and Joan Alison, John Byrne, Len Deighton, Hampton Fancher & David Peoples, The Firesign Theatre, Ian Fleming, Garrison Keillor, Stan Lee, Federico Garcia Lorca and Jim "Roy" Nichols, George Lucas, The Marx Brothers, Anthony Shaffer, Matt Wagner, H. G. Wells, and Herman Wouk.

Ferret
Jeff Burt

I had broken the chain of custody and the mawkish looks of the crowd assembled on the street made it seem like I had caused the universe to spin out of control, planets ending their orbits and wandering off from their suns, galaxies dissolving, black holes becoming neither black nor holes. I was a private eye under public view, and it didn't look encouraging. I had to find the gun.

In the crowded street, mothers glared at me as if a cup of mono had been passed from some other child to their own, or, worse, alcohol or a drug more volatile swimming in the Gatorade.

Fathers winced as if I had passed the ball to the closest defender thinking it was a teammate, neutralizing the taste of the nachos and salsa, flattening the beer.

Grandparents scowled as if I had passed my baby around a room of strangers.

Even the anarchists howled, who didn't believe in property, or assets, or anything surrounding possession, and look dismayed.

Now, the truth could not be told even though we all knew it was the truth. Anything could be altered, time, matter, energy, even the fifth element of the universe. All was in flux, or, rather, all was not in flux, because if all had been in flux, it certainly wasn't any longer, and if all had not been in flux, if things had been certain, they were certainly thrown back into flux. Punishment would not be a simple firing, or ostracism, or the rest of a life spent searching for a job more meaningful than mopping floors and cleaning urinals; punishment would be the hideous fear that somewhere, anywhere, sometime, anytime, a tube or a beaker or a blemish or a hair out of place would ruin someone's life.

I was damned, damned to hell, if hell was still the place of ruination, and it probably wasn't any longer, judging by the faces of the Pentecostal zealots on the curb.

I drank another Scotch, the whiskey unable to penetrate my perceptions any longer, though I cannot tell you if I see the world bleary-eyed or straight-eyed, it's been so long. I was always drinking, never seeming to finish a drink, not that anyone kept on pouring Scotch into my glass, but that I gulped the first few ounces and then had the drink in my hand forever while I talked and argued and tried to ferret out clues from my companions. Ferret out is an interesting phrase, because if you've ever seen a ferret do its thing, it's nothing like an investigator. Ferrets don't go around the edges—they identify their prey and go straight for it, usually straight after, and straight in it, like a hole or an outcropping of rock. They don't need subtlety, or wisecracks, or some serendipitous historical trivia to drop into their laps to know their prey.

Anyway, when I had Scotch, I ferreted. It seemed like anytime I needed to talk to someone, Scotch was in the room. With ice, like ice just lingered in the places I went to, or, in some cases, the ice had to be fetched from the kitchen, which gave me time to review the room and make esoteric connections with the pictures or the vases to the person to whom I was speaking.

Only sultry women drank Scotch with me. Strange? Hard industrialists, fellow criminals (I say fellow lightly—only because I break the law to enforce it, which is part of the investigators code of ethics, and might even be on the business license, which if I could afford one I'd tell you for sure), cops, bankers—they didn't drink Scotch. But put a .38 special or a .45 in the hand of a blonde in a tight dress with a steady gaze and hunger in the shiny glare of her fingernail polish on the fingernails you know she'd like to run down your back, and give her a name from the 50s like Dolores or Betty or some other name that reminded you of black nylon stockings, the kind that rolled up at the top, and garter belts, and there was a Scotch in her hand, usually bottoms upped before I could take my second sip, an acknowledgement of depression, of need, of desperation, that usually had nothing to do with the crime, a tour de force comparison between my vitality and their depravity brought by boredom. Yet I was never bored. I was seeking justice.

I looked out the window, imagined ambulances vying to park in the driveway, and cart the bodies away or a police van with several orange-suited criminals chained to the interior placing bets on which jurisdiction would get to claim the murders, any vehicle that could get me away. I would go shackled, manacled, ball-and-chained; the method didn't matter as long as it was perverse and heavy. Even a straitjacket would suffice, anything to mark me as more than the invisible spot of flesh behind the suburban walls I could no longer heat that were heading to foreclosure. I was starting to starve, my whole life now with a quickening pace towards dissolving completely, as if I had been road kill, a possum perhaps, and the bloating had passed and the body had been pierced, eyes yanked out of the sockets by crows to let the blocked gas escape, and now the deflated corpse was yielding to the forces of nature to rid the carcass of its shell and all but the skeleton inside.

The apartment had newly painted bedrooms, a squishy little living room with pillows on two sides and another room that looked like a family room that was all modern, networked, large screen TV, everything high def. Take one step from a bedroom into the old and the drafty, uninsulated floors took hold, and shit-kicking boots were a requirement, wool socks, and a willingness to let a German shepherd run around your legs waiting to do mayhem in the yard. The civility of the family room changed as well into cursing and cussing when the threshold was crossed. Caesar had his Rubicon; the victims had their kitchen.

I knew the officer was going to say it. You knew the officer was going to say it. The whole watching world knew the officer was going to say it.

You don't look so good, Tommy.

Of course, I didn't look so good. I'm a frickin' investigator.

My body had become a crash site, as in whatever goes up must come down kind of crash site. Is absolute zero a when, as when all molecular activity stops, or a where, where all molecular activity stops, or a how molecular activity stops, or, now, a whose, as in whose molecular activity has stopped, as in whose is me?

Of course, the mere thought of thinking disproves the absolute zero, unless thinking about absolute zero is zero activity, which in this case, seeing as how I recycled the thought for a seeming infinite amount of time I certainly gave myself every indication of total brain freeze. My entire body tingled, as if I had one giant artery and it had a kink, like a garden hose that supposedly never kinks gets a hook in it and the hook collapses and suddenly you've got a kink in the kink-less, and no water comes out at all, that's how my body tingled.

Yes, I didn't look good, no one who ferrets looks good, though I looked better than the two stiffs on the floor with needle tracks and a story of tattoos that spoke English, Chinese, Spanish, graphic novel, animal sex, and a rather pathetic emotional semiology I can only describe as seventh-grade doodling.

Anson, the person who shot the stiffs, was always fixing his nuts, and by nuts, I don't mean that he was nicking the nubs off some peanuts or scuffing the ends of an almond, or sorting a tin can of assorted widgets that go on bolts and screws. I mean he was adjusting his scrotum. By adjusting I mean he was the kind of guy who didn't turn away in a room full of guys and sent his hand into his pants like a soldier on a search and adjusted his nuts until he was comfortable, giving out a huge sigh when he finished, which I couldn't tell was a sigh of relief that he had adjusted them, or a sigh of relief that he had found them, that somehow not touching his nuts for an hour made them disappear. When women were around, he'd still adjust his nuts, but turn around, and the sigh became inaudible, though you could see it on his face, a certain anxiety passing to peacefulness, the kind of expression a woman doing sign language exhibits to get a point across. So here we were, him holding the gun, and I knowing that sometime in the next hour the gun would transfer from his right hand to his left and that right hand would submerge like a submarine into his trousers and I would get one chance to kick him in the hand and the nuts and take the gun away.

I let time pass. Not like I could prevent time from passing, which requires more effort than I can expend and usually some pills that I know about but have never carried with me, well, maybe carried with me but never used. It takes a long time for time to pass when all you are doing is sitting in a chair waiting for Anson to either shoot you or leave the place because you know after ten minutes the woman he keeps calling and never connecting with is never showing up. After about thirty minutes I even stopped fearing being shot, stopped ferreting, even stopped thinking about dying. I didn't think about living either, but merely stayed in the in-between of the two, became real Catholic mystic, Ignatius I think, or Aquinas, in limbo, my body kind of going on with the breathing and the perspiring and autonomic system functions, and my mind separated in this time warp of incredible detail and numbing lack of detail, like being able to see a tiny balloon spider up in the corner of the room and zoom in on it in a way that human eyeballs are not meant to do but not seeing the wall anymore, not even knowing I was in a room any more, not even knowing I was looking at a spider any more until Anson asked what the hell I was looking at.

A spider. Up in the corner. What're you looking at?

Nothing.

That was his answer to everything. Nothing. Like nothing was an answer. It was his answer for his future, his answer for the amount of his woman's passion for him, his answer for what he was getting out of killing two men, what he was going to do next, what he done in his past, what his motive was. Nothing.

And that's when I knew he was going for his nuts. He had to turn to look up at the spider and the gun had transferred finally from left hand to right, and as sure as the IRS rejects my itemized receipts every year for breakfast at Eddie's Billiards, his right hand went down to his crotch.

I came up from the chair fast and my right hand reached for the gun and took it like a baton in a relay race, like it was meant to be. Polished. Rehearsed. Michael Jackson—like, both my move and his crotch pull.

Then he bit me. He bit on the neck like a zombie or the living dead, not like a vampire all teeth-sinking and sexual, but blunt, like a mad cow might bite or a horse that's pissed off because you tickled his nose with a feather or a mule that might bite because it's a mule and mule's do that sort of thing once in a while. More like the mule, because he seemed randomly practiced at it. I grabbed the gun, and he bit me, like it was choreographed, liked he had worked on that maneuver knowing that someday he would be holding the gun in his left hand and some dick like me would grab it and he would need a response. He was quick and he was good at it, too. Like Michael Jackson.

I was pissed at being bit. I think at that time I might have welcomed being shot rather than having a dental impression. So I chased him out of the place and a little way after that and then threw the gun at him, and he picked it up and took off.

I know, I know. You don't throw a gun. But I was off balance. I'd sat in a chair for an hour. I'd been bit. My whole game was destroyed.

Your story sounds like you're hiding something, the lieutenant said.

Don't they always?

Yeah. Your story sounds pretty stupid, see. So I believe you. No one could make up a private dick throwing a gun at someone. You should have kept the gun. Now our forensic team will have a hole to fill.

Yeah, I said, yet that's my job. That's what a P.I. does, fills holes.

So that's what I need to do. P.I.s go around the universe filling holes. We find the missing piece of the puzzle, we put the last dirt over the dead, we blacktop the sinkholes of the heart caused by the tears of aching relatives.

Forensics was going to be all over my ass, except I could weasel, I could ferret, hell, I could mink if I had to. I'd broken the chain of custody, I'd created a hole, and had to find the link to fill the hole and put the universe back together. I looked at the seething crowd and rubbed the bite mark on my neck. I was ready.

I started to think about chaos theory, how if I had been 5 minutes earlier, if the traffic had been smoother, none of this would have happened. Or if they had been lovers, and loving, in the act of loving each other, this would not have happened. Or if a fire alarm had gone off. Or if loud music had blared. You know, the wing of a seagull in the Gulf of Mexico means Katrina ploughs into New Orleans instead of Galveston, or a tip of the leaf diverts the wind, or a frayed stitch on a baseball means a beaning that alters a career, or a single gamma ray on the drool of a bat in China creates a mutated virus that means a billion deaths. Chaos. Randomness. Ions with positive and negative additions sliding back and forth like credit cards in the transaction reader of time. Photons of light that are mass one nanosecond, waves of energy another nanosecond, and then no one knows what they are the next nanosecond.

Relativity.

I wasn't a detective for nothing. I was a detective to connect the dots, draw the line of responsibility from A to B. And I was good at that. I had been good at that since kindergarten. I knew that assessing responsibility mattered, so that in a universe of transformation and tendencies and eighty percent/twenty percent court decisions, that I could keep the crime moon in a state of constancy around earth. Someone pulled a trigger. Someone died. A to B. I was going to find the killer.

If string theory meant anything in quantum physics, it meant there was one end on one end, and one end on the other end. That's all I needed to know, and any ferret scratching his way down a hole doesn't need any more than that to go on. So I started scratching.

The Case of the Saintsville Cat
L.N. Hunter

"Nice Kitty. Good Cat," I struggled to keep the panic out of my voice. "You don't want to eat old Solly, now, do you?"

Of all the ways for my existence to end, being ripped apart by a four-hundred-pound panther came pretty close to the bottom of my list. I'd nearly drowned in the sewers one time, and only just avoided being burned alive another—both of which were undoubtedly worse ways to go, but only by a hair. I would've crossed my fingers for luck, but I didn't want to move and startle the nice kitty.

The big cat growled at me, showing eight inches of vicious canines. *Do felines have canines?*

I didn't think I'd be contemplating animal dentistry when the knock came on my door that morning.

She'd barged right in without waiting for an invitation, catching her nylons on the door frame and swearing in Afrikaans long and loud enough to make a Cape Town sailor blush. She was accompanied by a fog of perfume so thick it put up a fight with the odors of my fifth Lucky Strike of the day and the half-eaten egg-and-onion sandwich that formed my breakfast. I don't eat much, and extreme flavors are all my dead taste buds can perceive. She must've noticed the smell, but she didn't react. A real classy lady, this dame.

Behind a cloud of cigarette smoke, my eyes scanned her up and down, tracking from side to side to follow the curves—which took a while because, well, her curves had curves, if you get my meaning. I casually took a swig of bourbon, and then went for another look—but dropped the bottle cap. I scrambled to retrieve it with what I hoped was an air of casual sophistication.

Picking it up brought me overly close to the stubble peeking through her torn pantyhose. I shuddered and said, "Take a load off those gams, dollface."

She flumped onto the sofa across the office, which let out a long, plaintive *Wheeee-pffff* of protest.

"Solomon Granger?"

"Last time I checked, that's the name on the door. What's a dame like you need a PI for?"

I lit another cigarette and hauled my desk chair closer to the sofa—that didn't take very long, seeing how my office makes a walk-in closet for a naturist seem spacious.

As she sank deeper into the stricken davenport, her fur-lined collar gaped open, displaying more diamonds than anyone ought to be wearing in Saintsville. If the country was a human body, Saintsville would be its appendix—no one knows what it's for, but it can generate a lot of pain. And this was a broad who shouldn't be in anyone's appendix; with stones like that, she ought to be in the gallbladder, at least.

"Mr. Granger, I need you to find someone. My niece has disappeared."

"The police do missing persons." I didn't have anything against finding people—that made up more than half my business. What I wanted to know was if this would be an easy money job, or one that would wear out more shoe leather than even someone as well-heeled as this damsel in distress would be willing to pay for.

I didn't want to admit it, but I already knew I'd take the case—it would make a change from the run of missing pets I'd had recently. All of them unsuccessful. The most I'd managed to find of precious Tiddles or beloved Fido were a few collar tags. There were rumors of a dog-fighting ring, but I suspected that a more likely destiny for the pets was to become the major ingredient in Saintsville's street food.

The woman blushed, so much skin going bright red that I could feel the heat.

"No, I don't want to involve the police. The shame of it… Emily's a good girl."

So it's going to be one of these, I thought. I failed to conceal my smile at the cash register already ringing in my head.

The worst cases are where the cops have been on the job for weeks and found nothing, which typically means there's nothing to find. Unlike most PIs, I have nothing against cops—I used to be one, until I decided I wanted to pick my own jobs instead of being assigned them by a captain who always resented my return from the shootout in the cemetery. Well, my career prospects weren't helped by damaging the precinct's one car beyond repair—twice, and assaulting the aforementioned captain when I discovered he'd been bribed to send me to the cemetery in the first place.

"Tell me about your niece," I said, trying not to cough as her perfume cut right through the cigarette fumes and scoured the back of my throat. I thought about asking her if they did cologne as well—it'd help me cut down on the smokes.

Mrs. Darlington-Stevens—a name as substantial as the woman who wore it—told me Emily Gordon had disappeared two days earlier. She'd occasionally been out all night before, seeing unsuitable men, no doubt—I got the impression that *all* men were unsuitable in Mrs. D-S's book. However, the girl had an important meeting this morning and she wouldn't have missed it unless something was wrong—real wrong.

The dame started to cry, and I shoved a mostly clean handkerchief her way—mainly because I didn't want to see that makeup run. She waved the kerchief away and rummaged in her handbag, pulling out a photo and thrusting it at me.

My eyebrows mounted an expedition up my scalp as I looked at it. There seemed to be little linking the genetics of little Ms. Gordon and Mrs. D-S. The girl was a mid-twenties looker, with long black hair and blue eyes a man would let himself drown in before it crossed his mind to call for help. Her bright red lips had a knowing curve that would make a eunuch ask for advice on reversing the procedure. If I were several decades younger and less dead, I'd no doubt be one of those unsuitable men yapping at Emily's heels.

I scribbled down some more details, absentmindedly munching the rest of the curling egg-and-onion sandwich in between drags on my cigarette. Habits, known associates, favorite cafes and bars, all the usual drill. Totally useless, but it helped reassure clients like Mrs. D-S that I'd earn the dough she was about to fork over.

Unlike my usual clientele, she didn't blink when I told her my rate was forty bucks a day plus expenses—I should've gone for fifty. One of those expenses might be an appointment with the chiropractor, because I felt something in my back go click when I helped Mrs. D-S out of the davenport. I hoped my back was going to be easier to repair than my sofa.

After Mrs. D-S left, I washed down my sandwich with some more whisky, then topped up my hipflask, put on my somewhat battered fedora and my trench coat, turned the collar up and hit the pavement, lighting another Lucky on the way out.

Every PI in Saintsville knew the obvious places to look for missing persons, especially when the person in question was a looker like Ms. Gordon. Take the half dozen or so bordellos, for a start, and certain high-class hotels that didn't ask too many questions… not to mention the vampire mansion just outside of town.

But in this case, I figured the girl probably just wanted to get away from Auntie, so there's really only one place to go: the Evergreen Lodge motel, a one-star joint at the edge of Saintsville, the sort of dive where the bedsheets were changed once a week, and for clean ones most of the time.

"Your comfort and privacy are our pleasure," the sign on the hotel desk said, but the pimple-faced receptionist turned out to be more interested in a couple of greenbacks than in Ms. Gordon's privacy. Within two shakes of a love-smitten lamb's tail, my knuckles were treating her door to a rat-tat-tat.

"You're early, Iz—" she said as she opened the door. She did a double take. "You're not Isaac."

I tipped my hat. "No, ma'am. Solomon Granger, private investigator, at your service. Your aunt is concerned about your whereabouts."

"My aunt? Oh!" Emily put a hand to her cupid's bow lips, then grabbed my sleeve and pulled. "Come in, quickly. Did anyone see you?"

She sat me on the corner of the bed while she filled two glasses from the bar—which looked pretty thoroughly raided already. She held one of the drinks out with a shaking hand while gulping down the other.

"That woman's no aunt of mine."

"Now wait just a minute," I said. "How do I know you think you know who I know sent me?"

She stared at me for a moment, while we both tried to work out what had escaped my lips, and I did my best not to think about the things I'd like to do with hers.

"Mrs. Darlington-Stevens, right?" she said. "You do know that witch works for Tiny Tony?"

A chill ran down my spine, then turned around and ran back up, picking a spot behind my eye sockets to sit and throb. Anthony Tiny was Saintsville's gangster boss, a man with so many of Saintsville's high and mighty in his pockets he had no room left for his Altoids.

Gangster parlance being what it is, his moniker du jour became Tiny Tony. Anywhere else, that would be ironic, but Saintsville had neither the intelligence nor the patience for irony: Tony was baby-faced and all of three feet nada in his expensive Cuban heels. Two pints of evil in a half-pint jar, he had the temperament of a rabid terrier and the breath to match. We'd crossed paths in the past, and he'd promised to tap-dance on my liver as he strangled me with my intestines if I ever interfered in his business again.

I swallowed the drink and asked, "What have you got yourself into, lady?" *And how do I get myself out of it with my intestines still on the inside?*

"Tony's running a gladiator ring, and he wants me to fight."

My eyes widened and I gave her a once-over, and then a twice-over and a thrice-over because my eyeballs were enjoying the way her blouse stretched and wrinkled in time with her breathing. They say never mix business with pleasure, but then, I've never been so good at following advice.

"You don't look like much of a fighter," I told her.

She gave a wry smile, which did all kinds of exciting things to my blood pressure, and purred, "I have my talents, but—"

The door slammed against the wall and two thick-set goons sauntered in, while Mrs. D-S took up a position blocking the doorway. She smiled, displaying two rows of tombstone teeth.

"Thank you, Mr. Granger," she said. "You may leave."

While I was asking myself how I would do that, since there wasn't enough room for a breeze to slip past her, and I didn't figure on using the window as an exit, something hard cracked against the back of my skull. I crumpled to the floor like a marionette with cut strings.

My second to last thought before darkness overtook the sparkles in my mind was that the carpet needed to be cleaned. My last thought was that the hard thing that'd hit me was a two-and-a-half-pound lead-filled leather Wilkinson, a tidy, compact blackjack. I'd been hit on the head so many times that I got to recognize the weapons…

I came to with a rancid feline stench tweaking my nose hairs. When I opened my eyes, I found myself in a domed cage with one-inch steel bars. And I wasn't alone: a panther was gently snoring a few feet away, and it looked about twice the size a panther ought to be. Not that I'd spent much time around big cats, but still.

I scrambled back against the bars, and half my brain started screaming while the other half did its best to stop any sound escaping. The monster snored on. I reached into my pocket, pawing for my gun, before remembering that I'd lost it in a poker game in Reggie's Jive Dive a couple of nights before: my cheating hadn't been as skillful as the other guy's. In any case, the size of this monster, all the bullets would end up doing was annoying it.

I jumped when a match flared on the other side of the bars,

illuminating a small face and a large cigar.

"Solly, Solly, Solly," said Tiny Tony.

"Mr. Tiny," I squeaked, then cleared my throat and tried again. "Mr. Tiny—Anthony—what a lovely surprise, meeting you here."

When there's an elephant in the room you can do nothing about—or a four-hundred-pound panther, in this case—it's often wisest to ignore it in the hope that it'll go away before ripping your head from your shoulders. I was doing my best not to imagine tearing, slurping, crunching sounds.

Tony laughed and sucked on his cigar as he snapped his fingers.

Fluorescent tubes above the cage flickered on, bathing us in greenish light, revealing a ring of leering faces surrounding the cage. They seemed to be waiting for something, and my heart struck up a drum roll when I realized what their imminent entertainment was to be.

I glanced at the big cat, spotting a blouse and ripped slacks beside it—the clothes Emily had been wearing. The beast had eaten her and was sleeping it off. I could mourn the girl and raise a glass to her later—at the moment, my main concern was finding a way to escape the same fate.

"Tony," I pleaded, "you don't have to do this."

"No, I don't"—he rolled his cigar from one side of his mouth to the other—"but I want to."

If Luck was a lady, today must've been her time of the month. Tony snapped his fingers again, and one of his associates beat an iron bar against the bars of the cage.

The panther leapt to its feet, shaking its head angrily. It spotted Tony and growled, then turned in my direction.

I waved my hands in a placatory gesture as I slowly backed away.

And that's how I ended up in this mess.

The monster lurched towards me. I screeched like a panicked possum and leapt for the bars above my head. I managed to catch hold, then pulled myself up and scrabbled to the top of the dome. I clung on tighter than wet on water, while the panther paced back and forth below, making the occasional half-hearted swipe in my direction.

The spectators started to grumble, and Tony called, "Get down from there, ya cowardly bum. Take it like a man."

If being a man means getting shredded like an oversized cat's chew toy, put me in a dress and call me Sally.

The panther looked up and yawned, more bored than annoyed that its toy didn't want to play.

I loosened my grip enough to reach my hip flask, and, with a regretful sigh, poured what was left into the panther's gaping mouth.

It snapped its mouth shut, and swallowed instinctively. I like my bourbon with two ounces of pepper, ground chilies and vinegar—and I was betting my survival that would be more than this animal could handle. The beast sneezed, coughed, and sneezed again. It collapsed and started to paw at its snout, as tears seeped from its bloodshot eyes.

I cautiously eased myself to the ground and said, "Tony, you ain't going to get the fight you want. Lemme out, and we can talk about this like fully-grown adults."

Damnit! Did I really say "fully-grown?" My mouth just doesn't know when to stop. "Adults, Tony! I mean, like mature, sensible adults."

But the damage was done. Tony's eyes bulged, and he pulled out his gun. It was almost as big as he was.

He squeezed the trigger twice, ruining a perfectly good trench coat and making a mess of the torso behind it, and I crumpled beside the panther. *No, not a panther*, I thought. Too soft. I reached up to touch the animal, but felt smooth skin instead of fur and muscle. Then everything went black.

I came to in a dumpster. One advantage of being Saintsville's only undead PI is that it takes more than bullets to the chest to stop me. A second advantage, particularly when waking up in the sludge at the bottom of a dumpster, is a poor sense of smell—that's the main reason for the pungent food, the chain-smoking, and the additions to my booze. I could have done with a swig right then, but the flask was empty.

I hauled myself out, then emptied some unrecognizable semi-liquid from my fedora and attempted to reshape the hat, before popping it on top of my head. My temper was as wound up and vicious as a bear trap, and it was time to spring it on Tiny Tony.

I had no gun at the moment, but I did have the advantage that Tony thought I was dead. Which I had been for a long time, if you want to get technical. Point is, I was still moving.

If Saintsville was an angry pimple, Tony's Palace was the glistening head, and I was about to pop it. The gin joint's doorman flinched from my stench courtesy of the dip in the dumpster, giving me the opportunity to kick him where it hurts and follow it up with an elbow to the back of the skull. I grabbed the pistol from his belt and stormed in.

"Tony, I'm comin' for you," I bellowed, but no one paid any attention, accustomed as they were to fights in this place every night of the week here.

Tony's office was on the floor above, and that's where I figured he'd be. At the bottom of the stairs, I shot one of his bodyguards in the leg, but let the other run for it—I wanted to save the remaining lead for Tony.

I kicked the door open, then stopped. Even the noise from the speakeasy faded away.

I stared at Tony, Mrs. D-S, and… Emily. She was alive, unscathed—not so much as a scratch on the considerable amount of skin not covered by the minuscule black dress that had been painted onto her.

Tony stared back at me.

Mrs. Darlington-Stevens smiled her big-toothed smile. She held up a small wooden cat-shaped object, and brushing her sausage-like fingers over its surface, she said, "I was so disappointed earlier, but you're back to make up for it. How satisfying. Emily, my dear, you know what to do."

Emily raised her head and looked at me with sad, bloodshot eyes.

"I'm sorry," she said. "I can't help it—she uses the totem to make me do things…"

The young woman dropped to all fours, offering me a view of her decolletage I would've lingered over in less perilous times. Before I could so much as open my mouth to speak, her skin started to bulge and sprout dark hairs. The insubstantial dress ripped, and all of a sudden, I was face to face with the panther from before.

I'd like to think my astute subconscious was responsible for what happened next, but it's closer to the truth that I stumbled, pulling the trigger, sending a round of hot lead into the totem, shattering it.

The panther—Emily—paused, one foot raised, and I'm sure I saw a smile on that huge spectacularly-toothed face. She turned and leaped, ripping Mrs. D-S's face off. She grabbed the woman's shoulder and shook her like a ragdoll before discarding the body in a bloody heap. The cat jumped on Tony, pinning him to the ground with two enormous paws, then turned to look at me. Her eyes were like twin locomotives at the end of the tunnel.

My arms were still trembling, so I had to use both hands to hold the gun steady, pointing at Tony's forehead.

Emily backed off, and changed back into human form with a lot of unpleasant clicking and squishing.

Being a sophisticated gentleman of a PI, I tried not to peek as I shuffled out of my coat and handed it to her. Tried, but failed. If my salivary glands hadn't dried up years ago, drool would've been pouring from my mouth.

I croaked, "Are you all right?"

She nodded, holding her breath—I guessed the rank smell of my coat had more effect on her sensitive semi-feline nose than it could ever have on mine. I turned my attention back to Tony.

"Now what do I do with you, Mr. Tiny?"

Tony held up both hands, palms towards me.

"Look, Solly, it's just business. I put on shows for the local plugs, and when Ms. Gordon turned up with her particular talent, well, what could I do?"

My finger tightened on the trigger, and I growled, "You could've *not* let that witch control her."

Emily put a hand on my arm, which sent tingles up long-dead nerves. "There's been enough killing."

"Listen to the skirt, Solly. What's the point of killin' an old mug like me?"

Lots of thoughts crossed my mind, but then I sighed and let the gun droop. "You know something? You're right," I said, "it wouldn't be long before someone else stepped into your Cubans, and at least I know how you tick."

"That's right," he nodded eagerly. "We're pals, like you said. Let's forget all about the whole mess. I'll stay outta your business and you turn a blind eye towards…" His voice faltered as glared at him with my dried-up eyeballs.

He gulped. "OK, I'll stay out of your business, and you do what you need to."

I turned to leave. "Come on, Emily."

We went back to her hotel room, where she showered and dressed, while I smoked my way through the rest of my pack and drained her room's bar one bottle at a time.

When she finished, I showered—it wouldn't do much for my body-preserving parfum de formaldehyde, but it would get rid of the detritus from my dumpster dip—while she stepped out to buy me a new trench coat, fedora and the rest. My old clothes went into a laundry bag which she disposed of along the way to do her shopping.

When we were both feeling more human, if that's a term that could be applied to either of us, I asked how she became a were-panther, or whatever she was.

She shrugged. "A couple of months ago, I was a reporter for the *Johannesburg Daily Times* working on a story on the recent rise in ivory poaching. An American company seemed to be involved, and when I went to meet their local administrator, a woman called Mrs. Darlington-Stevens, I was attacked and thrown in an animal pit. I expected to die, but despite the pain and the terror, I survived, and that witch brought me back as her plaything. And now I'm free, thanks to you."

An unusual story, but not the strangest I've ever heard. Once you've dug yourself out of a grave after six days in the ground, not much surprises you.

"So, whaddya s'pose you'll do now?"

She shrugged again. "Another city, another state. And hope no one finds me. Maybe back to Africa."

She looked me in the eye and said, "You could come with me, you know."

The corners of my lip twitched up, then fell back down again. "Someone needs to look out for all the sinners in Saintsville."

Saintsville was where I lived, and where I died. And where I came back to the un-life I'm living now. I couldn't leave. If Saintsville was a dame, then I was her chump of a lover… unable to give her everything she needs, but unwilling to let her go.

Adjusting my hat to shade my eyes, I shuffled to the door. I opened it and turned to the girl.

"See you around, doll."

The door closed with a soft but final click.

The Usual Unusual Suspects

Daryl Wood Gerber is an Agatha Award-winning author best known for her nationally bestselling mysteries, including the _Literary Dining Mysteries, Fairy Garden Mysteries,_ and _Cookbook Nook Mysteries._ As Avery Aames, she penned the popular _Cheese Shop Mysteries._ In addition, Daryl writes suspense including the well-received _The Son's Secret, Girl on the Run,_ and the popular Aspen Adams suspense novels. Her short stories have appeared in a number of anthologies including _Mystery Most Theatrical, Infinity, Fish Tales,_ and more. Fun Tidbit: as an actress, Daryl appeared in "Murder, She Wrote." She loves to cook, garden, read, and walk her frisky Goldendoodle. Also she has been known to jump out of a perfectly good airplane. You can learn more on her website: https://darylwoodgerber.com

Don Magin, husband (of 1), father (of 5), grandfather (of 15), great-grandfather (of 2, _so far_), retired chemist (reborn as science and math teacher), and Santa-Claus-look-alike, lives in Bon Air, Virginia with his wife of 55 years. He has had stories and poems in _Grand_ Magazine, _Guide_ Magazine, _Short Humour, Central Virginia Poetry Bard_ Magazine, _Microhorror, Flashes in the Dark, Necrotic Tissue, The Shine Journal, Sylvia,_ Pure Slush Books, Westwood Quarterly, _Creatopia_ and other online and print publications and anthologies.

James Donzella lives in Northern California. He is an active member of the UCLA Wordcommandos Creative Writing Workshop for Military Veterans and is currently building his first collection of short stories. He's worked as an ad copywriter, actor and screenwriter.

J. T. Seate states that after reading a few early stories to his parents, they booted him out of the house. Undaunted, he continues to write everything from humor to the macabre, spanning a gulf between such publications as *Horror Novel Review's Best Short Fiction Award* to the *Chicken Soup for the Soul* series.

His first *Crimeucopia* appearance is in *We'll Be Right Back — After This!*

S. B. Watson lives in Keizer, Oregon, USA — and has had numerous pieces published in *Spinetingler Magazine, The Dark City Mystery Magazine, Mystery Magazine, Mystery Tribune,* and *Punk Noir Magazine.* His first *Crimeucopia* appearance is in the historical *Through The Past Darkly.*

Wil A. Emerson has been on the writing path for approximately 15 years. While not fresh out of college to write the Best Seller, she spent her early years as a Registered Nurse. Now on the fringe of being overlooked due to the inconvenient late start, she's successfully published in anthologies and has one novel under her belt. *Taking Rosie's Arm*, a Five Star, Thorndike publication, recounts the story of an elderly woman who befriends a troubled, but determined young girl. Writer, artist, traveler, cook: soup's on.

Wil's recent work is mainly mystery and women's fiction, and her first appearance is in *Crimeucopia — Careless Love*, with her piece, *The Driver* — followed by the 'second installment' *The Road to Reconciliation* in *Crimeucopia — Crank It Up!*

Also a struggling artist, her art can be viewed on her website. *www.wilemerson.com*

Michael Bracken's short fiction has appeared in *Alfred Hitchcock's Mystery Magazine, Ellery Queen's Mystery Magazine, The Best American Mystery Stories,* and in many other anthologies and periodicals. He recently appeared in *Crimeucopia — Let Me Tell You About....*

Glenn Francis Faelnar is a writer from Cebu in the Philippines, who has been writing fiction for the last 8 years. His recent work has appeared in such diverse places as *Storyberries* and *Daily Science Fiction*. He first appears in *Crimeucopia — Totally Psycho Logical.*

Michael Thomét is a mystery writer hailing from dusty Arizona. His characters are queer because he's queer, and he's not sorry about it. His work recently featured in SFWG's *Nightmare Fuel.* Michael writes for games as his "day job" and otherwise, he's often playing narrative games—usually murder mysteries. You can learn more about Michael at *https://michaelthomet.com.*

The first *Bear and Bird* short fiction appears in Crimeucopia — The 'I's Have It. *Bear and Bird in the Snow* was originally placed in the sadly uncompleted *Crimeucopia — An Alternative Line Of Inquiry* — hence the delay in it seeing publication.

John 'Jay' Andrew Connor has been writing and publishing under a menagerie of names and genres since the late 1970s — sometimes even professionally. He's worked at a variety of jobs, in various locations, and has also published small press, and semi-pro magazines in the past. Sadly, even though he is now on full time medication, he's at it again.

Memindip and the Persian Poet is the second in the *Memindip Quartet — The Death and Life of an Unwilling Investigator* series, set in an 'alternative' North African city, in 1969. The first of the four — *Memindip Solves a Problem* — appears in *Crimeucopia — We'll Be Right Back — After This!*

Martin Zeigler writes short fiction, primarily mystery, science fiction, and horror. His stories have been published in a number of anthologies and journals, both in print and online.

Every so often (okay, twice), he has gathered these stories into a self-published collection. In 2015 he released *A Functional Man And Other Stories.* More recently, in 2020, a year we will all remember with fondness, he released *Hypochondria And Other Stories.*

Besides writing, Marty enjoys the things most people do. And besides those, he likes reading, taking long walks, and playing the piano.

Marty makes his home in the Pacific Northwest.

Michael J. Ciaraldi*'s Film Blank* is the first in a series of stories about Summer Cum Laude, College Detective. Other parts of the series includes *Two Graves* and *Hunted* — both of which have been produced on stage at WPI, the university where he used to teach computer science, robotics engineering, and playwriting. At present he is working on *My Old School* and *The Spy Who Googled Me.*
Mike is a three-time winner of the Alfred Hitchcock's Mystery Magazine Mysterious Photograph Contest. He lives in Shrewsbury, MA with his wife and a chihuahua.

Jeff Burt lives in Santa Cruz County, California, with his wife and a July abundance of plums. He has contributed to *Gold Man Review, Williwaw Journal, Red Wolf Journal,* and *Brazos River Review.* He won the Cold Mountain Review 2017 Poetry Prize. His work can be found at *www.jeff-burt.com.*

L.N. Hunter*'s* comic fantasy novel, *The Feather and the Lamp* (Three Ravens Publishing), sits alongside works in anthologies such as *Best of British Science Fiction 2022* and *Hidden Villains: Arise,* among others, as well as several issues of Short Édition's *Short Circuit* and the *Horrifying Tales of Wonder* podcast. There have also been papers in the IEEE *Transactions on Neural Networks,* which are probably somewhat less relevant and definitely less entertaining. When not writing, L.N. occasionally masquerades as a software developer or can be found unwinding in a disorganised home in Carlisle, UK, along with two cats and a soulmate.
Get in touch via:
https://linktr.ee/l.n.hunter or
https://www.facebook.com/L.N.Hunter.writer

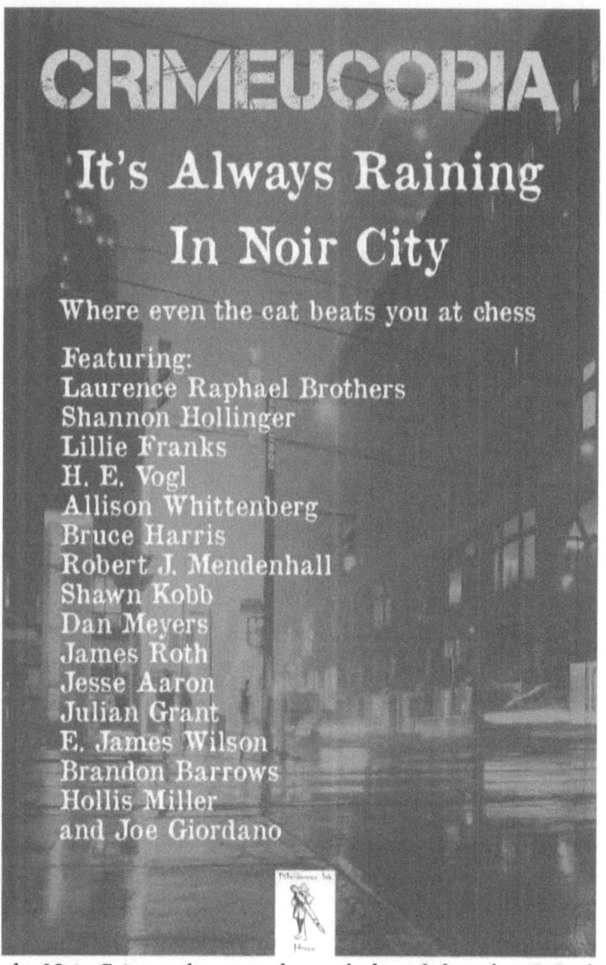

Is the Noir Crime sub-genre always dark and downbeat? Is there a time when Bad has a change of conscience, flips sides and takes on the Good role?

Noir is almost always a dish served up raw and bloody - Fiction bleu if you will. So maybe this is a chance to see if Noir can be served sunny side up - with the aid of these fifteen short order authors.

All fifteen give us dark tales from the stormy side of life - which is probably why it's *always* raining in Noir City....

Paperback Edition ISBN: 9781909498341
eBook Edition ISBN: 9781909498358

It Was In The Year Of....

Historical/Period Crime short fiction ranging from Cosy. Noir, PIs, Narrative Crime, and a whole spectrum of Crime sub-genres in between

21 authors — Gary Thomson, Edward St. Boniface, Terry Wijesuriya, Frances Stratford, Dennis E. Delaney, Joan Leotta, Hope Hodgkins, Karen Odden, J. F. Benedetto, S. B. Watson, Hal Dygert, Merrilee Robson, John G. Bluck, David Hagerty, Avi Sirlin, Karl El-Koura, Penny Hurrell, Kai Lovelace, Maddi Davidson, J. Aquino and Kirk Landers — take you from 420 BC through to AD 1969, and give you a criminal history, laid out in a case by case Crimeline.

Paperback 9781909498587 eBook 9781909498594

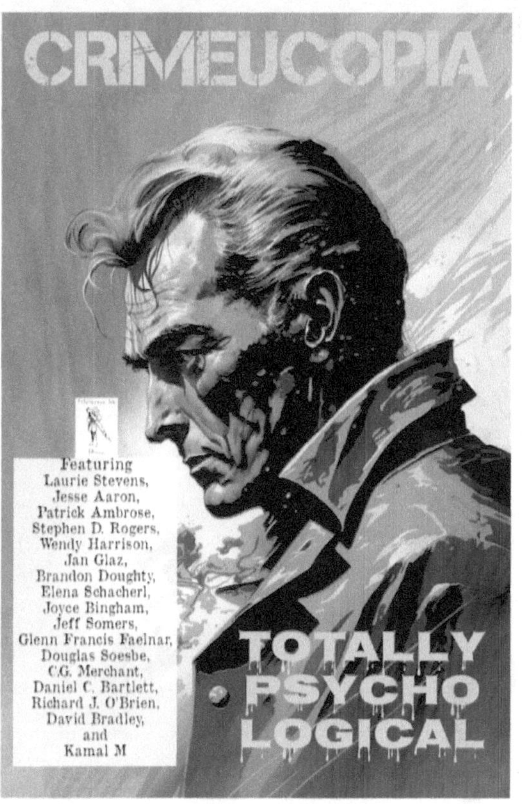

Totally — *adverb:* completely; absolutely. Used to emphasize a clause or statement. "He/She is totally bat-shit crazy!"

Psycho — *noun:* an unstable and aggressive person. "Don't you know? My ex is a total psycho!" — *adjective:* exhibiting unstable and aggressive behaviour "There's some kind of psycho nut job on the loose out there!"

Logical — *adjective:* characterised by or capable of clear, sound reasoning. "His/Her logical mind? Are you nuts or something?"

But are all psychos 'nut jobs'?

Laurie Stevens, Jesse Aaron, Patrick Ambrose, Stephen D. Rogers, Wendy Harrison, Jan Glaz, Brandon Doughty, Elena Schacherl, Joyce Bingham, Jeff Somers, Glenn Francis Faelnar, Douglas Soesbe, C.G. Merchant, Daniel C. Bartlett, Richard J. O'Brien, David Bradley, and Kamal M present 17 cases for the defence.

Paperback 9781909498563 eBook 9781909498570

CRIMEUCOPIA

Let Me Tell You About...

If Looks Could Kill, She Would Have Been An Uzi...

...Or more likely a shotgun. I mean, Lawd knows what those two ever saw in each other in the first place, and that's a fact. Don't believe me? Well, let me tell you about the time when.... But that's how it usually starts, doesn't it? Someone says something, which reminds someone else about.... And so the anecdotal avalanche begins.

This time there's 19 storytellers: **Vinnie Hansen, V.S. Kemanis, David Krugler, Robert Jeschonek, Beverle Graves Myers, Kirk Landers, James Lee Proctor, Victor Kreuiter, K. Arlington Andrews, Michael Bracken, Kevin R. Tipple, William Flores, Robert Sumner, Jim Guigli, James Roth, Michael Zimecki, Sebastian Corbascio, Martin Zeigler, and John Bertram Fawet III**

All gathered around the front counter of the Crimeucopia *Shots to Hell* Bar & Grill — and more than willing to tell you about how it is, or was, or even will be....

So, over the background sounds from an old jukebox loaded with worn out 45s (vinyl rather than the likes of a Px4 Storm), settle back and take in their individual stories – and we guarantee there's going to be Crimesapleanty indeed...

Paperback Edition ISBN: 9781909498600 — eBook Edition ISBN: 9781909498617
Amazon Paperback Edition ISBN: 9798337923338